PENGUIN BOOKS

THE PENGUIN BOOK OF
WELSH SHORT STORIES

Alun Richards has lived most of his life in Wales, apart
from service in the Royal Navy and a brief period as a proba-
tion officer in London. He is the author of several novels,
including the much-praised *Home to an Empty House* and
Ennal's Point. His collection of short stories, *The Former Miss
Merthyr Tydfil and Other Stories*, which is to be published in
1978, is a selection from two volumes of short stories: *Dai
Country*, which received the Welsh Arts Council literary prize
for 1974, and *The Former Miss Merthyr Tydfil*, which was
equally well received. Alun Richards is also the editor of *The
Penguin Book of Sea Stories*.

He has also written a number of plays for the theatre, including *The Snowdropper* which was recently produced in
London and Cardiff. His collected stage plays, *Plays for
Players*, were published in 1975. He is perhaps best known
outside Wales for his many television plays and adaptations
of the works of well-known writers, such as H. G. Wells and
W. Somerset Maugham, on the national networks, and he has
also made frequent contributions to such popular series as
The Onedin Line.

Alun Richards is married with four children and lives in
Mumbles, near Swansea.

The Penguin Book of Welsh Short Stories

EDITED BY
ALUN RICHARDS

PENGUIN BOOKS

Penguin Books Ltd, Harmondsworth, Middlesex, England
Penguin Books, 625 Madison Avenue, New York, New York 10022, U.S.A.
Penguin Books Australia Ltd, Ringwood, Victoria, Australia
Penguin Books Canada Ltd, 2801 John Street, Markham, Ontario, Canada L3R 1B4
Penguin Books (N.Z.) Ltd, 182–190 Wairau Road, Auckland 10, New Zealand

—

This collection first published 1976
Reprinted 1978

This collection copyright © Penguin Books Ltd, 1976
All rights reserved

—

Made and printed in Great Britain by
Hazell Watson & Viney Ltd,
Aylesbury, Bucks
Set in Linotype Georgian

CONTENTS

CONTENTS

INTRODUCTION

It was an American wit who listed one of man's greatest virtues as the art of making the long story short, but he was saying nothing about the short story which has its own necessary length, neither too long, nor too short, and is – in this editor's view – at its best when it presents a revealing insight into a person in a particular situation. What interests me most is being at the core of another life, seeing new light thrown upon it through the mind and world of the central character. It is a help if I am so involved at the outset that my attention does not wander and that my sympathies are immediately engaged, but, ultimately, I must know more at the end than I did at the beginning. Now and again, let it also be stated, I can certainly do with a smile.

These stories have been chosen to fulfil such requirements where they can be met, but they are, in addition, of a place and a time. The place is Wales and the time is this century, since the short story is a comparatively new arrival here. They reflect Wales, not always flatteringly, as it is and has been. English writers, it has been said, are often refugees from society, but almost all the stories in this book written by Welsh men and women show a concern for a particular landscape or community. It is as if Welsh writers cannot escape this involvement, and often there is also a sense of characters off stage, present but unseen at the story-teller's elbow. Perhaps the reason for this awareness of others is that so many of us have lived in such crowded places, and, while it is not always healthy, it is a part of the Welsh experience which is very different from that of our neighbours.

I have not been able to define a specific characteristic of the Welsh short story which makes it immediately identifiable, save for the nationality or place of residence of the writer, but it should be pointed out that some Welsh writers writing in English have faced particular difficulties when they have felt the need to emphasize their difference from

English counterparts. Often this need has led to exaggerations of speech, the whimsicality of which gives the lie to thought. At the back of it, one suspects the seductive pressures of those who like to see their Welshmen as clowns or 'characters', but it should also be said that many Welshmen have woven myths about themselves and their country with mischievous delight, and one doubts if they needed much encouragement. Of course this forced use of language can be detected in other literatures, some of them colonialist, and it is perhaps the inevitable consequence of the dominance of a distant metropolis. Having said that, it is only fair to note that many of the short-story writers who write in English received their first encouragement in Ireland or England, and indeed some of them, like Alun Lewis, represented here by an almost unknown story of Army life, are at their best away from home. In his case, he was probably more searching as an observer with a foreign eye, and his stories dealing with English life were perhaps more acutely observed than those dealing with his native South Wales. It is an arguable point, but, as with Rhys Davies and Kate Roberts, there is an abundance of riches from which the anthologist may choose and my task has been made easier by the selections of other editors whose choices I have tried not to duplicate where possible.

I have said that these stories were chosen because they please one reader and are of a place and a time, but I have also had a number of other considerations in mind and I have tried to represent all Welsh writers, including those whose work belies the concept of Wales as a homogeneous society. Thus Brenda Chamberlain finds her place here alongside the savage satire of Caradoc Evans or the sermonizing of T. Hughes Jones who, like Kate Roberts and D. J. Williams, writes exclusively in Welsh and for whom Welsh is the first language. All arguments about degrees of Welshness I find to be fruitless; for me, the story is the thing, although, on re-reading so many stories in preparing this volume, I could not help but detect the security of so many writers in the Welsh language which has freed them from painful attempts to emphasize their nationality, a strain which affected the work of some of their counterparts writing in English for a time.

Ironically this freedom seems to be in danger of ending and, judging by some of the stories made available in translation, appears to have been replaced by the aim of political conversion, to the detriment, in my view, of the storyteller's art. However, the representation of writers in the Welsh language and here translated is varied enough to warrant a further anthology comprised entirely of stories translated from the original. Nevertheless it is my hope that the Wales of the past and the present is well represented in this volume, together with the world of work and workmen in some of our more ravaged terrains, an aspect which has tended to be neglected in the past.

Finally I should like to express my gratitude to the Welsh Arts Council for their generosity in making funds available for translations, to numerous Welshmen for their suggestions, and also to Dr F. G. Cowley of the University College library at Swansea for his help in unearthing so many stories, long forgotten and out of print.

                                        ALUN RICHARDS

ACKNOWLEDGEMENTS

For permission to reprint the stories specified we are indebted to:

Curtis Brown Ltd and William Heinemann Ltd for Rhys Davies's 'The Fashion Plate' from *The Collected Stories*;

Glyn Jones for his own story 'The Golden Pony' originally published in *Chance*;

Mrs Gwenno Lewis and George Allen & Unwin for Alun Lewis's 'Acting Captain' from *The Last Inspection*;

David Higham Associates Ltd and Jonathan Cape Ltd for Geraint Goodwin's 'Saturday Night' from *The White Farm*;

Kate Roberts for her own story 'The Loss';

Gwyn Jones and the Oxford University Press for his own story 'The Brute Creation' from *Shepherd's Hey*;

J. M. Dent & Sons Ltd, the Trustees for the Copyrights of the late Dylan Thomas and New Directions Publishing Corporation for Thomas's 'Extraordinary Little Cough' from *Portrait of the Artist as a Young Dog*;

J. D. Lewis & Sons Ltd, Gomer Press, for D. J. Williams's 'A Successful Year', Eigra Lewis Roberts's 'An Overdose of Sun' and Islwyn Ffowc Elis's 'Black Barren';

Victor Gollancz Ltd for Gwyn Thomas's 'The Teacher' from *Gazooka*;

Hughes & Son and Christopher Davies Ltd for E. Tegla Davies's 'The Strange Apeman' and for T. Hughes Jones's 'The Squire of Havilah';

Dennis Dobson for Caradoc Evans's 'Be This Her Memorial' from *My People*;

Neville Chamberlain for the late Brenda Chamberlain's 'The Return' from *Life and Letters Today*, vol. 54;

V. Davies for B. L. Coombes's 'Twenty Tons of Coal' originally published in *Penguin New Writing*;

Moira Dearnley for her own story 'The House in Builth Crescent';

Jane Edwards for her own story 'Blind Date';

Harri Pritchard Jones for his own story 'Morfydd's Celebration';

Atlantic Monthly for Leslie Norris's 'A Roman Spring';

The New Statesman for John Morgan's 'A Writer Came to Our Place'.

Ron Berry for his own story 'Before Forever After' originally published in *Planet*;

Michael Joseph Ltd and Alun Richards for his own story 'Hon. Sec. (R.F.C.)' from *The Former Miss Merthyr Tydfil*;

Secker & Warburg Ltd and Emyr Humphreys for his own story 'Mel's Secret Love' from *Natives*.

Acknowledgement and thanks are also due to those who provided new translations for this volume and to the Welsh Arts Council which generously paid their fees.

The Fashion Plate

RHYS DAVIES

I

'The Fashion Plate's coming –' Quickly the news would pass down the main road. Curtains twitched in front parlour windows, potted shrubs were moved or watered; some colliers' wives, hard-worked and canvas-aproned, came boldly to the doorsteps to stare. In the dingy little shops, wedged here and there among the swart dwellings, customers craned together for the treat. Cleopatra setting out in the golden barge to meet Antony did not create more interest. There was no one else in the valley like her. Her hats! The fancy, high-heeled shoes, the brilliantly elegant dresses in summer, the tweeds and the swirl of furs for the bitter days of that mountainous district! The different handbags, gay and sumptuous, the lacy gloves, the parasols and tasselled umbrellas! And how she knew how to wear these things! Graceful as a swan, clean as a flower, she dazzled the eye.

But, though a pleasure to see, she was also incongruous, there in that grim industrial retreat pushed up among the mountains, with the pits hurling out their clouds of grit, and clanking coal wagons crossing the main road twice, and the miners coming off the shift black and primitive-looking. The women drew in their breaths as she passed. She looked as if she had never done a stroke of work in her life. Strange murmurs could be heard; she almost created a sense of fear, this vision of delicate indolence, wealth, and taste assembled with exquisite tact in one person. How could she do it? Their eyes admired but their comments did not.

Yet the work-driven women of this place, that had known long strikes, bitter poverty, and a terrible pit disaster, could not entirely malign Mrs Mitchell. Something made them pause. Perhaps it was the absolute serenity of those twice-weekly afternoon walks that nothing except torrential rain or snow-bound roads could prevent. Or perhaps they saw a vicarious triumph of themselves, a dream become courageously real.

There remained the mystery of how she could afford all those fine clothes. For Mrs Mitchell was only the wife of the man in charge of the slaughterhouse. She was not the pit manager's wife (indeed, Mrs Edwards dressed in totally different style, her never-varied hat shaped like an Eskimo's hut). Mr Mitchell's moderate salary was known, and in such a place no one could possess private means without its being exact knowledge. Moreover, he was no match to his wife. A rough-and-ready sort of man, glum and never mixing much in the life of the place, though down in the slaughterhouse, which served all the butchers' shops for miles, he was respected as a responsible chap whose words and deeds were to be trusted. Of words he had not many.

The women wished they could curl their tongues round something scandalous. Why was Mrs Mitchell always having her photograph taken by Mr Burgess in his studio down an obscure yard where he worked entirely alone? But nobody felt that suspicion of Mr Burgess, a family man and chapel deacon with a stark, knobbly face above a high stiff collar, sat comfortably in the mind. The bit of talk about the two had started because one afternoon a mother calling at the studio to fix an appointment for her daughter's wedding party found Mrs Mitchell reclining on a sofa under a bust of Napoleon. She was hatless and, in a clinging dress ('tight on her as a snake skin') and her hands holding a bunch of artificial flowers, she looked like a woman undergoing the agonies of some awful confession. Mr Burgess certainly had his head under the black drapery of his camera, so everything pointed to yet another photograph being taken. But to have one taken *lying down*! In the valley, in those days, to have a photo taken was a rare event attended by tremendous fuss. Accompanied by advising friends or relations, one stood up to the ordeal as if going before the Ultimate Judge, and one always came out on the card as if turned to stone or a pillar of salt.

The whispering began. Yet still everyone felt that the whispering was unfair to Mr Burgess. For thirty years he had photographed wedding parties, oratorio choirs, and silver-cup football teams in his studio, and nothing had ever been said against his conduct.

Mrs Mitchell, coming out of her bow-windowed little house as out of a palace, took her walk as if never a breath of scandal ever polluted her pearl ear-rings. Was she aware of the general criticism? If so, did she know that within the criticism was homage? – the homage that in bygone times would begin a dynasty of tribal queens? Was she aware of the fear, too, the puritanic dread that such lavishness and extravagance could not be obtained but at some dire cost greater even than money?

II

This afternoon her excursion was no different from the hundreds of others. It was a fine autumn day. The tawny mountains glistened like the skins of lions. She wore a new fur, rich with the bluish-black tint of grapes, and flung with just the right expensive carelessness across her well-held shoulders: it would cause additional comment. With her apparently unaware look of repose she passed serenely down the long, drab main road.

Down at the bottom of the valley the larger shops, offices, a music hall, and a railway station (together with Mr Burgess's studio) clustered into the semblance of a town. She always walked as far as the railway station, situated down a hunchback turning, and, after appearing to be intent on its architecture for a moment, wheeled round, and with a mysterious smile began the homeward journey. Often she made small domestic purchases – her clothes she obtained from the city twenty miles away – and as the ironmonger's wife once remarked: 'Only a rolling-pin she wanted, but one would think she was buying a grand piano.'

Today, outside the railway station, she happened to see her young friend Nicholas and, bending down to his ear, in her low, sweet voice breathed his name. He was twelve, wore a school satchel strapped to his back, and he was absent-mindedly paused before a poster depicting Windsor Castle. He gave a violent start and dropped a purple-whorled glass marble which rolled across the pavement, sped down the gutter, and slid into a drain. 'It's gone!' he cried in poignant astonishment. 'I won it dinner-time!'

'And all my fault.' Her bosom was perfumed with an evasive fragrance like closed flowers. 'Never mind, *I* have some marbles. Will you come and get them this evening? You've been neglecting us lately, Nicholas.' She was neither arch nor patronizing; he might have been a successful forty.

'I'll have to do my homework first,' he said with equal formality.

'Well, come in and do it with us. You shall have your own little table, and I'll be quiet as a mouse.'

They lived in the same street and, though no particular friendship existed between the two households, he had been on visiting terms with the Mitchells, who were childless, for a couple of years. The change from his own noisily warring brothers-and-sisters home to the Mitchells', where he was sole little king, nourished him. To his visits his mother took a wavering attitude of doubt, half criticism, and compassion; before becoming decisive she was waiting for something concrete to happen in that house.

That evening Mrs Mitchell had six coloured glass marbles ready for him on a small table on which, neatly set out, were also a crystal ink-well, a ruler, blotter, and pencils and – yes! a bottle of lemonade with a tumbler. Very impressed by the bottle, which gave him a glimpse of easy luxury in a world hard with the snatchings and blows of his brothers and sisters, he made little fuss of the glitteringly washed marbles, which he guessed she had bought in Watkins's shop after leaving him – and in any case they had not the value of those won from bragging opponents kneeling around a circle drawn in the earth.

'Is the chair high enough, would you like a cushion? ... You must work hard if you want to get near the top of your class, but you must *enjoy* working... There! Now I'll do my sewing and not say a word.'

Hers was not big, industrious sewing, complete with bee-humming machine, as at home. She sat delicately edging a tiny handkerchief with a shred of lace, and on her face was no look of minutes strained to their utmost; she had the manner of one who never glances at a clock. The house was tidy, clean, respectably comfortable. But it was shabbier than his own home. And somehow without atmosphere, as if it was left alone to look after itself and no love or hate clashed within its shiny darkly papered walls. Occasionally this lack of something important vaguely bothered the boy. He would stand with his lip lifted, his nostrils dilated. He had never been upstairs, and he always wanted to penetrate its privacy. Was the thing he missed to be found there? Did they live up there and only come downstairs when there were visitors? Down here it was all parlour and Sunday silence, with for movement only the lonely goldfish eternally circling its bowl.

Mr Mitchell came in before the homework was finished. 'Good evening, *sir*,' he greeted Nicholas. 'Doing my accounts for me?' He seemed to look at the boy and yet not look at him. And he was not a jocular man. He had a full, dahlia-red, rather staring face of flabby contours, sagged in on its own solitude, and the eyes did not seem to connect with the object they looked at. His face had affinities with the face of some floridly ponderous beast. He had a very thick neck. It was strange, and yet not at all strange, that his work had to do with cattle.

'Do you want a meal now,' Mrs Mitchell asked in the heavy silence, 'or can you wait?' Her voice was crisper; she stitched in calm withdrawal; she might have been an in-different daughter. Though bent at the table, the boy sensed

the change. There was a cold air of armistice in the room, of
emptiness. Nervously he opened his bottle of lemonade. The
explosion of the uncorking sounded very loud.

'I'll go upstairs,' Mr Mitchell said. 'Yes, I'll go upstairs.
Call me down.'

'You'll hear the dishes,' she said concisely. The boy turned
and saw her stitching away, like a queen in a book of tales.
Mr Mitchell went out bulkily; his head lolled on the fleshy
neck. It was as if he said 'Pah!' in a heavily angry way. His
footsteps were ponderous on the staircase.

Had he come straight from the slaughterhouse and was
weary? Had he a short time ago been killing cattle?
Nicholas, like all the boys of the place, was interested in the
slaughterhouse, a squat building with pens and sties in a
field down by the river. Once he had been allowed inside by
an amiable young assistant who understood his curiosity,
and he saw in a whitewashed room hung with ropes and
pulleys a freshly dead bullock strung up in the air by its
legs; it swayed a little and looked startlingly foolish. Blood
spattered the guttered floor and some still dripped from the
bullock's mouth like a red icicle. In a yard another young
man was rinsing offal in a tub filled with green slime. 'No,
we're not killing pigs today,' he replied to Nicholas's inquiry.
Because of the intelligent squeals and demented hysteria of
these intuitive beasts as they were chased from the sties into
the house of death, pig-killing was the prized spectacle
among all the boys. But few had been fortunate enough to
witness it; the slaughtermen usually drove them away from
the fascinating precincts. Nicholas, an unassertive boy on
the whole, had never liked to take advantage of his friendship with the Mitchells and ask to be taken to the place
properly, an accredited visitor on a big day. He wondered if
Mrs Mitchell went there herself sometimes. Could she get
him a pig's bladder?

She did not bring in supper until he had finished the
homework. 'There, haven't I been quiet?' She smiled. 'Did
you work easily? I can see you're studious and like quiet. Do
you like lobster too?'

'Lobster?' He looked at her vacantly.

She fetched from the kitchen an oval dish in which lay a fabulous scarlet beast. Cruel claws and quiveringly fine feelers sprang from it. At first he thought that Mr Mitchell must have brought it from the slaughterhouse, but when his excitement abated he remembered they came from the sea. 'How did you get it?' he asked, astonished.

'I have to ask Harris's fish shop to order one especially for me. I'm the only customer here that wants them.'

'Do they cost a lot?'

Over the fiery beast she looked at him conspiratorially. 'Nothing you enjoy ever costs a lot.' She smiled.

Mr Mitchell must have heard the dishes. But he came down looking more torpid than ever. 'Lobster again!' he said, sombrely. 'At night! There's stomachs of cast-iron in this world!'

Mrs Mitchell looked at him frigidly. 'If you encourage nightmares they'll come,' she said.

'You're not giving it to the boy?' he said.

'Why not? You'll have a little, Nicholas?' Of course he would.

'I have dreams,' said Mr Mitchell, his heavy, dark-red face expressionless. 'Yes, *I* have dreams.'

'Do you?' Her husband might have been an acquaintance who had called at an inopportune time. 'A little salad, Nicholas? Shall I choose it for you?' In delightful performance she selected what seemed the best pieces in the bowl; with deft suggestions she showed him how to eat the lobster. He enjoyed extracting from inside a crimson scimitar shreds of rosily white meat. The evening became remarkable for him.

And it was because of it that he added to the local legend of Mrs Mitchell. When he told them at home about the lobster, there was at first silence. His mother glanced up, his brothers and sisters were impressed. He felt superior. A couple of weeks later, while he waited to be served in Watkins's shop just after Mrs Mitchell had passed the window on her return from her walk, he heard a collier's wife say: 'Yes,

and they say she has lobsters for breakfast nearly every day.
No doubt her new hat she wears at breakfast, too, to match
them.' Despite his sense of guilt, he felt himself apart, an
experienced being. No one else in the place was known to
have dealings with the exotic fish.

'She'll be giving him champagne next,' he heard his father
say to his mother. 'Mitchell, poor devil, will be properly in
the soup some day.' And his mother said, troubled: 'Yes, I
do wonder if Nick ought to go there—'

III

That winter Mrs Mitchell won a £100 prize in a periodical
which ran a competition every week. You had to make up a
smart remark on a given phrase and send it in with a six-
penny postal order. A lot of people in the place did it; someone else had won £10, which set more members of both sexes
running to the Post Office. It seemed quite in order that Mrs
Mitchell, who dressed like no one else, should win a cracker
of a prize, but everybody was agog the day the news got
around.

'You'll be going to see her every day now,' Nicholas's
eldest brother jeered, adding offensively: 'Take your money-
box with you.' And his father said to his mother, in that
secret-knowledge way which roused an extra ear inside one:
'If she's got any feeling, she'll hand that prize to Mitchell
straight away.' To this his mother said: 'Not she!'

A week later, with Christmas not far off, Mrs Mitchell took
her afternoon walk in a new fur coat. It shone with opulent
gleams, as if still alive, and its owner walked with the composure of one who owns 365 fur coats. It was treated to a
companionable new hat into which a blue quill was stabbed
cockily as a declaration of independence. Her red-tasselled
umbrella, exquisitely rolled, went before her with a hand
attached lightly as a flower. The women watchers down the
long, bleak road gathered and stared with something like
consternation. Surely such luxury couldn't proceed for ever?
The God of Prudence, who had made his character known in

abundant scriptures, must surely hurl one of his thunder-bolts right in her path some day.

That same evening Nicholas visited the Mitchells' house. And he found Mrs Mitchell delicately shedding a few tears into a lacy wisp of the finest linen. He could not take this restrained sort of weeping seriously. Especially as she had just won a big prize. 'Have you got a headache?' he asked.

She blew her pretty nose and dried her eyes. 'I'm glad you've come. It keeps Mr Mitchell quiet.' Pointing to the ceiling, she whispered dramatically: 'He's just gone up... Oh dear!' she sighed.

'What is he always doing upstairs?' It did not now take him long to adjust himself to being treated as a grown-up.

'Oh, only sleeping... He's a man that seems to need a great deal of sleep. He says he gets bad dreams, but I believe he likes them.' She smiled at him with dainty malice. 'Do you know what he wanted? ... My prize!' Nicholas looked thoughtful, like one privy to other knowledge. She went on: 'Week after week I worked so hard at those competitions, and he never helped me, it was all my own brains.' Her eyes shone with that refined malice. 'To tell you the truth, *he isn't clever*. Not like you and me.' She giggled. 'Oh dear, don't look so solemn, Nicholas; I've had a very trying day.'

'I have too,' he said.

'Have you, darling? Would you like a chocolate?' She jumped up and fetched a ribboned box from the sideboard. They ate in release from the stress. But he could see that her attention was on something else, and presently she resumed: 'He found out today that I had spent the prize on a fur coat. Oh, good gracious, such a fuss!' She rummaged for other chocolates. 'An almond one this time? Nougat? I don't like the peppermint ones, do you? We'll keep them for Mr Mitchell... Of course, people do criticize me,' she said, wrinkling her nose. 'You must not repeat what I've said, Nicholas.'

'Oh no,' he said, decided but flushing. Memory of the lobster affair still obscurely troubled him.

'Gentlemen do not,' she said. 'As you know.'

'I'm going to visit my grandmother after Christmas,' he said awkwardly.

Suddenly footsteps sounded on the stairs, descending with pronounced deliberation. And Mrs Mitchell seemed to draw herself in, like a slow, graceful snail into its shell. The door opened, and Mr Mitchell stood there in a bowler hat and overcoat, bulky and glowering. Even his ragged moustache looked as if it was alive with helpless anger – anger that would never really shoot out or even bristle. 'Am going out,' he said, in a low, defeated growl. Of Nicholas he took no notice. 'Going out,' he repeated. 'Yes.'

'You are going out,' she murmured, remote in her shell. Her eyelids were down as if against some rude spectacle.

'Yes.' Something in his heavy neck throbbed, making it thicker. Yet there was nothing threatening in his mien. His slow, ox-coloured eyes travelled from his wife's face to the large pink box of chocolates on her knees. 'I hope,' he then said, 'you'll always be able to afford 'um.'

She asked faintly: 'What time will you be back? Supper will—'

'Going to the slaughterhouse,' he said sullenly. 'Got a job to do.'

'—will be ready at nine,' she said.

'Ha!' he said. He stared at her shut face. But the heavy glaze of his unlit eyes threw out no communication. The boy looked round. Feeling at a loss, he glanced uneasily at Mrs Mitchell, and saw that a peculiar, almost dirtily grey, tint blotched her face. 'Ha!' repeated Mr Mitchell. The large, sagged face hung down over his swollen neck. For a moment he looked vaguely menacing. Then he tramped into the hallway. The front door slammed.

Mrs Mitchell opened her eyes wide at the slam. 'Oh dear!' she wailed faintly. Her eyes were different, darker, almost black. 'He never says very much,' she fluttered, 'but he stands there *looking*... Good gracious!' She bit a chocolate mechanically and winced in chagrin as if it held a flavour she did not like. 'It seems he's having a very busy time in the slaughterhouse,' she went on erratically; 'some sheep have come in... Ah well!' She jumped up again. 'You haven't seen my new photographs.'

Once again they sat over the album; she inserted a copy of the new photograph. There she was in about thirty different representations, but whether she was sad or smiling, dreamy or vivacious, aloof or inviting, it was clear that the eye of Mr Burgess's camera found itself in concord with its elegant object. For nearly an hour she pored over the album with an exaggerated, detailed interest, demanding once more his opinion. Her voice was high, her manner hurried. 'Isn't this your favourite? It's mine too. Why do you like it so much?'

He thought carefully. 'You look as though you're just going for a holiday to the seaside,' he said finally.

'It's true I was happy that day. At the time I thought we were going to move to London... Then Mr Mitchell refused to take the job he was offered there.' Her voice sharpened remarkably. 'He refused... The fact is, he has no ambition.' Suddenly she snapped the album shut, rose with a bright restlessness. 'Will you come down to the slaughterhouse with me, Nicholas?'

At last the invitation! He agreed with alacrity and thought of the envy of the other boys.

'If you are with me, Mr Mitchell won't be so disagreeable.' She hurried upstairs, and returned in her new fur coat and the coquettish toque. 'Come, I didn't realize we had sat here so long... I can't have him sulking and going without his supper,' she explained.

The starlight night was cold. There were few people in the streets. The secret mountains smelled grittily of winter. Somewhere a dog barked insistent, shut out from a house. The public-house windows were clouded with yellow steam, and in a main-street house a woman pulled down a blind on a lamplit front parlour where sat Mr Hopkins the insurance agent beside a potted fern. They crossed the main street and took a sloping road trailing away into waste land. Odorous of violets and dark fur, Mrs Mitchell walked with a surprisingly quick glide; Nicholas was obliged to trot. They heard the icy cry of the river below, flinging itself unevenly among its stone-ragged banks. She said nothing now.

The slaughterhouse stood back in its field, an angular array of black shadows. No light showed there. Mrs Mitchell fumbled at the fence gate of the field. 'I've only been here once,' she said, 'when I brought down the telegram saying his father had died.' She paused doubtfully. 'There's no light.' But the gate was unlocked.

'There are windows at the back,' Nicholas urged; 'there's a little office at the side.' But he himself was disappointed. It seemed unlikely that slaughtering was proceeding among those silent shadows.

They walked up the cobbled path. There was a double door leading into a stone-floored paddock; it swung loose. Inside, a huge sliding door led into the main slaughter chamber; this did not yield to their push. Then Nicholas remembered the smaller door at the side; he turned its knob, and they walked into a whitewashed passage lit at the end by a naked blue gas-jet. 'The office is down there,' he said. He felt morose and not implicated. He remembered glancing into the office during his previous visit; it was no more than a large box with a table and chair and files and ledgers. They walked down the stone-flagged passage. She stopped. He heard her breathing.

' Go back,' she said.

Sharpened by her tone of command, he looked up at her. Her nostrils, blue in the gaslight, were quivering. He looked down quickly. From under a door a stream of dark, thick liquid had crawled. It was congealing on the stone flag into the shape of a large root or a strand of seaweed. He looked at it, only distantly conscious of her further cry and her fingers pressing into his shoulders. 'Go back; go home!' she exclaimed. He did not move.

She stepped to the door as if oblivious of him. But she carefully avoided the liquid root. She turned the brass knob, slowly pushed back the door. Still the boy had not moved.

He could not see inside the door. She gave a queer cry, not loud, a low, hunted cry, broken in her mouth. And Nicholas never forgot the gesture with which her hand went to her throat. He ran forward from the wall. At the same time his feet instinctively avoided the dark smears. 'Let me see!' he cried. But she pulled back the door. 'Let me see!' he cried. It was then he became conscious of another odour, a whiff from the closing door mingled with the perfume of fur and violets.

She violently pushed him back. 'Go home at once!' There was something like a terrible hiss in her voice. He looked up in confusion. Her face, blotched with a sickly pallor, was not the elegantly calm face he knew; the joints and muscles had loosened and were jerking convulsively. It was as if the static photograph of a pleasing face had in some nightmare way suddenly broken into ugly grimaces. For a moment he stared aghast at that face. Then he backed from her.

Her eyes seemed not to see him. 'Go!' she screamed, even more startlingly. Then he swiftly turned and ran.

IV

Three days later, carrying a large bunch of chrysanthemums from his mother, he walked down to the Mitchells' house. He went with a meek unwillingness, but not unconscious of the drama in which he was involved. All those three days the place had hummed with talk of the Mitchells. Within living memory there had been only one local suicide before.

Already there was pre-knowledge of the bailiffs who were only waiting for the coffin to leave the house before taking possession. The dead man's affairs were in shocking condition. Besides forcing him to mortgage his house several years ago, the Fashion Plate had bullied him into going to money-lenders... And, no, she was not a nagging woman, but she got her way by slyly making him feel inferior to her. She had done him honour by marrying him and he must pay for what was necessary to her selfish happiness.

At first Nicholas's mother had said he must not visit the

house again. Then that evening – the inquest had taken place the previous day – she told him to take the flowers. His unwillingness surprised her and, oddly enough, made her more decided that he should go on this compassionate errand. He frowned at the flowers but sheltered them from the wind. He wondered if it was true that the Mitchells' house was going to be sold up, and if so could he ask for the goldfish.

When Mrs Mitchell opened the door he looked at her with a furtive nervousness. But, except for the deep black of her shinily flowing new frock, she was no different. 'Oh, Nicholas darling!' she greeted him, with the same composed smile as before the event. And she accepted the flowers as if they were for an afternoon-tea vase. She was alone in the house. But twice there was a caller who was taken privately into the front room for a short while.

'You haven't brought your homework with you?' she asked. He was a little shocked. Upstairs lay the dead man in his coffin. She sat making calculations and notes in a little book. A heap of black-edged stationery lay on the table. The pit hooter sounded. There were silences. He looked at the goldfish eternally circling its bowl. 'What do you feed it with?' he murmured at length.

'Black gloves,' she said inattentively; 'do you think I could find a decent pair in this hole of a place!'

Out of the corners of his eyes he kept on glancing at her, furtively. Once she remarked: 'You are very distant this evening, Nicholas.' Then, as his silences did not abate, she asked suddenly: 'Well, have you forgiven me?' He looked confused, and she added: 'For pushing you away so rudely in the slaughterhouse.' The cloudy aloofness in his mind crystallized then, and he knew he indeed bore her a grudge. She had deprived him of something of high visual interest. In addition he was not yet reconciled to the revelation of how she had *looked*. . . 'Oh, it doesn't matter,' he mumbled, with hypocritical carelessness. He stared again at the goldfish. 'What do you feed the goldfish with?' he repeated.

'You must take that goldfish away with you tonight. Other-

wise those dreadful men will stick a number on the bowl
and get half a crown for it... Would you like to see Mr
Mitchell now?' As he did not reply at once but still looked
owlish, she said: 'Well, come along upstairs.' He rose and
followed her, in half forgiveness. 'I don't like being de-
pressed, it doesn't suit me,' she complained; 'I feel quite old.'

Her fresh poplin skirts hissed as she climbed. 'Poor Mr
Mitchell,' she sighed, 'I do wish I could feel more sorry for
him. But I'm afraid his nature made him melancholy,
though I must say as a young man he wasn't so difficult...
And he used to be quite handsome, in a footballer kind of
way... Ah!' she said, shaking her head, 'these beefy sports-
man types, they're often quite neurotic, just bundles of
nerves... Oh, it's all been so unpleasant,' she went on, with
a dainty squirm of repudiation, 'but I must own he had the
decency to do it *down there.*'

Upstairs there were the same four rooms as in his own
home. She took him into the end back room and turned on
the light. It seemed to be the room where they had slept;
there were brushes on the dressing-table and a man's jacket
was still flung across a chair. On the bed lay a coffin. It sank
heavily into the mattress. The lid lay against a wall. 'You won't
want to be here long,' she suggested, and left him to his
curiosity. He saw her go across the landing to the main front
room and put on the light there. She left both doors open.

He looked into the coffin. Mr Mitchell wore a crisp white
shroud which somehow robbed him of the full powerfulness
of being a man. And his face, with the dark red flabbiness
drained out of it, was not his. He looked as if he had been ill
in bed for a long time but was now secure in a cold sort of
health. Round his throat a folded white napkin was tightly
swathed. This linen muffler, together with the shroud, gave
him an air of being at the mercy of apparel he himself would
not have chosen. Nicholas's round eyes lingered on the napkin.

He left the room feeling subdued and obedient. The cold
isolation of the dead man lying helpless in that strange
clothing made him feel without further curiosity; there was

nothing to astonish, and nothing to startle one into fearful pleasure.

Mrs Mitchell heard him come out and called: 'What do you think of this, Nicholas?' He went along the landing to the fully illuminated front room and saw at once it was where she slept. The room was perfumed and untidy with women's clothes strewn everywhere. Hadn't Mr and Mrs Mitchell used the same room, then, like other married people? He looked around with renewed inquisitiveness. A large cardboard hatbox lay open on the bed. From it Mrs Mitchell was taking a spacious black hat on which the wings of a glossy blackbird were trimly spread in flight. Standing before the mirror, she carefully put on the hat.

Even he could see it was an important hat. She turned and smiled with her old elegant brilliance. 'I'm wearing it to London as soon as Mr Mitchell is buried. My sister is married to a publican there... Do you like it?' she asked in that flattering way that had always nourished him and made him feel that he was a full-size man of opinions.

The Golden Pony

GLYN JONES

FOR the moment the child was at peace and in another world and the terrors of the island were forgotten.

The sun shone warm through the thick glass of the lattice window into the small schoolroom where the heads of the children were bowed over their work. The only sound was the dry creak of the teacher's chair. Then a bluebottle on the window diamonds let go his hold and tumbled droning off the panes about the shabby room. The teacher himself, a hot-skinned man with hob-nailed boots and hair like ginger wool, was drowsing in the airless heat with his chair tilted back and his huge hands locked across his belly. He would sometimes, when he had finished writing with them, lay down his things on the front desk where Rhodri sat, and now in the groove were a fresh stick of white chalk and a new red-ink pen, the wooden holder varnished brown.

Rhodri glanced round the desks. The dozen boys and girls who composed the school wrote round him in silence. He pushed the teacher's piece of chalk forward in the groove, so that the broader part, the white disc of its base, approached the domed end of the shining penholder. The sun poured powerfully onto the desk and the chalk emitted in its radiance a strong reflection, a powerful glow of white light beamed out of the flat disc and illuminated the rounded end of the varnished holder. As the child slowly withdrew the chalk back along the groove the shine on the pen was dimmed and as he slid it forward again the varnish lit up and glowed white in the beam of the oncoming radiance. Rhodri continued to slide the white stick slowly to and fro in grave ecstasy.

The sight called up for him the world which he inhabited

with the golden pony, and his heart glowed. Whenever he was completely absorbed, whenever his eyes, his ears or his heart were filled and satisfied, he seemed to have fallen beneath the spell of that gentle golden-coated creature to whose world he attributed all loveliness and joy.

He meant to look up to see if the teacher was still drowsing but a thread of gossamer drifting out of the gloom of the schoolroom corner caught his eye; slowly it writhed from the shadows into the bright sunlight and suddenly hung burning there brilliant as a firework before floating out into the dimness again.

The edges of Rhodri's exercise book seemed hairy in the clear sunlight as a white cat. He picked up the teacher's pen. The nib was still wet with red ink. He placed it vertically on its point right dead centre of the dazzling clean page of his exercise book. There it cast a long clear shadow across the bright blue lines of the page; and when he tilted it towards him the shadow lengthened, it seemed to become more slender and elegant, the nib tapering into a point of the greatest fineness and delicacy. And the red ink in the slit glowed, both in the nib and in the firm image of its shadow, it burned with a wet ruby brilliance like a bead of scarlet wine. Rhodri was oblivious of everything. Only the pen and its shadow on the dazzling page existed for him, they absorbed his whole being, and the golden naked horse moved round his mind in a glowing ring, casting upon it the radiance of its strange loveliness.

To reassure himself that the varnish of the new pen tasted bitter as his own usually did he placed the end of the holder between his teeth and gently bit it. Small scales of varnish fell with a sharp taste on to his tongue and he wiped them away with the back of his hand. Then he erected the pen again on its nib and continued to slope it this way and that, with his index finger firm on the domed end, watching with complete absorption the altering shape and intensity of the shadow and the jewel-like brilliance of the scarlet bead glowing on the sunlit paper.

And then he stopped. A shadow had fallen on his desk,

completely darkening his sunny exercise book. He lifted his
eyes, and close before them was the guttered belly of the
hot-faced teacher, a bone button and a thick powdering of
chalk in every groove of his waistcoat. The other children
must all have been watching Rhodri because when he raised
up his head and saw the teacher glaring down at him they
all began to laugh.

'Leave things alone,' shouted the teacher in his harsh
voice, and Rhodri felt a stinging blow fall on the side of his
head.

*

The child had come to live in the island at the death of
his parents. His grannie had fetched him from the mainland and they had crossed the sea in stormy weather. As
they came down the path to the beach his heart was heavy,
he could not keep his tears back with loneliness and fore-
boding. His grannie walked beside him in her torn and
shabby cloak muttering to herself. Whenever she kicked
against a stick on the path she picked it up and put it under
her cloak. The child had never seen her before. She had
a wild brown face and her hair was in disorder. Her large
flat eyes were staring and pale, they were fixed wide open
and silverish in the darkness of her face. She said nothing
to the child but muttered endlessly as she trod in sightless
absorption along the path.

The air was heavy around them and utterly still, and the
clouds over the whole sky had turned smoky with thunder.
Above the sea's horizon a great raw patch was spread as
though the outer skin of the heavens had been removed
and the angry under-flesh laid bare, crimson, the sombre
blood heavy behind it. Then a tree shivered and the sudden
cold wind raised a fin of dust along the path. The old
woman's cloak burst open. The cold lead-like rain began to
fall, but she paid no heed to it. The child could see the
ferryboat before them, low in the water, loaded down with
people returning from the mainland. The two crossed the
pebbles and found room in the stern. The people sat round

them in silence and dejection expecting the storm, their dogs
and their baskets at their feet.

In the gusty rain the whole air turned cold and dark as
nightfall. Seabirds flashed sideways through the wind. The
boatman was drunk and his face hideous with a purple disease. He wore black oilskins and cursed the people as he
pushed the heavy boat off the pebbles. The rain came in
oblique gusts as though shooting out sideways from slits in
the sky. The island lay smouldering in the distance, charred
and sombre in the darkness, like a heaped fire gone out on
the sea. Once the boat was out of the shelter of the land, the
rain fell steadily upon it. The mast growled. The brown sail
was out over the water and the rain poured off it into the
sea. The sodden ropes, becoming taut, surrounded themselves with a mist of fine spray.

Out in the smoky channel the boat began to rise and fall,
she shuddered from end to end as the waves exploded under
her and the sea-wool boiled up onto the surface. The child,
cold and wet, looked up in apprehension at his grandmother.
She was heedless of the storm, she stared straight in front
of her, her eyes hard and white and overlaid with an im-
penetrable glaze like mirrors. She muttered endlessly to herself. Her bonnet hung by its ribbon around her neck and her
stiff disordered hair was being plastered down on to her head
by the rain.

The people looked at one another in fear. They no longer
tried to shield themselves from the pelting rain and their
sodden clothes shone like black silk. They were silent. Some
covered their faces with their wet hands. The dogs shivered
and whimpered and were not reproved. Suddenly the boat
banked steeply on its side as though it would turn over, and
the sea smoked over it. Several voices cried out in terror.
Rhodri's grandmother stopped muttering and looked about
her. She left her seat. She knelt down in the water at the
bottom of the boat and began a wild prayer. The boatman
cursed her and pointed through the rain to the sea-plastered
crags of the island. The child trembled with misery and fear.

The woman sitting on the other side of him lifted her cloak and put it over him, covering his head. There, in the utter darkness, he could smell the sweat and camphor of her hard body. He could hear the quarrel above the storm, his grannie's voice screaming and the boatman shouting in reply. The boat plunged and shuddered and from time to time he heard a blow fall upon the taut cloak in a splashing thud as a wave came over the side. He drowsed. He could not remember landing. The next morning he woke up in his grannie's house.

*

A dog was yelling in unremitted agony. The child opened his eyes and heard some creature scampering rat-like across the hot roof sloping close above his head. Instantly he remembered and looked about in confusion. The grimy whitewashed bedroom was bare but filled up with sunlight. The window was a latched square of cobwebbed glass. He thought with a heavy heart of the meeting with his grandmother and the terrible crossing of the water. Hurriedly he got up from bed and looked out of the window. His eyes were on a level with a large vegetable garden where everything was green and glittering like tin in the sun. The dog was not to be seen but the cries continued in a high-pitched voice, the creature yelled hysterically and then sank into a series of agonized whimperings. The child, in deep distress, went down into the kitchen.

There it was dim and stifling, because a large piece of brown paper had been pinned over the window to keep the sun off the fire. He could not see his grannie. The room was bare but a great chained kettle hung boiling over the fire. His clothes were drying on a chair-back. He opened the kitchen door and looked out into the yard. The crying at once redoubled in intensity and he heard a drumming noise and the sound of a chain being rattled. The yard was a square of soft mud and dung with decaying out-houses surrounding it. In one corner was a barrow-load of dung over-

grown with shoots of new grass. Near the kitchen door a
great heap of his grannie's twigs leaned against a broken
fragment of brickwork.

It was an agony like a tearing of the flesh to hear the
crying mount up again to a fresh climax of howls and yells.
Soon it was plain the clamour came from an old out-house
on the far side of the yard, a broken-backed pig-sty with a
roof under heavy dock and feverfew. The door shook as it
was thumped from the inside and the chain rattled.

An old man trudged into the yard at a stoop leading a
hulking ginger horse. He was wearing corduroy trousers
and a ragged black jacket. An old hat was pulled down over
his eyes. The mare had been working in traces and her
chains jingled as she placed her great hairy hooves down
in the mud. The dog heard the jingling and his crying increased in anguish. The child closed his eyes, he felt utterly
engulfed, quite overborne and annihilated.

When he looked again, the old man had begun to pile
the mare's harness on the bank. The child could see the
sweat dark on her naked coat the same shape as the harness.
The old man gave no sign that he heard the dog. Slowly he
leaned one hand against the mare's flank and with the other
began to milk her. As he plucked beneath her a rigid stream
of warm milk fell with a splashing sound upon the mud.
The child felt a deep stirring of his bowels. The anguish of the
dog's crying was unheard as the white milk flowed over the
mud and dung of the yard. In a moment the old man gave
up and crossed to unbolt the stable. His movements had the
clumsy ungainliness of an aged animal. The door of the pig-
sty rattled under its battering as he trudged past, but he did
not turn his head.

Out of the stable a beautiful golden foal bounded into
the sunlight. The child's eyes opened with wonder and delight at the sight of her. She was the most beautiful thing
he had ever seen and she was alive, she was moving and
sunlit, and in his presence. Her coat was a pale limpid golden,
a flamy honey-colour that seemed to flash off its fluid brilliance into the sunlight as she moved. Her mane and tail

were already long and plentiful, to him they were as white as snow, but her muzzle had the dull smoky look of dark velvet. Her coming was a gap of ecstasy and pure silence. She trotted uncertainly into the middle of the yard, shying and prancing on her beautiful long legs, bewildered by the unsheltered brightness of the world. Then with a whinny she made for the great mare standing motionless and indifferent beside the bank and began to take suck. The child stared in blissful fascination. The marvel of the golden foal filled his heart, his delight ran through him like some great shaking draughts of ecstasy. Everything around him, while he gazed, fell under a spell of unassailable silence.

The old man, long-armed and high-shouldered, turned his back on the horses. Some cinders had been thrown down on the mud to form a path and he advanced over them with a stiff tread towards the house. His hoarse breath came with difficulty. He walked head down with a great hump-backed stoop, so that he was almost at the doorstep before he saw the child. Slowly he raised his eyes and Rhodri felt a sharp stab of anguish at the sight of them. They were dark as jet but the long lashes surrounding them were almost white, they were very thick and long, as dense as the hair of an animal, like a fringe of long yellow fur surrounding the edges of the dark lids. The face was rugged and bony, but the mouth hung open, the thick flesh of the lips seemed too slack and shapeless to cover up the hideous teeth. The old man said nothing, he stood and blinked at the child in morose suspicion, his great bony shoulders rising and falling as he gulped breath hoarsely through his wet mouth. Because of his stoop, the shining collar of his coat went out in a wide loop behind his neck and the sun shone on it in a half circle. He took off his hat and placed it on the sill. His long brown teeth showed and the broad back of his nose became loaded with a mass of wrinkles as he frowned into the dazzling sunlight. The child noticed the top of his head was hairless and not brown like his face, the dark skin ended abruptly where his hat had been and the pale scalp was thickly covered with beads of sweat. He lifted up his large

bony hands and placed them with a clumsy action like a
cap on the crown of his head. He held them there for a
moment gasping for breath. Then he moved them slowly
down over his soaking skin. The drench of sweat was
squeezed forward along his scalp, it ran off his head before
his hands and poured down over his face.

The child stared at him with the silent regard of complete
fascination. Clogs clattered across the kitchen flags behind
him and he could see his grandmother in the dimness
beckoning with sud-gloved hands. Her stiff hair was wild
and her eyes in that gloom seemed to have become completely sightless and transparent. The child went in towards
her with fear. Behind him the explosive yelling of the dog
broke out with unabated frenzy.

Soon the old man followed, bringing mud and dung into
the kitchen. He sat down as though with exhaustion at the
table. When he had replaced his sweat-sodden hat he began
to eat in stolid silence. His hands were large and stiff, like
great rigid claws falling upon his food. The child, seated
opposite him, tried to eat his own breakfast, but he could
not. He was in fear, his soul filled with utter confusion and
bewilderment. He saw the old man breathing heavily and
turning his food round in his slack mouth; he saw the beautiful foal springing golden into the sunlit yard; and he heard
the incessant yelling of the chained-up dog. He began to
pray in silence that the agony might be remitted.

'Mamgu,' he said at last, looking round at his grandmother, 'Mamgu, why is the dog crying all the time?'

She came towards him with a look of puzzlement in her
eyes. 'Crying?' she repeated, and turned to face the old man.
She mumbled something which the child failed to catch.
The old man shook his head slowly and resumed his chewing. The dog howled throughout the meal, and the chain
rattled with agonizing repetition.

When he had finished, the old man got up and went out
without speaking, a thick brown scum around his mouth.
Rhodri said: 'Mamgu, is he my grandfather?'

She looked at him again in wide-eyed puzzlement. Then she nodded her head.

*

The child's cave, although it overlooked the sea, was not one of rock. It was a hollow under a grove of elders and, wearing only his ragged trousers, he sat at the mouth of it looking out over the water. The dog lay down panting at his feet and the golden pony, swishing her tail, cropped the green turf of the slope. The afternoon was still and silent, every leaf and blade of grass stood out brilliant and petrified in the intense heat. On an unsheltered rock cropping out of the turf the sun had kindled its uncoloured bonfire. The blue of the sky was flawless, it stretched out tranquil and unsoiled to the horizon and there was not a white cloud in it to cast the stain of a shadow upon the sea. From time to time, as the child watched, the breeze beat the water gently with ferns. At the foot of the slope, where the hill went into the sea in dark crags, the snowy gulls floated, they heaved gently upon a sea-swell that washed the black rocks in the milk of an endless caressing. The child had been bathing; before the tide was full he had ridden the golden pony naked along the lonely beach, splashing in the shallows of the sea.

The child came to his cave for safety and solitude. Every day now he was with the beautiful pony. At first he would stand by her when she was having suck and when she had finished she would come to him with milk on her mouth, blinking the dark globes of her eyes, black and lustrous. He was a little timid of her but she was gentle and gay and he soon learned not to fear her. He would put out his hand and stroke the soft sooty plush of her unquiet muzzle. When she had been weaned and placed in a field by herself, he used to go to the gate, before school and after, to speak to her. Directly she saw him she would throw up her head, point out her rigid ears and trot towards him with breeze-borne mane and outfloating tail. It was bliss to see her move rapidly over the grass with the grace of a great golden

bird and the radiance of sunlight. She became more beautiful. Soon all the rough tufts of foal-fur had disappeared even
from her long slender legs. Her white mane thickened, her
creamy tail almost reached the ground. Her coat assumed
a polish like brushed and smoothed silk, it was a golden
orange colour, but in some lights paler, almost honey yellow,
or caramel, and then sometimes again the rich bronzy lustre
of old gold.

Often when he came to the gate she was waiting for him,
standing with her glowing flank against the bars. Then he
would speak gently to her and give her sugar or an apple,
and sit astride her back. Round and round the field they
went, she placing down the pure white horn of her unshod
hooves delicately upon the grass and tossing her dense and
snowy mane off her neck at every step; he speaking gently
to her her own praises, bending forwards to pat her neck
with his hand beneath her mane. Her beauty and gentleness
filled his imagination day and night. He loved the brown-
eyed spaniel, but the mare was like a great flame of delight
flaring up in the centre of his being. In his cave he crossed
seas with her, climbed mountains, rode triumphantly
through fallen cities. She accompanied him everywhere on
the island. She dispelled the hauntings of the eyes, the
animal stare of his long-lashed grandfather and the insane
and transparent eyes of his grandmother.

One night the child had climbed out of his bedroom window into the moonlit garden. He found the dog, a little
black spaniel, on a short chain in the ruined pig-sty crying
pitifully to himself. The whole floor was under an oozing
mass of pigs' dung. He held the dog against his body to
comfort him and the little creature leaned up against him,
shivering and whimpering softly. His nose on the boy's
cheek was cold and moist, like the touch of a snail. In a few
moments he began gently to lick the child's face with his
rough tongue. Every time Rhodri moved, the dog seemed
to cling to him and his crying began again, but now it was
only soft and plaintive. The child unfastened the chain and
took the dog into his bedroom. They both slept. The next

morning he tossed the chain into the nettles. Later he raked out all the stale dung off the floor of the pig-sty, and was sick. His grannie came and watched him at his work, she stood at the door of the kitchen, her great flat eyes fixed immovably upon him, but she said nothing.

Rhodri's grandfather spoke seldom and never to him. The island was rocky and he laboured in silence. Once on the little beach below the farm the child sat down and began building a model in sand. It was large and elaborate, part temple, part fortress, part palace, with courts, arches, and towers, all ornamented with cockle-shells and glittering chips of glass-like quartz. The weather was sunny and he worked for several hours with the spaniel panting beside him. He had built it beyond the reach of the tide, so that he could return to it. At last, when he looked up, he could see the sun was lying down close to the water, its great red eye glaring across the flat sands, and he knew he would not be able to complete his work until the next day. As he moved back to admire the square-built walls, and the pebble-studded windows, he saw his grandfather driving the cart across the sands. The hulking mare was in the shafts and she came out of the sunset at a smart trot. The old man was standing up stooping, his hat over his eyes, but Rhodri could feel he was looking at him. The great horse approached at a good pace, her hooves clacking and her harness jingling. His grandfather drove straight on towards him. The mare went heedless over the sand-building and kicked it to pieces. The child sat down and hung his head. His grandfather had not turned to look after him. The cart rolled on. The spaniel, seeing the child with his head bowed in misery, came up and began to lick his face, in his eagerness to bring comfort he destroyed all that was left of the model.

The child's cave faced the sea. It was on the steep and barren side of the island where no one lived. He spent much of his time near it because the boys who persecuted him would never pursue him to this distance. To the cave he came to escape from his sense of solitariness and his un-ceasing desire to escape from the cruelty of the island. Here he forgot his fear of the brutal schoolmaster, and of the boys who hated him; here he was not haunted by the watchfulness of his grandfather and his grandmother's muttering and her screaming in the night. It was to the cave he came to eat the fruits he found on the island, the bilberries and the little wild strawberries and once or twice when he had fallen into the sea he had lit a fire there to dry his clothes. But he would not light a fire in it now. A robin had built a nest in the overhead boughs and her little brood had already hatched.

From time to time a swallow cut over the grass, capering around the heels of the grazing pony. The pony's coat was honey-yellow, and where the light fell upon her back it shone like a saddle of pure silver. She had been rolling and upon her shoulder was a pale grass-stain, like a green patch of the most delicate verdigris. With her head drooped forward on her arched-out neck, a thick lock of mane hung between her ears on to her brow the colour of the froth of meadowsweet. Her muzzle had a dusty look as though it had been thrust into dark pollen. Her wavy tail broadened out and then tapered irregularly to a point that almost touched the grass. The boy did everything for her now. One day he would ride her through the world and everyone would recognize her beauty. The crowds in the streets would see him astride her with his legs along her golden flanks and as she trotted by they would acclaim the fluttering of her mane, and the elegant alighting of ivory hooves, and the soft swansdown floating of her tail. She had begun to cast her glow and enchantment upon everything that existed with her in his imagination, and objects and sensations were recreated for him in her image. When he opened his eyes in his bedroom, the morning was a great horse, green and naked, ravaging the world outside his window. Watching the snow alighting gracefully, flake by flake, curving in the wind towards him over the hedge, he saw the beautiful stepping of white ceremonial hooves, advancing with delicacy out of the weather. And each day he saw in her more clearly the symbol of his escape.

In the evening the weather became chilly. A gull, perching on a rock near by, recalled him with the screeches of the splayed nib of her beak. Inside the cave the little robins opened their beaks as he paid them his final visit. He watched the pony gracefully curving her front leg forward on the slope and rubbing her muzzle against the inside of it. He whistled and her head came up and her ears stood erect. Then he made for the house with the dog and the golden pony following him.

*

After school the child went to look at the nest. He had known of it from the beginning, when it was merely twigs and a bowl of smooth mud, like a large acorn-cup. He had seen the six warm-hued eggs laid in it and he had visited the young ones almost every day to watch them grow. Soon they would be fledged. On the way he noticed that three of the boys who persecuted him were coming at a distance behind him. The boys had one day chased the golden pony to annoy him by making her sweat. They cornered her in the field and as she broke out one of them ran behind her clutching at her tail. She cast up her hooves and at one kick the boy's arm snapped like a candle. Since then they had attacked him constantly.

To throw the boys off his track he hurried down the path leading towards the bay. In a little he glanced behind again and he found he was no longer being followed, so he turned up the cliff in the direction of the cave. He wondered if the little robins would have learnt to fly. They completely filled up the nest now, they seemed to repose quite motionless on top of one another, forming a dome of smoky-coloured fluff enriched with a gleam of jewel-like eyes and with six yellow mouths that opened wide whenever he approached.

Rhodri stooped and went into the cave. He looked into the recess between the boughs where the birds were. He found only a heap of twigs with moss and horsehair hanging from it. His heart went cold, he felt an iciness lipping over into every part of his body. He dropped to his knees and saw the robins lying dead on the floor. Some had their heads cut off and others had been squashed with heavy stones. He groped his way out of the cave bewildered with rage and anguish. Standing on the path were the three boys who had followed him. They were stolid and old in their long, frayed trousers, their heavy faces dull and expressionless. One of them came up to him and gripped the front of his jacket. 'Robbing nests,' he said.

Rhodri tried to get away. He was afraid of the boys. They were bigger than he was, they worked on the land after school and were strong. The boy held him firmly by the coat, his face thrust close, heavy and repulsive. 'Let me go,' said Rhodri. 'I didn't rob the nest. It was my nest. It was you who robbed it. I know you robbed it.'

One of the boys came on to the path and spat on Rhodri's coat. Then he laughed. The child's heart thumped as though it had increased to many times its normal size. He tried to wrench off the hand that was holding him, but the boy pushed him over backwards and bore him onto the ground and lay heavily upon him.

At the pain of the fall the fear of his tormentors seemed to leave him and his flesh was possessed by an overwhelming frenzy of hatred. He writhed and struggled in the dust, try-ing to bite. He heard coming out of his own throat the scream of his demented hate, in its mastery he thought only of destroying the iron weight and the smell of the boy astride him. He lashed out savagely with his feet, he wanted to claw at the dull expressionless eyes, to smash into a pulp the bones and flesh of the stupid face. But he could not wrench his hands free, his wrists were held to the ground as firmly as with fetters. And gradually to his dismay he felt the great wave of lust and power ebbing from him. The knowledge that he had been impotent, even when nourished with this unaccustomed strength and ferocity, filled him with humiliation. He began to gasp for breath although all the time his lungs seemed full and bursting. He heaved his body up again convulsively and tried to squirm out from under the powerful unbudging body, but the passion had deserted him. Tears of dismay and frustration burned in his eyes. His body became limp. When he was quite still and the tears were running freely, the boy astride him leaned forward and struck him in the face. 'You pig,' he said, and slowly the immovable body was lifted.

Then the two other boys who had watched the struggle in silence and indifference came closer. One of them said: 'He's mad, like his grannie.' The other kicked the dust near Rhodri's head so that it fell over his face. The three then went away.

Rhodri crouched on the ground. His wrists burned like fire where he had been held down and he felt limp and weak, as though with long hunger. He made no attempt to rise. He sobbed bitterly on the path until his throat ached like a wound. No one came near. Presently a chill wind began to blow. He shivered. He had sweated during the struggle and now his bruised flesh seemed turning to ice. He felt sick and giddy. He crawled to the door of the cave and sat down in utter wretchedness, his face in his hands. His head throbbed. He would leave the island. He had no money but he would swim across to the mainland at low water and the golden pony should go with him. He wiped his face, and made his way back to the farm. His determination to escape filled his mind and his misery was overborne by it. Near the house he passed his grannie collecting sticks in her apron. She glanced at him from her staring eyes but did not stop or speak. He hurried on. The house was wide open and empty. He went upstairs and lay down on the bed, waiting for the darkness.

*

At midnight the child came down the beach with the pony behind him. In the distance, beyond the sea, was the dark mainland with a few lights sprinkled on the backs of the hills. A full moon glowed rosy in the sky as though an unseen fire were lit against her curve. The tide was like black glass. It had gone out a long way and as the child went over the wet sand the moon was fragmentary in the little water-

filled grooves and depressions of the beach, rapidly its light
splintered into bright fragments and as rapidly flashed together again into one shining disc as the brilliant image was
momentarily whole in a wide pool.

The child stood at the edge of the sea, wearing only his
shirt and trousers. The night was calm and silent and very
warm. The water in the straits lay motionless before him
except for a strip of tide near the mainland where the current was running out strongly. Down the shelving sand into
the sea he waded and the pony came after him. The water
rose over his bare feet, over his knees, over his loins. In spite
of the mildness of the night the sea was cold. When he was
over his shoulders, he heard the pony snort behind him and
begin to swim. She came alongside with only her head out
of the water. Her mane floated and her nostrils were wide,
shaped out like the mouths of trumpets. The boy flung his
arm over her back as she passed him and kicked out. Together they went along, swimming side by side through the
silent water. The child's heart was filled with unutterable
joy. He was no longer fearful. He was escaping and the
golden pony would be with him, she was bearing him away
in the moonlight for ever from the island. Before long they
would touch together the sands of the mainland. Many times
he had swum in this sea but never so tirelessly and with
such elation as now. The moon gave them ample light. His
arm lay in an easy grip over the back of the pony, her white
mane floated and the water swished up against her body
as she kicked out with her hooves. Calmly, in perfect unison,
they approached the middle of the straits.

There the current became stronger, soon the child could
feel it beginning to wash his body away from the flank of
the pony. She too felt the strain and although her pace did
not slacken her breathing became heavier. Presently he had
to clutch fiercely at her neck and mane to prevent himself
being swept away, and he feared this might bring her head
under. The sea was no longer silent, it began to rush with
the roar of a great river, deep ridges appeared along the
current as though the water were being miraculously

ploughed. His body was dandled about from wave to wave. He thought that if he could get to the other side of the pony then the current would drive him against her flank and not away from her as it was doing at present. They had drifted a long way below the nearest point to the island, the outward-jutting rock on which he had hoped to land, and the force of the current showed no sign of diminishing. And in spite of the powerful swimming of the pony they did not seem to be getting any nearer the land; instead they were being swept along parallel to it. The child feared that in this swift and rough water they would soon become separated. He determined to risk diving under the pony's head so that he could rest against her other flank. He was beginning to tire, but there all his energy could be used in swimming forward, not in holding on to the pony.

He drew himself up close to her, his arms around her neck. She went on swimming bravely, her wide-eyed head rising and falling as she went across the current. He whispered her praises and then dived. He tried with the ends of his fingers to maintain contact with her coat under water, but his hands were numb with cold and directly his head was submerged she was swept out of his reach. When he came to the surface she was nowhere to be seen.

The glaring of the moon troubled him and the splashing of the moonlit torrent in his eyes. He found himself moving along faster than ever. The gutter-like current lifted him on to the crest of a ridge and he glanced rapidly over his shoulders. The pony was behind him. She was still swimming strongly in the direction of the land but she did not seem to have made any headway. She seemed rather to be further out from the rocks than when they had become separated. The child realized that when he had dived he had not gone beneath her head at all. The current had hurled him forward and now its force was separating them more widely every minute.

He tried hard to swim parallel to the pony's head but he made no progress, the powerful rush of the broken water bore him along past the land. Soon he would be swept out to sea. He struggled afresh, but he was cold and nearing exhaustion. His lungs seemed to be inflated all the time, and hard. His head went under constantly and the water roared in his ears. Each time he came to the surface the moon appeared to be held right against his eyes, dazzling bright and yellow as candle-flame. He spun round like a leaf on a cobweb. Rising suddenly out of the water, he glanced rapidly around again. In that hurried glimpse he saw the golden pony rising out of the sea; somehow she had reached the land and was slowly making her way up the beach, shining like silver in the moonlight. The golden pony was safe. What would she do alone on the shore? Would she wait for him? He had to reach the land, he was bound now to get ground under his feet again, so that they could be together.

And then gradually he felt the current diminish. He had been swept round into a small bay, behind which stretched out a large dark fan of land. The tide seemed to have run out completely and the waters to have become slack. With what strength he had left he struck out in the direction of the land. He had not gone far when he found his arms touching the floating fronds of seaweed. His feet sank to the rocks. He staggered forward, falling and slipping among the underwater boulders. He found he was naked. In utter exhaustion and wretchedness he climbed over the rocks and reached a cut field bordering the sea. There he pulled a haycock over himself and took sleep into his body like a drink.

When he awoke the sun was shining brightly. The loud morning rang like strings with birdsong. His body ached. He could scarcely move. But the thought of the pony gave him no rest. He dragged himself out of the hay and stood upright. There in the distance lay the island floating lightly upon the varnished sea, calm and beautiful in the morning sun. Far out in the channel was the ferryboat, making for the island under her brown sail. And behind the boat was a small black object moving along at the same pace. The child recognized it at once. It was the head of the golden pony. They were swimming her back to the island.

Acting Captain

ALUN LEWIS

THE detachment was a very small one, a single platoon sent
from the battalion to guard the dock gates and perimeter,
but they had a bugle. Acting Captain Cochrane, the detachment commander, had indented persistently for one, and
after two months' nagging on his part, D.A.D.O.S. had
grudgingly coughed up a brand new one. It was hanging
over old Crocker's bed in the fuggy blacked-out Nissen hut
in which the administrative staff were sleeping. There was
Crocker, an old soldier who had served in Flanders, Gallipoli,
India, and the Far East; he was the cook, Acting Lance-
Corporal, C.3, and used to it. Next to him Taffy Thomas was
snoring; the air had grown slowly thicker and more corrupt
with fumes from the stove, last night's fish and chips, cigarettes and beer, and all the coming and going since black-out
time on the previous evening; so you couldn't breathe it into
your lungs without a snore as it squeezed and scraped past
your uvula. The fire was still flickering under a weight of
grey ash and cinders in the stove.

For no apparent reason Crocker woke up, groaned,
yawned, pushed his dirty blankets off, and sat up, vigorously
scratching his thin hair. He was wearing his thick winter
vest and long pants with brown socks pulled up over the legs
so that no part of his flesh was showing except where the heel
of his sock was worn through. He listened a moment, to discover whether it was raining; then, finding it wasn't, he un-
hooked his bugle from the nail above his head, turned the
light on to make sure that the office clock, which he always
took to bed with him, indicated 6.30 a.m., put out the light
again, shuffled to the door, spat, breathed in, closed his lips
inside the mouthpiece of the bugle, and blew reveille. He

found he was blowing in E instead of G, but, after faltering an instant, laboured through with it in the same key. It was too dark for anyone to notice; not a streak of grey anywhere.

'Gawd curse the dominoes,' he grumbled, shuffling back to his bed. He shook Taffy Thomas hard, relishing the warm sleeping body's resistance.

'Get up, yer Welsh loafer,' he shouted in his ear. 'You'll 'ave the boss on yer tail if you don't get down there wiv 'is shaving water double quick. Get up. You ain't got yer missus besidejer now.'

Taffy didn't get up as philosophically as Crocker. He was still young enough to resent and rebel against things the old cook had long ago ceased thinking about. Most things were a matter of course to Crocker; air raids, sinkings, death were as normal as cutting rashers of bacon in the dark and peeling potatoes in his ramshackle corrugated-iron cooking shed.

However, Taffy got up. He put his hand on his head to feel how hot his hangover was, and then in a fit of irritated energy pulled on his trousers and pullover and searched about for his razor. 'Well, we're a day's march nearer home,' he said, dipping his shaving brush in the jam-tin of cold water he kept under his bed and lathering his face in the dark.

'You pups are always thinking about leave,' Crocker said, fed-up. 'D'you know I didn't see my old lady for three and 'alf years in the last bust-up, nor any English girl. Plenty of dusky ones, of course, and Chinese ones that'd scarcely left school—'

'Yeh, I know,' Taffy interrupted. 'You're a real soljer. I know.'

'Well, I didn't want to write 'ome every time I found a flea under my arm,' Crocker scoffed. 'I've sat in the mud scratching my arse from one Christmas to the next wivout arsking to see the O.C. abaht it.'

'It wasn't your fault we didn't lose the war, then,' Taffy said, wiping his shaved face in his dirty towel. 'And if you're moaning about me asking for leave and asking for a transfer, you'd better shut your trap, old soljer, 'cause I'm not going

to sit in this dump doing nothing while my missus freezes in
the Anderson and coughs 'er heart up every time Jerry
drops a load on Swansea.'

'What you going to do, then?' Crocker taunted. 'Stop the
war?'

'No,' Taffy answered hotly. 'Win the bleeding thing.'

'Garn,' Crocker laughed jeeringly. 'Get off and polish the
cap'n's Sam Browne. Win the war, be damned. What was you
doing at Dunkirk if it isn't rude to ask? We never scuttled
out of it, we didn't.'

'Aw, shut up and get a pail of char ready for the lads,'
Taffy said. 'I reckon you'd still be in your little dugout if
somebody hadn't told you the war was over.'

He slammed the door after him, pulled his cycle from
under a ripped tarpaulin, and, tucking his bag of cleaning
kit under his arm, pedalled through the muddy pooled ruts,
past the sentry shivering in his greatcoat and flapping
groundsheet like a spider swollen by the rain, down the lane
past the knife-rest and Dannert wire obstacle that ran from
the sidings to the quay where the Irish packet boat lay
moored, and out onto the bleak tarred road that was just
beginning to reflect a mildew-grey light along its wet surface. The detachment commander was billeted in an empty
house on the hill above the harbour. Taffy's first job was to
boil him some water for shaving and tea, make a cup of tea
with a spoon infuser, shake him respectfully, salute, collect
his Sam Browne and yesterday's boots or shoes, and retire
to the scullery to clean them up. Then he swept the downstairs rooms, looked round to see whether there were any
chocolate biscuits hidden in the trench-coat pocket, threw
his sweepings outside for the starlings to swoop and grumble
over, and then go back upstairs to fold the blankets and
sheets, empty the wash basin and jerry, and let the clean air
of the ocean revitalize the room. The whole operation was
conducted in silence, broken only by odd grunts and mono-
syllables from the officer and a sort of absent-minded
whistling by the private. Taffy knew his man well enough to
leave him alone while he pulled himself together; a glance at

his reflection in the shaving mirror was enough to inform
him as to the patient's condition. He had a young face, but
his narrow grey eyes and almost pointed teeth, combined
with the thin bony forehead and cheeks, gave him an
astringent intolerant sharpness that only wore off after he
had warmed up to the day's task. He was a regular officer
who had been commissioned a few months before the war
began, and because of his martinet appearance and the
facility with which he could fly into an abrupt temper he
had spent most of the war drilling recruits on the square at
the regimental depot. He had got the square in his blood
by the end; muddy boots or tarnished buttons, an indifferent
salute, the lazy execution of a drill or an order provoked him
immediately to a violent reprimand; all his actions were impatient and smart, his appearance immaculate and important, his opinions unqualified and as definite as they were
ill-informed. His nature was bound to insist sooner or later
on action; he had got into a bad state at the depot and asked
to be posted to a battalion. He considered it a rebuff when
he was posted to this small harbour on the featureless north-
west coast, and it hadn't improved his frame of mind to consider that a further application for posting would be im-
politic while an indefinite stay in his present post could only
blur the image of a forceful disciplined soldier which he had
so assiduously striven to impress on the depot command. He
endured his inactive isolation with some acerbity and sought
compensation in other quarters. He was careful of his career,
knowing how easy it is to fall down the Army ladder; he paid
court to the daughter of the battalion's colonel with the
same regard for tact and proper keenness as he employed in
his conduct towards his senior officers. But he was not of a
firm enough mould to subsist on long-term expectations of
advancement. He had to have his fling. And, what with one
thing and another, he usually got out of bed on the wrong
side and had to work a little blood out of his system before
he could sit on his table and argue politics or swop dirty
jokes with Sergeant Crumb, his principal stooge, or Private
Norris, his clerk general who had a classics degree, an LL.B.,

a mind of his own, and a stoop that barred him from pro-
motion.

'Quiet night last night, sir,' Taffy said amiably when the
hair-combing stage had been reached and a measure of
civility might be expected.

'Was it, hell!' the O.C. replied, wincing his face. 'Mix me
a dose of Andrews' Health Salts, Thomas. They're in my
valise.'

'Very good, sir.'

'What sort of morning is it?'

'Nothin' partic'lar, sir. What do you want for tonight, sir?'

'My S.D. suit and my Sam Browne; best shoes and walking
out cap. I don't want any silvo stains on it, either.'

'Very good, sir.'

The vexed look left the harsh young face as he tilted the
bubbling glass down his throat; beads hooked to the un-
combed hairs of his moustache; it was pink at the roots and
gold-brown at the tips. 'Gosh!' he said, 'it makes you want
to live a clean life always, tasting this stuff. God bless Mr
Andrews.'

Having returned and breakfasted with the rest of the lads
on old Crocker's lumpy porridge and shrivelled bacon and
greased tea, Taffy strolled off to collect his wheelbarrow and
begin his second task, cleaning the lines. He had sharpened
a beech-stick to pick up the chip papers and litter; Curly
Norris had suggested the idea, saying it gave the camp a
better tone, made it more like a royal park. Curly also wanted
to indent for a couple of fallow deer, or if D.A.D.O.S. refused
to supply them, purloin them from the grounds of Magdalen
College, Oxford. He said Taffy should lead the raiding party,
singing the War song of Dinas Fawr.

'You will probably be put on a charge,' he said. 'But what
is a charge *sub specie aeternitatis*?'

He was always laughing behind his twinkling spectacles,
and even if you didn't know what he was talking about,
which was most of the time, his gaiety infected you and you
laughed as well or wrestled with him.

When Taffy arrived outside the office Curly Norris was just completing his housework. The office was swirling with smoke from the newly lit fire and dust from the floor. Curly's first task was to sweep all the dust from the floor onto the tables and shelves and files. This ritual was always performed alone, before Sergeant Crumb arrived for the day.

Taffy halted his barrow and respectfully tapped the office door.

'Any old match-sticks today?' he shouted. 'Any old match-sticks?'

'Take your dirty boots off my porch,' Curly shouted. 'A woman's work is never done, don't you men know that yet?'

Taffy jumped in and screwed his arm round Curly's neck. They were wrestling on the table when Sergeant Crumb appeared. At his bull's bellow they stopped.

'What the hell d'you think this is? A tavern?'

'Sorry, sarge.'

'You'll apologize to the O.C. if I catch you at it again, either of you.' He smoothed the underside of his waxed moustache with a nicotine-stained forefinger. 'What sort of a mood is he in this morning, Thomas?' Sergeant Crumb always arranged the morning programme on the basis of Taffy's report.

'Got a liver on this morning, sarge,' Taffy replied. 'Shouldn't be surprised if it turns to diarrhoea.'

'I saw him in the Royal at closing time,' Sergeant Crumb said. 'He was buying drinks all round, so I expected he'd be off his food. Get cracking, Norris. Get the correspondence sorted out, let's see what there is. Then get down to the stores and warn Rosendale to appear before the O.C. I saw him in town last night when he should have been on duty. Make a charge-sheet out before you go. Section 40 – conduct prejudicial to good order. Get weaving.'

Curly thought it a pity there wasn't a mantelpiece for the sergeant's elbows and a waistcoat for his thumbs.

'Very good, sarge.'

'And you get down to cleaning the lines, Thomas. What are you hanging about here for?'

'Want to see the O.C.,' Thomas said.

'Too busy,' the sergeant replied, stiffening his weak chin. 'Get out.'

'I can see the O.C. if I want to,' Thomas replied.

'A-ha!' laughed the sergeant, his shallow blue eyes turning foxy. 'Getting a bit Bolshie, are you? What with you and Rosendale in the detachment we'd better hoist the Red Flag, I'm thinking.' He straightened up, blew out his chest, hardened his characterless eyes. 'Get out!' he shouted.

Curly wasn't laughing now. He looked serious, bothered, and unhappy. The way these foolish and unnecessary rows blew up, these continual petty litigations springing from bad temper and jealousy and animosity; why did they allow their nerves to become public? Why couldn't they hold their water?

Taffy stayed where he was, stubborn and flushing. He had a bony ridge at the base of his neck, a strong chin and a knobbly receding forehead. Huge-shouldered and rather short and bandy in the leg, he gave the appearance of animal strength and latent ferocity.

'That was an order,' the sergeant said.

'O.K.,' Taffy replied. 'But I'm asking to see the O.C. You can't refuse.'

The sergeant began to hesitate, grew a little sick at the mouth, fiddled with the paper-cutter.

'What d'you want with him?'

'I want to get into a Commando,' Taffy said.

'You'll get into a glasshouse, maybe,' the sergeant laughed unpleasantly, not at all sure of himself now.

'Yes, for knocking you between your pig's eyes,' Taffy said.

An immediate tension, like the shock of an electric charge, and silence.

'You heard what he said, Norris,' the sergeant snapped. 'I'll want you as witness.'

'Hearsay doesn't count as evidence,' Curly said quietly.

'What did you say?' Sergeant Crumb swung livid on him. 'You bloody little sea-lawyer, are you trying to cover him?'

'No. I'm not covering anybody. I simply happen to know that legal procedure excludes my repeating something alleged to have been said by a person not formally warned.'

Sergeant Crumb wrote some words on a sheet of paper.

'We'll see,' he said, uncertainly. 'Now get out.'

Taffy shrugged his shoulders and slouched out. He hadn't meant to say that. Not out loud. All the same, it was O.K. by him. He pushed his barrow down the muddy path to the stores shed.

Rosendale was shaving in his shirt-sleeves. His mirror was a splinter of glass an inch long stuck into a packing case. There was a heap of straw in one corner of the shed; the men were changing the straw of their palliasses; he, as store-man, was in charge; he gave more to some than to others – not to his friends, for he had none, but to the important people, the lance-jacks and the lads with a tongue in their heads who determined public opinion in the camp. Rosendale was very sensitive to public opinion, partly because it affected his own advancement, partly because he was politically conscious and wanted to form a cell to fortify his somewhat introvert ideas. He was inept as a soldier, too untidy and slow to get a stripe; consequently he posed as a democrat refusing to be bought over to the ruling classes by a stripe, as one of the unprivileged millions who would be deprived of power and exploited by the boss class for just as long as they were content to endure it. He wasn't making much headway in his campaign. His ideas were too dogmatic to convince men who saw life as a disconnected series of circumstances and poverty as a natural ill and active political opposition as both unpatriotic and unpleasant, something that might get you C.B., or your application for a week-end pass rejected. He was popularly known as Haw-Haw.

'Morning, Rosie,' Taffy said, having recovered his equanimity. 'Had a tidy sleep, love?'

'Be damned I didn't,' Rosendael grumbled. 'I slept in that bleeding straw in the corner there and a goddamn mouse

crawled under my shirt and bit me under my arm. I squeezed
him through my shirt and the little sod squirted all over
it.'

'Well, you'd better brass yourself up, Rosie,' Taffy commented, ''cause the snoop has pegged you for being out of
camp last night when you were on duty. I'm on the peg, too.
So don't start moaning.' At such moments Rosendale lacked
the dignity and calm bearing of the representative of the
unprivileged millions. He became an anxious, frightened
little man seeking an excuse, a lie, an alibi. 'Curly'll come
down with the charge in a minute,' Taffy said reassuringly.
'He'll tell us what to say, Curly will.'

Curly brought the mail with him when he came. There
was a letter for each of them. Rosendale was too het up to
read his letter; he threw it without interest onto the table
and bit his nails until the other two had read theirs. Taffy
was a slow reader. Rosendale fiddled and shuffled, tears
almost touching the surface of his eyes. 'My missus is bad
again,' Taffy said, staring at the soiled cheap paper on which
a few slanting lines had been pencilled in a childish scrawl.
Big crossed kisses had been drawn under the signature. 'She
can't touch her food again and her mouth is full of that yellow phlegm I told you about, Curly. And the rain is coming
in since the last raid.'

'Why doesn't she go into hospital?' Curly said. 'She's on
the panel, isn't she?'

'I don't know proper,' Taffy said, rubbing his face wearily.
'I used to pay insurance when I was in the tinplate works,
an' she's been paying twopence a week to the doctor. But *he*
don't know what's up with her. I fetched him down last time
I was on leave; anybody could see she was bad. All yellow
and skinny, pitiful thin she was. Not eating a bite, neither,
not even milk or stout, but only a drop of pink pop when
she was thirsty. I made her bed for her in the kitchen to
save her climbing the stairs. I stayed in every night with
her. Had to go drinking in the mornings with my brother
and my mates. And she was spitting this yellow stuff all the
time, see? Very near filled the pisspot with it every day.'

'Well, you've got to get her to hospital,' Curly said. 'What the hell is that doctor doing? It sounds criminal to me.'

'I told her to see another one,' Taffy went on. 'But my mother-in-law it is, she swears by him, see? He's delivered all her kids for her, and he helped my missus through with the twins. So she won't change him. She won't go against her mother, see, Curly?'

'What the hell does a mother-in-law matter?' Curly said sharply. 'Look here, Taff. You've *got* to get home and *carry* her to hospital *yourself* if you don't want her to die. D'you understand? Especially with all these air raids. It's cruel to leave her alone.'

'But what about the kids? She can't take them to hospital with her.'

'Get them evacuated. Or send them to your mother-in-law's.'

'What? That bastard?'

'I'd like to knock your head off, Taffy,' Curly said with cold and exasperated anger.

'I wouldn't care much if you did,' Taffy replied, suddenly plunged in despondency. Like his temper, which had flared against the sergeant, his blues came on him without warning.

'Come on,' Curly insisted crossly. 'Pull yourself together. It doesn't matter about you. It's your wife and kiddies I'm thinking about. Get up to the office and show this letter to the O.C. You've *got* to get home.'

'Catch him giving me a forty-eight hours' leave after Crumb has told him what I said,' Taffy said, hang-dog.

'I'll see Crumb at once and ask him to hold the charge back,' Curly said, turning to go.

'What about my charge?' Rosendale asked. He had been hanging round the fringe of Taffy's trouble, like an uncomfortable curate with a dyspepsia of his own. 'Can't you talk it over with me, Curl?'

'Your charge isn't important,' Curly said, hurrying out.

'Bloody intellectuals! They're all the same, the pack of them,' Rosendale muttered.

Sergeant Crumb was already closeted with the O.C. when

Curly got back to the office. The Nissen hut was divided into two rooms by a central plywood partition with a door. Curly stood by the door listening.

They were talking about Sergeant Crumb's wife. It was a matter of long standing, and Curly knew enough about it from the sergeant's occasional confidences to see that he had been ruined by it so gradually and completely that he himself didn't know the extent or nature of the damage. He had joined the Army eight years back to get away from a powerful woman who had him tucked into her bed whenever she wanted him and who was pushing him to divorce his wife. He was afraid of ruining his business, a small garage, by the publicity of a divorce; moreover, he wasn't in love with either of the women though he slept with each in turn. So he joined up to let time and distance settle the mess. Oddly enough it was still unsolved. His wife had gone back to a factory job and taken a small flat. After several years he had called on her on leave, having been discarded by the other woman who preferred a civilian lover. He was very proud of that night. He had wooed his wife back to him; Gable had nothing to show him, he told Curly, recounting in some detail. So things reverted to the old ways for a while, until he received information from a sister of his who lived near his wife that his wife had another man, somebody in the works, a young fellow in a reserved occupation. It wasn't definitely established; Sergeant Crumb wasn't one to beard lions; he hadn't asked his wife point-blank, nor did he intend offering her a divorce. He preferred to use the welfare machinery of the Army. Through the O.C. he had got in touch with the regimental paymaster and requested him to investigate his wife's conduct through the local police with a view to stopping her allowance, to which he contributed fourteen shillings a week, if her guilt could be established. Meanwhile he continued to prove his manhood and independence by making love promiscuously wherever he was stationed, and displaying a definite penchant for married women. His heart wasn't affected by the affair any more, his affections weren't involved. That was the whole trouble, it seemed to Curly. It was simply a matter of pride, of getting his own back. He took it out of his staff in the same way, blustering at them, telling the O.C. of their disloyalties and delinquencies, keeping well in with his chiefs, at once toady and bully. At the same time he was efficient and hard-working, smart at drill and a master of office routine and military redtape. His files were neat and complete, correspondence properly indexed, A.C.I.s and Battalion Orders always to hand. Messing indents, pay rolls, men's documents were all open for inspection. The only man who knew that Sergeant Crumb depended entirely upon Private Norris, his clerk general, was Curly Norris himself. And because of his peculiar comic outlook on life he had no desire to split. It amused him to contemplate the sergeant's self-importance and it paid him to be useful in a number of small ways. He could get a week-end pass for the asking. He could use the office at nights to type out his private work – some learned bilge he was preparing for a classical quarterly – and as the war was a stalemate and the Command board had rejected his application for a commission after one look at his stoop, he had grown to consider these small amenities as perhaps more important than the restless discontent that produces poets or heroes or corpses.

Having discussed his marital affairs and got the O.C. to write another letter to the paymaster, Sergeant Crumb, as was his wont, made deposition against the malcontents, on this occasion Rosendale and Thomas. He suggested that each should be charged under section 40 of the Army Act. Curly, hearing the O.C. melt under the sergeant's reasoned persuasion, shrugged his shoulders and lit a cigarette. He knew it was poor look-out for Mrs Thomas's cancer of the throat. Certainly it was no use making any application at the moment. The O.C. had given him two week-ends' leave in the last six weeks, after air raids, to see that his wife was all right. It was Taffy's own fault, the fool, for not getting her into hospital when he was home last. And now they had no money. Curly had already lent him his last train fare, and had no more cash to spare.

Rosendale came in with a pail of specially sweet tea at that moment, hoping to mollify the powers. But Sergeant Crumb's voice was unsweetened as he told him to get properly dressed and be ready to answer a charge in five minutes' time.

The upshot of it was that both men got seven days' C.B. and Curly a severe unofficial reprimand for attempting to shield Thomas. The O.C. always enjoyed a little adjudication. It gave him strength.

'Sod the Army!' Rosendale moaned, bitter and outraged. 'King's Regulations be damned. Better if they'd spend their time in strengthening the League-a-Nations or finding a living job for the unemployed or making things better somewhere, not pottering around with King's Regulations.'

'What wouldn't I do to Mr bleeding Crumb if I met him in Civvy Street after the war,' Taffy murmured fondly.

'A lot of use that is to your wife,' Curly snapped.

'Go on. Rub it in,' Taffy flared up, goaded to feel anguish at last. Disconsolate, he wheeled his barrow off to the incinerator, and Curly returned to the office to write letters to his friends.

Acting Captain Cochrane was sitting on the clerk's table, tapping his swagger cane against the brown boots Taffy had brought to a nice shine and chatting to Sergeant Crumb over a cup of lukewarm tea.

'Well, Norris,' he said with a sardonic grin. 'You see what comes of playing the barrister to a pair of fools.'

'They're not particularly fools, sir,' Curly replied with proper deference. 'They're both men. Thomas has worked in pits and steel-works, he's taken the rap in Belgium, he's trying to maintain a wife and two kiddies – that's more than most of us have done.'

'He's still a fool,' the O.C. said. 'He's like the rest of the working people. They've been too blind and stupid to help themselves when they had the chance. They could have had Socialism any time in the last twenty years. They've got the vote. Why don't they use it to get a Labour government? Because they can't be bothered to lift a finger for their own interests. I'm a Socialist at heart, but it's not a bit of good trying to help the people. They don't want to be helped.'

'It isn't entirely their fault, sir,' Curly replied. 'The middle class hasn't helped them very much – the teachers and clergy and newspaper proprietors and business executives. They've all thrown dust in their eyes, confused or denied the real issues and disguised selfish interests and reactionary politics to appear progressive and in the public interest, as they say. They keep the world in a state of perpetual crisis in order to crush internal opposition by the need for national unity, and they buy off their critics by giving them minority posts in the Cabinet. Appeasement at home and abroad; give the beggar a penny and expect him to touch his cap.'

'Hot air,' the O.C. answered, offering Curly a cigarette. He always came in for a chat after giving anybody a dressing down; Curly surmised that it was a maxim of his that a man who is alternately severe and humane wins the respect as well as the affection of his subordinates. As a matter of fact the men distrusted his geniality and called him two-faced. They never knew how to take him; before asking a favour of him they always consulted Taffy or Curly about his mood. They were nervous of him in a surly way; not from fear, but because they disliked being treated curtly without being able to retort on natural terms. 'Would you like England to become Communist?' he continued.

'I should be quite acclimatized to the change after serving in the Army,' Curly replied. 'We live a communal life here; all our clothes and equipment are public property; nobody makes any profits; we serve the state and follow the party line.'

'You think the Army is based on Lenin's ideas, do you?' the O.C. said. 'That would shake the colonel if he knew it.'

'He needn't worry,' Curly said, laughing. 'The Army hasn't got a revolutionary purpose. It has no ideas worth speaking of except a conservative loyalty to the throne and a professional obligation to obtain a military victory. King Charles I's ideas with Oliver Cromwell's efficiency. That's England all over. They never settle their differences, they always keep both sides going. The Royalists were beaten in the field, yet they dominate the Army. The Germans were licked, yet they've got Europe where they want it. There's plenty of class distinction in the Army, black boots versus brown shoes, but no class conflict. I could go on quite a long time like this, sir. It's more interesting than football.' He laughed to hide his seriousness. He hadn't been speaking in fun, but he preferred to be taken lightly. He knew himself to be a perpetual student, introspective, individualist, an antinomian with a deep respect for the privacy of others. His gentle and slightly neurotic liberalism took the edge off his revolutionary convictions. He lacked the strength to defy what is powerful in men, and he had no heart for extreme action. So he always preferred to be left in peace, to think and observe; his conflicts were within him. He had his own anguish.

'I tell you what's wrong with you, Norris,' the O.C. said largely. Curly felt something wince in him. To be told again what was wrong with him. People were always presuming to do that, nearly always people who knew too little about him and about themselves. It wasn't so bad if they spoke from kindness and a desire to help; that hurt, but it was understood by him. But when a man, like this young fascist type with his muddled democratic ideas and his desire to exercise his power over men, proffered him advice, he writhed like a split toad.

'You haven't got enough *push*, Norris. That's what's wrong with you. Too soft-hearted, not enough keenness. You don't go for things as if you wanted them.'

Curly laughed.

'My ambitions aren't as tangible as yours, sir,' he replied.

'Well, get some ambitions, then, for God's sake. Your life won't go on for ever. Get cracking.'

'Very good, sir. I'll submit my scheme for defeating Germany to Sir John Dill immediately.'

The O.C. shrugged his shoulders, confessing to himself that here was another man who wasn't worth helping because he refused to be helped. He was browned off with fools.

'If you want to help anybody, you might help Thomas to get his wife into hospital, sir.'

The O.C. snorted and narrowed his eyes.

'I know the difference between seven days' C.B. and a week-end leave,' he said curtly. 'Thomas won't pull that old gag over me again.' Curly hadn't enough vigour to insist. He clenched his fists on the table, knowing how important it was that Taffy should get leave, knowing it suddenly with anguish. But, as so often, the conflict smashed itself up inside him like two contrary tides, and he said nothing because the intensity of his feelings made him impotent.

The door opened and Sergeant Crumb came in, followed astonishingly by a very dashing young lady. The sergeant was all smiles and deference, inclining his body courteously to her and pointing with a wave of his hand to the O.C. Curly stood to attention. The O.C. stood flushed.

'Lady to see you, sir,' Crumb said urbanely.

'Hector,' the lady said, her rouge parting in a slow private smile. She held out her gloved hand, letting her fur coat fall open.

'But – but come in,' the O.C. stumbled. He pushed open the door of his room and she swept through in a swirl of fur and silk and interesting perfumes. He closed the door after her, humbly.

'Gives you the impression of expensive cutlery,' Curly said softly, 'though I doubt whether she is stainless.'

'It's the colonel's daughter,' Crumb whispered, his head inclined and movements subdued as though he were in the presence of the saints.

Curly hoped she wanted some love, so that he'd have a little peace to write his letters. But he had scarcely started when the door opened and she came out again.

'Don't trouble to see me to the gate,' she said. 'I'm sure you're busy. This private will escort me.'

'Not at all,' said the helpless captain, following her out with her gloves.

'Stand easy, stand easy,' Crumb said as the door closed

behind them. 'She must have been jilted or something,' he sneered.

The O.C. came back in a hell of a tear.

'Where's that bloody fool Thomas? Tell him to go to my billet and polish my shoes and Sam Browne till he can see his face in them. And tell Rosendale I want him to take a message for me. At once.'

'Very good, sir,' Sergeant Crumb leapt to it, realizing the situation was urgent. The room was suddenly in a turmoil, as though the young lady had been a German parachutist.

The O.C. took a sheet of paper and scribbled a quick note, put it in an envelope, and threw it into the OUT tray.

'Tell Rosendale to deliver that when he comes, Norris.'

He put on his service cap, took his stick and gloves, and went out. He was excited and flustered. Probably going to cool off by catching the sentry sitting down or the cookhouse staff eating the men's cheese rations, or the fatigue party throwing stones into the cesspool they were cleaning.

Rosendale came and collected the letter.

'Forgot to lick the envelope,' he said. 'What is it? Is there a war on?'

'Run away,' said Curly, weary of everything.

Rosendale cycled out of camp and down the road till he was out of observation. Then he opened the letter and read it through.

Dear Eva, [it said] Sorry I can't meet you tonight as we arranged. I'm on duty again and won't be able to see you this week. I seem to have so little free time these days that I doubt whether it's worth our while carrying on any more. What do you think? Affectionately yours, Hector Cochrane, Capt.

'Hector Cochrane, Capt.,' Rosendale repeated, curling his lip. He cycled down coast to the town, knowing where to go; he had been to the little street behind the gasworks on other occasions. Miss Barthgate was the name, and very nice, too. Smart little milliner, deserved better luck than to fall in love with *him*. Rosendale's mind was working by devious ways. He'd seen the flash dame in the fur coat with rich smells about her. Maybe he'd get a bit of his own back for that seven days' C.B.

He knocked at the door, propping his cycle against the wall. She worked in the parlour; he could see the sewing machine through the window. But the place sounded quiet today, as though she hadn't started working yet.

There was some delay before she opened the door. She was in a loose-fitting frock let out at the waist. Her face was nervous, her dark eyes looked dilated. Her beauty seemed agitated, on pins. 'Yes?' she said, almost breathing the word, at the same time holding her hand out for the note he held between his fingers. Grinning a little, Rosendale handed it to her, watched her read it, waited a long time while she tried to raise her head. . .

At last she looked up. She wasn't bothering to hide anything. He could see it clear as daylight.

'There's no answer,' she said.

'No,' he replied. 'No answer.' He shuffled, half turning to go. Then he looked up at her shrewdly.

'He isn't on duty,' he said. 'I thought I'd tell you. I shouldn't mind about him if I were you.'

'No,' she said, looking at him vaguely with her unutterable distress.

He had intended to say more, but her look confused him. He turned, mounted his cycle, and pedalled off. She didn't move all the time.

There was a new sensation buzzing through cookhouse, stores, office, and guardroom when he returned. The sentry told it him as he cycled through the gate; and because of it he decided to withhold his own bits of gossip till the chaps would be readier to appreciate it. He didn't want any competition.

The news was that Taffy Thomas couldn't be found anywhere. His denim overalls were on the floor by his bed, his best battledress and respirator were missing. He hadn't answered Crocker's quavering version of Defaulters bugle, he hadn't come forward to shine the O.C.'s Sam Browne. He'd done a bunk.

Curly was waiting for Rosendale with another message, this time for the Swansea police, asking them to visit Taffy's house at night and instruct him forcibly to return by the next train. The O.C. had said something about a court-martial; it would be the colonel's charge at least. That meant probably twenty-eight days' detention and no pay for him-self or his wife. It was a bad business, all things considered; but Curly was glad Taffy had gone. Perhaps he'd save his wife's life; twenty-eight days was cheap at that price.

Acting Captain Cochrane had a considerable liver by the end of the afternoon. The men had been dozy and idle all day. He'd gone round bollucking them right and left. The latrines hadn't been cleaned, the washbasins were still lit-tered with rusty blades and fag-ends when he inspected them after lunch. The cesspool stank and the fatigue party com-plained that there wasn't any hot water for them to clean up afterwards. All the plugs for the washbasins were missing, the kit was untidily laid out on the beds, the rifles hadn't been pulled through since he inspected them last. He was in no mood to be accosted. When he saw Eva waiting for him at the bottom of the lane, he had already had too much.

She was wearing a plain mackintosh, a loose-fitting Bur-berry, and a little green hat with turned-up brim like a schoolgirl. Her hands were in her pockets, her eyes on the ground. He knew she'd seen him, but she wasn't able to look at him approaching. He walked smartly towards her, very military in his swish greatcoat and service cap flat over his eyes. His face looked narrow and sharp under the severe cap, his fair moustache and rather pointed teeth giving him a stoatlike appearance. When he was within a couple of yards, she looked up and her eyes were wide and lambent, looking at him for some sign.

'Well, Eva,' he said. He coughed and looked at his wrist-watch. 'You got my letter, didn't you?'

She stayed looking at him with her pale searching face

and her dark transparent eyes. Damn it all, she had a nice face. Was she going to cling? Why did she take things so seriously?

'Well? Say something, Eva.'

His voice was softer, the least bit softer.

'I got your letter,' she said. 'That's why I came to see you.'

'Well, you know I'm on duty, then?' he tried it out, not so sure that he wanted to finish it for good just yet.

'That's what you said,' she replied.

He flushed, but she had turned away from him.

'Well?' he queried, his voice hardening. He wasn't going to be pried into. If his word wasn't enough for her, O.K. chief!

She looked up again. He noticed she hadn't powdered herself very carefully; her nose had a thick patch on it.

'Hector,' she said, putting her hands on the immaculate breast of his greatcoat. 'Don't you understand, darling?'

He was swept with impatience. His success with women was about equal to his ignorance of them. He wasn't going to have any sob stuff, thank you.

'How the blazes do you expect me to understand?' he said roughly.

'Well,' she said. 'There is something to understand.'

He quailed under her sudden precision of mood; she knew what she was going to do now; she wasn't leaning on him, beseeching him with her eyes. She was very quiet and firm.

She looked at him and he got scared.

'There's nothing serious, Eva, is there?' his fear prompted him.

'It is serious,' she said.

'Darling,' he gasped.

He was horrified of the consequences, infuriated with her for getting into this mess, and, for the first time in his life, even if only for a minute, in love.

He spoke slowly, stopping to think.

'Can't you see a doctor, Eva? There are some doctors, you know—'

'I don't want to,' she said, still with this ridiculous composure.

'But – but you ought to,' he said.

'I can do as I choose,' she replied.

He said nothing, sensing a hopeless deadlock.

'Eva,' he said at last.

'Well?'

'We could get married at the Registry Office next weekend if you like,' he said, slowly, never taking his worried eyes off her. She was silent, as if listening to his words again and again in her mind.

He felt a growing exhilaration, a new and wonderful simplicity in him, like sunlight slowly breaking.

'Shall we?' he asked, holding his hand out.

She looked up again. This was always the most active thing she did, disclosing her eyes. Her hands all the time in her Burberry pockets. She was reluctant to answer; there was a sweetness in the possibility, a reflection of his own momentary sincerity. It was what she had come for, to hear him say that; because he had said these words she was happy. She had no sense of tragedy or of shame. She felt indifferent to the future.

'No, we can't get married,' she said slowly at the last.

Something in him was suddenly overpoweringly relieved. He had no sense of a durable daily happiness, of a long companionship in love; but only romantic impulses, like sunlight, and harsher emotions.

'But why not?' he asked, trembling.

'Because – oh well,' she mumbled, seeking blindly to bind up her thoughts into the certainty that was still inchoate in her, 'because you – don't—' she turned away, and in profile he saw her lips finish the sentence – 'love me.'

Her courage shamed him into a greater confusion. He flushed and lost his head and was just about to gallop into the breach with protestations of devotion when a four-seater army car swung round the bend and pulled up with a screech and shudder.

'Christ,' he gasped, this time in a real fluster. 'Look out.'

He sprang to the car and saluted.

The colonel half-opened the door.

'Just coming to see you, Cochrane. Expected to find you in your office, not flirting on the roads.'

'Yes, sir.'

'Hop in. Quickly. I want to get back.'

'Yes, sir.'

The car surged forward.

Eva watched it go. By herself. She pushed her hair back, rubbing her cheeks, rubbing the cold sweat off her forehead. Heavily she turned and walked slowly along the road.

The colonel looked into the first Nissen hut.

'These bricks round the fireplace,' he said. 'I sent an order to all detachments that they be whitewashed. Why haven't you done it?'

'No whitewash, sir.'

'Get some. Christ. What are you here for?'

He picked up a pair of boots from one of the men's beds.

'These boots. Burnt. Look at the soles. Burnt through. Drying them by the fire. Is this man on a charge?'

'Er, no, sir.'

'Why the hell not? Nation can't afford to waste boots every time they get wet. Christ. Send him to me tomorrow under escort.'

'Yes, sir. I don't believe they *are* burnt, sir. The man has been waiting for a boot exchange for five weeks. He's worn them out—'

'I tell you they're burnt. Christ man, you're not a cobbler, are you?'

'No, sir.'

'Then talk about something you know.'

By the time the old man drove off Captain Cochrane was utterly emasculate. He saluted with so pathetic and servile a gesture that the colonel didn't even return the salute. And so his day ended. The duties of the evening confronted him. Dinner in mess, then dance attendance on the old man's daughter. Poleworth was the name. Less respectfully, when

the subalterns were hidden away in a pub, the name was
sometimes garbled to Polecat. She certainly had a pungent
odour. Still, hardy men said she was a good sport. She liked
to play, they hinted, twisting the yellow ends of their moustaches. Captain Cochrane emptied his whisky flask before
deciding on his tactical plan. Marvellous thing, whisky.

Curly took a walk after drinking his mug of tea and eating
a piece of bread and marge and a Lyons' fruit pie. He didn't
wash or brass up. He wasn't going to town. He wanted some
peace of mind, along the sand dunes running from the harbour to the boarding house promenade where the ferro-
concrete seaside resort began. Faintly, as though his tedious
preoccupations had taken a musical form, the distant sound
of hurdy-gurdy jazz songs blaring in the fun-fair touched
his quietness, accompanying him unobtrusively as he
climbed the loose sand. Thinking of the industry of pleasure,
he watched the sea, fuming like a thin grey smoke far far out
beyond the mudflats, and it seemed as though the purpose
of the town had been lost, the balance between sea and land
ruined, the fundamental element forgotten. Pleasure had
broken away from simplicity, the penny-in-the-slot machine
had conquered the sea, people had turned their backs and
were screaming with laughter. Watching the sea fuming and
grey he found himself suddenly investing the solitary person
walking slowly and with downcast head across the wet worm-
cast mud with all the attributes which humanity, he decided
this evening, had rejected. He wanted to speak to this lonely
person; it was a woman; heavy she was; heavy with the rejected attributes of humanity; pregnant she must be, and
pale with a serious beauty, bearing so much in her.

Following his fantasy, he walked down from the dunes and
across the slimy front towards the girl. He walked quickly,
keeping his attention on her, refusing to allow the usual in-
hibitions to stop him accosting her.

Eva felt no particular strangeness at his approach. A little
soldier with spectacles and curly hair like a wire brush. It
was quite natural. She said good evening. She was glad he
had come.

'I was standing on the dunes,' he said. 'And there was no-body but you anywhere at all. And so you became important to me, so that I came to ask you something.'

'Don't ask me anything,' she said.

'No, I don't want to,' he said thoughtfully.

'Will you take me back to the land?' she said, looking at him, holding her hand out to him uncertainly.

Her face was as he had imagined it, young and hollow, large hollow-eyed, luminous and vague with distress.

He took her cold hand and led her back to the firm land, the grass and rocks and walls and telegraph poles and houses. In silence.

'Have you ever tried to die?' she asked.

'Yes,' he said.

'What shall I do now, then?' she asked again.

'Walk,' he said. 'Pick a flower. Hurt your shin against a rock. Keep doing things like that for a bit. Do you like coffee?'

'Yes,' she said, thinking back to the taste of such things. 'Yes. I like coffee.'

'Shall we go and have some, and some chocolate biscuits, in the Marina?' he asked.

'Yes,' she said, very seriously. 'That would be nice.'

She looked at the people having coffee and peach melbas and spaghetti on toast at the little green tables, soldiers and girls, commercial men, ponderous wives on holiday with children past their bedtime. The waitresses rustling and slender and deft, rotund and homely and competent; the warm shaded lights falling on the flowery wallpaper. The strangeness and the fear gradually left her eyes like sugar melting in a lemon glass. She tasted the hot coffee slowly, and its warmth led her to smile.

'Why do you look so serious?' she asked Curly.

He looked at her all the time. She could see the gathering of his thoughts in the dark blue eyes magnified and concen-trated by the curved lenses of his spectacles.

'Funny, you having blue eyes,' she said.

Looking at each other over the wispy coffee steam, each

wanted to be confessed in the other, each desired to share a
new yet ancient community of interest. Neither of them
could think now of how different they were, the one from
the other, how insulated by separate compulsions and circumstances.

'I live near here. Shall we go and sit by the fire?' she asked.

'I'd like to,' he answered. . .

'It's only an electric fire,' she said, as he opened the glass
door for her.

There were two photographs on the mantelpiece of her
little bedsitter. Curly noticed they were both men in uniform.
Brothers? Or lovers? Also a sewing machine and dresses half
finished. A reading lamp and *Picture Post* and *Lilliput* and
a *Sunday Pictorial*.

'I haven't got a shilling for the meter,' she said.

He produced one.

'You're very good,' she said to him, putting the shilling
in the slot, bending down as she spoke. 'You stopped me
committing suicide and now you've given me food and
money and – and what else?'

'What else?' he repeated, his sensitive mind crushed by
the sledge-hammer blow of her casual confession.

'I don't know,' she said, standing up and smoothing her
navy skirt down, picking bits of fluff off her knees. 'I don't
know what I'm talking about.'

Her sick soul was in her eyes.

He stayed with her till late in the night, putting another
shilling in the meter, going and queuing outside the chip
shop for some fish cakes for their supper while she set the
little table and boiled the kettle and cut some bread and
butter. The reading lamp on the table, and she telling him
about dress-making, and the poverty she was in now there
was no material purchasable, and the requirements of her
clients, and their sexy confidences. She was recovering herself and he watched her judgement returning gradually as
her comments on people and things reached further and
further out from the touchstone of herself, radiating like
ripples from a stone dropped into a pond. She had no politics

or plans, no criteria; except herself, her intuitions and feelings, aversions. He wanted to restore herself to her, so that she could continue living from day to day, thought to thought, with continuity.

They were talking about the army; tonight it seemed a remote, unreal topic, a social problem which could be discussed or dropped as they chose. In the same unreal mood she said:

'My husband liked the army. He's the one on the right there. He had a good time in France, till suddenly it all happened.'

Curly crossed to the mantelpiece and looked at the smiling R.A.C. sergeant in his black beret; a powerful, smiling man, confident and untroubled.

'He never bothered about things,' she said. 'He liked tanks and so he liked the war. I don't think he bothered about dying, or being away from me. He just married me one leave, that's all. He wouldn't have a baby. It never occurred to him. And now he's dead. A whole year now he's been dead. I've forgotten nearly everything about him.'

Curly looked from the second photograph in consternation.

'You know Captain Cochrane?' he asked.

'He's been coming here a lot,' she said. 'He's had enough of me now, though.'

How weary she sounded, telling him all these elemental facts in a flat, indifferent voice.

'I should have thought you'd had enough of him,' he said. 'He's a poor piece of work. You shouldn't have let him take you in. He's nothing at all, just cardboard and paste.'

She smiled, lighting one of his cigarettes.

'Would you have saved me, if you'd known me six weeks ago?' she said. 'I met him in the Plaza at a dance, just six weeks ago. Would you have stopped him touching me?'

'It's your own affair,' he said. 'If I'd known you I would have.'

'Could you have?' she teased him. 'Could you make love as gifted as he did?'

'I don't suppose so,' he said. 'I'm not a cinema fan. Nor am I very enthusiastic about that sort of thing. You know what he used to say? He used to say he had a lot of dirty water on his chest and he knew a woman who would swill it out for him.'

'You're not preaching to me, anyway,' she said. 'You're hitting hard, aren't you?'

'I could hit much harder,' he replied.

'I can't help it now,' she said, dejected. 'He offered to marry me; there's that to be said for him; only he didn't mean it.'

Curly went hot and sticky, as though there were filthy cobwebs all over him. And at once the old despair touched him with its dry unavailing fingers, as when he had tried to get a short leave for Taffy Thomas to see to his wife.

It was difficult for him to go now. Yet she didn't want him to stay. She was normal again, and consequently beginning to understand the task that was on her, the mess she had made, the immense fatigue. She turned on the wireless, late dance music, mawkish and sticky. They both stood up.

'Shall I come and see you again?' he asked.

'Yes,' she said. 'Yes. Unless I go away from here.'

'Where to?'

'I don't know,' she said. 'Where do you go to have a baby? Are workhouses open for that? Or I'll go to my sister-in-law. She evacuated to her father's farm in Borrowdale. I won't go yet. Not for a few months. Perhaps I won't go at all.'

She was only talking round and round.

On his way downstairs he bumped into somebody, stood against the wall to let him pass, recognized Captain Cochrane, smelt his hot whisky-sweet breath, and hurried out into the black streets and the unhurried stars.

Anglo–German hostilities, held in abeyance during the daylight, resumed at a later hour than was customary this particular night. The operational orders of the Luftwaffe gave a certain unity to the experiences of Taffy Thomas, Curly Norris, Captain Cochrane and the women with whom they were connected – a unity which would not have existed otherwise. Taffy reached Swansea on a lorry conveying sheep skins from slaughterhouse to warehouse just as the first Jerries droned eastwards along the Gower coast, droned lazily towards the dark sprawling town, and released beautiful leisurely flares into the blackness below. Taffy was hungry and thirsty and broke, not even a fag-end in his field dressing pocket. So he didn't mind a few extra inconveniences such as air raids. Life was like that at present. He wasn't expecting anything much. He hurried past his habitual pubs, past the milk-bar where he had eaten steak-and-kidney pies on his last leave and been unable to get off the high stool on which he sat, drunk at one in the afternoon and his kid brother just as bad at his side, bloody all right, boy; and, as the first bombs screamed and went off with a sickening shuddering zoomph down the docks way, he turned into his own street and kicked the door with his big ammunition boots. It was about the same time as Curly went into Eva's flat, and Captain Cochrane bought the Polecat her first gin and lime. Taffy's missus was in bed on the sofa in the kitchen; she couldn't get up to let him in, she'd gone too weak. He had to climb the drainpipe to the top bedroom and squeeze through the narrow sash. She knew who it was as soon as he kicked the door with his big boots, so she wasn't frightened when he came downstairs; only ashamed, ashamed that she was such a poor wife, so useless a vessel for his nights, skinny thighs and wasted breasts and dead urges.

'Hallo, mun,' he said with his rough vigour, picking up the newspaper and glancing at the headlines. 'Still bad? Where's the kids? Up in your mother's?'

'She fetched them up after tea,' she said. '' gainst there's a raid.'

'By yourself, then?' he said. 'Good job I come. Got anything to drink?'

'No,' she said, ashamed at being such a poor wife. 'I'd 'ave asked mam to go down the pub for a flagon if I'd thought you was coming.'

'What about yourself?' he asked. 'Still drinking that old pink lemonade? Can't you drink a drop of milk or tea or Oxo or something yet? Still spitting that old yellow phlegm up, too, by the looks of that pisspot. I don't know, bach.' He sat on the edge of the sofa and put his hand idly on her moist tangled hair. 'I don't know what to do. Curly said for to take you to the hospital. I think I'd better, too. Shall I carry you tonight?'

'No,' she said, frightened. 'You can't now. It's blackout and there's bombs again, and I doubt there won't be a bed there. And you got to pay, too.' She pushed her bony hand slowly across the soiled sheet and touched his battledress. 'I don't want to go there,' she said.

She was too weak to wipe the tears out of her eyes.

'Oh Jesu!' he said, getting up in a temper. 'Don't cry, then. I was only suggestin'. Do as you like. Wait till tomorrow if you like. Only I was thinking the redcaps will be coming round to look for me tomorrow.'

'Never mind about tomorrow,' she said.

'The cat's been pissing in the room somewhere,' he said, sniffing about him. He sat down again and wiped her eyes with the sheet.

'You got to mind about tomorrow,' he said.

'Remember you was jealous of me in a dance at the Mackworth when we was courting?' she said. 'You took me out and slapped me in the face, remember?'

'What about it?' he asked slowly, nonplussed.

'Slap me now, again,' she said.

He laughed.

'I'm not jealous of you no more,' he said. 'You get better, and then p'r'aps I'll get jealous again, see?'

She smiled and let her neck relax on the cushion.

'You'll never be jealous of me again,' she said, looking at him with her far-away eyes.

Her soul was in her eyes, and it wasn't sick like her body.

The bombs had been falling heavier and heavier, and neither of them seemed to notice. Till the light went out, and then he cursed filthily. The fire was nearly out, it was cold sitting with her all the time. He tucked her icy hands under the blanket.

'I'm going out for some coal,' he said.

'There's none there,' she said. 'The coalman's killed.'

'Christ, there's plenty more men not killed,' he said. 'I'll get some from next door, then.'

'Don't go,' she whispered.

The house shivered and plaster fell in a stream of dust, as if from an hour-glass.

'Can't sit in the cold all night,' he said. 'And the dark. I won't be a minute.'

He slipped the latch and went out into the burning night, straight out into a screaming bomb that tore the sky with its white blade and flung him onto his face in the little back-yard and brought the house crashing down with its mighty rushing wind.

The Luftwaffe's secondary objective concerned Captain Cochrane's harbour. The raid began at midnight, by which time Swansea had nothing to do except stop the big fires spreading and wait for the morning to come. Taffy had called at his mother-in-law's, and seen the children; and at the police station, to tell them his wife was buried and ask them to inform his unit; and he was just walking around, trying to keep himself from freezing and crying and lying down in a doorway, when Captain Cochrane, who had also suffered some emotional disturbance, was getting out of Eva's bed and hastily pulling on his shirt and trousers in the dark. When he was half dresed he pulled the blind back to see what was happening. The searchlights were stretching their white dividers over the harbour; and yes, by God, they had a plane in their beam, a little tinsel plane, and the red tracer bullets were floating up at it from the Bofors by the sidings. Christ, it was a marvellous sight. He was thrilled stiff, trembling to sink his teeth into it, to draw blood. Where the hell were his shoes?

'I'll have to run,' he said brusquely, grabbing his cap and greatcoat.

Eva, motionless and dark in bed, said nothing at all. Of course he had to go; a soldier like him.

'Good-bye,' he said, stumbling on the stairs.

Eva lay quietly, heavy and as though waterlogged, thinking of the Germans and the English, the soldiers of both sides, her husband and the excitement, the professional coolness with which, firing his two-pounder from the revolving turret of his pet tank, he died. And Hector Cochrane – she always thought of his surname as well as his Christian name – that boy with glasses was right; he wasn't much of a man. When he had come in tonight, drunk and abased, begging her forgiveness – as if *that* was anything to give or to withhold – her infatuation had dissolved like a sudden thaw, leaving everything slushy. And as she stroked his spiky Bryllcreamed hair and let him sob into her lap she had felt how small and worthless the two of them were, clumsy bungling people of no moment, passive and degraded by their own actions. She had let him take her to bed. Anything was as good as nothing. He had written her a cheque.

Captain Cochrane had a haggard jauntiness, arriving at the office the next morning. The ethical code of his profession forbade a man to allow a hangover to take the edge off his morning smartness. He behaved in the exemplary manner of a commissioned officer, inspecting the sleeping huts and the cookhouse and the sump, chewing up slovenly old Crocker for overflowing the swill bins, chasing the fatigue party who were rat-hunting round the sump, getting a shake on everywhere. Then to the company office for his morning correspondence. Ration indents, pay requisition, arrangements for boot and clothing exchange, a glance at the medical report to see who was scrounging today. Sergeant Crumb had everything in order, non-committal and deferential, soothing.

'Damn good show last night, sergeant,' he said when he had finished his business. 'Got a cigarette?'

'Certainly, sir.' (Bloody cadger). 'The Bofors crew are going on the beer tonight, sir, to celebrate knocking that Jerry down.'

'Yes. Damn good show it was. All burned to death, weren't they?'

'Yes sir. The plane was too low for them to parachute.'

'Well, that's burned their fingers for them. Something towards winning the war.'

'Yes sir.'

A phone message. Thanks. Captain Cochrane speaking. Good-morning, sir.

This is Swansea police. A private Thomas from your company, sir. Yes? Called in at 0025 hours last night, sir. Said his wife had been buried under a bomb, sir. Christ, has she? That's bad luck. Have you confirmed it yet? Not yet, sir. Check up on it, please. He's a bit of a scrounger. If it's O.K., put him in touch with the barracks. They'll give him all the dope he needs. Money. Railway warrant. O.K.? Yes sir. If he's bluffing hand him over to the redcaps. He's absent without leave. Very good, sir. Good-bye. Good-bye, sir.

'Thomas's wife. Killed. They must have had a raid as well.'

'That's bad luck, sir. I'll look up the A.C.I. about coffins. I think the civil authorities supply them, don't they, sir? R.A.S.C. only issue them to soldiers. She was ailing anyway, sir, I know.'

'Check up on it, sergeant. Also ring through to battalion and inform them. We'll send him a leave pass if necessary. Keep the charge sheet, though. He'll have to go before the colonel for absence without leave just the same.'

'Very good, sir.'

'Anything else, sir?'

'No. I don't think so. Oh yes, there's that return to the adjutant about anti-gas deficiencies. I'll inspect all respirator contents at 1100 hours.'

'Very good, sir.'

'Christ, that reminds me. I've left mine in town .Where's Norris?'

'Up at your billet, sir, I sent him to clean your kit, sir, being that Thomas your batman isn't available.'

'Send a runner up, then. Tell him to go to this address' – he scribbled it down, Sergeant Crumb hiding the faintest

wisp of a smile as he did so – 'and ask for my respirator. Miss
Eva Barthgate is the name.'

He smiled, too. They were both men.

'Very good, sir.'

Sergeant Crumb saluted smartly and withdrew.

Captain Cochrane yawned and put his feet up for a few
minutes, and thought, well, that was that.

Maybe he'd ask the old man to put him in for a transfer
to the Indian Army. There were better prospects out there,
on the whole.

Saturday Night

GERAINT GOODWIN

He had arranged to meet her at The Cross, but now he thought it was a bit too obvious. After all, things had not gone quite so far as that – he was only 'walking out'. But meeting at The Cross, in the very centre of the town, where the whole load of it debouched, and this on a Saturday night of all times, was putting it about.

And he did not like people eyeing him so closely; the procession went past him with an eye raised and all the younger ones, as was their way, chirped in with the: 'How do, Len?' The 'how do' was just the town all over – the cheek of it and the nastiness. He had to endure it, but he was pained.

But perhaps he was a little too conspicuous – for them. He had on a very lush imitation Homburg hat, which he had struck rather jauntily across his head, and his bow was tied loosely and drooped a little, which took the shine out of the celluloid 'butterfly'. The ready-made bows were only eight-pence halfpenny from the Emporium, but this one he had tied himself – that was what made the difference. Otherwise he was smart – the lower extremities, the pin-striped trousers which had been under his bed for a week – the double-breasted waistcoat, and the black alpaca coat, were meant to advertise his neatness, his impeccable taste. The hat and the tie were meant to show that he was different – that he went beyond them. They called him 'Lord Horton' because of his manner. He knew his nickname but did not mind it, was secretly flattered. But the little bit of difference he reserved for himself.

He kept tapping his malacca cane on the pavement in his annoyance. She was late. He craned his neck up to look at the town clock, but people were watching him. So he sauntered up the High Street casually, as though nothing were the matter.

She was always late, and he did not like it; and then, when she did turn up she would burst out laughing and catch him by the arm in a sweep of emotion, as though nothing had happened. It was some sort of an outrage – on himself.

Late for the pictures was one thing – they only missed the Pathé Gazette, but late for the opera was another. He felt in his breast pocket for the two reserved tickets and twiddled them about. Never before, within his memory, had there been an opera in the town. Even now it was hard to believe, but there before him on the hoarding, reaching all the way down, already torn and scribbled on, read *La Traviata*, *Pagliacci*, *Carmen*, *Cavalleria Rusticana*, *Madame Butterfly*, and now, on the Saturday, *Faust*. It was really one of the greatest days in his life – and she was late!

He wondered what he would say to her – and then it was no good saying anything. It was like water on a duck's back – she just went on in her own sweet way and nothing would alter her. He did not understand her – but it was a pity that she did not understand him.

And she supposed to be musical! She carried off every prize at the local eisteddfods, and people were saying she should have her voice trained.

'Why?' she said, when he asked.

'Well ... to get on.'

'It's not good enough,' she said, shaking her head.

'It might be.'

'It might not. What will poor Megan do then, do then?' she laughed. Then she pretended to cry – making a great show of sobbing into her handkerchief. That was her all over.

'You mean you don't want to,' he said stiffly.

'Perhaps not,' she said in her simple way.

That had been the end of the matter. He did not know her, but all this talk about her, and the overwhelming way she had, provoked him out of himself. He was sure that he loved her – only he wished that she was somehow different. But then, the Welsh were such a queer lot – and a bit too theatrical. He did not like being taken unawares – and he was not sure that she was not laughing at him all the time.

He walked up to The Cross again, past the loafers who were always spitting and chaffing one another on the kerbside. The town was lighting up, with the worn, subdued festive air of a Saturday. Everybody was about the streets. Women unseen from week-end to week-end were out with little baskets, probing around the stalls, hovering round the shops, or walking with their husbands, two by two, in an unending line.

He went out to meet her, feeling that he should not go, but going. At the last lamp-post he waited. Beyond that the road trailed away into Wales; the garishness of the little town was cut off as though with a knife. Beyond him the road went off into the mountains, lurching up there at the valley's end.

He struck the lamp-post with his cane and pranced about. There were still the 'good night, Lens' of the passers-by. It was showing him up! He would give her five minutes and then go without her. He *thought* he would go without her, but he knew in his heart that he would not. Without her his little world came down on him and oppressed him – it was the town, the last lamp-post, the 'good night, Lens'. But she made it all so different – then there were no borders to it, there was another world, something remote and all-encompassing – beyond even Shrewsbury and Wolverhampton; there was 'life' which worked in him like a dull ferment – there was everything. And yet he did not like her because she laughed at all those things he held sacred – made him feel small. She was always pulling his leg – and it was not right.

But when he saw her hurrying down the road a load came off him. He knew it was her by her walk – the urgent sweep about it, as though her feet were too slow to carry her. But he bristled as she came on towards him; it was too bad.

She was only nineteen, but she was a woman. Her figure had filled out and her breasts were heavy with a certain sweeping proud grandeur of her own. She was not pretty, with her rather pale face inclined to muddiness, and her features were not regular, but her large, wide open eyes and the edge of jet black hair like a frame to it, redeemed them. She was 'striking' as they said, but she was not pretty. And she did not seem to care. Her father was only a 'ganger' on the railway and her mother was dead and she had care of the family. She had not time for anything else.

'What's the game?' he said, beside himself.

She caught him by the arm in her impulsive way, but he shook it free. Her eyes clouded and then hardened.

'Well . . . ?'

'We got ten minutes to get there.'

'Well – plenty of time.'

'What about me?' he said. 'I don't count!'

'Don't be silly,' she said, laughing.

'Silly!' he said, his lips tight. 'I like that!'

'Don't you want me to come?' she said, her wide eyes open.

'I don't care,' he sniffed.

'Right!' she flashed and turned round.

'Megan . . .' He ran after her and caught her by the shoulders. 'Look – look here,' he said, 'it's too bad. Be fair.'

'Too bad!' she mimicked, pursing her lips and screwing her face up.

'Well – it is!'

'Of course!' she said. 'Too bad for you! That our Emrys has got the croup – that I ought not to come, that's nothing.'

'How was I to know?' he asked, shamefaced.

'By having a think,' she said. She stamped her foot.

'But you're always late,' he replied. 'You've no idea of time.'

'What if I haven't?' she flashed. 'You want things your way – all wrapped up nice and proper. I've had about enough.'

'No,' he said, 'I didn't mean it – not really.'

He felt himself lost before her, defenceless. She went right over him in her overwhelming way, and he could only stutter. He felt that she was right – because she was always right. It was only afterwards that he felt that she was making him feel small. He did not like it, and he did not like her because she was the cause of it. But when she was there – standing before him, with her wide eyes open and a temper to her like a sprung blade – then he felt lost and bewildered. He felt that if he let her go there would be nothing worth having.

'Come on,' he said, linking his arm through hers, 'let bygones be bygones.'

One brief, derisive look, the curl of a smile, and then she melted. That was just like her – she was all hot or cold, and she never let anything rankle. They walked back into the town, she talking away gaily, the words tumbling out in the uprush of emotion.

'Can you afford it, Len?' she said, her eyes raised. 'I mean ... really?'

'Can I!' he said in a sudden proprietary way, giving his cane a swing. 'Can I!' he said again. 'You bet! Look here,' he went on, lifting the flap of his overcoat, and showing the top of the box.

He patted it with a wink.

'Why, Len – it's a pound box!'

'Perhaps,' he said casually.

'There's extravagant! You ought not to.'

'Why not?'

'Well, you ought not to – that's why.'

He wanted to say something more – the words came up in a sudden rush and choked him. He could have got them out if they weren't walking so fast; as it was, he could not get them out. People would stop and look at them, would smirk and snigger and wonder what was the matter. They were in the High Street, with its shops and stalls, and flooded windows, the tradesmen shouting and the people jostling.

He had never felt like that before. It eased off a bit, but the surging, triumphant feeling kept coming up in him. The thought of the opera, and she beside him, perhaps holding

his hand – the costumes and the singing, and the light and
glitter of it; that far away, magnificently remote world rose
up before him.

'It's *Faust*,' he said, in his exuberance.

'Oh,' she said; no more.

'Don't you like it?' he went on, peeved.

'How *can* I tell? – and me never heard it? You are funny,'
she added.

He remembered that he had not, either. But it upset him
quite a lot that one could talk about *Faust* like that, whether
one had heard it or not. *Faust* was *Faust*.

'Dad says it's the best,' he went on.

He was on firm ground again. His father was first violin
in the local musical society. He always said: 'Ah ...
Gounod!' and gave his little imperial beard a tug, and
rolled up his eyes. The front-room piano was loaded with
operatic numbers. To his father, who was a clerk as he was,
music was life, and, though he himself did not play any in-
strument at all, he was sure that music was something that
could not be discussed. He would like to have told her a lot
more, only he was afraid to – he could not forget that she
was a singer of 'rare promise'. Ever since the local paper had
described her so, he was sure that he loved her; now that he
knew that he did love her, he wished that she was like anyone else, for the bitter knowledge of it – that she did, and
he only 'knew' – left him bare and naked; this little closed
door, this secret little loft in his mind, had somehow become
of no account, littered up with odds and ends that belonged
to nobody, were of no use to anyone. It was some sort of
sacrilege.

So he said again – 'That's what Dad says.'

'Well – your father knows!'

He did not like the way she said it, and looked sideways
at her. But he was not sure.

'You're ... you're sure you're going to enjoy yourself?'
he reached out.

'Oh, Len – if I do, I do. How *can* I say?'

They walked up the length of the High Street, keeping

on the edge of the kerb, and often finding themselves buffeted off into the roadway.

As it was Saturday night the place was full to overflowing. Up and down the roadway went the young people of the town in long lines, arms linked together, laughing and shouting – a row of youths and a row of girls, giggling behind, with some sort of traffic between. The opera was not for them, he thought with a certain pride – they had been done out of their night at the pictures. A good job too.

They turned at the bridge, down the alley-way to the Public Hall, now the cinema. The operator had run up a line of lights over the porch – red and blue and pink – and the big hoarding announcing *Faust* stood propped up against a portico. There was a picture of a man with a beard and another with a sword, and then in big block capitals the list of the cast. He had seen them come in on the ten train on Monday, all huddled together, and Ernie Weaver, the porter, wheeling the cane hampers up behind them. He stood in the office window and watched, stemming down the secret sense of shame he felt – that so much could look so little. They stayed at The Golden Rule, which was the theatrical digs in the old days, in the heyday of the throbbing flannel mills, when they got the same companies as Oswestry, and it had gone around that they could knock back port and lemons one after another, and no one was quite sure who was the husband of who. That was just like the town – football results and pictures, and what did Art mean? They thought it a joke. Well, let them snigger.

Inside, the hall had been transformed. They had brought chairs into the 'threepennies' and moved off the benches. The best seats were in front, instead of at the back, as at the pictures. He was pleased that it was so – this sense of difference. But the chairs were too far apart for his liking, and when, after a time, he tried to move nearer, to get within the sense of her, his chair screeched over the polished parquet floor and people looked around at him. He thought he would try again when the lights went down, but then he remembered that the lights would not go down.

She was enjoying it all like a child at a peepshow – waiting for the people to come out. When they did, she leaned forward in her chair, screwing up her programme.

'Listen to the orchestra,' he said, with a quiet nudge. 'Gounod . . . !' he added.

Marguerite was a thin-chested woman, with a face drawn and pasty and great daubs of rouge like raddle on her face. She sang in a sort of defiance – of the audience, of everything. The hero was a fair man with a wheeze and a waddle, and the pressure of his paunch had blown out his hose. He was sweating a great deal and by the end of the scene his face shone through the grease paint. And there was some argument going on *sotto voce* between them and Faust at the curtains. But they'd got the house all right. The people had never seen anything like it before. He clapped his hands until they hurt, and then began to stamp on the floor. Once or twice he shouted 'Bravo!' But the people in front looked round again and the word died in his throat.

'All right?' he said as an afterthought, turning to her.

'Grand!' she said, with a nod. 'How long does it go on for?'

'Don't you like it, then?' His jaws came together in a clip.

'Why – of course.'

'We're only halfway through,' he said, waving his programme as the curtain went up. 'The duel next,' he whispered. He pushed the box of chocolates across to her in his urgency.

'How's he going to fall down?' she said, catching him by the arm. 'Oh, Len! When he dies!'

'Shish!' he said, reaching forward in his seat, his eyes fixed on the slot of light on the stage.

The fat man expired slowly. His sword dropped to the boards in a clatter and he swung around, his arms aloft. He went round twice with an anxious eye on the sword, and then let his legs bend; very slowly he went down on his haunches and then let himself out on the floor. But the duel had taken too much out of him; his paunch rose and fell in his breathlessness. Nothing he could do would stop it rising and falling; slowly he reached for his cape and drew it round him, and so expired.

'Oh, Len – look; do look!'

Very gently, like a poplar nodding, the scenery began to bend. The big canvas slat reached over the stage, and then straightened itself.

The dead man saw it and reached his neck up, turning his bloodshot eyes up anxiously.

'Mind out!' someone shouted from the gallery. The house began to titter.

The fat man was dead again, but he couldn't keep his head down; he felt uneasy there on the floor and, try as he would, he kept reaching his neck up.

Faust moved across and got his backside against the canvas, and Marguerite went on singing.

'Watch out, Surrey!' rang out the same voice, and the dead man's head was raised as though jerked.

This time there was no doubt about it. The slat had heeled over at an alarming angle. Faust took it on his shoulders and as the weight bent him, slid his feet on the board floor to get a foothold. Marguerite ran prancing over the stage, both arms outstretched, and put her weight to it. And Faust, feeling the weight too much for him, said something to the fat man which was heard all over the hall. But the fat man could not get up, try as he would; he was like a beetle on its back.

The house let itself go in a roar.

'Louts!' said Len through his teeth.

Slowly, with infinite menace, the big slat drooped downwards. The fat man, seeing it coming, did a roll, but he could not roll far enough; instead, he put his feet up in the air to break the fall, and waved his hands hopelessly. Faust was bent double under the weight; it was only a question of time. Suddenly his feet slid on the boards and the big canvas toppled over him. It came down with a resounding whack, sending up a cloud of dust – this old worn piece, that had been down in the cellars of the Public Hall for twenty years. When the cloud of dust had lifted the fat man was discovered impaled, his head through it, and, farther down, his leather buskins sticking up. He looked like a man on the stocks stretched horizontal.

The house was roaring.

'Go it, Surrey,' the lads were shouting. 'Mind theeself.'

And in its fall it had brought with it the scene hands whom they all knew: the manager and the cinema operator and the little lad in buttons who sold programmes, all of whom had been holding on behind. They were flung forward in a heap and then began to walk sheepishly up the slat into the safety of the wings, but their feet went through it like men in the snow.

The house went on roaring; people shouted encouragement to them, calling on them by name. And then they all walked in a troupe to the fat man and pushed his head back through the canvas and out of sight. But the dust and grime of years was too much for him – it bobbed up again through the hole. And this time he began to use language which, although not heard in the uproar, was plainly understood.

'Oh, Len. Look! look!' she screamed. She caught him by the arm. She was bent double with tears streaming down her face.

'Funny?' he said, shaking his arm free.

Her wide open eyes turned to him, steady:

'Why, Len . . . ?'

'Funny?' he said again, his face grim and set.

'Len! Whatever *is* the matter?' she asked, hurt.

'We'd better go,' he answered briefly. He reached down for his coat under the seat and picked up his stick.

'If you like,' she said, her voice changing.

They hustled along the row of seats and he pushed the swing doors open for her rudely. All up the High Street he said no word. She walked along beside him, keeping pace with his long strides.

'This is the end,' he said at last.

'Whatever *is* the matter?' She had waited for him to speak.

'Let's leave it at that,' he said, his lips tight shut.

'Are you mad?' she asked, unbelieving.

'I've had enough.'

'What do you mean . . . *enough*?'

'Of . . . of everything.'

'Oh. I see. So that's it!' She stopped in her stride. 'Well, you can go,' she said, nodding her head. 'I know my way.'

'I'll see you home,' he answered grandiloquently.

'Thank you,' she said, very tight and drawn. 'I'm particular.'

They stood there toe to toe in the lighted street. But he could not let her go.

'Why did you?' he implored. 'Like them!' he jerked a finger over his shoulder.

'Don't be a fool,' she said, her spirit rising. 'That's what you are – a *fool*!'

'Perhaps,' he sniffed.

'No perhaps. A fool!' She stamped her foot.

'We shall see,' he said, turning his head up and sniffing again.

'Will we?' she flashed. 'You poor . . . mutt!'

He bowed under the storm, very superior.

'If I am a mutt . . .' he began.

'Yes . . . a mutt,' she shouted, stamping her foot again. 'That's just what you are! Dead from the neck up – so now you know!'

She turned on her heel, her eyes flashing and her bosom lifting, and then strode off up the road.

'Megan,' he called after her, seeing her go away from him – out of his life. 'Be fair now – be fair!'

'*Ach!*' she shouted in her frenzy, tossing her head up. 'Fair! Keep your fair!'

When she got out of the town she felt easier. All the way along the streets, with their thin, fitful lamps alight, the whiff of the slums and 'courts' in their foul cluster; the weight of it, the sense of it, oppressed her. She felt as though she would choke, that she was too tight to breathe; her breasts rose and fell in her choler and her hands gripped and loosened themselves as she went.

But once without the town she felt better. There was a big round harvest moon that went on steadily across the sky, a ripe edge to it, and the little fleeces of cloud hung draped about like streamers. When it came right out of the cloud the valley all before her rose up out of the darkness, very gently, in a swill of light: the fields and the tall nodding elms of the Plas, and the Severn in a long white streak and the hills all around about, very quiet and still; and then there, up beyond her home, the ragged edge of mountain framed up in the sky. It was all so still and quiet, with that first autumnal breath on it – the soft, subdued light-in-darkness of the autumn. She stood there on a stile, the anger gone out of her like a puff. Anyhow it was all over.

All over – a faint fear, an unalterable little dead weight of dread, came to take possession of her. What did it matter – she did not love him, she told herself. Did she? No – how could she? But she felt sorry now – sorry for him, sorry for herself, sorry for life, sorry for eveything.

Right up the valley the moonlight went, flooding it – the clear crisp fields, empty now with the harvest gathered, the brown, ripe stubble like the squares on a quilt, holding the texture; the ripe, brittle ends of a life that had gone, slowly to moulder into the earth with the rain and snow of winter. The winter was coming – but then there would be spring again soon, and then the summer and another harvest – and then winter again.

She did not love him – not really. How nice it would be – to be really in love, with somebody. . .

The tears were streaming down her face. She pretended not to notice them but the whole of the world before her was blurred and hidden. She rubbed her eyes and saw there, on the edge of sight, the old mountains up against the sky, very grey and ancient.

She heard her brother crying and hurried across the field to the little cottage by the level crossing. There was no other sound in the house: her father must have gone out on the spree, then – it was Saturday night. She ran breathless over

the last field and let herself in. One of the children was on
the stairs, his face wan and frightened.

'Our Emrys is fine and bad,' he said, trying not to cry.

'Hush. Go to bed. This min-nit!'

'Was it nice?' he said, disappearing.

'Go to bed,' she shouted as he scampered up.

She hurried up to the cot and took out the little figure
swathed in flannel and pressed him to her.

'There, there,' she crooned. Her breasts filled and her voice
came out warm and rich and infinitely tender.

She rocked the child backwards and forwards in her arms,
humming the while.

'Our Meg!' he pleaded, reaching up his hot face. 'This
wance?'

'Will you be good then?' she asked, setting him down and
bending over him. 'Getting spoilt, you arr!'

'*Pant Corlan,*' whispered the other brother from the door.

'*Will* you go to bed!' she shouted. 'Playing a game you
arr – the lot of you.'

'*Pant Corlan,*' he begged again.

'Oh dear. You arr wans. All of you,' she said. She wanted
to laugh. The little one, free from the attack, was sitting up
in bed again, waiting, his big round eyes winking.

'You *arr* bad, I must say,' she laughed. Everything was all
right again now. She felt daft in the sudden rush of her joy.

The elder children had crept in from the other room and
sat around her in a ring, their white anxious faces raised.

So she sang for them, as she promised, an old Welsh folk
song, *Pant Corlan yr Wyn,* about the shearing, and then gave
them, as a special treat, a song called *Hen Aelwyd Cymru*
(The Old Welsh Hearth), her heart full to brimming. Her
breasts had gone out in the flood-tide of her emotion and the
old *hiraeth* came up in her throat; her eyes were half shut
in the longing, and her beautiful contralto voice, clear and
low, went out with an infinite tenderness.

'There now,' she said at last, as she sent off the elder children to their room. 'That will be three-and-sixpence if you
please. Front seats!'

As she tucked up the little one for the night he said, half awake:

'Our Meg...?'

'Hush.'

'You're... not going to go away?'

'There's silly!' she whispered.

'Fine and nice,' he said, turning over drowsily, the songs still with him.

That was to be her recompense.

The Loss

KATE ROBERTS

(translated by Walter Dowding)

THE engine of the bus was throbbing, throbbing, and Annie's heart throbbed with it. So much so, to her mind, that she feared her husband, sitting beside her, would hear it. She tried to make conversation.

'Isn't it fine, Ted?' she said.

'Yes,' he answered, 'it's a great day.'

Before her eyes stretched the mountains about Creunant, and a smile came over her features as she thought of the happiness they could have that day, by the lake shore amongst the hills.

The sun shone warmly on the windows of the bus, and she turned her cheek to it, to obtain all its heat, at the same time trying to keep her other cheek as close as she could to her husband, so that she might catch every word from his lips. She could think of nothing but the afternoon they would spend in the mountains. The passing scenery was uninteresting, nothing compared with that which awaited her, and so she paid little attention to it. She was aware of branches of the hedge sweeping against the glass of the bus, and she closed her eyes, fearing they would strike her. She was conscious, too, of the engine of the bus vibrating under her feet, and of her husband at her side, his head inclined towards her, and the scent of tobacco on his clothes.

Her idea in making this trip to the mountains, on a Sunday like this, was to see if she could recapture something of the time of her wooing. It was a year and a half since their marriage and Annie was not altogether happy. With her romantic nature, she had expected married life to be an extension of courtship, though she had passed thirty years when she married. Her husband had become more prosaic after marriage. To him, in the terms of his native town, marriage was 'a settling down' – slippers, a fire, tobacco, the newspaper, and his wife completing the picture by sitting on a chair opposite, knitting. It never occurred to him that there was need to use the language of courtship after marriage. And Annie felt she had lost a lover in gaining a husband.

Ted Williams was his name, but 'Williams' he was called everywhere, except on his medicine bottle and by his wife. 'Mr Williams' was on the bottle, and 'Ted' was what his wife called him, though if Ted was on her tongue, it was as 'Williams', the man, that she thought of him.

To counteract all this she determined to get a day in one of those spots they had most loved to frequent during their courtship, and she had been fortunate in this opportunity to persuade him to a trip on Sunday, for Ted normally went to Sunday School; was, in fact, a Sunday School teacher.

But for once he was glad in his soul to leave the town, and especially to leave Lloyd and the Teachers' Meeting. Of late, no matter what was the subject of discussion in the Teachers' meeting, Lloyd would be certain to oppose him. It was high time Lloyd left, he thought – or died, it would make little difference which! Williams did not know how the people of the chapel allowed him his way in everything, and he only a stranger come into the place. And the previous Sunday Lloyd had been more perverse than usual. The question of the Sunday School Trip was before them. While everyone else was scratching his head to see to which town in North Wales it would be best to take the children, Williams ventured to propose Rhyl, for the sake of getting it over and going home to tea. As though he had been suddenly struck by the idea, Lloyd proposed that they should not have a trip this year, but should have a tea party instead. A trip would go very dear and, more than this, there were fearful accidents happening every year to Sunday School Trips. He laboured the point as much as possible. And, with all the accidents that ever happened to every Sunday School Trip in the world on his visage, sat down. Lloyd's amendment carried, and Williams went home cursing in his bosom, and hoping every child would have a slight attack of measles on the day of the tea party. Of course, his wife had the history of the Teachers' Meeting for cream with her currant tart over the tea. She laughed heartily about such things. But they weighed heavily on Ted, and during the week, at his work in the Post Office, Lloyd blotted out the sun for him. It was not surprising, therefore, that he readily agreed when Annie proposed Llyn Creunant to him in lieu of Sunday School the following Sunday. She knew exactly how he felt, but of her thoughts he was quite unaware.

With the swift motion of the bus, Lloyd faded from the mind of Williams, and in his place was the pleasure of seeing the hay cascading in the meadows and the honeysuckle and roses speckling the hedges. And in a little while he, too, began to look forward with pleasure to sitting beside Llyn Creunant. The walk from Llanwerful, the bus terminus, up to the lake was hot, and it was good to sit down on the shore, despite the midges that played about their faces. But having reached the lake Annie saw two things which displeased her. The first was three motor cars drawn up at the lake shore, cars of well-to-do people.

'Why couldn't these people have left their cars at Llanwerful, instead of coming right up to the lake with them?' she said.

'Yes,' answered Ted. 'It would do those double-chinned folk good to walk, and the landscape would be better without their cars – or them for that matter.'

The other thing which annoyed Annie was a small chapel, a few yards from the lake. It was a very miniature affair, two windows and a door, but Annie was afraid it was enough of a chapel to remind her husband of Lloyd. But to Williams a chapel in the country was not the same thing as a chapel in town, and it had not the effect on him that his wife feared.

They sat, half reclined, on the lake shore. Before them the great mountains stood like giants between them and the horizon, the purple of the heather and the yellow of the gorse shading into a lavender grey. At their feet lapped the waters of the lake, incessantly, like a cat gently pawing a knee to attract attention. It was a view to drink and not to be described, a landscape which intoxicated and made light-headed. From the corner of her eye Annie could see the little chapel. What was going on there, she wondered. Was there a Teachers' Meeting, and folk all getting fussed up? No, there could not possibly be more than one class, nor more than one teacher!

'Why do people need to go to chapel in a place like this?' she said. 'One would think they could never cease from worshipping in the middle of all this beauty.'

'Well, I don't know. Unless they go to pray. They must want to go somewhere to pray, after seeing so much loveliness,' said Ted.

'Sure enough. But they haven't much room in this old chapel.'

'No. It must be terribly small inside. One cough from John Ifans, Eglwys-bach, would be enough of a service for them for a month.'

Annie laughed, and turned her head towards the chapel. Looking at it now, she thought it did not seem so much out of place after all. If there were a chimney on it, it would look sufficiently like one of the houses. Possibly those who worshipped there did not see one another from one Sunday to the next, she reflected. It was like that in the country. Then she saw the people were coming out, a mere handful, and they went off each to their own home, spreading out in all directions like the legs of a spider. She followed them in her imagination, and amused herself by wondering what they would have for tea. Apple tart or currant cake, certain. And the moment she thought of this she could smell all the scents of a farmhouse kitchen on a Sunday afternoon – a mixture of farmyard, dairy, potatoes baking in the oven, and apple tart. And a longing came over her for her old home, as it used to be when she worked in the Post

Office at Colwyn Bay, and she went home over the Sunday.

She took a deep breath of happiness. 'Isn't it wonderful here?' she said to her husband.

'It's heaven on earth,' he replied, his eyes following a bird that skimmed the surface of the water.

'Do you remember the Whit Sunday we came here a good time back?'

'I do, well enough.'

'Do you remember what we talked about?'

'Quite well. I said I preferred being with you to anything else in the world.'

'Do you still feel like that?'

'I do!'

'In spite of everything?'

'Despite everything – and the devil!'

Williams was not in the habit of swearing, but in his own mind he was giving a last kick at Lloyd. And more than that, Annie looked uncommonly pretty, looking into her eyes in this place! She had a very shapely neck and bosom. Not a hollow anywhere, and one or two curls had strayed from under her hat on to her forehead.

They went off hand in hand to get tea. They knew a little cottage, right on the shore, where an old lady, living with her brother, supplied teas.

Arrived there, they saw the old woman busily carrying teapots and hot water out to the people belonging to the motor cars. They took a table and sat down.

'I will be back to you in two minutes – only finish with these,' cried the old lady.

'These' had two double chins each! And the old woman was kept busy quite a time, carrying hot water out to them. They had brought their own food.

Presently, the old man, her brother, came along, carrying a pitcher of water, and went with it into the house. He looked as though his real pleasure would be to pour it over some-one! Carrying water – that was his work in summer time. Lord knows what he did in the winter.

He came back out of the house, having deposited his

pitcher, and went to sit in a little field behind. Annie could
not restrain herself from turning to look at him. She felt
there could be only one man like this in the whole round
world! On his head was a Jim Crow hat, rusty with age. He
wore side whiskers, in fact his whole mode of dressing was
Victorian. His features seemed chiselled in marble. His eyes
were narrow and almost expressionless. Annie could hardly
turn away from watching him sitting there, brooding on
nothing.

'What do you suppose the old man is thinking about?'
she asked Ted.

'Dunno. Religion, perhaps,' said Ted.

'He couldn't be thinking of religion every minute of his
life.'

'There's nothing else for him to think of – unless he thinks
of the water he will have to carry next summer!'

Annie laughed at this.

'I wonder has he ever had a sweetheart!' she said mus-
ingly.

'Dunno, but it's hard to believe he had. Look at his eyes!'

'One couldn't judge from his eyes,' said Annie.

'Oh well, I wouldn't ever believe he had had a sweetheart,'
replied Ted. 'He's too fond of his own company.'

At this point the old woman returned to them. Her manner was intimate, and she had a motherly expression.

'I'm sorry to be keeping you waiting like this,' she said.
'Those people wanted a terrible lot of attention.' And she
continued, 'I haven't seen you two for a very long time.'

'No,' answered Ted. 'We're married now, you know.'

'Well, dear, dear!' exclaimed the old woman. 'Nobody
would know. You look just like two sweethearts still.'

Annie and Ted looked at each other with shy pleasure.

They enjoyed the tea, and particularly the homemade
bara brith which the old woman served them. Then, when
they had finished, they went to sit on the fence in front of
the house. The old man in the field behind continued to
brood, opening and shutting his eyes like a cat.

Presently a thin mist crept over the mountain and soon

it reached and curled about them. They started down to
Llanwerful, walking sharply, because by now it was getting
chilly. The mist dripped in small drops, like dew pearls, from
Annie's hair.

When they got home they saw a man walking up and
down in front of the gate like a sentry. Ted recognized him
immediately. It was Jones-the-Druggist.

'Where on earth have you been?' was Jones's greeting to
Annie and Ted. 'I've been searching everywhere for you
since four o'clock.'

'Oh, a bit of a jaunt,' said Annie.

'Well!' exclaimed the man. 'I was in the Teachers' Meeting this afternoon. It would have been worth you being
there. Humphrey got up and raised the matter of the trip
again and Lloyd went mad – he was like an angry wasp. He
called Humphrey every name he could think on! But the
biggest surprise ever was young Morgan, you know, he's an
apprentice with Humphrey – a shy, quiet little creature,
afraid of his own shadow almost. Well, he stood on his feet
and *made Lloyd sit down*. Somehow or other, perhaps
astonished at being told to sit down by such a crwtyn, *Lloyd
sat down*, and couldn't say any more. Everybody looked
dumb with surprise, and then the President got up and
said, "The Grace of our Lord, etc." '

Annie did not hear all of this. She hurried on into the
house to prepare supper. She was too happy even to remember to ask Jones to come in to supper with them.

Presently her husband came in. There was a different look
on him somehow, thought Annie. While he ate he said
nothing, but just looked down at his plate of meat. Annie
looked at hers, but her thoughts were far away. She was
going over and over every small happening, every word and
every look that Ted had given her that afternoon. She was
happy, happy! Ted was 'Ted' after all.

Then, later, Williams looked up and said, 'I would give
the round world to have been in the Teachers' Meeting this
afternoon.'

She all but choked. Great tears flowed into her eyes. But

she did not cry. In a few seconds she was laughing uncontrollably, peal after peal resounding through the house. Her husband stared at her in mute surprise.

The Brute Creation

GWYN JONES

THIS was the Field. The white tents, the four hundred yards
of grass, the hurdles, and the pens flashed at his eyes, the
flags and the bright dresses of the women. The first dogs had
already gone out. He was suddenly sober, a shepherd with
a job to do. He knew that most of his fellow competitors disliked him, and that some of them feared him, but to be
feared was honey on his tongue. He knew, too, how they
hoped to see everything go wrong for him this afternoon: he
wouldn't trust those scabs down the field not to loose a tough
one when his turn came. They said it was the run of the
game, the sheep a man had to work; he growled to think how
often he got bad ones. Some of these farmers, squat, basin-
bellied, fat-legged, he'd like to see them on the mountain.
That's where you showed whether you could handle sheep,
not on a green handkerchief like this.

He was a red-headed one from the farmstead up under
Creigiau: the Rocks. A scurfy, thin-soiled place with the
whole mountain for a sheep-run. Sometimes he had a woman
up there, but never for long: they could stand neither the
place nor its tenant. The tall, black rocks rose up behind the
cottage like a claw; the mountain sprawled away thereafter
in bog and stream and the rush-hidden grass of the grazing
grounds. Lonely – too lonely for everyone save him – too
lonely sometimes even for him. That was when he would
come down to the town and haggle with some sly or trampled
creature to come up for a week, a fortnight – no one had ever
stayed longer than that. And they all left him the same
way: they waited till he was far out on the mountain after
sheep and then fled downwards, from home field to path,
from path to mountain road, and so to where the lower farms

spotted the slopes round Isa'ndre. Fled, they would say, as if the devil were behind them, a devil with big hands and red hair.

He lumbered his way to the stewards' table. There were thirty or forty dogs entered for the different classes, the air quivered with their excitement. Their merits and failings were as well known here as those of their masters, and even more discussed. He saw men eyeing his black-and-white bitch as she moved close behind him. 'Novice?' asked one of the Isa'ndre shepherds, jerking his thumb. 'Novice!' he sneered, and then, savagely: 'Open! The Cup!'

The Cup! That tall white silver thing on his shelf for a year, his name on it for ever. A wide smile covered his face and he looked down at the bitch. 'You better,' he said. 'You better, see!' Her tail went tighter over her haunches, her eyes seemed to lose focus.

They were ticking his name off at the stewards' table. They were looking down at the bitch, a fine-drawn, thin-faced youngster. 'You ought to have entered her for the Novice. It's not fair to a young 'un.' 'She's going to win,' he told them, grinning. 'She better!'

He was walking away, swinging his stick. Behind him they shook their heads, shrugged, went on with their business. He grew restive and arrogant among men who seemed always to be moving away from him. Crike, he'd show them.

And then he was out at the shepherd's post, and far down the field they were loosing the three sheep which he and his bitch must move by long invisible strings, so that his will was her wish, her wish their law. A movement of his fingers sent her out to the right on a loping run which brought her well behind the three sheep. She sank instantly, but rose at his whistle and came forward flying her tail and worked them swiftly through the first hurdle. No one of them attempted to break as she ran them down towards the shepherd, turned them neatly round to his right, and then at a wave of his stick fetched them down past his left hand and so away to the second hurdle. They were now running too fast, and he whistled her to a stalking pace while the hurdle was still seventy yards away. The sheep halted, their heads up, and at the whistle the bitch proceeded with short flanking runs which headed them into the gap.

The shepherd was now five separate beings, and yet those five integrated so that they were one. He was the shepherd, he was the bitch, he was the three sheep together and severally; he could hardly distinguish between them as aspects of himself. The sheep had been turned across the field towards the hurdle in front of the spectators' benches at a moment when a string of children ran madly towards a stall selling drinks and ice-cream. As they faced the benches, the shepherd could feel alarm and irresolution grow in the sheep. The bitch felt it, too, and showed by a short, furious spurt that she was worried. Her worry moved simultaneously within the shepherd's mind.

The bitch steadied on his whistle, crouched, rose again, and raced out to fetch a straggler back. At once a second sheep broke away on the other side. By the time she had them once more in a group her anxiety was apparent to every shepherd on the field. They broke again and it looked as though they would pass round the hurdle, but a fierce whistle helped her cut them off. The pattern renewed itself; yet again the sheep faced the hurdle and the fluttering benches behind, yet again the bitch sank in their rear. The time was going by, she had lost the benefit of her quick work at the beginning and the shepherd brought her once more to her feet. She raced to their right, but grew confused on his signals and sank at the wrong time, letting a sheep escape. The crowd began to laugh, for she seemed little better than a fool to them now. She collected the sheep for the last time, but they at once strung out across the face of the hurdle, and at the shepherd's furious whistle she openly cringed and began to creep away from the sheep. Hoots of laughter and miaowings pursued her across the field; only the shepherds were silent.

The red-headed man turned from the post, his face like murder. The time-keeper's whistle had blown to clear the field, and at his own whistle the bitch came slowly to within thirty yards of him. Nearer she would not approach. 'That bitch,' said the steward who had spoken to him before, 'you want to go quiet with her. She'll make or break after this.' The red-headed man hardly looked at him, but gripped his stick and made for the gate.

First he went to eat food and then began a round of the back streets, the spit-and-sawdust bars where the legginged touts and copers drank, and where the policemen walked in twos. When he entered a pub he moved ponderously, swinging his weight from side to side like a Friesian bull, and he had a bull's eyes, gleaming, reddish, ill-tempered. At the Hart he pushed across the counter a corked medicine bottle. 'Fill this! All whisky. No water.' He slid his ten-shilling note into a spill of beer, grinning into the landlord's cloudy face.

Behind him, wherever he walked, slunk the bitch. She was hungry and thirsty, but too terrified even to lap water. From time to time he stopped and looked at her; he had no need to threaten; her bones had softened inside her. He could wait for the reckoning; delay would add to the pleasure. And the more he drank the blacker-hearted he grew. She'd made him look a fool before them all – all right, they'd see.

Late in the evening he went down to the woollen mills where before now he had found someone hardened or needy enough to accompany him back to Creigiau. He avoided the women who knew him, and struck into a bargain with someone he had not seen there before, a woman in the early thirties with an old, used face, dressed in country black. 'Come back to my place,' she wheedled. 'We can talk there. P'raps I will, p'raps I won't. We can settle it after.' They were both smiling, his face cunning, brutal, hers set in a mirthless coquetry. 'All right,' he said thickly, his hands opening and shutting. 'Where?'

They were walking down a dingy low-fronted street. 'There's a dog following us,' she said.

He began to curse the bitch, his luck, everything that had happened that day. 'Eh,' she said, 'you don't want to take it that bad. She looks frightened.' She patted her knee, clicked her tongue to call the bitch to her, but the creature stayed at the same distance, sitting and shivering.

'Leave her,' he growled, 'she'll follow. She better!'

The bitch turned away at his tone, but when they went on to the woman's room she trailed them behind, like a lost soul. Hours later when the woman went to the window overlooking the street the bitch was still there, outside the house, lying uneasily at the edge of the shadow. Behind her the redheaded man stretched and groaned in his sleep and she looked round at him, his huge lardlike shoulders, the thick neck and hairy hands. 'Swine,' she whispered, 'filthy swine!' Moonlight fell through the window with a pale green radiance, so that she could stare down the swollen whiteness of her body to her spread feet and the greasy fringe of the mat on the floor. 'Great God,' she whispered, 'Great God in heaven above!' She went quietly to the cupboard in the corner and hunted through her food-shelf till she found a piece of meat and a cake crust. She was back at the window with these when he sat up and asked what she was doing.

'The dog's outside,' she said, afraid of him. 'I was giving it food.'

'She don't eat tonight,' he told her. 'Nor p'raps tomorrow.' He leaned back against the bed-head, savouring her fear of him. 'I'm a bad 'un to cross. She got to learn it.'

'P'raps I got to learn it too, up at your place.' She reached for her raincoat and pulled it over her. The action, the covering her nakedness, gave her resolution. 'You can get moving, and the sooner the better.'

He shook his head. 'I don't take orders. Not from muck like you, I don't.'

'I'm muck,' she said bitterly, 'Christ knows, but I'm too good for you at that. I'm wise to you anyway, and I'm not coming.'

He closed his fist. 'I got a mind—' he began but she had opened the door and stood half on the landing, staring in at him. 'Don't try anything,' she said. 'If I call, I got friends.'

'You!' he jeered. 'Friends!' But he got slowly out of bed

and dragged on his clothes, swaying with exhaustion and drink. 'Muck like you,' he said, tying his laces. 'Friends!' He coughed and hawked with his heavy laughter.

Warily she watched him out of the room, backing away from the head of the stairs. He began to clump his way down, his boots hammering the boards, making all the row he could in that listening house. Then he was through the door with a shattering slam. She went back to the moon-filled window and looked into the street. For a half-minute she saw him leaning against the wall below her, then he began to walk away. The bitch emerged from shadow and, disregarding her low whistle, slunk after him.

The night air, cool and clean, drew him briskly forward. His head felt loose and large, but his legs moved steadily, his weight back on his heels so that his progress rang and echoed between the houses. He felt he could walk a hundred miles. A brief good humour filled him. Hadn't he been too clever for everyone? That landlord! He rumbled with beer and satisfaction. The woman too! If only he'd had a fair deal in the Field!

His good humour was gone. He looked round for the bitch. That woman. The judges. That blasted landlord scowling at him. Crike, he'd take it out of someone before he was through.

The houses had changed to hedges. There was no pavement, nor now a strake of dusty grass to walk on. The ring died out of the road; his boots were beginning to drag. He struck angrily at an ash branch which had missed the hedger's bill. If only it were that woman, the judges, the landlord – he thrashed it till the branch hung torn and a faint bitter odour of greenery tinged the air. He turned and called to the bitch but she kept her distance, her haunches tight, her head hanging forward.

It was then that he heard the clopping of a horse, the scrape of wheel rims, and saw away behind the bitch the yellow blob of a headlamp. He went into the middle of the road, stood waiting with his stick raised.

'You, is it?' said the man in the trap. The words were uncordial, the voice unfriendly. 'All right, get in. I'll take you to the usual place. That your bitch behind there?'

He was a compact, dried-out man nearing sixty, spry with gaiters, side-whiskers, and a hard hat, a big farmer from higher up the valley. He was a great one with the chapel and the local bench, and the red-headed man at once despised him and stood in awe of him, for he was the kind who could put the police on to you. The kind who would, too, if you touched his pride or pocket.

'She won't come,' he said sullenly.

'Not the first time today she made a fool of you,' said the farmer coolly. 'All right, if she won't ride I reckon she can run.'

He drove the mare smartly, as though she were before judges in a ring. The hedgerows were dipping past them, the mare's hooves tapped sleep into the red-headed man's brain. First his head rolled sideways and then he was canted on to the floor, groaning with discomfort, the sourness of drink rising into his mouth and nose. He was thinking, or dreaming, of the woman in her room when the shaking of the trap became so intolerable that he must open his eyes and struggle up. But the trap was stationary, and it was the farmer kicking hard at his feet to wake him. 'We are there. I was just going to tip you off.' He snaked the whiplash out sideways, gathered it neatly back to the handle. 'This bitch of yours now—'

'Where is she?'

He pointed with the whip to where she lay gasping thirty yards down the road. 'I'll take her off your hands as a favour.'

For a moment the other couldn't take this in; he stood staring at his hands as though they should contain something. Then, 'Not for sale,' he said abruptly.

'I'm not talking about a sale.' His hard little eyes stared into the red-headed man while he reached for a wallet with a wide rubber band round it, opened it, and drew out a note. 'Still, I'll make it legal.'

'Legal, hell,' said the red-headed man. He leaned so

heavily on the back of the trap that the mare pawed uneasily. 'She's worth five, ten pounds. What's this? A scabby
ten bob!'

'Take it,' said the farmer. 'I'm doing you a favour.'

'Favour, hell. I'll see you stuffed first!' He leaned forward
into the trap, closed his fist. 'I got a mind—'

The man in the trap had made his decision. Instantly his
whip cracked and the mare bounded forward so sharply that
the red-headed man fell floundering onto the road. He came
onto all fours, cursing and threatening, but the trap was
disappearing round the next bend before his hand could
close on a stone. 'Chapel bastard!' he swore, and turned to
the bitch. This was her fault. Everything that had happened
today was her fault. He'd see that she paid. 'Come here,
damn you!' he called.

Suddenly he thought of the whisky in his pocket. The
medicine bottle was undamaged and he took a long, noisy
suck at it. Whisky was a whip, he told himself, and began to
lurch up the mountain road.

But tired! After three hundred yards on the steep road he
felt that till tonight he had not known what tiredness was.
His legs were moving against rather than with his will. Only
the pattern of resentment shaping in his mind drove him on.
All the faces of the day, he saw them staring at him, landlords, stewards, judges, the woman who'd thrown him out –
he ought to have smashed his fist into their grinning mugs.
He'd been too soft, he'd let them outsmart him. Tomorrow
he'd go back and find them, his fist like this, see, smash
them all. Smash, smash, smash!

His head swayed with thought. The bitch was the cause
of it. Well, that was something he could take care of tonight.
When he came to the path, to the peat stream, there'd be a
pool big enough. He turned to look at her. 'Come here then,
little 'un,' he said, wheedling and hoarse. 'Come to the old
man.' Exulting in his stratagem, he began to coax her forwards with soft words and endearments. Once she moved so
much as a foot she was lost; she was powerless against the
god she recognized in him, helpless against her craving for

kindness after so horrible a day. 'Well then,' he said at last, stroking her head and slipping the leash on to her collar, shoving her frantic tongue from his face; 'We shan't be long now.'

Crike, but he was tired. 'I'm drunk,' he said aloud, and she wagged her tail with joy. 'Owl drunk. Where's the whisky? Crike, but I'm drunk!'

This was it! He must find a stone, a big stone. There it was, shining in the water, black with a glitter on it, just under the surface. Careful, he said, careful now. He heard a curious slapping sound and was puzzled what it could be. It was the bitch, drinking. 'That's right,' he grinned. 'Plenty of water.'

He slipped the leash because it wasn't long enough for him to hold the bitch and reach the stone. But she wouldn't run away. She was ingratiating herself with him, frisking her tail, fawning and slobbering.

'Crike!' he said vexedly. There was a bright ringing weight in his head from where he had been stooping. And dimly he was aware that this was no real pool, just a couple of inches of water over pebbles, and they moved treacherously under his feet.

He shouldn't have stooped. He reeled as he straightened up, and saw a blinding moon flash from the heavens. His heels shot from under him, and he fell face down into the water. Still the great moon flashed and pealed, only it was all about his head now. He must get his head up out of the moon. It blinded and deafened him. He heaved with his back, thrust with his great hands, for a moment his mouth gasped air.

From the bank the bitch watched his play with increasing excitement and delight. She was barely a year old. She dabbled the water with her forefeet, whined and then yapped her pleasure. She wanted to join in the game. Emboldened now and dizzy with joy that the black of the day was behind her, she leapt for his arching back, and stood proudly with her two paws on his shoulders. She could feel him moving in muscle and lung, and she tried ecstatically to lick his face. But always her muzzle was repelled by the water; so she retreated to the bank and sat for a while wagging her tail in expectation that he would play with her again.

The shadows had shifted a broad handbreadth when she paddled out to him a second time and sniffed at the back of his head. Soon her paws were once more on his shoulders, for long seconds she sniffed and whimpered. Then the hair rose along her backbone, the muzzle pointed, and briefly she moaned in her throat before her long and lonely howl went tingling to the moon.

Extraordinary Little Cough

DYLAN THOMAS

ONE afternoon, in a particularly bright and glowing August, some years before I knew I was happy, George Hooping, whom we called Little Cough, Sidney Evans, Dan Davies, and I sat on the roof of a lorry travelling to the end of the Peninsula. It was a tall, six-wheeled lorry, from which we could spit on the roofs of the passing cars and throw our apple stumps at women on the pavement. One stump caught a man on a bicycle in the middle of the back, he swerved across the road, for a moment we sat quiet and George Hooping's face grew pale. And if the lorry runs over him, I thought calmly as the man on the bicycle swayed towards the hedge, he'll get killed and I'll be sick on my trousers and perhaps on Sidney's too, and we'll all be arrested and hanged, except George Hooping who didn't have an apple.

But the lorry swept past; behind us, the bicycle drove into the hedge, the man stood up and waved his fist, and I waved my cap back at him.

'You shouldn't have waved your cap,' said Sidney Evans, 'he'll know what school we're in.' He was clever, dark, and careful, and had a purse and a wallet.

'We're not in school now.'

'Nobody can expel me,' said Dan Davies. He was leaving next term to serve in his father's fruit shop for a salary.

We all wore haversacks, except George Hooping whose mother had given him a brown-paper parcel that kept coming undone, and carried a suitcase each. I had placed a coat over my suitcase because the initials on it were 'N.T.' and everybody would know that it belonged to my sister. Inside the lorry were two tents, a box of food, a packing-case of kettles and saucepans and knives and forks, an oil lamp, a primus stove, ground sheets and blankets, a gramophone with three records, and a table-cloth from George Hooping's mother.

We were going to camp for a fortnight in Rhossilli, in a field above the sweeping five-mile beach. Sidney and Dan had stayed there last year, coming back brown and swearing, full of stories of campers' dances round the fires at midnight, and elderly girls from the training college who sun-bathed naked on ledges of rocks surounded by laughing boys, and singing in bed that lasted until dawn. But George had never left home for more than a night; and then, he told me one half-holiday when it was raining and there was nothing to do but to stay in the wash-house racing his guinea-pigs giddily along the benches, it was only to stay in St Thomas, three miles from his house, with an aunt who could see through the walls and who knew what a Mrs Hoskin was doing in the kitchen.

'How much farther?' asked George Hooping, clinging to his split parcel, trying in secret to push back socks and suspenders, enviously watching the solid green fields skim by as though the roof were a raft on an ocean with a motor in it. Anything upset his stomach, even liquorice and sherbet, but I alone knew that he wore long combinations in the summer with his name stitched in red on them.

'Miles and miles,' Dan said.

'Thousands of miles,' I said. 'It's Rhossilli, U.S.A. We're going to camp on a bit of rock that wobbles in the wind.'

'And we have to tie the rock on to a tree.'

'Cough can use his suspenders,' Sidney said.

The lorry roared round a corner – 'Upsy-daisy! Did you feel it then, Cough? It was on one wheel' – and below us, beyond fields and farms, the sea, with a steamer puffing on its far edge, shimmered.

'Do you see the sea down there, it's shimmering, Dan,' I said

George Hooping pretended to forget the lurch of the slippery roof and, from that height, the frightening smallness of the sea. Gripping the rail of the roof, he said: 'My father saw a killer whale.' The conviction in his voice died quickly as he began. He beat against the wind with his cracked, treble voice, trying to make us believe. I knew he wanted to find a boast so big it would make our hair stand up and stop the wild lorry.

'Your father's a herbalist.' But the smoke on the horizon was the white, curling fountain the whale blew through his nose, and its black nose was the bow of the poking ship.

'Where did he keep it, Cough, in the wash-house?'

'He saw it in Madagascar. It had tusks as long as from here to, from here to ...'

'From here to Madagascar.'

All at once the threat of a steep hill disturbed him. No longer bothered about the adventures of his father, a small, dusty, skull-capped and alpaca-coated man standing and mumbling all day in a shop full of herbs and curtained holes in the wall, where old men with backache and young girls in trouble waited for consultations in the half-dark, he stared at the hill swooping up and clung to Dan and me.

'She's doing fifty!'

'The brakes have gone, Cough!'

He twisted away from us, caught hard with both hands on the rail, pulled and trembled, pressed on a case behind him with his foot, and steered the lorry to safety round a stone-walled corner and up a gentler hill to the gate of a battered farm-house.

Leading down from the gate, there was a lane to the first beach. It was high tide, and we heard the sea dashing. Four boys on a roof – one tall, dark, regular-featured, precise of speech, in a good suit, a boy of the world; one squat, un-gainly, red-haired, his red wrists fighting out of short, frayed sleeves; one heavily spectacled, small-paunched, with indoor shoulders and feet in always unlaced boots wanting to go different ways; one small, thin, indecisively active, quick to get dirty, curly – saw their field in front of them, a fort-night's new home that had thick, pricking hedges for walls, the sea for a front garden, a green gutter for a lavatory, and a wind-struck tree in the very middle.

I helped Dan unload the lorry while Sidney tipped the driver and George struggled with the farmyard gate and looked at the ducks inside. The lorry drove away.

'Let's build our tents by the tree in the middle,' said George.

'Pitch!' Sidney said, unlatching the gate for him.

We pitched our tents in a corner, out of the wind.

'One of us must light the primus,' Sidney said, and, after George had burned his hand, we sat in a circle outside the sleeping-tent talking about motor-cars, content to be in the country, lazing easy in each other's company, thinking to ourselves as we talked, knowing always that the sea dashed on the rocks not far below us and rolled out into the world, and that tomorrow we would bathe and throw a ball on the sands and stone a bottle on a rock and perhaps meet three girls. The oldest would be for Sidney, the plainest for Dan, and the youngest for me. George broke his spectacles when he spoke to girls; he had to walk off, blind as a bat, and the next morning he would say: 'I'm sorry I had to leave you, but I remembered a message.'

It was past five o'clock. My father and mother would have finished tea; the plates with famous castles on them were cleared from the table; father with a newspaper, mother with socks, were far away in the blue haze to the left, up a hill, in a villa, hearing from the park the faint cries of children drift over the public tennis court, and wondering where I was and what I was doing. I was alone with my friends in a field, with a blade of grass in my mouth saying 'Dempsey would hit him cold,' and thinking of the great whale that George's father never saw thrashing on the top of the sea, or plunging underneath, like a mountain.

'Bet you I can beat you to the end of the field.'

Dan and I raced among the cowpads, George thumping at our heels.

'Let's go down to the beach.'

Sidney led the way, running straight as a soldier in his khaki shorts, over a stile, down fields to another, into a wooded valley, up through heather on to a clearing near the edge of the cliff, where two broad boys were wrestling outside a tent. I saw one bite the other in the leg, they both struck expertly and savagely at the face, one struggled clear, and, with a leap, the other had him face to the ground. They were Brazell and Skully.

'Hallo, Brazell and Skully!' said Dan.

Skully had Brazell's arm in a policeman's grip; he gave it two quick twists and stood up, smiling.

'Hallo, boys! Hallo, Little Cough! How's your father?'

'He's very well, thank you.'

Brazell, on the grass, felt for broken bones. 'Hallo, boys! How are your fathers?'

They were the worst and biggest boys in school. Every day for a term they caught me before class began and wedged me in the waste-paper basket and then put the basket on the master's desk. Sometimes I could get out and sometimes not. Brazell was lean, Skully was fat.

'We're camping in Button's field,' said Sidney.

'We're taking a rest cure here,' said Brazell. 'And how is Little Cough these days? Father given him a pill?'

We wanted to run down to the beach, Dan and Sidney and George and I, to be alone together, to walk and shout by the sea in the country, throw stones at the waves, remember adventures and make more to remember.

'We'll come down to the beach with you,' said Skully.

He linked arms with Brazell, and they strolled behind us, imitating George's wayward walk and slashing the grass with switches.

Dan said hopefully: 'Are you camping here for long, Brazell and Skully?'

'For a whole nice fortnight, Davies and Thomas and Evans and Hooping.'

When we reached Mewslade beach and flung ourselves down, as I scooped up sand and it trickled grain by grain through my fingers, as George peered at the sea through his double lenses and Sidney and Dan heaped sand over his legs, Brazell and Skully sat behind us like two warders.

'We thought of going to Nice for a fortnight,' said Brazell

– he rhymed it with ice, dug Skully in the ribs – 'but the air's nicer here for the complexion.'

'It's as good as a herb,' said Skully.

They shared an enormous joke, cuffing and biting and wrestling again, scattering sand in the eyes, until they fell back with laughter, and Brazell wiped the blood from his nose with a piece of picnic paper. George lay covered to the waist in sand. I watched the sea slipping out, with birds quarrelling over it, and the sun beginning to go down patiently.

'Look at Little Cough,' said Brazell. 'Isn't he extraordinary? He's growing out of the sand. Little Cough hasn't got any legs.'

'Poor Little Cough,' said Skully, 'he's the most extraordinary boy in the world.'

'Extraordinary Little Cough,' they said together, 'extraordinary, extraordinary, extraordinary.' They made a song out of it, and both conducted with their switches.

'He can't swim.'

'He can't run.'

'He can't learn.'

'He can't bowl.'

'He can't bat.'

'And I bet he can't make water.'

George kicked the sand from his legs. 'Yes, I can!'

'Can you swim?'

'Can you run?'

'Leave him alone,' Dan said.

They shuffled nearer to us. The sea was racing out now. Brazell said in a serious voice, wagging his finger: 'Now, quite truthfully, Cough, aren't you extraordinary? Very extraordinary? Say "Yes" or "No".'

'Categorically, "Yes" or "No",' said Skully.

'No,' George said. 'I can swim and I can run and I can play cricket. I'm not frightened of anybody.'

I said: 'He was second in the form last term.'

'Now isn't that extraordinary? If he can be second he can be first. But no, that's too ordinary. Little Cough must be second.'

'The question is answered,' said Skully. 'Little Cough is extraordinary.' They began to sing again.

'He's a very good runner,' Dan said.

'Well, let him prove it. Skully and I ran the whole length of Rhossilli sands this morning, didn't we, Skull?'

'Every inch.'

'Can Little Cough do it?'

'Yes,' said George.

'Do it, then.'

'I don't want to.'

'Extraordinary Little Cough can't run,' they sang, 'can't run, can't run.'

Three girls, all fair, came down the cliff-side arm in arm, dressed in short, white trousers. Their arms and legs and throats were brown as berries; I could see when they laughed that their teeth were very white; they stepped on to the beach, and Brazell and Skully stopped singing. Sidney smoothed his hair back, rose casually, put his hands in his pockets, and walked towards the girls, who now stood close together, gold and brown, admiring the sunset with little attention, patting their scarves, turning smiles on each other. He stood in front of them, grinned, and saluted: 'Hallo, Gwyneth! Do you remember me?'

'La-di-da!' whispered Dan at my side, and made a mock salute to George still peering at the retreating sea.

'Well, if this isn't a surprise!' said the tallest girl. With little studied movements of her hands, as though she were distributing flowers, she introduced Peggy and Jean.

Fat Peggy, I thought, too jolly for me, with hockey legs and tomboy crop, was the girl for Dan; Sidney's Gwyneth was a distinguished piece and quite sixteen, as immaculate and unapproachable as a girl in Ben Evans's stores; but Jean, shy and curly, with butter-coloured hair, was mine. Dan and I walked slowly to the girls.

I made up two remarks: 'Fair's fair, Sidney, no bigamy abroad,' and 'Sorry we couldn't arrange to have the sea in when you came.'

Jean smiled, wiggling her heel in the sand, and I raised my cap.

'Hallo!'

The cap dropped at her feet.

As I bent down, three lumps of sugar fell from my blazer pocket. 'I've been feeding a horse,' I said, and began to blush guiltily when all the girls laughed.

I could have swept the ground with my cap, kissed my hand gaily, called them señoritas, and made them smile without tolerance. Or I could have stayed at a distance, and this would have been better still, my hair blown in the wind, though there was no wind at all that evening, wrapped in mystery and staring at the sun, too aloof to speak to girls; but I knew that all the time my ears would have been burning, my stomach would have been as hollow and as full of voices as a shell. 'Speak to them quickly, before they go away!' a voice would have said insistently over the dramatic silence, as I stood like Valentino on the edge of the bright, invisible bull-ring of the sands. 'Isn't it lovely here!' I said.

I spoke to Jean alone; and this is love, I thought, as she nodded her head and swung her curls and said: 'It's nicer than Porthcawl.'

Brazell and Skully were two big bullies in a nightmare; I forgot them when Jean and I walked up the cliff, and, looking back to see if they were baiting George again or wrestling together, I saw that George had disappeared around the corner of the rocks and that they were talking at the foot of the cliff with Sidney and the two girls.

'What's your name?'

I told her.

'That's Welsh,' she said.

'You've got a beautiful name.'

'Oh! it's just ordinary.'

'Shall I see you again?'

'If you want to.'

'I want to all right! We can go and bathe in the morning. And we can try to get an eagle's egg. Did you know that there were eagles here?'

'No,' she said. 'Who was that handsome boy on the beach, the tall one with dirty trousers?'

'He's not handsome, that's Brazell. He never washes or combs his hair or anything. He's a bully and he cheats.'

'I think he's handsome.'

We walked into Button's field, and I showed her inside the tents and gave her one of George's apples. 'I'd like a cigarette,' she said.

It was nearly dark when the others came. Brazell and Skully were with Gwyneth, one on each side of her holding her arms, Sidney was with Peggy, and Dan walked, whistling, behind with his hands in his pockets.

'There's a pair,' said Brazell, 'they've been here all alone and they aren't even holding hands. You want a pill,' he said to me.

'Build Britain's babies,' said Skully.

'Go on!' Gwyneth said. She pushed him away from her, but she was laughing, and she said nothing when he put his arm around her waist.

'What about a bit of fire?' said Brazell.

Jean clapped her hands like an actress. Although I knew I loved her, I didn't like anything she said or did.

'Who's going to make it?'

'He's the best, I'm sure,' she said, pointing to me.

Dan and I collected sticks, and by the time it was quite dark there was a fire crackling. Inside the sleeping-tent, Brazell and Jean sat close together; her golden head was on his shoulder; Skully, near them, whispered to Gwyneth; Sidney unhappily held Peggy's hand.

'Did you ever see such a sloppy lot?' I said, watching Jean smile in the fiery dark.

'Kiss me, Charley!' said Dan.

We sat by the fire in the corner of the field. The sea, far out, was still making a noise. We heard a few nightbirds. '"Tu-whit! tu-whoo!" Listen! I don't like owls,' Dan said, 'they scratch your eyes out!' – and tried not to listen to the soft voices in the tent. Gwyneth's laughter floated out over the suddenly moonlit field, but Jean, with the beast, was smiling and silent in the covered warmth; I knew her little hand was in Brazell's hand.

'Women!' I said.

Dan spat in the fire.

We were old and alone, sitting beyond desire in the middle of the night, when George appeared, like a ghost, in the firelight and stood there trembling until I said: 'Where've you been? You've been gone hours. Why are you trembling like that?'

Brazell and Skully poked their heads out.

'Hallo, Cough, my boy! How's your father? What have you been up to tonight?'

George Hooping could hardly stand. I put my hand on his shoulder to steady him, but he pushed it away.

'I've been running on Rhossili sands! I ran every bit of it! You said I couldn't, and I did! I've been running and running!'

Someone inside the tent put a record on the gramophone. It was a selection from *No, No, Nanette*.

'You've been running all the time in the dark, Little Cough?'

'And I bet I ran it quicker than you did, too!' George said.

'I bet you did,' said Brazell.

'Do you think we'd run five miles?' said Skully.

Now the tune was 'Tea for Two'.

'Did you ever hear anything so extraordinary? I told you Cough was extraordinary. Little Cough's been running all night.'

'Extraordinary, extraordinary, extraordinary Little Cough,' they said.

Laughing from the shelter of the tent into the darkness, they looked like a boy with two heads. And when I stared round at George again he was lying on his back fast asleep in the deep grass and his hair was touching the flames.

A Successful Year

D. J. WILLIAMS

(translated by Glyn Jones)

THE rent of Pant y Bril was two pounds ten a year, and Rachel paid it every rent-day from what she got for the calf. So the day the cow calved was one of the big events of the year for her – the most important but one, and *that* was the day for selling it. Only once did the cow fail to calve, and Rachel hardly got over the financial loss of that year for the rest of her life. She talked so often about the price she was likely to get for her calf that the farmers living near, owners of many calves some of them, could almost calculate the coming year's success or failure by the amount of money Rachel was going to be paid. Two pounds twelve and six and it was going to be a successful year, with everybody able to pay his way. Two pounds fifteen and the year was going to be unusually prosperous, with a few unexpected weddings taking place. On the other hand, if Rachel's small hard hand was slapped for two pounds seven and sixpence – then a thin year was in store. And if the price should happen to fall as low as two pounds five, it was fully time to think of the chapel holding a service of intercession.

Rachel, having just finished her drop of broth for dinner, was sitting knitting a stocking out in the garden and pondering on all this while the fitful sunshine of April warmed her little red cheeks. Near her was her bitch Cora, with her little tail in a yellow ring on her back, sniffing from smell to smell. Somehow these confused scents were more to her taste than the remains of her mistress's meal that had been put down for her earlier. The magic of spring was in the air. Rachel saw the young buds opening out on every hand, in the cur-

rant and gooseberry bushes, and in the mass of red roses
near the back of the cottage. She looked at them all, the
miracle of sudden awakening, as though she had never seen
it before, unconsciously relating it to the circumstances of
her own life. Was there for her, too, to be new hope like
this? Or was what lay ahead only a continuation of that
long Autumn, which began at the height of her life's Summer, when she was left, fifteen years ago, a childless young
widow, to mourn the death of a sickly husband? Fifteen
years of working her fingers to the bone to scrape a bit of
food, yes, and often having to deny body, and soul too. Still,
she had lived as decently as she could during that time. Not
always to perfection, perhaps. But King David, as she heard
in that sermon the previous Sunday, had yielded to temptation and then repented, and so had received forgiveness for
his sins. She herself felt she must have gained complete
absolution that afternoon because she was conscious somehow of a marvellous sense of well-being, a lightness of spirit,
without the smallest regret for anything she had ever done.

She glanced down at herself: she was wearing a little white
shawl across her shoulders, a check apron pleated with her
flat-iron, and her best pair of boots – however that was to be
accounted for on a week-day – shining upon her feet. She
had given herself a hasty glance in the mirror on the way
out of the cottage and had thought the small, ominous criss-
crosses under her eyes were less in evidence than she had
seen them for some time. And, with the gentle warmth and
the fresh green life shooting out everywhere, her spirit made
a leap, as it were, ten years into the past.

The next moment she found herself somehow listening
attentively to that sermon of the previous Sunday once again.
She blushed, although she did not quite know why. Then
immediately there followed an urge, as inexplicable as the
blush, a fancy to go into the house and to change into her
clogs and her canvas apron, and then to clean out under the
pig. This job was long overdue, as she had noticed that
morning when she had given him his bit of food. But before
she could decide what to do she heard a rough voice that

startled her badly for the moment, addressing her from beyond the garden gate. At the sound of it Rachel turned into a lump of icy virtuousness.

'Hullo, girl, how's things?' said the voice, with a suggestion of beery slurring in it. 'I've called by to buy your old calf this year again.'

'Here's this old rowdy come at last as I was afraid he would,' Rachel said to herself, trying to slip behind the thick currant bushes near by. In making the move, her eyes fell, with a certain amount of guilt, upon her shining best boots.

'Hullo, playing peep-bo, are you, good girl? Come on out for me to have a look at you. You're looking very pretty this afternoon, aye indeed you are.' And the speaker came on and rested his elbows in a leisurely way on the top bar of the garden gate. It was obvious he knew that standing there he was master of the only entry into the garden, if it came to a question of siege. He knew, too, that many gold sovereigns and half-sovereigns lay snugly in the gussets of his long brown purse at the bottom of his trousers pocket. A real old dawn-fox was Teimoth, coming around every spring long before the snowdrops arrived even, to inquire into the prospects of the first-born among the little calves of the district.

'I'm not selling the calf this year, not to you or to anybody else,' Rachel said abruptly, forced to come out from behind the currant bushes, her annoyance rising in a hot flush in her face. 'So get about your business.'

'Oh, so that's it, is it? Retiring, I s'pose, and living on what's in the old stocking, like Griffiths Tŷ Sych. Or better still, rearing the old calf to be a bull! Rachel Evans, Pant y Bril. One-Ex Bull!' And Teimoth laughed in his most jeering way at his own joke.

'You old blockhead! It's a heifer calf the cow's got this year again, as usual. And I'm going to keep her because her mother's getting old.'

'Well, whatever's happening to the old cow, *you* are getting younger every year,' Teimoth said, his small black eyes dancing mischievously in his head. 'Come on, let's have a look at how those best boots of yours are fitting you, and what sort of a job you've made of those pretty little pleats in your apron,' he went on, attempting, in his clumsy way, to come in through the gate.

'Teimoth,' said Rachel, raising her voice, 'if you come one inch nearer, I'll set Cora on you. Cora-Cora-Cora!' she shouted rapidly. But Cora had just made some important discovery in the bottom of the hedge and was burrowing with too much deliberation in pursuit of it to pay the slightest attention to anything else – even to something as sacred as the safety of her mistress.

'It's not a bit of good calling Cora. Cora knows me before today, don't you, old girl?' said Teimoth, making a soft soothing sound with his lips to attract the bitch's attention. 'Come on, girl, come on,' he continued, casting a sort of knowing wink in the direction of the cow-shed. 'Let's have a look at the calf. We won't fail to come to an agreement this time, any more than in the past.'

Rachel had been digging the garden that morning, and at those words a lump of turf flew just past Teimoth's head – then a second lump – and a third.

'You come near my house again without my asking you, that's all, you old nuisance,' Rachel shouted, righteous indignation possessing her completely. Teimoth was a pretty crafty one usually, but he realized he had misjudged the weather somewhat this time. He judiciously went off up the road, mumbling something about, 'That queer old girl, oh,' and marvelling at the strangeness of women.

The first thing Rachel did, when she saw that Teimoth was far enough away, was to go into the house and give thanks that she had had enough strength to drive the Evil One out of the garden. She sat in her armchair by the fire, shedding a few tears in the excitement of her victory. With Satan thus put to flight the voice of her conscience, which had been reproaching her with a few uncomfortable reminders now and then ever since that sermon the previous Sunday, was now at peace. But in her rejoicing Rachel forgot one important

thing: that the devil is never more dangerous than when he
has just been routed. Before the warmth of her thankfulness
had completely disappeared from her heart other less serious
thoughts began to gather there. She recalled Teimoth, like
some old black boogy-boo striding up the narrow lane, and
over the top of the hedge the clods of earth falling in a
heavy shower around his ears. She began to laugh and she
laughed until her eyes watered; to think that she, a little bit
of a thing as she was, could put old Teimoth to flight like
that! What if the neighbours knew, she thought, smiling.
No, there was no need for the whole neighbourhood to know
either, fair play to old Teimoth too. And somehow she began
to feel her heart warming towards him. There were worse
people than Teimoth to be had, after all, although his tongue,
like his whiskers – his funny whiskers! – was a bit rough
sometimes. But what right had he got all the same to jeer
at her for wearing her best boots on a week-day, exactly as
though he thought she had put them on just for his special
benefit? If he came back that night – and, come to think of
it, it was quite possible he would, because he had hardly ever
bought a beast without going away from the house, and then
coming back, perhaps two or three times, to squeeze the
price down a few pence – if he should come back, she would
put some salt on his tail where the price was concerned,
that was certain. And Rachel's temper ruffled up and almost
boiled over again in an upsurge of offended virtue. But then
peace entered her soul once more, because the kettle just at
that moment began singing.

*

Rachel's guess was correct. The little lamp, home-made out
of an old bottle, a twig and a cork, had been put on the table
some time. Rachel played idly with a little spill in the flame
of the fire, ready to light it. She considered very seriously
what had happened, half blaming herself by now for her
rashness that afternoon, perhaps losing her best chance to
sell the calf, and the rent already overdue at that. She was

suddenly roused from her musings by a bumping sound coming from the cow-shed which formed the end of her cottage. Going to the division between her living quarters and the shed, and peeping over the stall that separated them, she saw Teimoth's massive hand feeling the back and the ribs of her calf, and the little creature in her innocence hollowing her back and slowly raising up her tail as though she was thoroughly enjoying these attentions.

'Indeed, Rachel, you've got a lovely little calf this year again,' Teimoth said, after both of them had come out into the yard. He showed not the slightest ill-feeling after the unpleasantness of the afternoon.

'Yes, she's a good little calf. But she's too dear for you to buy this year all the same,' said Rachel in a meaningful voice.

'Come on, come on, don't be so awkward, woman. State some reasonable figure so that we can have something to bargain about. It's getting dark, can't you see, and old Teimoth has got a good bit of a way to go still.'

'There was no need for you to have come back to pester me like this anyway,' Rachel replied, sharp and no-nonsense.

'Come on now, come on. Don't waste time. I know very well that you're dying to get rid of the little calf and you wouldn't have slept a wink tonight if I hadn't come back. Give me your hand on two pounds ten, since it's you.'

(Secretly Rachel marvelled to herself that he was starting the bidding at such a high price. But she said nothing.)

'Now look here,' Teimoth went on, his face becoming very serious, 'if I was to eat my hat, I won't get two quid for your calf next Saturday, after I've dragged her all those miles to Carmarthen mart. No indeed I won't, not if I was to drop down dead by here. Two pound ten.'

'Two pound fifteen,' said Rachel, her little round chin as rigid as a harp-string.

'I'll tell you what I'll do with you,' said Teimoth, plunging his right arm into the depths of his trousers pocket. 'We'll split the difference. Half a crown off your price and it's a bargain. Come on, let's go in for me to have a nice cup of tea with you. I've got a terrible thirst on me after walking all this way.'

'Two pound fifteen,' said Rachel, determined, 'and not a farthing less, not if you stayed here all night.'

'No, no, woman. And come on, that cup of tea. You're asking too much now.'

'Stop talking nonsense, will you?' Rachel answered.

A lot of hard bargaining went on for a long time over that next half crown, Teimoth swearing on his oath that he would bring the judgement of heaven upon his head for daring to offer such an exorbitant amount for such a tiny little weakling, and the poor calf becoming smaller and smaller with every thruppence his offer went up. She was still too young to understand the meaning of the way Teimoth was belittling her, or she would have felt small enough very soon to try to escape down the mousehole in the wall in front of her nose. The old lady her mother stood by in disdainful surprise, in the middle of chewing her cud. Rachel actually said very little, but she held on stubbornly to her price with her lips set firmly – although her teeth were watering to get rid of the calf.

'Well, since you're so mulish tonight,' said Teimoth, wearying at last of his unavailing eloquence, 'come on, give me your hand on it – three pounds less five bob. Two pounds fifteen, for goodness' sake. And come on inside for me to count the money.' And he tried to catch hold of Rachel's arm so that he could slap the palm of her hand to seal the bargain.

'Now look here, Teimoth,' Rachel said, freeing herself quickly from his grasp, 'don't try any of your tricks with me. Three pounds *less* five bob indeed! Three pounds *plus* five bob I've been saying from the beginning!' She added this shamelessly, laughing in his face. And before Teimoth could get his wind back Rachel had run into the house, holding the door slightly ajar after her.

'You silly old fool,' she shouted, 'if you hadn't jeered at me because of my best boots, you could have had the calf this afternoon for two pound ten, as you did before. As though I'd worn my best boots and my little shawl just to please Teimoth, the important gentleman!'

'Well, heaven knows!' said Teimoth, speechless with fury, unable to say another word.

'Yes and *I* know well enough too,' Rachel said sharply. 'It's my turn to do the dealing now, if you please. You can have the calf for three pounds if you want her – and a cup of tea, perhaps, into the bargain. Say quick, before I shut the door.'

'You can keep your old calf, until her horns grow out through the roof!' shouted Teimoth.

The door slammed shut.

Teimoth had hardly gone out of the yard before a very unfortunate shower of heavy April rain began to fall. He turned up the collar of his coat and hurried to shelter under some old holly trees near by, his feelings as stormy as the weather. He was angry with Rachel, and angrier still with himself – that little handful making a fool of *him*, old Teimoth. Overhead he could see the black sky moving swiftly and loaded with many a sharp downpour. To his right, out from under the shelter of the branches, there were the long miles of the overland journey, through soaking valleys and across the unsheltered hills. To his left a warm beam of light stretched out in his direction. It was near enough for him to see the heavy rain falling through it as it shone out of the cottage window. He imagined Rachel inside, in her clean apron and those shining little boots of hers that had cost him so dear, preparing herself a cup of tea. A fierce battle was fought in his heart: pride against avarice – his emotions meeting in a hand-to-hand struggle and the rain falling faster through the holly trees as though each one of them had turned into a sieve.

Suddenly he heard a doorlatch lifting. His heart almost stopped. A broad slice of light shot out, shining on the rain. In this illumination he saw Rachel quite clearly, her hand shading her eyes, trying to see out into the darkness. The last words he heard were those of that old money-grubber that ruled his heart. 'You remember now, Teimoth,' that old skinflint said, 'three quid's a lot of money to give for a bit of a calf like that.'

Yes, the story is quite true. That year is remembered even today as the most prosperous in the history of the locality.

The Teacher

GWYN THOMAS

Mrs Monroe had taken the history teaching post after the departure of her husband, Mr Glen Monroe. The cool wisdom and gentleness of that man still haunted our minds and the rooms of the school. He was the only person we had met who had thought himself into a state of serenity on this earth, and in his presence we marvelled and gave thanks. Often when we had been in the lower school, badgered into a lethal rawness by some teacher who had long since ceased to regard teaching as anything but a squalid trap for himself and the taught, Mr Monroe would come in with his smile and his quiet voice and we would, in seconds, be soothed back into tolerance, then contentment. His was the sort of humanity which, laid like a kiss upon any phase of the far past, would make death and folly apologize for their crass obstructiveness, bow and make way for the healed and resurrected dead.

Then he himself had vanished into the gullet of time and change. We could still remember him and Mrs Monroe from the days before the war addressing meetings in this vestry, that hall, on behalf of peace, collecting signatures for the Peace Pledge, convinced that no man, however mad for his own power and the pain of others, would want war again. War came, and we watched the sad, stricken face of the man as he walked through the school, masking the outraged fury of his heart with a quiet melancholy. In lessons he would fall oddly silent at places where before he would have attempted a defence, an apology for some bit of vile destructive violence on the part of the world's strange ringmasters.

'Life has been and still is,' he would say, 'in a state of

fever. The germs of fear, greed, frustration still burn in its blood. The fever will pass. The body will grow cool. The mind will become normal and will address itself to the task of living with the affectionate brotherly humility, which we in this room expect from ourselves. Always think of mankind as one body, with limbs that move jerkily, ridiculously now, but to be treated with the same love and patience as you would give to a cripple of your near acquaintance.'

In 1942 he was called up. His wife, Mrs Monroe, came to take his place at school. With her we had the same mental experience as we had with him, the same attempt to lay a soothing unguent of tolerance and understanding on the raw hot places of our past. In 1943, in the autumn, he came under heavy shell fire in a tank in Italy. His chest and face were shattered. In 1944 he was brought back to a military hospital which had wards for the unseeable, the virtually dead, the survivors by miracle and irony. It was about seven miles from Mynydd Coch, a lovely village called Tremscott. We had often walked there by way of a path that led through the sea of ferns on the plateaux above the town. In 1945, on an October day, Mrs Monroe called us, our group in the fifth form, Wilfie, Spencer, Bosworth, Sam, Leo, and the rest of us to her side.

'I've been to see Mr Monroe today.'

'How is he, Mrs Monroe? When will he be back?'

'He's just the same. He won't be back for some time.'

'We'd like to go and see him, Mrs Monroe.'

'That's what I wanted to talk to you about. He kept talking about that outing he did with you to Caerphilly Castle.'

We remembered Mr Monroe had promised to take us on that trip when we first began the study of Norman castles in the second form. But something had always cropped up to prevent it. When Mr Monroe had gone into the army we thought we would never make the pilgrimage, for Mrs Monroe, out of school, was always busy with her mother who was ailing. And then quite suddenly, one summer afternoon, Mr Monroe, in uniform and on his embarkation leave before going to Africa, came into the classroom where we were sitting. He asked the headmaster if he could take the boys who had originally put their names down for the trip to the castle.

We travelled by bus, through the valleys and over the moorland. He pointed out the huge defensive details of the ruin, somewhat impatiently, for the whole apparatus of violence bored him and made him ill at ease. He looked at the great circle of the surrounding hills and described how Owen Glyndwr and his men had poured forth from their fastnesses to break their hearts and bodies upon this fist of stone.

'The clenched fist of fear,' he said. 'Look at it. The defensive stranger in a strange, hating land. For such there is no victory. Owen in his grave is a prettier sight than this mausoleum. Man will ache, man will bleed, for as long as even one member of his tribe knows he has some power, some wealth that is not rightly his and keeps his finger for ever on the gun. If the rapacious lout were only rapacious and willing to go when his crop is full, all would be well. But he is stupid also, and proud, and will not withdraw.'

Then he took us to a café and treated us to a meal that took us an hour to eat, spam, chips, ten sorts of cakes and four sorts of cordial as well as tea. As he raised his last cup of tea to his lips he stared at his khaki sleeve, smiled and said:

'Each age hugs to its heart its own brand of Black Death. We are not happy without a pestilence. I wonder what my germ will be.'

He urged us to clear the cakes, especially Sam who had barely eaten a mouthful. Since he started in the school, Sam had hung on Mr Monroe's every word.

'But never mind,' said Mr Monroe; 'remember what I told you. Mankind, one body. Even if it stumbles and mortally crushes you, remember that its limbs are still strange to one another, its brain in fragments, kept in fragments for aeons longer that has been strictly necessary. If it bleeds, clean the wound, let no dirt remain in it to rankle. If it falls, never snarl at it for clumsiness. Smile at it, lift it to its feet, tell it its legs are getting stronger, its directions surer.'

Then we walked briefly once again in silence and failing light around the ruin, across the rough neglected ground close to the walls, allowing our senses to be touched by the hazards and outrages of dead time. At my side Leo Warburton was full of pouting reservations, for he had always believed in the placing of a cold authoritarian fist on the hot fuss of our kind. No one was in a mood to argue and Leo said nothing.

On our way home from the castle the hilltop road along which we travelled was upheld in the great golden glow of an all-out sunset. We sang in snatches. For a while Mr Monroe listened to our singing and smiled at us. Then he looked at the red sunset and his smile vanished in a thoughtful silence. We said good night to him on Mynydd Coch Square and we had not seen him since.

'He would like to have you visit him,' said Mrs Monroe to us, 'you boys who went with him to the castle.'

'Yes, Mrs Monroe, we'd like to very much.'

'Shall we wear our best suits, our dark ones?' asked Bosworth Bowen.

'He won't be able to see you.'

Bosworth looked stricken and turned away.

We made the journey to Tremscott by bus, covering in part the same hill road we had taken on our way to the castle, driving through the serene fern-sea that had movements of light trembling over it in the fitful sunlight of the afternoon.

In the hospital, approached through a thick and lovely wood, we walked through long corridors, bringing an unnatural noisiness and jollity with us. Mr Monroe was in a small room, alone. Of his face we could see nothing through the helmet of bandage. His arms were in sight. He said nothing. We looked in a pain of wonder at him, at Mrs Monroe, at each other.

'Just talk,' she said. 'About yourselves, about the school.'

We were silent. We could feel our stupidity bore its way right through to the end of time.

'He wanted to hear you, your voices, all together,' said Mrs Monroe. 'He finds it hard to talk today.'

All the silence on earth was around us and it had the unmoving white helmet on the pillow for its core. I heard Leo begin a slow stiff formal declaration of gratitude to Mr Monroe for all he had done for us. Leo had heard his father, a councillor, pass these votes of thanks so often he was a master of them. There was hardly a sector of life in Mynydd Coch that Mr Warburton had not covered with his thanks at one time and another, and we had been told that even at table when he thanked Mrs Warburton for a meal he got Leo to second the vote. Leo droned on, coldly. The rest of us fidgeted, marvelling that amidst the pelting tears of things Leo should so invariably be the boy with the blotter.

A nurse peeped in at the door, stared and nodded at the bed with a look of unhappy preoccupation and went away again. For myself I was remembering the afternoon in our first year at the school when we had been taken by Mr Wilkins, the small, trembling man who had taught us chemistry. We had been at the school long enough to realize that most teachers have a wound, some special ineluctable bit of rawness, and ever since we made the discovery we were to be seen wheeling sacks of salt up the school drive to speed on the work of mortal aggravation. Mr Wilkins's mania was a conviction that humanity was covertly muttering about his lack of natural strength and dignity, the failure of his voice to penetrate to the room's corners and to ours, his inability to make plain the magic which he knew to lie at the heart of his subject, to have it take wing before us and lift us out of the pool of shabby mischief and malice. Then there were his tremors, hesitancies and minutes of downright, abject silence in which he seemed to go below surface and stare his defeat and sickness in the eye. To torment him, we would, whenever his eye fell on us, engage in a bit of prison-style, side-of-the-mouth whispering with a neighbour. That afternoon we had driven him into an evangelical frenzy. He appealed to our honour, our pity, our friendship. He explained to us how ill he became if ever he was vexed or ill-tempered. His gestures were big and intense. They struck us as comic, and our laughter was loud and savage.

'Boys, boys, boys!' It was not so much an appeal as a note on the nature of hell.

Then he became silent and greenly pale. His jaw dropped and his eyes bulged. His hands pawed helplessly in front of him as if he were trying to jostle away the evil that was plainly smothering him. He slipped out of sight behind the desk in a faint. As he fell he gave out a moan that shocked us. At that moment Mr Monroe came into the room. He rushed down the aisle calling for some water. It was brought. He leaned over Mr Wilkins, helped him to revive and half carried him to the staff-room. We waited for Mr Monroe's return, speechless and dismayed, our eyes full of prophecies of blood upon the moon, of heads banged together with such force there would be a quick exchange of teeth. But when Mr Monroe re-entered the room, he merely looked around with his usual grave mildness.

'The march out of barbarism,' he said, 'is the widening and deepening of the power to be kind. Accept no definition more complicated than that. I will now select an incident from history that will help you, though still utterly barbarian, a little more swiftly along that road.'

Then, in the tiny ward, Spencer's voice cut across Leo's. 'You know what a boy Sam is for sweet stuff. When he gets his pay from Turner the greengrocer on Saturday night he goes into Jacko Galeazzi's shop and puts down six of those chocolate biscuits that are off points.'

'You're a bright one to talk,' said Sam. 'The way I've seen you shovel it away in that dining-hall in school. If you spent Saturday lugging a loaded bike up and down hills you'd bite a bit off Jacko's arm as well.'

'No doubt,' said Spencer. 'Well, there was Sam, the day Mr Monroe took us to the castle. He was thinking over what Mr Monroe had said about the way the hill people had shattered their lives against those bastions and he was very broody. Mr Monroe had got him a plateful of those cream slices that are very special in that café. Mr Monroe had said: "We have known so much of things like castles, brutal mindless things, that there is a defensive castellated zone of dread in every heart, barring the way to the perils and glories of a full comradeship." Do you remember that, Mr Monroe?'

I thought I saw a movement of the head, but it may have been an illusion due to having stared for so long at the whiteness of the bed.

'Well, Sam,' went on Spencer, 'was struck quiet as a mouse by this notion and he was busy working out what it meant and drawing up a list of elements in Mynydd Coch who might well be called Offa for the dykes they carried around in this connection. He asked Leo if he ever felt a strong sense of mortar in his emotions. Then Sam noticed the cream slices and his eyes lit up. But Bosworth and me kept asking him leading questions about this thesis, and every time Sam got worked up over a fresh point Bosworth or me would nip in and whip a slice.'

There was some more talk. Wilfie gave an account of his dealings with Mr Rawlings, the second senior assistant master, in the matter of Bible readings in the hall for the morning assembly and Wilfie wondered why Mr Rawlings always kept picking passages of intense fury from the Old Testament denouncing adultery when this was not yet an important activity in the school. Leo explained some new suggestions made by Mr Rawlings for bringing greater dignity and uniformity into the dress of the prefects.

'He says it's about time somebody struck a note of pomp in Mynydd Coch. The place is so deficient in a sense of hierarchy it's no wonder it suffers from a sort of social rickets.'

'He said its feeling for the ceremonial was bandier than any corgi.'

Then Sam related the tale of a persecution maniac called Elmo Allen living in Minerva Meadows, his street, who had chased his entire household around the western side of Mynydd Coch shouting that he would rather see the world perish by conscious personal malignity than by the impersonal idiocies of war and hunger. Elmo grew tired, for his family was fast and the hatchet a great weight, and he called in at the Library and Institute to listen to a debate on the mechanics of love and pity before handing himself over to the constable.

'He had a point,' said Mrs Monroe. 'But I am disappointed to hear of him trying to enforce it in just that way.'

'About Minerva Meadows,' said Bosworth Bowen, 'they are nearly all jingles, with Sam giving out the beat mostly.'

A nurse came in and said we should go. A slight convulsion shook the figure on the bed. He raised his arms. We shook his hand in pairs. Then we left.

On the way back a night full of rain clouds fell rapidly. We spoke little. Mrs Monroe, staring out at the plateau which stretched towards the tall rounded hills that stood between us and the west, said nothing.

As we began the downhill road into Upper Mynydd, the rain began to beat around the bus in a temper. We got a sense of dangerous desolation, exposedness, from the thorough ferocity of the large plastered drops against the panes. We were alone in the bus except for its conductor, Galway Davies, who had been at school with us, a few years ahead.

Then Mrs Monroe threw her head against the back of the seat before her, loudly, hurtingly. She broke into a storm of weeping as wild and without curb as the downpour outside. We signalled to Galway Davies to stop the bus. We filed out, leaving Mrs Monroe to herself. The bus resumed its way and soon disappeared into the hissing shadows. For a few seconds we saw the face of Galway Davies looking out at us from the back window of the bus, darkened and bewildered. We continued our journey down into Mynydd Coch, soaked. Our thoughts gave out the same strong dank smell as the ferns, dripping on either side of us.

Two days later, Mr Monroe died. They held a special service in the assembly hall. Mr Rawlings had all the prefects lined up in the front of the whole assembly. Leo, Bosworth, and Pendennis Vaughan all stood rigidly to attention as the Head, in a voice that moved with the jerky anguish of an arthritic limb, read that passage about a new heaven, a new earth, and no more pain, no more death, a truce to pain and an end to tears. But Sam, Spencer, and myself, our bodies seemingly relaxed by a sorrow that struck us in some way as familiar, well worn, stooped slightly forward. Sam's face was ashen, inconsolable in a basic and terrible way. Our voices, when we came to the hymn, were low, uncertain and full of dark-tipped reservations, as we came to the lines urging a shroud of acceptance for the outrage of goodness betrayed, the pushing away of lives still creative into the darkness of death and waste.

The Strange Apeman

E. TEGLA DAVIES

(translated by Wyn Griffith)

A DAY of teeming rain in the great forest, the apemen hunched up against the tree-trunks, so close to the trees that they seemed part of them, their arms like branches in shape and colour. There they squatted, watching the heavy rain-drops falling lifelessly to the ground. The water formed into pools under the trees, and the pools rose and met, until the marshy ground became a lake and each apeman stood on a small island little larger than his foot.

At times a light puff of wind rustled the leaves and a rush of water fell from them; here and there an apeman climbed the trunk of his tree as his island vanished under him. Soon there remained but one upon the ground – the strange ape-man whose behaviour troubled them all. As his island shrank, they watched him bend down to reach a large stone still above the water-level, dragging it towards him and thrusting it against the tree-trunk, standing upon it when his island disappeared. They parted the leaves and stared at him vacantly. Whenever they were in trouble his actions were inexplicably strange to them. Sometimes they showed their gratitude by rubbing their cheeks against his, but more frequently he roused a feeling of perplexity and imminent danger, and then they sought his blood. His skill in devising a new way of escape or defence saved him.

One day, when the monster was pursuing them closely and they had neither refuge nor forest at hand, nor were they numerous enough to attack tooth and limb, it was he who scaled a crag quickly to loosen a great boulder so that it fell on the head of the beast and killed him. They had not imagined that boulder and crag could help them, nor did they understand how it happened then. They knew that the stone this strange apeman had loosened fell upon the monster's head and saved them, and that the fall of the stone came after his climb. For a while, they expected this to happen each time he scaled a crag, and, as it did not take place, they grew more confused and avoided him whenever possible.

Now that they saw him standing on the stone instead of climbing the trunk, they feared him and they crept each to the other side of his own tree, so that the trees that sheltered them might protect them from him. As the rain fell, they peered past the trunks and through the large heavy leaves at this strange apeman on his stone. But the water rose and covered the stone, and he was compelled, against his will, to climb his tree. They were relieved when they saw that he had to do as they had done, and they moved once more towards him and made him one of themselves again. There they sheltered, each in his tree, mute and still as images, listening to the rain, with no sign of life but an occasional blink as a stray raindrop fell between the leaves and on their heads.

In spite of the downpour the leaves stood firm and unbent, giving good shelter; rarely did any drops penetrate, but in the gaps between the trees the rain fell straight to the ground in a mighty deluge. For a long time the leaves withstood the tempest although the water accumulated in them, but in the end they gave way, for all their strength, and they began to droop and the water to fall upon the creatures below. This continued until there was little to choose between tree and open ground, the one with its steady rain and the other with its periodical drenching. Gradually the leaves took the shape of the wings of giant birds, wounded in their joints, hanging limply, rain pouring from their tips; the trees ceased to give shelter and the apemen closed into the places where the boughs branched most thickly.

Terrified at their helplessness, they forgot the strange apeman until one of them chanced to look in his direction

and saw him seizing the leaf-stalks and shaking them free
of water, plaiting them clumsily into a fairish roof above his
head, stout enough to shelter him. The watchers' grunt of
surprise drew the attention of the rest, and they stared at
him in amazement, pressing against the tree-trunks, closely
following his movements as he plaited until at last he was
content to rest and gaze at the downpour. They began to
scowl, their hands to twitch with desire to rend him could
they venture near; a few gnashed their teeth, and others
were so bemused that they left their shelters and moved to
the ends of the boughs nearest to him, until the sagging of
the thinner boughs beneath their weight and the weight of
the water on the leaves brought a deluge on their heads and
roused them to retreat.

Thus they remained, closing in to the trees for shelter
while the rain fell down the leaves and into the lake below.
No rustle, no cry, no sound but the sad drip of water on the
trees, dripping again from tree to lake, until the very sound
of it became silence in their ears. Suddenly it was broken by
the uneasy stir of a great bird sheltering near by and shrink-
ing from the rain that penetrated the leaves, flapping its
wings when a large leaf emptied its burden. A viper rustled
its way out of the dust that was turning into mud, and swam
in the lake to clean itself. The apemen, even the strange
apeman, looked disconsolate and cowardly as they stared
at the falling rain, the lake rising round the trees, the great
birds and the vipers growing restless.

The strange apeman began to sniff and to look this way
and that, the others following him, their chests rising and
falling quickly, sniffing frantically until the noise rivalled
the sound of the rain. A heavy stench of mud reached them
and brought new terror to them. Their eyes opened wide and
turned red, and they scowled in their panic as they vainly
sought another refuge. For they were creatures of the
ground, clumsy in their movements upon the trees to which
they resorted in emergency only.

The monster roamed in search of prey, and the stench
arose from the deep mud of the marsh as his feet squelched

through the crust, wave after wave of stench as he lifted his feet. The apemen sniffed violently, for the strange apeman had located the source of the odour, and a new fear came upon them with the new sound, the vile sound of feet in the mud. They forgot the rain and began to descend, but the lake lay below and they turned back into their shelters on the trees. If the monster reached the trees, it would be hard to hold to the branches when he began to shake a tree, as he had so often done in the past, until he uprooted it, and then woe betide whoever trusted to the tree. In days gone by, escape would have been easier, but now the ground below had become a lake, and the unsubmerged land was a bog more dangerous than the lake.

Drenched and despondent, the apemen looked at each other in fear, barely able to grip the slippery branches. The strange apeman, they observed, rose and shook himself, looked at them and then leapt on to another tree in spite of the danger of slipping; as he landed, a torrent of water fell from the leaves. They were afraid to do likewise, until they saw him leap again a moment later, and after he had leapt several times in safety, they ventured to follow his example. For this was their only means of escape, and they dared not take to the lake below them. He leapt from tree to tree, and they followed him. A screech re-echoed through the forest, and in their sudden panic they clung to the nearest branch. But one of them fell and sank until they saw nothing but his head and arms vainly striving to reach the trunk of his tree; the strange apeman leapt upon one of its branches and forced it down within reach of the creature until he seized it and climbed up again, the others staring confusedly at him and at each other. A glimmer in their eyes showed that they relied upon him for salvation.

As the water fell from the trees after each leap, the hideous cry of the monster tore through the air until the forest seemed to quake in terror, for the falling water revealed their position and he drew nearer to them, the stench rising and the sound of his squelching feet growing louder. The strange apeman leapt forward from tree to tree steadily and safely,

ever in the same direction, and they followed him heedless
of the wet and of the danger of slipping, so great was their
desire to escape.

Soon they reached open country with rising ground a
short distance ahead, and from the last tree the strange
apeman leapt on to a knoll. They followed him up a rocky
spur on to a high crag, climbing from ledge to ledge, crossing the many torrents, quickly disappearing into a cave
half-way up its face. There they tried to shake themselves
free of water, looking now at the strange apeman who led
them, now at one another, with a trace of something not
unlike a smile on their faces. They stood at the mouth of the
cave watching the heavy and monotonous rain falling lifelessly, with nothing to break the monotony but the occasional fall of a stone loosened from the crag and hurtling
down from ledge to ledge until it reached the water below,
for all the land from the crag to the forest and beyond was
one vast sea. They squatted at the cave-mouth in long and
sullen silence, listening intently.

When at length the rain stopped, the silence was profound,
for there was no wind blowing. But the dread sound rose
up again, the squelching feet of the monster approaching,
the stench of mud heavy on the air. Huddled together, they
were still as the dead, listening to every movement as the
monster sniffed about at the foot of the crag uncertain of
their position and half submerged in the water.

The sky cleared, and the sun was setting. Towards the
horizon the tints merged their beauty and wisps of cloud
crossed the sky. The apemen saw it all, unmoved and un-
comprehending, as they had watched the falling rain. But
the strange apeman looked upon this beauty open-eyed,
stirring uneasily as if lost in contemplation, while the others
glared at him angrily each time he moved, although he
made no noise in moving. Under the spell of this new marvel
of colour changing before his eyes, he forgot his scowling
companions, the monster sniffing to and fro below the crag,
the terror awakened by the squelching feet, and he stepped
forward.

Suddenly, forgetting his peril, oblivious of his surroundings, the strangest 'Oh!' that apeman ever uttered burst from his lips, and the monster bellowed in reply to this betraying cry. His companions turned upon him and tore him limb from limb and cast him down; they fled from the cave, rushed up the crag into safety, leaving his limbs to the monster to devour. Each in his own crevice in the rock-face, they stared contentedly at the vain efforts of the monster to climb towards them, rid of their peril and of the strange apeman. On their faces, as they sucked their fingers and licked their chops, was a look of ease; the world turned bright.

So died the first man, and a myriad years passed before a second man appeared.

Be This Her Memorial

CARADOC EVANS

MICE and rats, as it is said, frequent neither churches nor poor men's homes. The story I have to tell you about Nanni – the Nanni who was hustled on her way to prayer-meeting by the Bad Man, who saw the phantom mourners bearing away Twm Tybach's coffin, who saw the Spirit Hounds and heard their moanings two days before Isaac Penparc took wing – the story I have to tell you contradicts that theory.

Nanni was religious; and she was old. No one knew how old she was, for she said that she remembered the birth of each person that gathered in Capel Sion; she was so old that her age had ceased to concern.

She lived in the mud-walled, straw-thatched cottage on the steep road which goes up from the Garden of Eden, and ends at the tramping way that takes you into Cardigan town; if you happen to be travelling that way you may still see the roofless walls which were silent witnesses to Nanni's great sacrifice – a sacrifice surely counted unto her for righteousness, though in her search for God she fell down and worshipped at the feet of a god.

Nanni's income was three shillings and ninepence a week. That sum was allowed her by Abel Shones, the officer for Poor Relief, who each pay-day never forgot to remind the crooked, wrinkled, toothless old woman how much she owed to him and God.

'If it was not for me, little Nanni,' Abel was in the habit of telling her, 'you would be in the House of the Poor long ago.'

At that remark Nanni would shiver and tremble.

'Dear heart,' she would say in the third person, for Abel

was a mighty man and the holder of a proud office, 'I pray for him night and day.'

Nanni spoke the truth, for she did remember Abel in her prayers. But the workhouse held for her none of the terrors it holds for her poverty-stricken sisters. Life was life anywhere, in cottage or in poorhouse, though with this difference : her liberty in the poorhouse would be so curtailed that no more would she be able to listen to the spirit-laden eloquence of the Respected Josiah Bryn-Bevan. She helped to bring Josiah into the world; she swaddled him in her own flannel petticoat; she watched him going to and coming from school; she knitted for him four pairs of strong stockings to mark his going out into the world as a farm servant; and when the boy, having obeyed the command of the Big Man, was called to minister to the congregation of Capel Sion, even Josiah's mother was not more vain than Old Nanni. Hence Nanni struggled on less than three shillings and ninepence a week, for did she not give a tenth of her income to the treasury of the Capel? Unconsciously she came to regard Josiah as greater than God: God was abstract; Josiah was real.

As Josiah played a part in Nanni's life, so did a Seller of Bibles play a minor part in the last few days of her travail. The man came to Nanni's cottage the evening of the day of the rumour that the Respected Josiah Bryn-Bevan had received a call from a wealthy sister church in Aberystwyth. Broken with grief, Nanni, the first time for many years, bent her stiffened limbs and addressed herself to the living God.

'Dear little Big Man,' she prayed, 'let not your son bach religious depart.'

Then she recalled how good God had been to her, how He had permitted her to listen to His son's voice; and another fear struck her heart.

'Dear little Big Man,' she muttered between her blackened gums, 'do you now let me live to hear the boy's farewell words.'

At that moment the Seller of Bibles raised the latch of the door.

'The Big Man be with this household,' he said, placing his pack on Nanni's bed.

'Sit you down,' said Nanni, 'and rest yourself, for you must be weary.'

'Man,' replied the Seller of Bibles, 'is never weary of well-doing.'

Nanni dusted for him a chair.

'No, no; indeed now,' he said; 'I cannot tarry long, woman. Do you not know that I am the Big Man's messenger? Am I not honoured to take His word into the highways and by-ways, and has He not sent me here?'

He unstrapped his pack, and showed Nanni a gaudy vol-ume with a clasp of brass, and containing many coloured prints; the pictures he explained at hazard: here was a tall-hatted John baptizing, here a Roman-featured Christ pray-ing in the Garden of Gethsemane, here a frock-coated Moses and the Tablets.

'A Book,' said he, 'which ought to be on the table of every Christian home.'

'Truth you speak, little man,' remarked Nanni. 'What shall I say to you you are asking for it?'

'It has a price far above rubies,' answered the Seller of Bibles. He turned over the leaves and read: ' "The labourer is worthy of his hire." Thus it is written. I will let you have one copy – one copy only – at cost price.'

'How good you are, dear me!' exclaimed Nanni.

'This I can do,' said the Seller of Bibles, 'because my Mas-ter is the Big Man.'

'Speak you now what the cost price is.'

'A little sovereign, that is all.'

'Dear, dear; the Word of the little Big Man for a sover-eign!'

'Keep you the Book on your parlour table for a week. Maybe others who are thirsty will see it.'

Then the Seller of Bibles sang a prayer; and he departed.

Before the week was over the Respected Josiah Bryn-Bevan announced from his pulpit that in the call he had discerned the voice of God bidding him go forth into the vineyard.

Nanni went home and prayed to the merciful God:

'Dear little Big Man, spare me to listen to the farewell sermon of your saint.'

Nanni informed the Seller of Bibles that she would buy the Book, and she asked him to take it away with him and have written inside it an inscription to the effect that it was a gift from the least worthy of his flock to the Respected Josiah Bryn-Bevan, D.D., and she requested him to bring it back to her on the eve of the minister's farewell sermon.

She then hammered hobnails into the soles of her boots, so as to render them more durable for tramping to such capels as Bryn-Bevan happened to be preaching in. Her absences from home became a byword, occurring as they did in the hay-making season. Her labour was wanted in the fields. It was the property of the community, the community which paid her three shillings and ninepence a week.

One night Sadrach Danyrefail called at her cottage to commandeer her services for the next day. His crop had been on the ground for a fortnight, and now that there was a prospect of fair weather he was anxious to gather it in. Sadrach was going to say hard things to Nanni, but the appearance of the gleaming-eyed creature that drew back the bolts of the door frightened him and tied his tongue. He was glad that the old woman did not invite him inside, for from within there issued an abominable smell such as might have come from the boiler of the witch who one time lived on the moor. In the morning he saw Nanni trudging towards a distant capel where the Respected Josiah Bryn-Bevan was delivering a sermon in the evening. She looked less bent and not so shrivelled up as she did the night before. Clearly, sleep had given her fresh vitality.

Two Sabbaths before the farewell sermon was to be preached Nanni came to Capel Sion with an ugly sore at the side of her mouth; repulsive matter oozed slowly from it, forming into a head, and then coursing down her chin on to the shoulder of her black cape, where it glistened among the beads. On occasions her lips tightened, and she swished a hand angrily across her face.

'Old Nanni,' folk remarked while discussing her over their dinner-tables, 'is getting as dirty as an old sow.'

During the week two more sores appeared; the next Sabbath Nanni had a strip of calico drawn over her face.

Early on the eve of the farewell Sabbath the Seller of Bibles arrived with the Book, and Nanni gave him a sovereign in small money. She packed it up reverently, and betook herself to Sadrach Danyrefail to ask him to make the presentation.

At the end of his sermon the Respected Josiah Bryn-Bevan made reference to the giver of the Bible, and grieved that she was not in the Capel. He dwelt on her sacrifice. Here was a Book to be treasured, and he could think of no one who would treasure it better than Sadrach Danyrefail, to whom he would hand it in recognition of his work in the School of the Sabbath.

In the morning the Respected Josiah Bryn-Bevan, making a tour of his congregation, bethought himself of Nanni. The thought came to him on leaving Danyrefail, the distance betwixt which and Nanni's cottage is two fields. He opened the door and called out:

'Nanni.'

None answered.

He entered the room. Nanni was on the floor.

'Nanni, Nanni!' he said. 'Why for you do not reply to me? Am I not your shepherd?'

There was no movement from Nanni. Mishtir Bryn-Bevan went on his knees and peered at her. Her hands were clasped tightly together, as though guarding some great treasure. The minister raised himself and prised them apart with the ferrule of his walking-stick. A roasted rat revealed itself. Mishtir Bryn-Bevan stood for several moments spellbound and silent; and in the stillness the rats crept boldly out of their hiding places and resumed their attack on Nanni's face. The minister, startled and horrified, fled from the house of sacrifice.

The Return

BRENDA CHAMBERLAIN

IT isn't as if the Captain took reasonable care of himself, said the postmaster.

No, she answered. She was on guard against anything he might say.

A man needs to be careful with a lung like that, said the postmaster.

Yes, she said. She waited for sentences to be laid like baited traps. They watched one another for the next move. The man lifted a two-ounce weight from the counter and dropped it with fastidious fingers into the brass scale. As the tray fell, the woman sighed. A chink in her armour. He breathed importantly and spread his hands on the counter. From pressure on the palms, dark veins stood up under the skin on the backs of his hands. He leaned his face to the level of her eyes. Watching him, her mouth fell slightly open.

The Captain's lady is very nice indeed; Mrs Morrison is a charming lady. Have you met his wife, Mrs Ritsin?

No, she answered; she has not been to the Island since I came. She could not prevent a smile flashing across her eyes at her own stupidity. Why must she have said just that, a ready-made sentence that could be handed on without distortion. She has not been to the Island since I came. Should she add: no doubt she will be over soon; then I shall have the pleasure of meeting her? The words would not come. The postmaster lodged the sentence carefully in his brain to be retailed to the village.

They watched one another. She, packed with secrets behind that innocent face, damn her, why couldn't he worm down the secret passages of her mind? Why had she come here in the first place, this Mrs Ritsin? Like a doll, so small and delicate, she made you want to hit or pet her, according to your nature. She walked with small strides, as if she owned the place, as if she was on equal terms with man and the sea. Her eyes disturbed something in his nature that could not bear the light. They were large, they looked farther than any other eyes he had seen. They shone with a happiness that he thought indecent in the circumstances.

Everyone knew, the whole village gloated and hummed over the fact that Ceridwen had refused to live on the Island and that she herself was a close friend of Alec Morrison. But why, she asked herself, why did she let herself fall into their cheap traps? The sentence would be repeated almost without a word being altered, but the emphasis, O my God, the stressing of the *I*, to imply a malicious woman's triumph. But all this doesn't really matter, she told herself, at least it won't once I am back there. The Island. She saw it float in front of the postmaster's face. The rocks were clear and the hovering, wind-swung birds; she saw them clearly in front of the wrinkles and clefts on his brow and chin. He coughed discreetly and shrugged with small deprecatory movements of the shoulders. He wished she would not stare at him as if he was a wall or invisible. If she was trying to get at his secrets she could try till crack of doom. All the same. As a precautionary measure he slid aside and faced the window.

Seems as though it will be too risky for you to go back this evening, he said; there's a bit of fog about. You'll be stopping the night in Porthbychan?

—and he wouldn't let her go on holiday in the winter: said, if she did, he'd get a concubine to keep him warm, and he meant—

A woman was talking to her friend outside the door.

You cannot possibly cross the Race alone in this weather, Mrs Ritsin, persisted the postmaster.

I must get back tonight, Mr Davies.

He sketched the bay with a twitching arm, as if to say: I have bound the restless wave. He became confidential, turning to stretch across the counter.

My dear Mrs Ritsin, no woman has ever before navigated these waters. Why, even on a calm day the Porthbychan fishers will not enter the Race. Be warned, dear lady. Imagine my feelings if you were to be washed up on the beach here.

Bridget Ritsin said, I am afraid it is most important that I should get back tonight, Mr Davies.

Ann Pritchard from the corner house slid from the glittering evening into the shadows of the post office. She spoke out of the dusk behind the door. It isn't right for a woman to ape a man, doing a man's work.

Captain Morrison is ill. He couldn't possibly come across today. That is why I'm in charge of the boat, Bridget answered.

Two other women had slipped in against the wall of the shop. Now, four pairs of eyes bored into her face. With sly insolence the women threw ambiguous sentences to the postmaster, who smiled as he studied the grain in the wood of his counter. Bridget picked up a bundle of letters and turned to go. The tide will be about right now, she said. Good evening, Mr Davies. Be very, very careful, Mrs Ritsin, and remember me to the Captain.

Laughter followed her into the street. It was like dying in agony, while crowds danced and mocked. O, my darling, my darling over the cold waves. She knew that while she was away he would try to do too much about the house. He would go to the well for water, looking over the fields he lacked strength to drain. He would be in the yard, chopping sticks. He would cough and spit blood. It isn't as if the Captain took reasonable care of himself. When he ran too hard, when he moved anything heavy and lost his breath, he only struck his chest and cursed: blast my lung. Alec dear, you should not run so fast up the mountain. He never heeded her. He had begun to spit blood.

By the bridge over the river, her friend Griff Owen was leaning against the side of a motor-car, talking to a man and woman in the front seats. He said to them, ask her, as she came past.

Excuse me, Miss, could you take us over to see the Island?

I'm sorry, she said, there's a storm coming up. It wouldn't be possible to make the double journey.

They eyed her, curious about her way of life.

Griff Owen, and the grocer's boy carrying two boxes of provisions, came down to the beach with her.

I wouldn't be you; going to be a dirty night, said the man.

The waves were chopped and the headland was vague with hanging cloud. The two small islets in the bay were behind curtains of vapour. The sea was blurred and welcomeless. To the Island, to the Island. Here in the village, you opened a door: laughter and filthy jokes buzzed in your face. They stung and blinded. O my love, be patient, I am coming back to you, quickly, quickly, over the waves.

The grocer's boy put down the provisions on the sand near the tide edge. Immediately a shallow pool formed round the bottoms of the boxes.

Wind seems to be dropping, said Griff.

Yes, but I think there will be fog later on, she answered, sea fog. She turned to him. Oh, Griff, you are always so kind to me. What would we do without you?'

He laid a hand on her shoulder. Tell me, how is the Captain feeling in himself? I don't like the thought of him being so far from the doctor.

The doctor can't do very much for him. Living in the clean air from the sea is good. These days he isn't well, soon he may be better. Don't worry, he is hanging on to life and the Island. They began to push the boat down over rollers towards the water. Last week Alec had said quite abruptly as he was stirring the boiled potatoes for the ducks: at least, you will have this land if I die.

At least, I have the Island.

Well, well, said the man, making an effort to joke; tell the Captain from me that I'll come over to see him if he comes for me himself. Tell him I wouldn't trust my life to a lady, even though the boat has got a good engine and knows her way home.

He shook her arm: you are a stout girl.

Mr Davies coming down, said the boy, looking over his shoulder as he heaved on the side of the boat. The postmaster came on to the beach through the narrow passage between the hotel and the churchyard. His overcoat flapped round him in the wind. He had something white in his hand. The boat floated; Bridget waded out and stowed away her provisions and parcels. By the time she had made a second journey Mr Davies was at the water's edge.

Another letter for you, Mrs Ritsin, he said. Very sorry, it had got behind the old-age-pension books. He peered at her, longing to know what was in the letter, dying to find out what her feelings would be when she saw the handwriting. He had already devoured the envelope with his eyes, back and front, reading the postmark and the two sentences written in pencil at the back. He knew it was a letter from Ceridwen to her husband.

A letter for the Captain, said the postmaster, and watched her closely.

Thank you. She took it, resisting the temptation to read the words that caught her eye on the back of the envelope. She put it away in the large pocket of her oilskin along with the rest.

The postmaster sucked in his cheeks and mumbled something. So Mrs Morrison will be back here soon, he suddenly shot at her. Only the grocer's boy, whistling as he kicked the shingle, did not respond to what he said. Griff looked from her to the postmaster, she studied the postmaster's hypocritical smile. Her head went up, she was able to smile: oh, yes, of course, Mrs Morrison is sure to come over when the weather is better. What did he know, why should he want to know?

It was like a death; every hour that she had to spend on the mainland gave her fresh wounds.

Thank you, Mr Davies. Good-bye Griff, see you next week if the weather isn't too bad. She climbed into the motorboat and weighed anchor. She bent over the engine and it began to live. The grocer's boy was drifting away, still kicking the beach as if he bore it a grudge. Mr Davies called in a thin voice ... great care ... wish you would ... the Race and ...

Griff waved, and roared like a horn: tell him I'll take the next calf if it is a good one.

It was his way of wishing her God-speed. Linking the moment's hazard to the safety of future days.

She waved her hand. The men grew small, they and the gravestones of blue and green slate clustered round the medieval church at the top of the sand. The village drew into itself, fell into perspective against the distant mountains.

It was lonely in the bay. She took comfort from the steady throbbing of the engine. She drew Ceridwen's letter from her pocket. She read: if it is *very* fine, Auntie Grace and I will come over next week-end. Arriving Saturday tea-time Porthbychan. Please meet.

Now she understood what Mr Davies had been getting at. Ceridwen and the aunt. She shivered suddenly and felt the flesh creeping on her face and arms. The sea was bleak and washed of colour under the shadow of a long roll of mist that stretched from the level of the water almost to the sun. It was nine o'clock in the evening. She could not reach the anchorage before ten and, though it was summertime, darkness would have fallen before she reached home. She hoped Alec's dog would be looking out for her on the headland.

The wind blew fresh, but the wall of mist did not seem to move at all. She wondered if Penmaen du and the mountain would be visible when she rounded the cliffs into the Race. Soon now she should be able to see the Island mountain. She knew every Islandman would sooner face a storm than fog.

So Ceridwen wanted to come over, did she? For the week-end, and with the aunt's support. Perhaps she had heard at last that another woman was looking after her sick husband that she did not want but over whom she was jealous as a tigress. The week-end was going to be merry hell. Bridget realized that she was very tired.

The mainland, the islets, the cliff-top farms of the peninsula fell away. Porpoise rolling offshore towards the Race made her heart lift for their companionship.

She took a compass-bearing before she entered the white silence of the barren wall of fog. Immediately she was both trapped and free. Trapped because it was still daylight and yet she was denied sight, as if blindness had fallen, not blindness where everything is dark, but blindness where eyes are filled with vague light and they strain helplessly. Is it that I cannot see, is this blindness? The horror was comparable to waking on a black winter night and being unable to distinguish anything, until in panic she thought, has my sight gone? And free because the mind could build images on walls of mist, her spirit could lose itself in tunnels of vapour.

The sound of the motor-boat's engine was monstrously exaggerated by the fog. Like a giant heart it pulsed: thump, thump. There was a faint echo, as if another boat, a ghost ship, moved near by. Her mind had too much freedom in these gulfs.

The motor-boat began to pitch like a bucking horse. She felt depth upon depth of water underneath the boards on which her feet were braced. It was the Race. The tide poured across her course. The brightness of cloud reared upward from the water's face. Not that it was anywhere uniform in density; high up there would suddenly be a thinning, a tearing apart of vapour with a wan high blue showing through, and once the jaundiced, weeping sun was partly visible, low in the sky, which told her that she was still on the right bearing. There were grey-blue caverns of shadow that seemed like patches of land, but they were effaced in new swirls of cloud, or came about her in imprisoning walls, tunnels along which the boat moved only to find nothingness at the end. Unconsciously, she had gritted her teeth when she ran into the fog-bank. Her tension remained. Two ghosts were beside her in the boat, Ceridwen, in a white fur coat, was sitting amidships and facing her, huddled together, cold and unhappy in the middle of the boat, her knees pressed against the casing of the engine. Alec's ghost sat in the bows. As a figurehead he leaned away from her, his face half lost in opaque cloud.

I will get back safely, I will get home, she said aloud, looking ahead to make the image of Ceridwen fade. But the phantom persisted; it answered her spoken thought.

No, you'll drown, you won't ever reach the anchorage. The dogfish will have you.

I tell you I can do it. He's waiting for me, he needs me.

Alec turned round, his face serious. When you get across the Race, if you can hear the foghorn, he said quietly, you are on the wrong tack. If you can't hear it, you're all right; it means you are cruising safely along the foot of the cliffs. . . When you get home, will you come to me, be my little wife?

Oh, my dear, she answered, I could weep or laugh that you ask me now, here. Yes, if I get home.

Soon you'll be on the cold floor of the sea, said Ceridwen.

Spouts of angry water threatened the boat that tossed sideways. Salt sprays flew over her.

Careful, careful, warned Alec. We are nearly on Pen Cader, the rocks are near now, we are almost out of the Race.

A seabird flapped close to her face, then with a cry swerved away, its claws pressed backwards.

Above the noise of the engine there was now a different sound, that of water striking land. For an instant she saw the foot of a black cliff. Wet fangs snapped at her. Vicious fangs, how near they were. Shaken by the sight, by the rock death that waited, she turned the boat away from the Island. She gasped as she saw white spouting foam against the black and slimy cliff. She was once more alone. Alec and Ceridwen, leaving her to the sea, had been sucked into the awful cloud, this vapour without substance or end. She listened for the foghorn. No sound from the lighthouse. A break in the cloud above her head drew her eyes. A few yards of the mountaintop of the Island was visible, seeming impossibly high, impossibly green and homely. Before the eddying mists rejoined, she saw a thin shape trotting across the steep grass slope, far, far up near the crest of the hill. Leaning forward, she said aloud: O look, the dog. It was Alec's dog keeping watch for her. The hole in the mist closed up, the shroud fell thicker than ever. It was terrible, this loneliness, this groping that seemed as if it might go on for ever.

Then she heard the low-throated horn blaring into the fog. It came from somewhere on her right hand. So in avoiding the rocks she had put out too far to sea and had overshot the anchorage. She must be somewhere off the southern headland near the pirate's rock. She passed a line of lobster floats.

She decided to stop the engine and anchor where she was, hoping that the fog would clear at nightfall. Then she would be able to return on to her proper course. There was an unnatural silence after she had cut off the engine. Water knocked against the boat.

Cold seeped into her bones from the planks. With stiff wet hands she opened the bag of provisions, taking off the crust of a loaf and spreading butter on it with her gutting knife. As she ate, she found that for the first time in weeks she had leisure in which to review her life. For when she was on the farm it was eat, work, sleep, eat, work, sleep, in rotation.

I have sinned or happiness is not for me, she thought. It was her heart's great weakness that she could not rid herself of superstitious beliefs.

Head in hands, she asked: But how have I sinned? I didn't steal another woman's husband. They had already fallen apart when I first met Alec. Is too great happiness itself a sin? Surely it's only because I am frightened of the fog that I ask, have I sinned, is this my punishment? When the sun shines I take happiness with both hands. Perhaps it's wrong to be happy when half the people of the world are chainbound and hungry, cut off from the sun. If you scratch below the surface of most men's minds you find that they are bleeding inwardly. Men want to destroy themselves. It is their only hope. Each one secretly nurses the death-wish, to be god and mortal in one; not to die at nature's order, but to cease on his own chosen day. Man has destroyed so much that only the destruction of all life will satisfy him.

How can it be important whether I am happy or unhappy?

And yet it's difficult for me to say, I am only one, what does my fate matter? For I want to be fulfilled like other women. What have I done to be lost in winding sheets of fog?

And he will be standing in the door wondering that I do not come.

For how long had she sat in the gently rocking boat? It was almost dark and her eyes smarted from constant gazing. Mist weighed against her eyeballs. She closed her eyes for relief.

Something was staring at her. Through drawn lids she felt the steady glance of a sea-creature. She looked at the darkening waves. Over an area of a few yards she could see; beyond, the wave was cloud, the cloud was water. A dark, wet-gleaming thing on the right. It disappeared before she could make out what it was. And then, those brown beseeching eyes of the seal cow. She had risen near by, her mottled head scarcely causing a ripple. Lying on her back in the grey-green gloom of the sea she waved her flippers now outwards to the woman, now inwards to her white breast, saying, come to me, come to me, to the caverns where shark bones lie like tree stumps, bleached, growth-ringed like trees.

Mother seal, seal cow. The woman stretched out her arms. The attraction of those eyes was almost strong enough to draw her to salt death. The head disappeared. The dappled back turned over in the opaque water, and dived. Bridget gripped the side of the boat, praying that this gentle visitant should not desert her.

Hola, hola, hola, seal mother from the eastern cave.

Come to me, come to me, come to me. The stone-grey head reappeared on the other side, on her left. Water ran off the whiskered face, she showed her profile; straight nose, and above, heavy lids drooping over melancholy eyes. When she plunged, showing off her prowess, a sheen of pearly colours ran over the sleek body.

They watched one another until the light failed to penetrate the fog. After the uneasy summer twilight had fallen, the woman was still aware of the presence of the seal. She dozed off into a shivering sleep through which she heard faintly the snorting of the sea creature. A cold, desolate sound. Behind that again was the bull-throated horn bellowing into the night.

She dreamed: Alec was taking her up the mountain at night under a sky dripping with blood. Heaven was on fire. Alec was gasping for breath. The other islanders came behind, their long shadows stretching down the slope. The mountain top remained far off. She never reached it.

Out of dream, she swam to consciousness, painfully leaving the dark figures of fantasy. A sensation of swimming upwards through fathoms of water. The sea of her dreams was dark and at certain levels between sleeping and waking a band of light ran across the waves. Exhaustion made her long to fall back to the sea-floor of oblivion, but the pricking brain floated her at last on to the surface of morning.

She awoke with a great wrenching gasp that flung her against the gunwale. Wind walked the sea. The fog had gone, leaving the world raw and disenchanted in the false dawn. Already, gulls were crying for a new day. Wet and numb with cold, the woman looked about her. At first it was impossible to tell off what shore the boat was lying. For a few minutes it was enough to know that she was after all at anchor so close to land.

Passing down the whole eastern coastline, she had rounded the south end and was a little way past Mallt's bay on the west. The farmhouse, home, seemed near across the foreshortened fields. Faint light showed in the kitchen window, a warm glow in the grey landscape. It was too early for the other places, Goppa, Pen Isaf, to show signs of life. Field, farm, mountain, sea and sky. What a simple world. And below the undercurrents.

Mechanically she started up the engine and raced round to the anchorage through mounting sea spray and needles of rain.

She made the boat secure against rising wind, then trudged through seaweed and shingle, carrying the supplies up into the boat-house. She loitered inside after putting down the bags of food. Being at last out of the wind, no longer pitched and tumbled on the sea, made her feel that she was in a vacuum. Wind howled and thumped at the walls. Tears of salt water raced down the body of a horse scratched long ago on the window by Alec. Sails stacked under the roof shivered in the draught forced under the slates. She felt that she was spinning wildly in some mad dance. The floor rose and fell as the waves had done. The earth seemed to slide away and come up again under her feet. She leant on the windowsill, her forehead pressed to the pane. Through a crack in the glass wind poured in a cold stream across her cheek. Nausea rose in her against returning to the shore for the last packages. After that there would be almost the length of the Island to walk. At the thought she straightened herself, rubbing the patch of skin on her forehead where pressure on the window had numbed it. She fought her way down to the anchorage. Spume blew across the rocks, covering her sea boots. A piece of wrack was blown into the wet tangle of her hair. Picking up the bag of provisions, she began the return journey. Presently she stopped, put down the bag, and went again to the waves. She had been so long with them that now the thought of going inland was unnerving. Wading out until water swirled round her knees she stood relaxed, bending like a young tree under the wind's weight. Salt was crusted on her lips and hair. Her feet were sucked by outdrawn shingle. She no longer wished to struggle but to let a wave carry her beyond the world.

I want sleep, she said to the sea. O God, I am so tired, so tired. The sea sobbed, sleep, the wind mourned, sleep.

Oystercatchers flying in formation, a pattern of black and white and scarlet, screamed: we are St Bride's birds, we saved Christ, we rescued the Saviour.

A fox-coloured animal was coming over the weedy rocks of the point. It was the dog, shivering and mist-soaked as if he had been out all night. He must have been lying in a cranny and so missed greeting her when she had landed. He fawned about her feet, barking unhappily.

They went home together, passing Pen Isaf that slept; Goppa too. It was about four o'clock of a summer daybreak.

She picked two mushrooms glowing in their own radiance. Memories came of her first morning's walk on the Island. There had been a green and lashing sea and gullies of damp rock, and parsley fern among loose stones. Innocent beginning, uncomplicated, shadowless. As if looking on the dead from the pinnacle of experience, she saw herself as she had been.

She opened the house door: a chair scraped inside. Alec stood in the kitchen, white with strain and illness.

So you did come, he said dully.

Yes, she said with equal flatness, putting down the bags.

How sick, how deathly he looked.

Really, you shouldn't have sat up all night for me. He stirred the pale ashes; a fine white dust arose.

Look, there's still fire, and the kettle's hot. He coughed. They drank the tea in silence, standing far apart. Her eyes never left his face. And the sea lurched giddily under her braced feet. Alec went and sat before the hearth. Bridget came up behind his chair and pressed her cheek to his head. She let her arms fall slackly round his neck. Her hands hung over his chest. Tears grew in her eyes, brimming the lower lids so that she could not see. They splashed on to his clenched fists. He shuddered a little. Without turning his head, he said: Your hair's wet. You must be so tired.

Yes, she said, so tired. Almost worn out.

Come, let us go to bed for an hour or two.

You go up, she answered, moving away into the back kitchen; I must take off my wet clothes first.

Don't be long. Promise me you won't be long. He got up out of the wicker chair, feeling stiff and old, to be near her where she leant against the slate table. One of her hands was on the slate, the other was pealing off her oilskin trousers.

He said: don't cry. I can't bear it if you cry.

I'm not, I'm not. Go to bed, please.

I thought you would never get back.

She took the bundle of letters out of the inner pocket of her coat and put them on the table. She said: there's one for you from Ceridwen.

Never mind about the letters. Come quickly to me. She stood naked in the light that spread unwillingly from sea and sky. Little channels of moisture ran down her flanks, water dripped from her hair over the points of her breasts. As she reached for a towel he watched the skin stretch over the fragile ribs. He touched her thigh with his fingers, almost a despairing gesture. She looked at him shyly, and, swiftly bending, began to dry her feet. Shaking as if from ague, she thought her heart's beating would be audible to him.

He walked abruptly away from her, went upstairs. The boards creaked in his bedroom.

Standing in the middle of the floor surrounded by wet clothes, she saw through the window how colour was slowly draining back into the world. It came from the sea, into the wild irises near the well, into the withy beds in the corner of the field. Turning, she went upstairs in the brightness of her body.

He must have fallen asleep as soon as he lay down. His face was bleached, the bones too clearly visible under the flesh. Dark folds of skin lay loosely under his eyes. Now that the eyes were hidden, his face was like a death-mask. She crept quietly into bed beside him.

Through the open window came the lowing of cattle. The cows belonging to Goppa were being driven up for milking. Turning towards the sleeping man, she put her left hand on his hip. He did not stir.

She cried then as if she would never be able to stop, the tears gushing down from her eyes until the pillow was wet and stained from her weeping.

What will become of us, what will become of us?

Twenty Tons of Coal

B. L. COOMBES

IT happened three days ago. Three days have gone – yet my inside trembles now as it did when this thing occurred. Three days during which I have scarcely touched food and two nights when I have been afraid to close my eyes because of the memory that darkness brings and the fear which forces me to open them swiftly so that I shall be assured I am safe at home. Even in that home I cannot be at ease because I know that they notice the twitching of my features and the trembling of my hands.

That was why I forced myself to go along the street the first day after the accident. I wanted to go on with life as it had been before, and I needed the comfort and sympathy of friends. The first I saw was a shopkeeper whom I had known as an intimate for years. He was dressing the window so I went inside to watch him, as I had done many times.

I expect my replies to his talk about poor sales and fine weather were not satisfactory for he turned suddenly and looked at me before he said:

'Mighty quiet, aren't you? Looking rough, too. What's the matter, eh? Got a touch of flu?'

'No! I wish it was the flu,' I answered, 'I could get over that. I've had my mate smashed – right by my elbow.'

'Good Lord!' He is astounded for an instant, then remembers. 'Oh, yes. I heard something about it, up at that Restcwm colliery, wasn't it? That's the way it is, you know. Things are getting pretty bad everywhere. The toll of the road f'rinstance – makes you think, don't it?'

'The roads,' I answer slowly, 'yes, we all use the roads. Can't you realize that this is something different? He was under tons of rock, and everything was pitch dark. No chance to get away; no way of seeing what was coming; no – oh, what's the use? If you've never been there you'll never understand.'

'Don't think about it,' he suggests, 'you'll get over it in time. Best to forget about it.'

Forget! The fool – to think that I can ever forget. I know that I never shall and no man who has been through the same experience ever can.

I went back home; soon afterwards one of my friends called. When he saw me he exclaimed:

'Holy Moses! What the dickens has happened to you?'

He had been with me the evening before that accident but that night had written such a story of fright and fear on my face that he could hardly recognize me.

So I stayed indoors, hoping that time would ease my feelings but jumping with alarm at every sudden word or slam of the door, and dreading the coming of each evening when the darkness of night would remind me of that black tomb which had held my mate but allowed me to escape.

Then again, this morning, after I had heard the clock striking all through the night, I must have surrendered to my exhaustion and slept, for I did not remember anything clearly after four o'clock struck. At five o'clock someone hammered on our front door. In an instant I was wide awake; the bed shook with my trembling. That crash on the door was the roar of falling rock; the darkness of the room was the solid blackness of the mine; and the bedclothes were the stones that held me down. When the knocking was repeated I had discovered that I was safe in bed. In bed – and safe; how can I describe what I felt.

Then I pondered what that knocking could mean. It was obvious that another morning was almost dawning. Griff, that was my mate's name, used to knock me up if he saw no light with us when he was passing to work. Could it be that he was passing: that all else had been a nightmare that this sudden wakening had dispelled? No, I realized it had been no nightmare for I had helped to wash his body – what parts it had been possible to wash without them falling apart.

Then came another thought; could it be that he was still knocking although his body was crushed? I dreaded to look, yet I could not refuse that appeal. I stumbled across the room, lifted the window, then peered down into the darkened street. A workmate was there. He lived some distance away but was on his way to the pit. He had a message for me. He shouted it out so that there should be no doubt of my hearing:

'Clean forgot to tell you last night, so I did. They told me at the office as you was to be sure to be at the Hall before four o'clock today. The inquest, you know. Don't forget, will you?'

Will I – can I – ever forget? Yet so indifferent are we to the sufferings of others that this caller, who is old enough to know better, who is in the same industry and runs the same risks, and who may be in exactly the same position as I am some day, does not realize how he has terrified me by hammering at my door to give that needless message.

Forget it! Is that likely when a policeman called yesterday and, after looking in my face and away again, told me gently that I was asked to be at Restcwm before four o'clock tomorrow – he had to say tomorrow then, of course. Not more than an hour later the sergeant of police clattered up to our door and – very pompously – informed me that I was instructed to present myself at the Workman's Hall, Restcwm, not later than four o'clock on the afternoon of Friday the, etc., etc.

After the caller has gone to his work I get back into bed. I have been careful to put the light on because it will be a while before there is sufficient daylight to defeat my dread of the lonely darkness.

Be there by four – so I must start from here about two o'clock. Restcwm is a considerable distance away and I have other things to attend to before the inquest. I have to draw the wages for last week's work and I shall have to take Griff's to his house as I have been doing for years. Next week I shall be short of the days I have lost since the accident. I wonder if they will pay us for a full shift on the day that he was killed. I have been at collieries where one sixteenth of a shift was cropped from the men who took an injured man home just before the completion of the working day. I think our firm will not be so drastic as that; they are more humane in many ways than most of the coal-owners.

I lie abed, and think. The inquest will be this afternoon and I shall be the only witness except the fireman. This is the first time I have been a witness or had any connection with legal things and the police. I dread it all. I shall have to tell what happened in pitch darkness about two miles inside the mountain. They will listen to me in the brightness of the daylight and in the safety of ordinary life; and they will think that they understand. They may put their questions in a way that is strange to all my experience and so may muddle me.

I shall have to swear to tell the truth, and nothing but the truth. Nothing but the truth, it sounds so simple. I will try to recall what happened and whisper it to myself in such a way that I shall be question-proof when the time comes.

Griff was there before me that night, as usual, sitting near the lamp-room. He gave me the usual grin at our meeting, then when he had finished the last of that pipeful and had hidden his pipe very carefully under that old coal-tram near the boilers, he took a last look at the moon, then we stepped into the cage and were dropped down.

I remember him saying as he looked upwards before we got under the pit wheels:

'Nice night for a walk ain't it, or a ride through the country. Nice night for anything, like, except going down into this blasted hole.'

Griff is many years older than I am; I expect he is about fifty. We have worked together for many years. He is well built but quite inoffensive. He has a couple of drinks every Saturday night and chews a lot of tobacco at work because smoking is impossible. He is aware that things are rotten at our job and is convinced that someone could make them a great deal better if they wished to; but who should do it or how it should be done are problems too difficult for Griff to solve. Soon he is going to have one of his rare outings; he is one of a club that has been saving to see Wales play England at Rugby football.

We were two of the earliest at the manhole where the fireman tests our lamps and tells us what work we are to do that night, for we are repairers and our place of work is changed frequently. The fireman is impatient and curt, as always.

'Pile of muck down ready for you,' he snaps each word and his teeth clack through the quid of tobacco as he talks, 'there's a fall near the face of the new Deep. Get it clear quick. 'Bout eight trams down now, and you'd best take the hatchet and measuring stick with you because I s'pose as it's squeezing now.'

'Eight trams,' Griff comments as we move away, 'I'll bet it's nearer ten if it's like his usual counting.'

We hurry along the roadway, crouch against the side whilst four horses pass us with their backs scraping against the low roof, then move on after them. As we near the coal workings the sides and roof are not so settled as they were back on the mains. We hear the creak of breaking timber or an occasional snap when the roof above us weakens. The heat increases and our feet disturb the thick flooring of dust.

Where the height is less than six feet timber is placed to hold the roof but where falls have brought greater height steel arches are placed in position. They are like curbed rails, nine feet high to the limit and about the same width. Where they are standing we can walk upright but we must be wary to bend low enough when we reach the roof that is not so high. We have been passing engine-houses as we moved inwards. These are set about four hundred yards apart and become smaller in size as we near the workings. Finally we pass the last one where the driver is crouching under the edge of the arching rock.

The new Deep is the last right-hand turn before we reach the Straight Main. Our tools are handy to our work and we are glad to strip off to our singlets for they are sticking to our backs. We see at once that the official was too optimistic for the fall blocks the roadway and it is difficult to climb to the top of the stones.

'Huh,' Griff is disgusted, 'more like twelve it is. Eight trams indeed. I guessed as much.'

It is squeezing, indeed. Stones that have been walled on the sides are crumbling from the pressure and there sounds a continual crack-crack as timber breaks or stones rip apart. As we stand by, a thick post starts to split down the middle and the splitting goes on while we watch, as if an invisible giant was tearing it in half. Alongside us another post that is quite two foot in diameter snaps in the middle and pieces of the bark fly into our faces. The posts seem no better than matchsticks under the pressure and we feel as if we were standing in a forest – so close together are the posts – and that a solid sky was dropping slowly to crush everything under it.

'Let's stick a couple more posts up,' I suggest, 'because most of these are busted up. Perhaps it'll settle a bit by then.'

We drag some posts along the roadway, measure the height, then cut the extra off with a hatchet that must not be lifted very high or it will touch the roof. When we carry the timber forward we listen after every step, with our head on one side and our senses alert for the least increase in that crackling. We have measured the posts so that they should be six inches lower than the roof, then the lid can go easily between, but when we have the timber in position we notice that the top has dropped another inch. When we are tightening the lid we are careful not to hold on top for fear that a sudden increase in the pressure may tighten it suddenly and fasten our hands there. Ten minutes after the posts are in position turpentine is running from them – squeezed out by the weight.

The journey rider – this one is called Nat – comes along and we help him to repair the broken signal wires. He knocks on them with a file; there is a bang and rattle as the rope slackens and a tram is lowered to us. It seems that the roof

movement is easing a little so I climb on top of the fall to
sound the upper top. I have to stretch to my limit to reach
it although I am standing quite nine feet above the roadway. The stones above echo hollowly when I tap them with
the steel head of a mandrel so we are convinced that they
have weakened and may fall at any minute. The awkward
part is that we shall have to jump back up the slope and that
the tram will be in the way to prevent us getting away
quickly.

One of these trams holds about two tons and we had to
break most of the stones, so we were busy to get the first
tram filled in the first half hour. Nat signalled it to a parting
higher up where a haulier was waiting with his horse to
draw it along the Level Heading where the labourers would
unload it into the 'gobs'. Whilst Nat was lowering another
empty tram we noticed the small flame of an oil-lamp coming down the slope.

'Look out, you guys,' Nat warned us when he stopped,
'here's the bombshell coming and he'll want to know why
the heck we ain't turned the place inside out in five minutes,
you bet he will.'

It is the fireman and he came with a rush, stumbling over
a loose piece of coal and almost falling; whereupon Nat
turns away, partly as an excuse for not putting out his arm
to steady the official and partly to hide the grin that he has
started in anticipation of seeing the fireman go sprawling.
The fireman recovers, however, and he glares at Nat as if he
had read his thoughts. His hurry has caused him to breathe
gaspingly; drops of sweat are falling from the end of his
nose and the chew of tobacco is being severely punished. He
glares at the fall, then back at us as if he thinks we must
have thrown more on top of it.

'There's one gone,' I tell him, 'and a good nine left still.'

'Huh!' he grunts, 'don't be long chucking this one in
agen. There's colliers below and coal waiting.'

He rushed away to hurry the labourers. We were full
again when he returned in twenty minutes' time.

'While the rider's taking these trams up,' he ordered us, 'you roll some of these stones and wall 'em on the sides. Put 'em anywhere out of the way of the rails.'

Griff went to have a drink after we had filled the fourth. The water gurgled down his throat as it would have down a drain.

'Blinkin' stuff's got warm already,' he complained, 'and it was like ice when I brought it into this hole.'

His face is streaked with grey lines where the perspiration has coursed through the thickness of dust; when he wrings the front of his singlet the moisture streams from it. The fireman visited us every few minutes and upset us with his impatience. Even when he did not hurry us with words we could sense that he felt we were taking too long. It was nearly three o'clock in the morning when Nat arrived with the tram that would be sufficient to clear the roadway. It seems that the mountain always becomes uneasy about that hour and small stones had been flaking down like heavy raindrops. We peered out from under the edge of the hole and I said that these falling stones must be coming from the upper edge of the right side. I could see some stones there that had half fallen and become checked in their drop. I got the slender measuring stick – it was about nine feet long – and tried to reach those loose stones but when the stick was to its limit and my arms were outstretched I could not reach the upper top. I climbed upwards on some of the stones that had been walled near the side. When I had scrambled up to about eight feet high it was possible to tap the stones and they fell. It was warm down below but the heat was intense up in the hollow of the fall. The increase of temperature almost stopped my breathing; I noticed the warning smell that is like rotten apples. My head was so giddy that I could not climb down; I slid the last part.

'Phew!' I gasped. 'It's chock full up there. My head's proper spinning.'

'Full? What d'you mean?' the fireman demanded, although he knew.

'Full up of gas,' I replied, 'and there's enough in that hole to put us up to the sky.'

'What are you chirping about?' he snapped back at me, 'there's nothing to hurt up there.'

'Try it and see,' I suggested. 'I notice you haven't tested for any tonight.'

'Get on and clear that fall,' he said, 'there's nothing there.'

'Take your lamp up there,' I insisted, 'it's the only oil-lamp here. I know the smell of gas too well to be sucked in over it.'

Very reluctantly he began to climb but when he was nearly up he jerked his hand and the light was extinguished.

I had expected it, for that was better than showing there was gas present and he was wrong.

'Now just look what you've done,' he complained, 'I'll have to feel me way back to the re-lighter.'

I saved my breath because I knew further comment was useless. The official stayed sitting on the wall like a human crow and watched us while we went on with our filling. We were about half-full when I heard a sound like a stifled sob and the fireman slumped down, then rolled to the bottom quite near to Nat. The rider jumped back as swiftly as a cat, then crouched under the shelter of a steel arch.

'Now, where the devil did that 'un drop from,' Nat demanded. Then he turned to look at what had fallen. 'Good Lord!' he added, 'it ain't a stone – it's him. Out to the blinkin' world, he is. So there was some up there, all right.'

Our lights showed us that the fireman was breathing, although faintly.

'Let's carry him back to the airway,' I suggested, 'there's a current of fresh air there and he'll soon come round.'

'Too blasted soon, likely.' Nat was not sympathetic. 'The only time this bloke is sensible is when he's asleep. And why struggle to carry him when I got me rope as I can put round his neck and the engine as can drag him?'

After we had carried him to the airway we went on with our job. We had two pairs of steel arches to place in position and bolt together. We were anxious to erect them so that we could cover them with small timber in case any more stones

fell. Nat agreed to sit near the official and shout to us if
there was any undue delay in his recovering.

'Fan him with me cap.' Nat was angered when I suggested
it. 'Why the hell should I waste me energy on him, hey?
Let him snuff it if he wants to, I shan't cry.'

He seemed to be looking forward with delight to the time
when the fireman would open his eyes and see the sketches
that were chalked on the smooth sides of that airway. We
had some skilful artists in that district and no one could
mistake who was represented as waving that whip behind
those three figures who were carrying shovels.

We had the one arch solid and were well on with the
second before the fireman recovered enough to stumble up
the road towards us. He did not praise us for our speed in
erecting; I do not think he was very appreciative of anything
just then. He said nothing as he passed but climbed on to
one of the tram couplings. Nat warned him to hold tight in
a manner that showed that the fireman could fall off under
the trams if he liked, then they moved away up the roadway from us.

As soon as we had covered the steel arches we went to have
our meal. We moved to where the roof was stronger, covered
our shoulders with our shirts and sat on a large stone close
to one another. We leant back against the walled sides,
partly to ease the ache in our backs, and partly to lessen the
target if more stones should fall.

We were supposed to have twenty minutes for eating food
but we had finished before that. Griff looked at his watch;
it was ten minutes to four. I remember him stating the time
and remarking that we had not been disturbed at our food –
for a wonder. Hardly had he said that when we saw a light
coming towards us. We could tell by the bobbing of the
lamp that the one who was carrying it was running.

Whoever is coming it must be a workman because he is
carrying an electric lamp. We can hear him panting as he
comes and his boots hit the wooden sleepers with a thud.

'Something have happened.' Griff speaks my own thoughts,
'somebody have been hurt bad or—' He does not finish and

through the small coal on the floor of the heading. I a[...]
that fire flashed from my eyes, yet I felt at the same t[...]
be ice-cold all over. My legs were dead weights hangi[...]
hind me. When I breathed I swallowed the small coa[...]
was inside my mouth. My nose was blocked with d[...]
were my eyes. I felt about with my hands before rea[...]
that my face was against the floor and pushing dow[...]
arms to lift myself. I whimpered with relief when I fo[...]
could use my legs and so my back was not broken.

I could feel something running down my back; obvi[...]
it must be blood. Above, below, and around me every[...]
is black with not the slightest sign of light to relieve i[...]
whatever has happened the lamps must be smashed an[...]
can have no help from them.

I had just managed to get to my knees and start to co[...]
my thoughts when I heard a scuffle a few yards away. [...]
denly a new sound pierced the darkness. It was a sort of [...]
scream, half-squeal. At first I could not realize what [...]
terrible sound meant; I had never before heard a grown [...]
squeal with fear.

'Quick! Quick! Get me out!' It was the fireman scre[...]
ing, and he sounded to be quite near to me. It seemed [...]
he had been caught but was still alive. I did not hear [...]
least sound from Griff. I collected my strength and shou[...]
'Griff-oh! Are you all right?' I am far more concerned ab[...]
my mate than the official. Griff was near me when I was [...]
He was much more in the open than the fireman, who [...]
hosen a part that was sheltered alongside the stronger s[...]
had no reply from Griff, but the fireman heard my [...]
d I hear him sobbing with relief at knowing that I [...]
e and near to him.

ome here, quick,' he appeals. 'I'm held fast over h[...]
me out before more comes. Quick!'

isten for some seconds, trying to puzzle where G[...]
anding. I have lost all sense of direction. Am I nea[...]
of my mate or will I press a stone still harder upon h[...]
ve in that direction? While I hesitate the fireman [...]
is screaming. Small stones drip around me contin[...]

we wait, tensed, for the message ... The running man reaches us, pauses, then holds his lamp up to our faces. The shadow behind the lamp becomes more solid and I realize that it is Ted Lewis.

'Puff,' Ted blows his cheeks out, 'all out of wind I am. Been hurrying like old boots to get to you chaps.'

Already we are reassured because if someone was under a fall Ted would have shouted his message at once. After taking a deep breath he explains:

'Old bladder-buster sent me to fetch you chaps to clear a fall he did. Said to come at once and bring your shovels and a sledge.'

'Fall!' We are both annoyed. 'Making all this fuss about a blessed fall.'

'Aye, I know,' Ted insists, 'but it's on the main and in the way of a journey of coal. He's in a hell of a sweat about it, not 'arf he ain't. Told me to tell you to hurry up – to run along with your tools, he did.'

'Run! Huh!' Griff is disgusted. 'I s'pose as we'd best go, eh? Allus something, there is.'

With our tools under our right arms and our lamps hanging on our belts we hurry after Ted. We are careful to keep our heads down to avoid hitting the low places. Near the top of the third Deep we must meet the fireman, who swings around and walks in front of us. Suddenly he shouts back at us:

'There's ten full trams of coal the other side of this blasted fall and they won't be out afore morning if you don't shape yourselves.'

He is wasting his breath, for his threats and hurryings have lost their effect on us. His forcing is as much part of our working lives as the stones that fall or the timber that will break. Our lives are now a succession of delayed coal and falling roof; besides we are hurrying all we can. The sweat is dropping from our eyebrows; I feel it running over the back of my hand where a stone has sliced the skin away; it smarts as if iodine was smeared over it. The official stops suddenly and gasps:

'Just on by there. Not more'n four trams down and all stones, so it won't take you long. Look lively and get it clear.'

I judge the fall and decide that it is nearer six trams than four. My lamp shows me enough light to see to the top of the hole and to detect the stones that hang, half fallen, around the sides. There is a whitish glint over the shiny smoothness of the upper top. We call that type of roof the Black Pan; it will drop without the least warning.

'What's that smooth up above sounding like?' I ask.

'Not bad,' the fireman answers.

'Have you sounded it?' I ask.

'Course I have,' he answered, and I knew he had not.

'I'm going to do it for myself,' I stated, 'because you can't be too sure.'

I climbed on top of the fall, then tapped the roof with the measuring-stick. Boom – boom – it sounded hollow, as would a tautened drum. I scrambled back down.

'That upper piece is just down,' I said, 'it's ready to fall. Best to put some timber under it?'

'It's right enough,' the fireman insisted, 'and by the time we messes about to get timber here the shift'll be gone and it'll be morning afore we gets that coal by.'

'It would make sure that no more fell to delay us,' I argued, 'and it would be safer then.'

'And if you was to slam in it would be clear quicker,' he snapped, 'it seems as you're bent on wasting time.'

'I'm not,' I replied, 'only I wants to be as safe as I can. It's my body, remember, and a man don't want more than one clout from a stone falling from as high as that.'

'Get hold on the sledge, Griff,' he orders, 'and make a start. This chap have got a lot too much to say.'

Griff looks at the official, then at me. He is hesitant.

'Griff can do what he likes,' I said, 'but I'm not working under that top until it's put safer.'

'You'll do as I tells you or you know what you can do,' the fireman snarls, 'and that's pick up your tools and take 'em out.'

'I'll do that too,' I replied and threw my shovel on the side, 'and what about you, Griff? Are you staying?'

'Don't know what to do, mun,' he mumbles. 'P'raps it'll stay all right until we have cleared this fall. We've done it afore, heaps of times. Let's pitch in and clear away as soon as we can.'

I know that Griff has allowed the thoughts of his wife and family to overcome his judgement.

'Aye, that's the idea.' The fireman is suddenly friendly. 'Slam in at it. You won't be long and I'll stand up on the side and keep me eyes on the top. If anything starts to fall I'll shout and you can jump back.'

I know well that before the word of warning could have formed in his throat it would be too late. Griff looks at me in an appealing way. He will not start without me, but I do not want to feel that I am responsible for his losing the job. I decide to risk it with him but to listen and watch most carefully.

We start to work, breaking the big stones and rolling the back one on top of another until we have formed a ro wall that is about a yard from the rail. The roof is quie a while and so we work swiftly. The fireman keeps very because he can see we are working to our limit so can escape from under that bad piece, and he knows quieter he keeps the better we can hear. He sits on holding his lamp high and looking continually

We had cleared about half of the fall and I breaking a large stone when Griff asked me f hammer. Our elbows touched when I handed he hit with the sledge I lifted a stone on to slid down and dropped a couple of feet from a short pace after it, bent, then began to I was almost straightened up I felt air r something hit me a terrible blow or sound that seemed to start as a sob b was checked abruptly. The blow on I felt to be flung along the roadwa

ally, like the early drops of a shower of solid rain. Probably these are the warning that bigger stones are loosening but I cannot see what is above or which way to crawl and escape. I have lifted one eyelid over the other and the water from that eye has cleared away most of the dust. I can now open both eyes, but I can see no more than I could when my eyes were fast closed. I crawl towards the fireman, guided by his screams. Soon I find myself checked by what feels to be a mass of stone. I climb upwards, scramble over the top, then slide down. I call Griff again, softly, caressingly, as if to coax him to answer, whatever has happened, but no reply comes.

I press my shoulder against the solid side of the roadway so that it shall guide me, then I crawl forward, very slowly. The fireman knows I am nearing him and directs my movements – continually imploring me to hurry. Suddenly I touch something that is softer and warmer than stone. I run my hand along and know it is a human leg. My every nerve seems to grate when I decide it must be Griff's and that he is dead.

'That's the leg.' The fireman's scream relieves me. 'There's a stone on it as is holding me down. Lift it, quick.'

I feel for the stone and set myself to endure the pain of lifting. I might as well have attempted to move the mountain, for three attempts fail to shake the stone. The fireman is speaking near my ear; he is frantic; begs me to hurry; screams at me as would an hysterical woman. I feel about and find a stone that I can move so I push it tightly under the one that holds the leg. This fresh stone will ease some of the weight and will stop any more pressure coming on his foot.

I have realized that I cannot do more until I have help. I must crawl and get others. I tell the fireman so, but he begs me not to go. I know there is no other way, so I turn around and feel my way over the stones. My fingers touch the cold iron of a tram-rail, but as there is no sign of a tram on that side I am assured that this is the right way. I crawl alongside that rail, running my fingers on it for a guide.

'Don't you be long,' he screams after me, 'for God's sake don't be long.'

Above, in the darkness, I hear a sound that resembles the ripping of cloth. It is this noise that stones make when they are being crushed and broken by the weight that is moving above them. I must hurry, so that the fireman may be saved and to see if there is any hope for Griff.

I drag myself along a few yards, rest some seconds to ease the pain, then drag along again. I must have crawled more than two hundred yards before I saw a light in the distance. I could not shout, so I had to crawl close to the repairer who was at work there. He was some seconds before he understood the message that I was croaking, then when he did he became so flustered that he wasted some time hurrying back the way I had come before he realized it was useless going by himself. I lay in the darkness while he ran back to call the help that came very quickly. Soon the roadway was brightened by the lamps of scores of men, who hurried along and took me with them, and this time we had plenty of light to see what had happened.

I could see that at least another twenty tons had fallen and the hole under which we had been at work was now higher than ever. The place was all alive again, creaking above and around us. Posts back in the gob were cracking – cracking – as if someone was firing a pistol at irregular intervals.

The fireman was as I had left him. He had his back against the side. His right foot was free but the left one was held tightly under a large stone. We could see no sign of Griff. They lifted a rail from the roadway, then used it as a lever to ease the stone off the fireman so that he could be taken back from the danger. He was only slightly hurt because the weight had only been sufficient to hold him and the main body of the stone was resting on others. He would not sit down but wandered amongst the men continually telling them of his own fright and moaning, 'Who would have expected this?' They lost patience at last and someone told him to sit down and not delay the work.

Above the men who strained to clear the fall, huge stones several tons in weight had started to fall, then had pressed against other stones that were moving and each had checked the downward movement of the other. They had locked each other in that position and now remained balancing – partly fallen – but the slightest jar or movement of the upper top would send them crashing down to finish their drop on the gang of men underneath. There was a continual rolling above us like thunder that is distant. Little stones flaked from the larger ones and dropped on the backs of the men as they worked below. Each time a stone dropped all the men leapt back, for a smaller stone is often the warning from a bigger one that is coming behind.

Several of the men stood erect, with their lamps held high and their eyes scanning the moving stones up above. They kept their mouths open, so that the warning shout should issue with no check. The others, busy amongst the fall, tumbling and lifting whilst they searched under the stones, did not hesitate when a warning came – they sprang backwards at once and made sure that no man stood directly behind the other to impede that swift spring.

Men can lift great weights when fear forces their strength. These stood six in a row, then tumbled big stones away until only the largest one in the centre was left. This one needed leverage, so a man knelt alongside to place the end of two rails in position; they had to be careful not to put the end on a man's body. Several men put their shoulders under the rails then they prised upwards. As the stone was slowly lifted they blocked it up by packing with smaller stones, then started to lift again. When the stone was two feet off the ground they paused; surely it was high enough. There was something to be done now that each man dreaded; then, as if their minds had worked together, two men knelt down and reached underneath. Very carefully they drew out what had been Griff.

We retreated with our burden and left the sides to do what crushing, and the roof to do what falling, they wished. The pain of my back had been severe all the while, when the excitement slackened I felt sick and could not stand alone. I leaned against one of my mates for support and he placed his arm around me gently, as if I was a woman.

We all know the verdict well enough, but refuse to admit it. Griff seems to be no more than half his usual size. Some-one takes his watch from the waistcoat hanging on the side. They hold the shining back against what they believe is his mouth. Thirty yards away another stone crashes down on top of the others and the broken pieces fly past us whilst dust clouds the air. The seconds tick out loudly through that underground chamber whilst forty men watch another hold-ing a watch; when he turns around someone lifts a lamp near so that they can see. The shining back is not dimmed. We had all known, yet somehow we had dared to hope.

As we are going outwards I notice that the fireman tries to isolate me; he wants to talk. I avoid him and keep in the group. Some distance along I hear a queer sound and look back to see that he has collapsed. His legs have given under him and he cannot stand. He is paralysed with fright. Two of the men place their hands under him and they carry him along behind the stretcher. They have to lean inwards to avoid the sides and bend their heads down because of the top. The fireman senses the hatred that is in all our minds and he sobs continually but no one asks him if he is in pain.

When we reach the main roadway the journey of empty trams is waiting. We place the loaded stretcher across one tram and four men sit alongside it. The fireman is lifted into another tram and the rest of us scramble on.

Suddenly the fireman tries to reassert himself.

'All of you going out,' he complains, 'didn't ought to go, not all of you. That fall have got to be cleared so's to get the coal back first thing.'

It was as if he had not spoken. The rider knocked on the signal wires. We start to move outwards slowly, for the en-gineer has been warned that it is not coal he is drawing this time. The fireman starts his mumbling again and we realize that he will tell the manager that the men refused to listen to him. Already he has started to cover his tracks.

Outside, it is dark and raining. The lamps on the pit-mouth are smeared where the water has trickled through the dust on the globes. There is a paste of oily mud and wet small coal that squelches under our feet. The official limps away to the office. We notice, and comment on the fact, that he walks quickly and with hardly any difficulty. He gets inside the office and we hear him fastening the door before he switches the light on. He intends to be alone when making his report. We hand our lamps in, telling the lamp-men to note the damaged ones and we answer their inquiry as to 'Who is it this time?' They return our checks but put Griff's in a small tin box. A smear of light is brightening the sky but it is raining very heavily when we start on that half-hour's journey to his home. We feel our clothes getting wet on our bodies and the blankets on the stretcher are soaking. Water rushes down the house-pipes and it bubbles and glistens in the light of the few street-lamps.

All the houses near have their downstairs lights on, for news of disaster spreads quickly; besides, it is time for the next shift to prepare. The handles of the stretcher scrape the wall when we take the sharp turn to get through the kitchen door. This is the only downstairs room they have, so we prepare to wash him there. Neighbours have been busy, as they always are in this sort of happening. A large fire is burning, the tub is in, water is steaming on the hob and his clean pants and shirt are on the guard as if he was coming home from an ordinary shift.

I see no sign of Griff's wife. I remember her as small and quiet; a woman who stayed in her own home and was all her time tending to Griff and their five children. I do hear a sound of sobbing from upstairs and conclude that they have made her stop there, very wisely. Sometimes I hear the voices of the children too, but they are soft and subdued, as if they had only partly wakened and had not yet realized the disaster this dawn had brought to them.

I think that is all. I have re-lived that night fifty, yes, a hundred times since it happened, and each time I have felt that I hated the fireman more. Had that stone hit my back a little harder I would have been compelled to spend the rest of my days in bed with a broken back – and would have to exist on twenty-six shillings a week as compensation. Had I been a yard farther back I would probably be in similar state to Griff – then I would have been worth eighteen pounds, bare funeral expenses, as I would have been counted as having no dependants.

If I appear stupid at the inquiry, as a workman is expected to be, then I will answer the set questions as I am supposed to answer them and 'the usual verdict will be returned'.

Griff was my mate, and nothing I can do will bring him back to life again, but his wife and family are left. He would have wished that I do the best thing possible for them. If I remain quiet, they may be paid about four hundred pounds as compensation – which is the highest estimate of the value of a husband and father, if he is a miner. They will think that one of the usual accidents robbed them of the father, but if they are told he should not have died, it will surely increase their suffering.

If I speak what is true, the insurance company will claim that they are absolved from liability because we should not have worked there. Had we refused we should probably have lost our jobs. The insurance solicitor will be present – ever watching his chance – and will seize on the least flaw in the evidence.

So this afternoon I shall go to the office and draw two pay envelopes that should contain about two pounds sixteen each. One is mine, the other I will take to his house. There five silent children will be waiting whilst their dazed mother is being prepared to go to the Hall and testify that the crushed thing lying in the kitchen was her husband and that he was in good health when she saw him leave the house.

If the verdict is anything except 'Accidental Death' that pay packet may hold the last money she will have – unless it is the pension and parish relief.

Later, tonight, I shall have to face another fear; I shall have to go again down that hole and re-start work, but at four o'clock I will be at the inquest, shall kiss the Bible, and speak 'The whole truth and nothing but the truth' – perhaps. Would you?

The Squire of Havilah

T. HUGHES JONES

(*translated by T. Glynne Davies*)

I

I⊤'s likely that Daniel Jones, Rhos-y-grug, would have gone
to the harvest thanksgiving service even if it had been, as
usual, merely a prayer service. Every skeleton of a man would
try to drag himself to the thanksgiving, and in the back
seat, the one next to the door, you would see three or four
people who would never normally darken the door of the
chapel. They would come there early, taking their places
before anybody else. They would behave themselves dec-
orously enough during the service and then slide away
furtively before the dying strains of the last hymn, having
put a shilling each in the collection plate, the collection of
light. Although he was nominally a full member, the man
from Rhos-y-grug only dropped in at chapel from time to
time, and he always used to sit in the back seat – that unpaid-
for pew so proper for those who were, in the words of the
saints, on the common land of life.

Although Daniel Jones and the others had arrived early
for this particular service, they found that the chapel had
filled up quickly, and the back seat was already full. The
people of their particular parish knew them well and had
been gentlemen to the extent of leaving the seat vacant for
them, but many had come from neighbouring parishes,
ignorant of the unwritten rights of the inhabitants of the
Common Land. Daniel nearly turned away as he got to the
door, after his nose had crept in and his eyes had seen that
the seat was full, but the urge to hear the preacher from

America was greater than the desire to flee, and he strode on into the middle of the chapel.

It was Davies, Hyde Park, who had the inspiration of inviting the preacher from America. About forty-five years before that, Davies had gone, an impoverished boy from Pennant parish, to the milk business in London. There he made money as people make water, to use the unfortunate idiom of the local people, and he had come home to retire in his old parish, building a new house on the site of the old cottage where his father and mother had lived and where he had lived as a lad.

Glanrafon (Riverbank): that was the name of the old cottage, and 'Glanrafon', imprinted in gold letters, was the name on the frontage of his shop near Marble Arch, but after returning home it seemed essential to call the new house Hyde Park; that was Davies's conception of the propriety of things. At the first opportunity, he was made a deacon of the chapel. His London venture had kindled the imagination of those who competed with him for the honour and now he had channelled his energies into other directions, starting off with working out new concepts about 'running' (that was his word) the weak chapel Cause at Blaen-y-cwm. It was Davies's idea to hire the services of the preacher from America for the thanksgiving service. A London friend of his had told him about the American who had been preaching at some of the capital city's chapels, and Davies decided to woo him to Wales before he returned.

There were four deacons at Blaen-y-cwm chapel, and as a rule Davies had little difficulty in persuading two of them to do that which was obviously right. People used to say about one of them, Dafydd Ifans, that he knew his Bible backwards, and that he was a giant on his knees: he was the king of prayer at the chapel. Somebody said mischievously about another, Robert the Rock, that it was his almanac that he knew backwards. Before Davies returned to his native heath, Robert the Rock was the businessman of the chapel. However, the deacon who had most influence at Blaen-y-cwm was the fourth member of the fraternity, Ifan Jones, the

Castle, although he had not left his house for years because
of illness. His shadow spread over everything to such an
extent that no one dared take any action without the consent of Ifan Jones.

One Sunday night Davies mentioned the American
preacher to his two active co-deacons.

'I,' said Dafydd Ifans, 'had thought that we would have
a prayer meeting for thanksgiving, especially as it's war-
time, and to make it a kind of a meeting of humble supplication.'

'Come, come!' said Davies. 'You can't mix thanksgiving
and supplication; let's choose between the one and the
other!'

'But the Scriptures are on my side. In every thing by
prayer and supplication with thanksgiving let your requests
be made known unto God.'

'Well, if we have to change,' said Robert the Rock, 'what
about getting Mr Richards, Llanfair, to preach. He's a fascinating preacher and people like him. Bringing that man
over from America is like carrying water across a river.'

'Yes, like carting water across the Atlantic, if you like,'
said Davies, 'but everything depends on the quality of the
water.'

'Exactly!' said Dafydd Ifans, who had been engaged in
bitter battle with Richards in the Sunday School, 'if you cart
water at all, well, get it from far enough away!'

That was the eventual decision.

'But,' said Robert the Rock, 'what about Ifan Jones, the
Castle?'

'You leave,' replied Davies, 'you leave Ifan Jones to me.'

Davies's method of dealing with Ifan Jones was to put not
only ideas but also words into his head, as people said; that
is, he would attribute his own ideas and suggestions to Ifan
Jones in such a way that the latter would genuinely believe
that he himself had thought up the whole lot. Davies called
at the Castle that evening and before long the parish heard
that Ifan Jones, the Castle, was going to change the form
of the thanksgiving service and arrange for a stranger from

America to preach. That was an end to that; that was enough also to draw such a crowd to the chapel that Davies, Hyde Park, decided that the next step would be to build a gallery in the chapel.

The American preacher was not in the tradition of the Big Preachers: that was the opinion of the locality, and that was an opinion you could depend upon. 'All the man had was a sackful of "wit stories",' said Deio'r Cwm, one of the common-land residents. The 'wit story' was one of the most popular competitions in the entertainment meetings in that neck of the woods, and Deio meant the comparison to be a condemnation of the preacher.

The American was a small, well-set man with dark eyes that sparkled, and long black hair. He took his text from the second chapter of Genesis, from that part of the book that describes the geographical situation of the Garden of Eden, and he stressed mostly that verse which describes the river 'which compasseth the whole land of Havilah, where there is gold; and the gold of that land is good; there is bdellium and the onyx stone'. He started off by comparing this theory with the other theory about the location of the garden which eventually, after listing a number of definitive and infallible sources, he located in Mesopotamia, somewhere between the Tigris and the Euphrates. He used the name 'Mesopotamia' time and time again, using it as a bell to call the audience together, and occasionally threw into his sermon references to the Klondyke, the Yukon, and Johannesburg to make it a golden mixture. However, although the theology of his sermon was weak, the little man's stories captivated the congregation, and although it was a sultry night and the chapel windows were shut as usual, not one eye went to sleep. The rustic congregation's imagination was gripped by the novelty and the brilliance of the description of Havilah and the excellent produce of the land: the gold, the bdellium, and the onyx stone. It is true that towards the end of the sermon there was an attempt to draw some moral or other and that the people were urged to do something or other to better their earthly lives, but the thing

that Daniel Jones, Rhos-y-grug, and everybody else for that
matter remembered was the description of Havilah and its
amazing wealth.

The whole thing had slipped out of everybody's mind
very soon, except for that of Daniel Jones. Even on the way
home from the sermon some of the people were talking
about the man from Bwlch who had half his corn still un-
gathered in the fields as usual on the day of harvest thanksgiving, or about the good aftermath stubble and that kind
of thing, the land of Havilah having become a wisp of a
thing on the horizon. However, on his way home and
throughout the ensuing days Daniel Jones's mind was full
of thoughts about the riches of the desirable area between
the two rivers where the Lord God had planted a garden
for the man and woman He had fashioned.

Rhos-y-grug was a poor farm. As with most farm-names
in the district, the name, meaning 'the moorland of the
heather', was a good description of the farm itself. Originally
the place had been a *ty unnos*, a 'one-night' house, built in
the days when a man could become a house-owner if he
could build his house on common land overnight to the
extent that smoke could come out of the chimney by morning. Tradition had it that it was Daniel's great-grandfather
who had dug up the land, 'every inch of it', and had taken
from the earth the stones that he had used for the boundary
walls around the fields. However, the fields were still the
preserve of the heather, and Daniel used to love quoting an
old piece of doggerel :

> Gold 'neath the fern-leaves,
> Silver 'neath the gorse,

and then in a deep, doleful voice,

> Famine 'neath the heather.

Daniel was a bachelor about forty years old at this time,
living with his widowed mother; she always used to refer to
him as 'this boy of mine' even when he had become a grown
man. In the eyes of the neighbours, the son was rather aim-

less as a farmer. Instead of ploughing properly he would merely scratch the surface of the land. He would also sell a bullock before fattening it and do as little as he could to help nature with the tasks that came with the seasons of the year. After blundering through some sort of a day's work, Daniel's pleasure would be to leave everything at the end of the day to go to the village shop or the smithy for a chat with anybody who happened to be there. Rhos-y-grug was a secondary thing and, after the sermon delivered by the man from America, the poor destitute crops, the crooked trees, and the stony fields (stones always seemed to come from somewhere all the time) were far less real than the gold of Havilah and the bdellium and the onyx stone.

Daniel regretted that he had not stayed to speak to the preacher after the service, but the opportunity had gone. Neither had he heard of any other engagement undertaken by the stranger in the neighbourhood. 'It's likely that by this time he's on his way back to America,' reasoned the man from Rhos-y-grug. He did mention the matter to the minister of another chapel, but he had given the verses some allegorical interpretation, a very unsatisfactory interpretation in Daniel's view. Everybody had forgotten Havilah.

At the far end of the next parish there lived a character who had at one time been in the goldfields, and Daniel went to him to obtain more information about the land of gold and bdellium and onyx.

'Tell me,' said Daniel Jones 'what is your opinion of the gold there is in Havilah?'

'If it's gold you want, Ballarat is the place,' was the old prospector's reply as he ruminated over a series of romantic memories about Australian gold.

Daniel decided to make one more effort to direct the minds of the people of the parish, and particularly the minds of the chapel people, back to Havilah. The chapel *seiat*, or fellowship, met only once a month, and in the *seiat* the brethren often used to discuss the sermons of the month. Although Daniel was an inconsistent chapel-goer, he was still a full member and allowed to attend the fellowship meetings, not having committed a sin evil enough for him to have been excommunicated. His presence caused some consternation within the small gathering, and at last, after a great deal of discussion during which the thanksgiving service was not once mentioned, Robert the Rock said:

'We are very pleased to see you, Daniel Jones, in the fold with us tonight. May we have a word from you telling us what brought you here?'

'It was what the preacher from America said about the gold of Havilah!'

'Amen! Thanks be to Him!' shouted Beti the Hafod, who had been used to shouting such things ever since the great Revival of 1904–5 had enticed countless thousands of Welsh people to Chapel and to God, and although the saints by this time frowned upon such enthusiasm, she was never chastised, because she had been blessed with the root of the matter.

'Yes,' said Robert, quoting a hymn: 'Godliness in its strength is more precious to me than the gold of Peru!'

'It was the gold of Havilah that I said!' maintained Daniel, sticking to his guns and his text. 'I want to know more about that place Havilah!'

'The law of thy mouth,' said Dafydd Ifans, 'is better unto me than thousands of gold and silver,' and then, his tongue tasting biblical verses, he added: 'For the merchandise of it is better than the merchandise of silver, and the gain thereof than fine gold.'

'Yes,' said Daniel Jones, just as if he was in Sunday School, 'but who or what is that "it"?'

'Wisdom!' said Dafydd Ifans.

'And it would also be wisdom,' said Robert the Rock, 'for us not to waste more time on that rigmarole.' Actually Daniel had been at him before the *seiat* and had cornered him on the subject af Havilah.

By this time, Davies, Hyde Park, believed that he should say something, since it was he who had chosen the preacher, and he said:

'We are all glad that Daniel Jones clung to the sermon. That's our fault as religious people – we listen happily to the word and then let the devil steal it. I'm glad to hear our brother speaking about Havilah: the land of gold, wasn't it?'

It was too much for Robert the Rock to hear the shopkeeper from near Marble Arch talking about gold. He could see the *seiat* becoming a market place and a vanity fair, and hoisting himself in the Big Seat – a sign that he had something very important to say – Robert drew attention to the primary purpose of the *seiat* which was to warn the young people of the district not to go to the Hallowe'en Fair of Trewylan. Robert used to deliver this speech about this time every year, although few young people were there to hear it. 'Take care how ye walk!' thundered Robert, 'remember the eyes of the world are upon you. Because your adversary the devil as a roaring lion walketh about, seeking whom he may devour.'

Long before the speech ended, Daniel Jones had decided that he would go to the Hallowe'en Fair of Trewylan if only to spite Robert the Rock.

II

It may be that it was the devil who brought Daniel Jones to grief after all, albeit not in the form of a lion but in the form of the most unlikely creature anybody ever saw.

The Trewylan Hallowe'en fairday was one of the great days of the local calendar. Many years ago it used to be only a fair to hire farmhands and housemaids; some of the older people could remember seeing young men and girls standing in a row like bullocks and heifers at a mart, and the farmers and their wives passing judgement on them before attempting to hire them. This old hiring fashion had long since vanished, and the bargain for the ensuing year had been struck before the fairday, allowing that day to be free for pleasure and merriment – a careless and carefree day between the hard work of the year that had passed and the uncertainty of the one which was to come. However, instead of the old bargaining between master and labourer and between mistress and housemaid, there was now bargaining between sweethearts. During the afternoon you could see the young girls parading in their bevies, knowing that the eyes of the young lads were fixed upon them in their quest to choose the one with the prettiest smile and the grandest clothes. Between then and nightfall the groups would become smaller as the most attractive were whisked away one by one. Then, at night-time, everybody would go to the fairground to enjoy every form of amusement and jollity until midnight.

Daniel Jones always did go to the fair, but this time he went earlier than usual. Dafydd the Brake used to run two journeys to the fair – two in the morning and two returning journeys at night – and the early-morning journey used to be very early indeed and the last journey back very late indeed. Daniel went with the first brakeful in the morning when the town was beginning to prepare itself for the great day. Daniel thought before hoisting himself on to the wagon that Marged might be on the brake – Marged the Meadow. True, there was no permanent arrangement between them that they should meet on fairday, but somehow this always used to happen before it was time to go home. Everybody in the parish knew that Daniel and Marged had been courting after a fashion for years. It was a kind of an 'as-you-were' courting and the people of the area could not discern any change in the pattern of things as the years rolled by. The knowing ones said that Daniel was afraid of leaving his poor old mother, and that she for her part would allow no other female to partake of the government of Rhos-y-grug. And so, one year after another, you could see Daniel and Marged together at the eisteddfod, the singing festival and the fair. Marged had enough charm to attract other competitors – a fine figure, a ready tongue and by this time a fair amount of money, that is, if she had kept the wages she had earned as the chief maid at the Meadow, a position she had held for seven years now. Her seven-year tenure also entitled her to a pair of blankets as a wedding gift from her mistress.

Marged was not on the first journey. This did not worry Daniel too much because they had not arranged to meet anywhere in particular. She would be sure to be on the following journey and he would go to meet her deliberately accidentally. He wandered aimlessly around the streets for two or three hours, and then went to the place where the brake always ended its journey. There he saw Marged the Meadow in the company of Elis, the chief farmhand of Rhedynog. The two were merry and laughing all over the place. 'Marged!' said Daniel, but neither of them looked at him. Away they went, their every motion a forceful hint that it was all over for that particular Hallowe'en fair. Daniel watched them jinking up the street – Elis in his new breeches with shiny leggings, with his hat askew and a cigarette in his mouth, and Marged as happy as a flower opening out its petals in the heat of the sun.

Daniel went down to the seaside: there was a great stillness there. People said that it always rained on Hallowe'en fairday, but for once, at least, it was different. Perhaps it is necessary now and again to have the exception in order to prove the rule. The smooth surface of the sea seemed to second the appeal of the boatmen who were trying to entice people to go out in their boats, and Daniel almost went out himself. To him, however, as to many people from the country, there was a tremendous insecurity and danger about the sea. Supposing he was drowned and his neighbours said he had drowned himself deliberately because he had been disappointed by Marged the Meadow? 'No girl at all is worth that!' said Daniel out loud, and then, looking at the acreage of the sea, he added: 'There are plenty of other fish in the sea.' He started humming a Welsh folk song:

> Oh! If my darling sweetheart
>   Loves two other girls or three,
> And satisfies them truly
>   At every fair they see ...

Then he realized that he should have sung 'two other *boys* or three', but in Welsh the rhyming pattern meant that it had to be girls. Then he remembered one man who had sung the song at an entertainment meeting, calling it 'The Song of the Miller's Son' and not 'The Song of the Miller's Daughter' and he had changed the words to match the new title. Try as he would, Daniel could not remember those words. After long thought he found that he could sing a verse by re-arranging the lines:

> Oh! If my darling sweetheart
>   Loves two other boys or three,
> Then let her not imagine
>   Her antics worry me ...

Then, possibly, he could do the same thing with the lines that followed:

> And if she satisfies them
>   As every fair unfurls,
> I am as free as she is
>   To love three other girls.

'Come for a quick one!' said a voice at his side, and after putting a lid suddenly on his music Daniel could see Shaci the Smith by his elbow and the sign of the Black Lion immediately in front of him. 'Only just one small one.' The man from Rhos-y-grug was not teetotal: he would taste beer three or four times a year but never got drunk.

'I don't give a damn!' was the answer, and in they went.

As a rule, when you go into a public house, when it's full, you hear a deep excitement, the sound of half-a-dozen and more of different groups, every group with its own subject of discussion, and every discussion audible, sagacious and purposeful in its own circle, together becoming a meaningless murmur. The difference this time was that only one man was speaking in the Black Lion and he was in a soldier's uniform. He was talking about the war and everybody was listening to him astutely and with reverence. Shaci asked for two small ones quietly, and then they joined to listen to the man in military uniform. He was trying to prove that the reason for the war was not what people commonly thought: we were not fighting for Belgium. 'Belgium!' he said: 'What is Belgium to us?' and he clicked his fingers as if he was ridding the world of that unfortunate country with the emphatic click. 'No,' he said, 'the country we are really fighting for is Persia – and there's enough petrol there to keep this country going, and we have none in this country. You watch Persia! Why is Turkey in the war?' Everybody looked around for a minute at least, but nobody replied.

'And what,' asked Daniel Jones in the middle of the big silence, 'about the gold of Havilah?'

A great silence came over the whole room again. Daniel could hardly believe that it was he who had uttered the words: it was as if some power from without himself had got hold of him and made him a tongue for that power for the occasion. The soldier turned his gaze on him immediately, as did everybody else. Not a word was spoken because everybody was waiting to see what the soldier would say. At last, with a scathing look, and without any reference at all to what Daniel had asked, the soldier went on to talk about the true reason for the war.

Daniel Jones slipped out as quietly as he could, leaving his half pint of beer half full, but Shaci made sure that the rest of the beer was not wasted. Daniel nudged down the street furtively to the King's Head, determined to keep his mouth shut in one sense and to drink his beer quietly. A little later on he ventured into the street, feeling quite a bit more courageous and merry. By this time the people were edging towards the fairground, and Daniel himself followed the stream. Every merchant and showman was trying to draw complete notice to his own wares and at first the noises were enough to deafen anybody, but slowly you could segregate and isolate the different noises until you could make sense of them. As it was becoming dark, the whole area was lit up by naphtha, the naked flames being blown in every direction by the smooth breeze that moved across the field. Children, and people grown out of official childhood, were walking about squirting water from little metal bottles, aiming the thin streams of water at people's necks, particularly the nape. To be in the fashion, Daniel bought one and put it in his pocket.

In the middle of the fair, placed so that everybody could see it, was a tall pole with a bell at the top. The pole was marked with numbers that went up to 1,000 near the bell. The task was to strike with a large hammer at a piece of wood that could make the bell ring, that is, if anybody had the strength to send the piece of iron all the way up. Now and again the bell would ring to pronounce to all that somebody had succeeded.

'Come on!' shouted the man by the pole, 'try your strength; a penny a time and nothing to pay if you make the bell ring. Try your strength!'

Daniel stepped forward and grabbed the hammer; he lifted it up and brandished it while the onlookers held their breath as they always did when someone was about to strike the wood. Down went the hammer and up shot the piece of iron, but only to 750, no higher. 'Well tried, sir!' said the man, 'one more go!'

Daniel paid his penny and moved off as the showman was shouting to draw attention to an attempt about to be made by somebody else. Glancing over his shoulder, Daniel saw that it was Elis, chief farmhand of Rhedynog, about to put his hand on the hammer. Elis was so certain of his strength that he was going to use only one hand to hold it. This was the sort of exhibition that the crowd really enjoyed, and a few paces behind him stood Marged the Meadow looking at her hero with eyes that were full of admiration. Just as Elis was about to strike, Daniel remembered about the water squirter in his pocket and decided that it would be just as well to try it out. This he did just as the head farmhand was about to bring the hammer down with all the might of his arm; Elis felt a sting on the nape of his neck and then the cold water streaming down between his shirt and his skin. The strike was a clumsy one, the hammer hitting the edge of the wood at a slant and then following through, its full force being felt by the showman in charge of the pole. Raging in pain, he at once rushed at Elis and punched him until he fell to the ground. Elis had not seen it coming because he had turned around to see who had brought him to such shame. During the uproar and confusion, Daniel Jones slipped away, delighted to see two tall policemen strutting to the scene.

Daniel wandered around, looking at this thing and that. The games of chance were concentrated on the middle of the field, with a tent on each side, and hoarse showmen bawling in front of them. Daniel read the advertisements outside the tents – the ones about the fattest woman in the world, the calf with three heads (the only one of its kind in the world), the armless man (also the only one of his kind in the world), and the fortune-teller who was prepared, if you paid him, to prophesy the destruction of empires and the downfall of kings as well as explaining to girls who their husbands would be.

Daniel passed all these by, pausing for a while by the little wooden hobby horses as they whisked around in their confined circle in the glory of bright paint and fashionable tunes. From a tent near by came the roar of a lion, which roared in order to remind Daniel of Robert the Rock's warning about the devil going around as a roaring lion. 'The devil himself must be in that tent,' he said, laughing loudly at his own humour.

He had decided to go home when he heard something that stirred up old memories and his heart beat faster. Inside a big tent there were two tall black men in eastern clothes beating two big drums. Between them, wearing a thin linen jacket, a small man was inviting his listeners to go into the tent and pay threepence for the privilege. 'Now is the time,' he said, 'ladies and gentlemen, this is your opportunity to see the wild cat brought here specially from Mesopotamia.' When Daniel Jones heard the word 'Mesopotamia' he recalled immediately the goldfields of Havilah. The little man was obviously aware of the fascination of the word, because he used it at the end of every sentence, and every time he uttered it someone or other would edge nearer to the tent.

'This is the chance of a lifetime, ladies and gentlemen! Threepence for seeing the big cat from Mesopotamia, caught in the parched deserts by these two brave men,' at which time he bowed extravagantly to the two black men who in turn bowed to the audience. 'All the way from Mesopotamia to Trewylan – one of nature's wonders. Come to see one of the animals from the other side of the world! Come to Mesopotamia! Only threepence. The only. . .'

'Come to Mesopotamia!' To Daniel Jones, the call was like a heavenly summons: he paid his threepence and went in with the others. People were a little disappointed when they saw the 'big cat'; it was a skinny little furtive creature with different-coloured hoops around its body. It stalked around its cell, keeping far away from the iron bars at the front and bristling up every time the man tried to make it move.

Small wonder that Wil the Rhyd, who was standing behind Daniel Jones, shouted loudly: 'It's the old tom from the Rhyd, boys, painted for the fair! Puss! Puss! Puss!'

Daniel turned viciously on his heel. 'Shut up!' he shouted with such menace in the words that Wil obeyed instantly.

Daniel Jones could perceive an air of excellence about the little creature. Had it not come from the neighbourhood of Havilah, the land of gold, and the sides of its den were, perhaps, full of bdellium and onyx?

As the audience streamed out, mumbling its complaints, Daniel stayed behind, staring at the creature, the strange visitor from Havilah, until he heard the voice of the man in the linen jacket greeting him:

'Well! Haven't you had your money's worth? Anybody would think that you'd bought it!'

'Bought it?' echoed Daniel. 'I would like to buy the land that was this little thing's home. Was it you that caught it?'

'Yes,' replied the man, perhaps forgetting that he had just attributed that feat to the two black giants.

'Away in Mesopotamia?' asked Daniel.

'Yes, true enough.'

'The land's good over there, isn't it?'

'Oh, yes,' said the man, who by this time was losing his patience and using his most spiteful sarcasm, 'oh, yes, it's a land flowing with milk and honey, without anybody working there.'

'I knew that, I knew that,' said Daniel Jones, 'but nobody would believe me. Have you got a little land yourself now?'

'Yes, miles and miles.' The man's voice was full of scorn by this time, but it made no difference to Daniel Jones. 'Would you like to buy a little?'

'Buy?' His dream was coming to an end. 'I would like to buy a few acres in Havilah. That's in Mesopotamia, and that's the place you're talking about. Have you got any to sell?'

'As much as you want.'

'I only have twenty pounds, and I've left that at home.'

'You bring your twenty pounds and I will let you have twenty acres.'

'Freehold?'

'Yes, till the day of judgement.'

His patience was almost exhausted by this time, but he could not avoid the opportunity to play about with this rustic idiot. As for Daniel himself, he could not believe his luck. The landlords of Pennant were asking ten pounds for an acre for the poorest moorland at the top of the parish and this was the opportunity to get the gold of Havilah, not to mention the bdellium and the onyx, for a pound an acre.

'Will you hold on to the land until tomorrow?' asked Daniel. 'I shall bring the money tomorrow.'

'You bring the money and you will own the land.'

By this time the two black men had started beating their drums again and saying, 'That's it; sleep on it,' the man was half pushing Daniel out of the tent. Some had noticed that he had stayed behind, and when he came out Wil the Rhyd shouted: 'Boys! This is the wild cat coming, all the way from Mesopotamia!' Everybody laughed, but Daniel took no notice. He trod down the stairs and through the fair like a man who had seen a great vision.

He had little interest in the lights of the fair or in anything else; after walking into the town itself, he decided to walk the eight miles home rather than wait for the brake. How could he bear the clucking of idiots on a night like this? Was the company of the moon not better? He remembered a sermon which described the sun on its journey seeing everywhere and every country in the world – Japan, India, America, Australia, Britain. If that were so, was it not also true of the moon? And before the following night, she would have seen Havilah.

The keeper of the wild cat had the surprise of his life when he saw Daniel Jones in the fairground the following morning. Daniel knew that there was more than twenty pounds in his mother's old stocking, and he had taken the money out before going to bed. It was not easy to find an excuse to give his mother for another visit to Trewylan, but that morning he felt he could do anything.

Most of the people who had come to the fair had gone home with a gloomy look indeed on all their faces. In the morning the man who had worn a linen jacket was now wearing dirty working clothes, but Daniel recognized him easily.

'I have come to settle this business – about the land in Havilah.'

The man's impatience the previous night was nothing to compare with his intolerance now.

'Go home!' he said. 'I haven't got any time to talk to you.'

'But you promised to sell me the land, and here's the money, twenty pounds.'

The man changed completely as soon as he saw the twenty golden sovereigns. He had mentioned the previous night's discussion to another man who used to be an office clerk. He had said, 'If he comes back, let me know, and he can have his freehold.' It was to him that the man went again now, as soon as Daniel was safely out of sight.

'That idiot has come back again about the land in Mesopotamia.'

'And a policeman with him?'

'No, indeed, everything's right. I could see the money in his hands – twenty pounds for twenty acres – and he wants to buy.'

'Well, hold on to the fool for a while, and make sure there isn't a policeman about while I draw out the deeds.'

So, after much shaking of hands, Daniel Jones left the fairground to set off for home. In his pocket were the deeds proclaiming that the owner of Rhos-y-grug was from that time forth the owner of twenty acres in Havilah. Daniel was a weary man as he walked home for the second time, and two of the showmen from the fair were quite uneasy in their minds as they made for the next town, but he had the deeds and they the twenty pounds. In a way, honour was satisfied on both sides.

III

His neighbours started seeing a great change in Daniel Jones. He still neglected his farm as he had always done, but he now seemed to have a new interest they knew nothing about. The truth came out at the shop one night.

'Daniel here looks very satisfied with his lot!' said one. They had just been discussing the war-time complaints of the farmers, the utter stupidity of the bureaucrats, and the perplexity felt by every farmer. 'You look so happy; have you anything to say to lighten our darkness?'

'Perhaps he's courting a rich widow,' said one.

'Or maybe he's going to buy another farm!'

'Or this shop!'

'And perhaps,' said Daniel, weighing every word, 'perhaps,' he said again, determined to give every individual word its full stress, 'perhaps I have bought something that is enough to buy all your farms and this shop too.' It was Daniel's voice all right, but there was a strange stentorian air of authority about it. 'I have bought an estate in Havilah,' he said, 'and if you don't believe me, here are the deeds!'

He pulled out of his pocket a piece of paper with a red seal on the corner and tied with green ribbon. 'You read it,' he told the shopkeeper, 'to see that everything's in order.'

The shopkeeper read the paper more than once. The complicated English sentences had charm as well as authority. After a long silence, he turned to the others, nodding his head: 'He's right, he's right. He has bought twenty acres of land in Havilah, wherever that may be.'

'And that,' said Daniel Jones, 'is worth twenty thousand acres of Welsh land.'

Then some of the people in the shop remembered about the thanksgiving sermon and how it had been Daniel's main subject of conversation for weeks after that. 'There's no doubt about it,' said the shopkeeper, 'you are a squire!'

'Three cheers for the Squire of Havilah!' shouted one youth.

The company thought that this was taking things a bit too far, but the name stuck.

Towards the beginning of the year somebody decided that they should have a recruiting meeting in the parish. Only one of the local boys had joined the army – Roland Watcyn, something of a ne'er-do-well in the eyes of the parish. There was now a need for more soldiers, so one Sunday night Robert the Rock announced that there would be a recruiting meeting in the chapel on the Wednesday and that the fellowship would have to be postponed because of that. He announced that the meeting would be addressed by a popular preacher who had become an army chaplain, and also by an army officer. 'And come,' he added as he did whenever he made any announcement, 'come – all of you!'

The chapel was full on the Wednesday night. The deacons of Blaen-y-cwm considered it a good bargain to be able to hear the big preacher for nothing. It cost at least five guineas to obtain his services for a preaching meeting. Davies, Hyde Park, could now add another distinguished name to his list of big preachers who had stood in the Blaen-y-cwm pulpit. Davies was the chairman of the meeting. 'And since we are in a place of worship,' he said, 'we shall commence by singing the well-known hymn, "Guide me, O Thou great Jehovah".'

The singing was superb and the last four lines were sung over and over three times.

Davies was wise enough not to make a long speech. He uttered a few platitudes, as can anybody with experience in that line, and then called upon Colonel Sir Humphrey Llywelyn-Jones to address the meeting. The colonel's speech fell a bit flat after the enthusiasm of the singing. He could not bridge the gap between himself and this congregation. He had little oratorial power and even less command of the Welsh language, and everybody knew that his lack of the language would mean that his speech too would be a short one. He was therefore given what is so often wrongly called a perfect reception. Everybody was waiting for the Big Preacher to speak and in due course he was called upon. He was a tall, thin man with a thin, sallow face and black hair. He was in military uniform, his dog-collar a kind of a link with the old life before the war. He walked up the steps of the pulpit – the colonel had made his speech from the Big Seat – leaned on the Bible, and everybody expected him to introduce his text in the usual manner, saying: 'The text of my few observations is to be found in. . .' He stood upright, and without any preamble he said in a penetrating voice:

'I came not to send peace, but a sword.'

He started his sermon quietly and with deliberation as he started every time he preached. He spoke about the wars of the Old Testament, referring to exciting stories from the books of the Judges, the Kings, and the Chronicles, and he gave those stories the sort of treatment that only he could give. He followed this path, avoiding Isaiah's prophecy and the Sermon on the Mount. He showed that the biblical lands were once again at war. 'Our soldiers are fighting the infidels in Mesopotamia, on the earth of the Garden of Eden. The land trodden by our Saviour is in the hands of barbarians. They are calling us to release them.' The parish had heard about the Big Preacher's recruiting sermon, and particularly remembered the enthusiastic outburst that formed the end of his speech. As time went by, some members of the congregation were afraid that he would leave it out. But at last he came to that sweeping part of his sermon, starting with the words, 'But on Calvary Hill one Friday afternoon...' and he went on to captivate everybody's emotion. Beti the Hafod was shouting 'Hallelujah!' and 'Thanks be to Him!', and the old colonel was weeping like a child. And then, suddenly, the storm subsided and the preacher sat down.

The congregation thought that was the end of the meeting, but, as it was a recruitment meeting, the opportunity had to be given to anybody who had felt the call in his heart to come forward to enlist. Everybody moved around in the seats as they do at the end of a preaching meeting when the backsliders are asked to give themselves to Christ. On those occasions the people's eyes said : 'We have been saved; what about you sinners?'

But there was a noise and a flutter at the back of the chapel and Daniel, Rhos-y-grug, made his way laboriously towards the Big Seat as if he was a delegated sacrifice on the part of the congregation. Some smiled, one or two started laughing, but Daniel laboured on with some difficulty because benches had been placed in the aisles to accommodate such a large gathering. The old colonel got to his feet and went to meet him, holding Daniel by the hand to lead him into the Big Seat.

'I am very proud of accepting you,' he said in very broken Welsh. 'What is your name?'

'Daniel Jones.'

'I am proud again, Daniel Jones, of accepting you into the king's army. Very proud. Good fellow!' he added, smacking Daniel on the back. Nobody else came forward at all. Another hymn was sung to close the meeting, with Daniel Jones sitting in the Big Seat looking more like a repentant sinner than like a hero who had just answered the call of his country.

Before long, Daniel was called before the doctors to decide

whether he was healthy enough to join the army or not. They decided that they couldn't make a soldier of him, but they gave him some other work to do. A few weeks later Daniel came back to Rhos-y-grug because the authorities had decided that the heart of the country was the place for him rather than the field of battle. This was a bitter blow for Daniel: Havilah in danger and calling him, and he not allowed to go to Havilah's aid.

Ever since the night in the shop, Daniel had been known as the Squire of Havilah, and although he had been angry at first, he became proud of the name given to him in scorn. He had lost all interest in his farm. How could the owner of the Havilah goldfields possibly be concerned about the unfruitfulness of Rhos-y-grug? He went to the fairs regularly on the off-chance that he might meet the man who had sold him the land, but he never saw him. His neighbours started ignoring him; some went as far as showing him plainly what they thought of him, but neither their scorn nor their coldness could wither the blessedness of Havilah with its gold, bdellium, and onyx.

He still used to go to the shop to hear how the war was going on. The shopkeeper used to buy a daily newspaper and people would throng to the shop every night to hear the latest news. They were as acquainted with the names of the battles as they were with the big names of the Bible, and there used to be long and passionate arguments at times about the strategies and plans of the generals.

'Kitchener is the one they should have in France,' said one.

'Botha is my man,' said another.

'Give me the little man from Criccieth against all your generals,' was the observation of the third man.

One night, one of the people in the shop asked after Roland Watcyn, the parish's only serving soldier.

'He is somewhere near Kut,' answered the shopkeeper.

'And where's that Kut place?'

'In Mesopotamia.'

'That's where Daniel Jones's estate is! You'll have to look

out, Daniel, or the Germans will have taken all your land.'

'But it's the Turks who are at Kut,' said the shopkeeper, who went on to explain the campaign.

Daniel's opinion of Roland hadn't added up to much before he had gone to the army, but now he became an instant hero. Was he not fighting to keep his domain from being defiled? He found out Roland's address, and he wrote him a letter asking about Havilah. He put a pound note in the envelope as well. Roland knew well about Daniel's weakness and, in its time, back came a letter giving a vivid description of the country, making it out to be full of expensive and desirable things. Roland's letter was placed under the green ribbon to keep the deeds company. Within a month came the news that Roland had been killed and, in the memorial service at Blaen-y-cwm, Daniel Jones sat in mourning with the official mourners at the front of the chapel.

Few people had ever heard Daniel's views on the war, but now he started to criticize the leaders for wasting millions of soldiers to defend the watery land of Flanders in order to send only a few thousand to Mesopotamia. It was a black day indeed when the news came that Kut had been surrendered to the enemy, but Daniel's heart was lifted again when news came about General Maude's successful campaign in his march on Baghdad. When the final victory came in 1918 Daniel saw it not as the wisdom of generals but as the arm of the Lord punishing the defilers of Havilah.

IV

Immediately the war ended, there came the general election which showed that cooperation had been transient. There were three candidates in the county, every one with his own plans for the new world promised for the days after the war. Naturally enough all three came to the parish of Pennant in their turn to hold meetings, two Liberals and a Socialist. As it happened, the two Liberals held their meetings the same night and Daniel Jones asked them both for their opinion about the future of the goldfields of Havilah. Davies, Hyde Park, was the chairman of one of the meetings, and Robert the Rock was chairman of the other; because of this, neither spoke to the other for weeks after the heat of the election had gone. It was these two who had, at the meetings, tried to answer Daniel Jones's question, trying to shield their candidates at the same time. However, by the time the Socialist candidate came to the parish, friends had warned him about Daniel's question, and he went out of his way to give an answer that would give him one vote at least.

'That's a man who knows his onions!' said Daniel on his way home from the meeting, 'he's going to get my vote!' It was the Labour candidate who had his vote; it was he also who came third in the election.

His mother died before the winter ended and Daniel made no attempt to find anybody to take her place. Little did he realize her strength. Marged the Meadow had by this time been married to Elis for some while and she was Daniel's first and last sweetheart. He still held on to his little farm; it looked a little more respectable now because of the need for more ploughing as it was war-time. Yet, the mountain was only biding its time.

'What can you do with land like this?' asked Daniel, 'there's no heart in it.'

The more he thought of Havilah, the more he became dissatisfied with Rhos-y-grug. What were rushes and peat to compare with gold and bdellium, not to mention the onyx stone? Then he started going away from home. He told people that he was going to see about his property in Havilah. As the periods of his absence increased, he sold some of his stock until, in the end, he sold the lot and rented the fields to a neighbour, still holding on to the house itself. Sometimes, at night, people would see a yellow light in the window of Rhos-y-grug, and down in the valley they would say: 'The squire is back on his estate again!'

Before long, he sold the whole farm and Rhos-y-grug was bought by a neighbour who turned it into a grazing land for sheep which gave the heather another chance to inherit the earth that Daniel's great-grandfather had dug up inch by inch. Daniel found it interesting to compare the deeds with the deeds of his estate in Havilah, but the comparison ended with the scrutiny; on the one hand, dismal moorland with no charm, splendour, or pleasure; on the other, a land full of every kind of excellence, the land of gold, bdellium and the onyx stone. Everybody said that Rhos-y-grug had been sold for less than its worth, that the buyer had found himself a good bargain, but Daniel did not worry about that, for in due course he would get the wealth of Havilah.

About this time the parish decided to have a memorial institute in remembrance of the men who had perished in battle. During the war everybody in the parish had co-operated in every matter, forgetting the old divisions and quarrels. Things used to be so different when Pennant was notorious for its quarrels, with every newcomer eventually having to choose which side to join. Usually the differences arose between families, but this was not always the case: at the time of the post-war election you would see a wife opposing her husband and a son in opposition to his father. The election marked the beginning of the reversal to the old order of things and, when the time came to decide to do something about a memorial institute, the old divisions returned. The war had only been a layer of putty on the cracks, according to Shaci the Smith, and that was the truth.

The differences came to light over the question of deciding where the institute was to be sited. One section of the community wanted it at the bottom end of the parish, the other at the top end. Eventually it was decided to have a vote on the matter and, since most people lived at the bottom end, the decision, naturally, went their way. A public meeting was held to open a subscription fund. The chairman asked for those present to make their donations or their promises: 'We don't expect large sums,' he said, 'there is in this parish not one squire to put his name first in the book.'

'Only the Squire of Havilah!' shouted somebody.

'And he is...' started the chairman, but, before he could

finish the sentence, Daniel Jones stalked forward in his own dreamy way and put some papers on the table. The chairman stood up to say:

'Daniel Jones...'

'Havilah!' said Daniel.

'Yes, Daniel Jones, Havilah, fifty pounds; a gift worthy of a squire.'

There was a clapping of hands and a stamping of feet for a long time, and when the tumult finished there was no sign at all of Daniel Jones.

The work started on erecting the institute. At least, the site was bought and iron railings were put up around the spot, and that was as far as things went. The old differences of opinion came up again, some on this point, others on that. The people living at the bottom end of the parish started quarrelling, and old scabs came to light again. As the quarrels became more argumentative, so the weeds grew inside the railings on the site of the institute. The thistles, the dock leaves, and nettles were a perfect picture of the plunder and destruction wrought by war.

Daniel Jones's periods of absence from his parish grew longer and his journeys became longer too. Some people from the district used to come across him sometimes in the most unlikely places. One man came back after a motoring expedition in North Wales: 'And who do you think I saw sitting at the roadside at the foot of Snowdon?'

'I have no idea. Who?'

'The Squire of Havilah!'

Somebody else was coming over the Black Mountains late at night and, miles from nowhere, he saw the Squire ahead of him and asked him if he wanted a lift. 'No,' he said. 'I'm making for Liverpool; I know what time the ship leaves and if I walk like this I shall reach there in time.'

Another had seen him in Nant-yr-aur Pass at the foot of Plynlimon, above Cardigan Bay. Daniel pretended he did not know him, and looked, stupefied, westward. The other man also looked out to sea, and he saw it afire in the magic of the sunset.

Now and again Daniel would return to his old parish, calling always to see the intended site of the memorial institute. The local children were afraid of going there: their young imaginations had made it a forbidden place. However, when Daniel Jones came to stay overnight, as he often did in summertime, the children would ask:

'Where have you been this long time, Daniel Jones?'

'Been to Liverpool.'

'What did you see there?'

'I went to see whether the ship had left or not.'

'A ship going where?'

'A ship to Havilah.'

'Where's that, Daniel Jones?'

And so the conversation would go on, with the children asking endless questions.

Regularly on 11 November you could see him standing like a statue at about eleven in the morning in the desolation of the foundations of the institute. When the date fell on a Saturday one year, Daniel was there surrounded by a host of children, waiting for the observation of the two minutes' silence. He also used to come back to Trewylan every Hallowe'en fair, where he was always a kind of a laughingstock. Young people were always on the lookout for somebody to deride at fairtime and Daniel would walk around non-plussed, peering at individuals on the streets, staring particularly at any strangers, like a man looking for a long-lost friend.

One evening, at the beginning of October, the children of the parish were playing as usual near the foundations of the war memorial, outside the railings. Suddenly there was a wild shout: one of the children's footballs had been booted over the railings into the midst of the nettles and the other wild growth. It was a new ball given to one of the children as a gift, so that he climbed over the railings to look for it. Soon there was another wild shout and the boy ran for his life to his young friends. When he got his breath back, he told his friends that he had seen a man lying inside the enclosure and the children flocked together to tell Shaci the

Smith. Shaci went to the scene and looked over the railings. 'That's where he was!' shouted the boy, pointing to a corner. When Shaci got there, he stood as if petrified for a moment, and then said:

'The old Squire! The old Squire!'

There had to be an inquest, of course. The body was taken to the chapel house where it could easily be kept, as nobody lived there on week-days. Before the day ended, the policeman came from Llansulien to warn various householders that they were expected to act as jurors at the inquest. The following afternoon those who had been chosen could be seen walking slowly towards the chapel house. They were in their Sunday best; an inquest was an occasion of a lifetime and an occasion that demanded reverence and propriety. The last time an inquest was held in the district was about forty years previously after John Pen-y-Blanc had fallen into the lake on his way home from the fair. That was an incident to remember, because they had to take a boat to the lake and use grappling hooks to hoist the body from the water. One of the jurors at this inquest had also been present then.

The jury comprised the three deacons of Blaen-y-cwm and some of the most important farmers of the district. They had arrived at the chapel house long before time, because an inquest day, like a burial day, had to be given up entirely to the duty. They were the only ones in the small room apart from the Llansulien policeman who had taken his helmet off and undone the top buttons of his coat. While they were waiting for the coroner, they talked about many things: the harvest, the weather, and the state of the nation. It was the policeman who brought up the subject of the inquest.

'You will be foreman, Mr Davies,' he said to Davies, Hyde Park, turning around to the others to add: 'Somebody or other has to be made a foreman, as a kind of chairman.'

'And you would find nobody better fitted in the neighbourhood,' said a very small man.

'All right!' said Davies, 'I will do that much for the old

friend. After all, Daniel Jones's end was a very strange one, wasn't it?'

'No good came of him,' said one farmer, now that everybody was finding his tongue, 'ever since he started neglecting Rhos-y-grug. When a man starts prying about, putting his mind on far-off things, you won't get much out of him.'

'Whatsoever thy hand doeth,' said Dafydd Ifans, searching for a verse, 'do with all thy might.'

'I don't know about that,' said another juror, who suspected that the reference to 'prying' was aimed directly at him, 'there's a danger when a man cares too much about the things of this world. I could say that in one sense Daniel Jones put his mind on matters of the other world. . .'

'The other world!' exclaimed Robert the Rock.

'In a sense, I said,' replied the farmer; 'he had more pleasure out of Havilah than many a man gets from his farm.'

'You say what you will,' said Davies, Hyde Park, 'there was something very noble about the old Squire after all: he donated fifty pounds towards the memorial hall; yes, and there was the Havilah business, too.'

'There is a verse,' said Robert the Rock, 'about looking for the gold that will not perish.'

'Gold or no gold,' said Davies, suspecting that the last remark had been aimed at him, 'gold or no gold, no one at this inquest is going to try to make out that Daniel Jones was out of his mind or anything like that. I'm the foreman.'

'Remember, gentlemen,' said the policeman, 'that you haven't heard the evidence yet.'

At this point they could hear the coroner's car arriving, and the policeman put his helmet on and buttoned up his coat.

The coroner was a solicitor from the southern end of the county and he had brought a doctor with him.

'Do you want to see the body?'

Everybody nodded and all of them went into the next room, feeling as if they were facing something they could not explain. Then on they moved to yet another room. The coroner went ahead with his work without wasting any time. He called a distant cousin of Daniel Jones to identify the body, then the little boy who had discovered the body, and, when Shaci the Smith had told his story and the doctor had given his evidence, the coroner asked: 'Was anything found on the body?'

'Yes,' replied the policeman, 'a map and a will. Here they are. And ten pound notes as well.'

Everybody's imagination was fired by the mention of the word 'will', and as if he realized this and was determined to keep that exhibit until the end, the policeman took the map to the table. It was a map torn from some Bible or other, and it had fallen to pieces from being folded often. One part of the map was blacker than the rest of it, as if somebody had been pointing at that spot often. The coroner looked at the map.

'Mesopotamia looks very black,' said the coroner.

'That was the lightest part of the world for Daniel Jones,' said the foreman.

'And now,' said the coroner, 'for the will.'

The will had been drawn out by a solicitor in North Wales. In it Daniel Jones bequeathed twenty acres of land in Havilah to Blaen-y-cwm Chapel, as it was there that he had seen Havilah for the first time.

'What about this land in Havilah?' asked the coroner.

'The deeds are here with the will,' replied the policeman.

'I don't know what value there is to them,' said the coroner, 'but it would be better for them to go to the treasurer of the chapel.'

'I'm the treasurer,' said the foreman.

'Something to light the fire,' remarked the coroner.

Davies, however, was more far-sighted than that; he could see the fame that would come to Blaen-y-cwm in the wake of the will. No other chapel in the Monthly Meeting, nor in the denomination, thought Davies, would have any possessions to be compared with the fields of Havilah.

'Found dead,' was the verdict of the inquest.

Daniel Jones was buried in the Blaen-y-cwm cemetery by

the Reverend John Elis from Llansulien. John Elis had known him well and had spoken to him often. John Elis was a strange man at funerals. When he used to bury anybody well known for his godliness and virtue, he would hardly mention those qualities, but, if he were called upon to bury some worthless creature or lame sheep, he would let himself go to describe some of the good things in the life of 'our dear brother'.

At Daniel Jones's funeral, the old words were spoken: '... and the place thereof shall know it no more. But the mercy of the Lord is from everlasting to everlasting...' There followed the most popular Welsh funeral hymn about being able to see the whole journey of the desert from the hills of Jerusalem.

John Elis preached a sermon, using as his text the verse: 'The kingdom of heaven is like unto treasure hid in a field; that which when a man hath found, he hideth, and for joy thereof goeth and selleth all that he hath, and buyeth that field.'

The sermon flowed on and on through the mind of Deio the Hewl. Who would have thought that the Squire of Havilah would have merited the attention of the Lord?

An Overdose of Sun

EIGRA LEWIS ROBERTS

(translated by the author)

FOR the first time, ever, she had to move away from the sun. She had suffered it for an hour, only to spite the young ones on the beach. They had made it clear, right from the start, that she was not welcome; that the beach was their playground. They reminded her of the midges that used to swarm above the river on summer evenings. She would challenge the midges, determined to finish her journey, although longing for the feel of ice-cold water on her face. She would have challenged these, too, were it not for the sun.

Now they would assume that it was they, and not the sun, that had made her leave the beach. As she sometimes ran for a bus, the rain splattering against her legs, or as she fought the wind, she was still young. Some people believed that it was the early seasons of the year that showed one at his best. She found it easier to be young in winter, when the little vigour that remained within her was as evident as an evergreen in an avenue of withered trees. The sun was a cruel thing, revealing one's age as it did the dust on furniture.

Once she had welcomed it, greedily. She would inject it into her flesh, like a drug. If only she could again suck its warmth into her veins and feel it surge through her body. But she had lost her nerve and was afraid of its power.

On the edge of the promenade she was caught in a web of deck chairs, where the middle-aged sat, their legs entwined like cross-stitches. Here the past was bottled like perfume. How pleasant it would be to set her chair amidst them, its canvas between her and the sun. They would accept her as one of them; would let her proceed in their company. And they would willingly let her stop now and again to explore a new smell or to seek its sensation. But she was too heavily burdened and could not hope to catch up with them. Reluctantly she dragged herself past and made her way towards the benches.

There was room for one, right on the very edge. The beach could not be seen from the benches, only the very crown of the sea with the occasional sailing boat woven into it like hair ribbon. Its smell, too, was kept at a distance, and only an echo of it was caught as the gulls hovered above or as a child dripped past. The sun was trapped in the trees overhead. A few lukewarm drops would filter through every now and again.

It was here that the old people sat, a long line of them, linked together like a chain. By her side sat an old woman, her dress hanging loose at the waist – an old woman, flat-chested, long and tough, like a man.

Beyond her sat an old man, his stomach resting on his knees. She knew, if she chose to tickle him under the chin, that a gurgle of laughter would rise from his belly, like bubbles in a lemonade bottle. His eyes were sunken and a faded blue emanated from them, reminding her of the glimmer of light at the far end of a tunnel.

It was strange how men seemed to become gentler as the years passed, while the women became tougher. The men, as they remembered, content with licking the butter off the stale bread; the women eager to touch the bread, to crumble it between their fingers.

What were they looking for, she wondered, here in no man's land? Were old people greedier than they used to be? Her grandmother never ventured farther than the end of the lane. How disappointed she would have been if grandmother had ever insisted on deserting her world. Old people should stay at home, being tempered before their own fires; guarding treasures that they had accumulated over the years.

She, too, should have stayed at home. But others had

packed her case and pushed her on to a train. She could see them now, swarming into the station like a retinue; elbowing one another in their eagerness to reach her. Friends, who had been neighbours of hers, mind and body; relations who felt that they had a right to her, as blood was thicker than water.

They had tried everything before they had agreed to let her go: the numerous cups of tea, dark and sweet, and the sympathy, arranged delicately, and as sickly as cream cakes.

There was always someone there, as if they had agreed to do shift work. They would have respected a widow. Her memories would have been beautiful enough for her to have been left in their company. But a woman whose husband had left her was like a prisoner whiling away his days in a condemned cell, conscious that one life was coming to an end and that another was beginning; assuming that he could accept such beliefs.

They were ready to stand between her and the fiendish memories that could terrorize her at night. A sister of hers had insisted on lending her a child, as patronizing women share out library books in hospital, to make the sick forget their illness.

But she wanted to dwell on her illness; to remember how and when it had started; what it was like to be healthy. They treated their words as a quarryman would trim his slates, squaring the edges and smoothing the surface so that they would do no harm. They were determined to place a fancy label on her sickness instead of acknowledging it for the cancer it was. But she wanted to scratch the scabs off her memory, making past experiences bleed.

Once experiences were as easy to acquire as shells on a beach. There was little difference, then, between one shell and another, and in the sun they all had some virtue. She had loaded herself with them. What a shame that no one came around collecting memories as gipsies collected old rags. What a relief it would be to be able to hang the paper bags on a door knob and find, in the morning, that the bags and all their contents had gone.

They expected her to be able to leave her past on the beach for the tide to carry away. Its strength would surely succeed where their tea and sympathy had failed.

But she knew that she would have to follow each memory to its source before it could be aborted from her mind. She would have to see, not the young tree in the garden, but the hole that her husband had dug to uphold its roots in the early days of their marriage. She would have to hear their laughter as the soil yielded to the shoot; she would have to feel their concern when a straight young branch was severed by a storm.

She would have to see, not the bare finger, but the ring that had once adorned it. She would have to remember the cold sweat of his fingers on that challenging wedding day; the dryness and warmth that vibrated within them as their hands touched; remember the terror that she had felt, once, when she thought that the ring was lost; the cold biting into her finger like chilblains.

If it were not for them, she would, by now, have erased all her husband's finger marks; she would have opened the windows, wide, so that the wind would destroy all his echoes. She would have changed the course of the garden paths and would have filled the little pond with dirt and gravel.

Now they were waiting, to welcome her back, deaf and dumb, so that they could teach her a fresh vocabulary, lead her into new experiences. She would let them dress and adorn her like a baby doll, and would feel nothing.

One day she would come, again, and sit on a bench like this, with the old folk. And she would be flat-chested and wizened, like the old woman by her side. Perhaps she would walk past the people on her edge of the promenade; the ones who were content to place the canvas between themselves and the sun.

Standing there, she would see the beach that supported bold things, like the sun and the young ones. She would return to the bench and sit there, letting the past crumble between her fingers. And she knew now how hard and stale it would be.

The House in Builth Crescent

MOIRA DEARNLEY

THE house ought to have been handsome. Situated on a crescent favoured by the eminent Victorians of the town, it was three storeys high, with three rows of nicely proportioned windows and quite an imposing front door, with a modest flight of marble steps sheltered by a canopy with pillars. From the top floor you could glimpse, over the tree-tops and between the chimney-pots of the houses opposite, the sea. But the house also had a basement, and this basement was occupied by the Earnshaws who exuded ugliness. It was an ugly house.

Dr Mair Morgan, a Welsh witch with a certain amount of missionary zeal in her temperament, went down the area steps, placed a basket covered with a white teacloth on the doorstep, collapsed her umbrella, and rapped on the knocker. Mrs Earnshaw had a judas for inspecting callers, but even so appeared tardily, peeping over the six-inch chain that protected her from violent death, or worse. Dr Morgan identified herself in professionally sunny tones, and was welcomed effusively. Mrs Earnshaw was dressed for the great outdoors that threatened the Bastille barricades of her front door. The nobly savage head was swathed in a concertina of transparent plastic, the gross, pendulous torso and elephantine legs enveloped in a pink macintosh cape. Her mittened fingers darted through the slits in the cape and cradled the young woman's admired cheekbones. If it took courage to eradicate that smile full of green tombstone teeth, Dr Morgan was not one to flinch from suffering humanity. Guided by the mittened hands, she kissed the old woman on the lips.

Mrs Earnshaw had been expecting Dr Morgan's mother, Mrs Beatie Morgan, for days. The eyes that stuck out like

marbles on either side of a nose that had represented everything that was arrogant, moneyed, and possibly handsome
in the days of her youth, focused greedily on the basket. But
today was pension day. She had waited until the last possible
moment. But it was now half-past three, and it was essential
to get to the Post Office before the onset of coshing, raping,
robbing darkness on the trees and tall houses of Builth
Crescent. In the meanwhile, Albert would protect their
worldly wealth. The deeds of the house and a clutch of
documents and possessions whose value the world could but
guess at were locked into a Gladstone bag. A chain that was
padlocked to the handle of the Gladstone bag was padlocked also to Mr Earnshaw's right wrist. A chain that was
padlocked to Mr Earnshaw's left wrist was padlocked also to
the brass bed-post.

'They would have to kill him first,' triumphed Mrs Earnshaw.

The sacrificial victim had a thermos flask of tea set
charitably near his right hand which, despite the fetters,
was vouchsafed some flexibility. Dr Morgan would, of course,
run along to the Post Office later on. Mrs Earnshaw divested
herself of her outer garments and picked her way through
piles of yellow newspapers to end her husband's vigil, while
her visitor took another devious route to the study. The
Earnshaws lived in their bedroom; indeed, they lived in their
bed. Knowing them as well as she did, Mrs Beatie Morgan
might well have been shown into the bedroom. Even in those
days when Mrs Earnshaw was in her hale and hearty thirties,
Beatie's duties had revolved around her mistress's high brass
bedstead. (But Beatie had never so much as glimpsed the
rest of the bedroom furniture; it had always been shrouded
in dust-sheets.) Dr Morgan, knowing about the dust-sheets
and the human nest of a bed, was nevertheless prevented by
her youth and virginity from being invited into the bedroom. It had been different when Mrs Beatie Morgan was
a girl. She had been the maid-of-all-work, and privileged to
see all, starting the day as she always did by ascending three

flights of stairs with their breakfast tray, gourmet Cooper's Oxford marmalade and butter fresh from the churn at Free Fold Farm.

Carrying the basket that Mrs Earnshaw was hoarding for a ten-minute future of salivating anticipation, Dr Morgan entered the subterraneous study that smelt of grave-cold dust and mildewed books. She had visited that room with her mother once or twice a year since childhood, but this was the first occasion on which she had come alone. The pathos of those film-set folding canvas chairs and two Christmas cards on the mantelpiece (a brother in Harrogate remembered annually his brother in Builth Crescent, and Mrs Beatie Morgan remembered her old employers) had been lost on the child, Mair, who had sought along the bookshelves evidence of a saturnine but gigantic intellect. For Mr Earnshaw was well known, albeit the fact was whispered where little pitchers have big ears, to be an Atheist. The little girl, Mair, had found books on country matters, dustjackets decorated with sprays of cherry blossom or linoprints of cart-horses ploughing great corrugated fields. Before the war the Earnshaws had rented a house in the country, for weekends and the long, hot summers, from the very farm where Mrs Earnshaw's cousins still laboured for their living, and touched a cap to a woman whose father had made a fortune from wet fish and a later diversification into greengrocery. Mrs Beatie Morgan was known to expatiate on that country garden at Free Fold House (tended by one of the labouring cousins) where an abundance of fresh vegetables and luscious soft fruits came to early maturity; she was fond of recalling those shallow baskets of fungi, the dew-wet harvest brought home by Mr Earnshaw in the early morning: pale colours, ominous shapes, but not, after all, poisonous. Dr Morgan, idly remembering other people's lives, looked again at the books and found there the self-same orchards and simplistic rural delights. Still no evidence of the death of God. Mr Earnshaw had once presented her with a Hilaire Belloc, and she had found there the diabolical terrors that clever people's children not only enjoy, but understand. The Earnshaws had had no children to suffer agonizing, hilarious death.

His chains fell off, his heart rose free (Dr Morgan's mind rang with cheerful hymns), and Mr Earnshaw appeared in the wake of his wife. His head was as bald as a speckled egg, his velvet jacket was wine-coloured but greasy around the collar, and his trousers voluminously girded to a shrunken body by a leather belt. His sandals, also made of leather, suggested vegetarianism. Eyes gleaming mildly over half-spectacles, he presented himself with alacrity for Dr Morgan's kiss that smacked of loving-kindness.

'And how is your dear mother, Mair? *How* is dear Beatie? Nothing wrong, I trust?'

There was a great deal wrong. But the rich fruit cake and Christmas puddings had fortunately been made before the cancer was discovered, and Beatie's daughter was at least capable of making a few mince-pies and buying fruit and nuts and chocolate biscuits to fill the basket. But, Mrs Earnshaw complained, there was a great deal wrong with her legs, and nothing a clean, healing knife could do would put *them* right. Mr Earnshaw was ordered to the kitchen to make a cup of tea and to open a packet of Marie biscuits. The occasion warranted ceremony. Apart from breakfast foods, they had never kept much food in the pantry at Builth Crescent. Mrs Beatie Morgan, when she was Beatie Bevan and maid-of-all-work, usually fetched the lunches from Woolworth's. There was a special bag that took the pile of dinner-plates, and the dishes of hot pudding and custard on top. Mrs Earnshaw, explaining her symptoms to the young doctor, unpacked the Christmas fare and drivelled visibly. Mr Earnshaw returned with the tea.

'Dear Beatie always remembers my figs,' he said. 'Is she very poorly, my dear?'

'She's making a wonderful recovery,' replied Dr Morgan happily, convinced of the value of prayer and medical skills. 'Wonderful.'

'She's a wonderful person,' agreed Mr Earnshaw. 'Always was a wonderful girl, wasn't she?'

'Wonderful,' agreed Mrs Earnshaw emphatically. 'If scatter-brained.'

Mrs Beatie Morgan, when she was Beatie Bevan, was instructed by her mistress to make sure that on her way home from work she removed a rusty tin that a couple of hooligans had kicked on to the bottom marble step. Beatie, rushing home to change into a frock suitable for wearing to the pictures (she and Idris Morgan were courting), ignored the offending object until seven-thirty the next morning when, under cover of darkness, she dropped it into the ash-bin. Mrs Earnshaw, however, had already pinned a large notice to her bedroom door: I DO NOT WISH TO SPEAK TO YOU UNTIL YOU HAVE REMOVED THAT TIN. Thirty years after the event, Beatie still recalled the incident with tears of laughter running down her face. You needed a sense of humour, she told her family.

'Mair is the moral of her mother,' added Mrs Earnshaw. 'The very moral, isn't she, Albert?'

'Just like her mother,' agreed Mr Earnshaw. 'Your mother was a very pretty girl, Mair.'

'Yes, indeed. She was a very pretty girl, wasn't she, Albert?'

Mrs Earnshaw closed one marble eye in an arch wink, grinning widely at her fellow-conspirator, Dr Morgan. Her flesh under the layers of lacy-knit cardigans wobbled with silent mirth.

Mrs Earnshaw, Mrs Beatie Morgan remembered, had always been convinced that her husband was a lady's man. In those days he had had enough hair to arrange in the wrong direction over his scalp, and he had favoured a monocle. There had once been a fearful row over a cheque-book stub that was still extant, no doubt, in the Gladstone bag. Only a very stupid man would have scrawled Mrs Gwyn-Jones's name in such a place if he had been guilty. That he was innocent, that Mrs Gwyn-Jones had done him a small favour purely in a business sense (Mr Earnshaw dabbled for a while in local politics), could be proven. Documentary evidence as to the nature of the transaction was locked up in a bureau at Builth Crescent.

'TAKE ME TO BUILTH CRESCENT,' Mrs Earnshaw had thundered from the French window of the Free Fold House drawing-room, and advancing across the carpet she took a gloved hand out of her coat pocket, and stuck the short, hard weapon concealed in her glove under Mr Earnshaw's rib-cage.

Mr Earnshaw did as he was bidden. Beatie was commanded to follow: a mile along the lane from Free Fold House, between banks of primroses with lambs in the fields beyond, fifteen miles on the bus through the Easter countryside, with the weapon thrust into Mr Earnshaw's side, with Beatie aghast and agog in the seat behind them. They walked through the empty streets of the town, Mrs Earnshaw walking sideways to keep her husband covered, and Beatie trailing along behind. Mrs Earnshaw was inexplicably and vastly satisfied with the papers spread out for her inspection. With a wink and ecstatic grin, she had shown Beatie (but not Mr Earnshaw) the folded ruler in her glove.

Dr Morgan, required to hold a tea-cup and a Marie biscuit, removed her own fur-backed gloves. One pearl of modest price on a thin gold band on the ring finger of short, clean hands indicated her situation in life. The Earnshaws already knew of her engagement. They had preserved every issue of the local evening paper since their own betrothal in 1922. They offered their congratulations .

'Two doctors in the house,' smiled Mr Earnshaw tenderly, being the eighth person to make the joke.

'He wouldn't be a surgeon?' asked Mrs Earnshaw reverently, but looking down the rolling slopes of her body towards the swollen legs zipped laboriously into black suede bootees with astrakhan around the ankles.

'Oh good gracious no! We're both *very* newly qualified.' Mr Earnshaw looked hard at his wife.

'Not a great deal of money to start with,' he hazarded.

Riches untold, thought Dr Morgan, who had never had much of anything. But she held her peace, not liking to speak of money to people who now appeared to have none at all.

'Your husband-to-be is a local boy,' stated Mrs Earnshaw, having read her evening paper carefully, but there was a quizzical note in her voice.

'Well, not exactly. David comes from Port Talbot.'

They already knew this. But if they were to act wisely, they needed to know more. It was very nearly clear that Dr David Price must also be a product of the urban Welsh struggle to educate its sons and daughters. But there must be solicitors and dentists even in Port Talbot. They couldn't be absolutely certain that Dr Price's father existed in the momentary black-and-red glare and darkness of the steel works. Old-fashioned, open-hearth furnaces flared simultaneously in two pairs of inquisitive eyes, but Dr Morgan was studying the hen-like robin on the Christmas card from Harrogate.

'I used to go to Port Talbot on business,' observed Mr Earnshaw. 'Political business.'

Mr Earnshaw's business in South Wales hadn't been primarily political, however. He had come from Yorkshire to teach in a small bad school run as a private venture by a distant cousin. By virtue of birth alone, Mr Earnshaw was a gentleman. But the state of the family fortunes had made a university education and entry into one of the professions out of the question. At respectable lodgings near the school he rapidly engaged the affections of a fellow-boarder, Miss Sadie Jones, who was still at the Training College. Her parents, the fish-and-vegetable merchants, had just removed to an ostentatious villa in Twickenham. Miss Jones, who had never got on with her mother, preferred to stay in her home town. Mr Earnshaw decided that the eccentricities of a rich man's daughter were worth bearing, and his reward was the house in Builth Crescent, a wedding-present from her dutiful if not affectionate parents. There they lived in relative glory until the Furies hounded them to the basement in 1948.

'A very talented place, Port Talbot,' confided Mrs Earnshaw to her guest. 'Film stars and Trades Union officials.'

'And doctors, my dear,' added Mr Earnshaw, tenderly again, and his wife heaved with laughter.

'When is the wedding to be?' asked Mrs Earnshaw. 'They tell me young people don't save nowadays.'

'We hope to get married in the summer. July probably.'

'A white wedding?'

'Oh yes! All the trimmings.'

'Your mother had a very pretty wedding,' said Mr Earnshaw.

'Yes, but it was a pity about the war.'

Beatie Bevan, marrying Idris Morgan, had worn a floral dress with a sweetheart neckline, long tight sleeves, and a narrow belt with a buckle. She had also worn a hard white hat that shot up nine inches above the forehead and sloped quickly down to the nape of the neck. The Earnshaws had given her cut-glass cruets to put on the Utility sideboard.

'It'll be a big expense for your mother and father.'

'Indeed it will.' If there was the slightest wrinkling of the smooth forehead on that guiltless, blue-eyed face, it was momentary. 'But they want to do it. Naturally. They're very fond of David.'

Dr Morgan complacently patted the large fur hat where the fez of guipure lace would sit on sleek black hair in the summertime.

'We have always meant to do right by dear Beatie,' suggested Mr Earnshaw.

'The jewellery,' indicated Mrs Earnshaw. 'Indeed, I have already given over some of the lesser things during the course of my lifetime. Perhaps you were unaware, Mair? The rest is Willed.'

The lesser things consisted of a large medallion on a chain, with twin portraits, rather jaggedly cut out of sepia photographs, of the fish-and-vegetable merchant and his lady. This, together with one perfectly good cufflink in solid gold, and half a cufflink, also in solid gold, had been transported in the Gladstone bag in a taxi from Builth Crescent

to Tawe Road on a November evening in 1948. Mrs Morgan
had laid them carefully aside in case Mrs Earnshaw should
ever bring the Gladstone bag in another taxi to reclaim her
property.

'Perhaps I'll look out a little trinket for you to wear on
your wedding day,' smiled Mrs Earnshaw, revealing all those
long, grooved teeth. 'Something old. *I* wore a blue garter
above my knee and hoped it wouldn't show. Skirts were
very short in those days, dear!'

She had also worn one of those veils with a frill over the
eyebrows. All the brides of the era had had a slightly
neanderthal look.

'But jewellery,' suggested Mr Earnshaw, more to his wife
than to his guest, 'is neither meat nor drink. Certainly not
a roof over one's head.'

He jerked his eyes towards the ceiling so that his wife
was sure to understand.

'But lovely to have,' soothed Dr Morgan.

'Did you ever see over the house?' asked Mr Earnshaw.

The change of subject was sudden, but Dr Morgan was
polite, interested.

'Just once, I think. When I was a little girl.'

She remembered sunlight on bare, blanched floorboards
and a view over a tangled garden at the back of the house.
There had been an excursion up shallow, cracked paving
stones to the summer-house, and small, hard, unripe apples
lying in the green grass. The fruit was full of wriggling
maggots. Nothing there for a small child.

'Would you care to see it again? Young women like
houses, I believe.'

'Albert is very proud of my house,' explained Mrs Earnshaw.

'I'd love to,' enthused Dr Morgan, flexing her cold feet,
glad to move.

'Now? It'll be getting dark soon.'

'Love to,' she beamed, pulling on her gloves again. 'A
quick look round and then I'll pop along to the Post Office
for you.'

'Just like your mother,' said Mr Earnshaw, placing his cup very carefully beside the robin. But it clattered a little in the saucer.

'I'll stay put,' said Mrs Earnshaw. 'My legs.'

At the top of the basement stairs, the floor of the main entrance-hall was laid with maroon and emerald tiles. The staircase spiralled elegantly to the floors above. Beatie Bevan, on call for ten hours a day to perform a myriad petty duties, had never had to break her back with hard work, she would allow that. The Earnshaws had never been house-proud. The bedding, for instance, was collected weekly by van, while the long woolly under-garments favoured by Mr Earnshaw and the ballooning underwear favoured by his wife, were attended to by the mistress herself. The soap, sold expensively wrapped in oiled paper, was rubbed long and lovingly over every square inch of every noxious garment. Each garment was put to soak separately in an individual bowl. The tower of bowls was left in the kitchen for a week, ten days, longer sometimes. Solid jelly, Beatie recalled. Then, coming in to work long before it was light, she would become aware of dim presences on high. Mrs Earnshaw would have threaded her lines criss-cross from banister to banister, the huge garments hung to drip down the well of the staircase on to a soggy mat of newspapers – expendable newspapers, provided by Woolworth to keep the dinners hot. Dr Morgan wondered fleetingly whether Mrs Earnshaw ever washed clothes nowadays. Both the Earnshaws smelt sour.

'Shall we go up?' invited Mr Earnshaw. 'We'll start at the top and work down.'

There was scarcely enough light. Flexes hung crookedly from ceilings, empty of light bulbs. Mr Earnshaw held on to the banister, putting both feet on a step before attempting the next one. Dr Morgan took his arm. She was lithe, healthy. She supported him up to the first floor and on up to the second. As they climbed, he assured her several times (panting a little) that she mustn't worry about his being chained to the bed. He found it wise to humour his wife's little ways as she wasn't too well these days. Mair would have noticed that. Dr Morgan had indeed noted symptoms of paranoia, but she preferred to make soothing noises to her host.

The rooms opening off the landings were shadowy and empty, for the Earnshaws had fallen on hard times eventually. It was, as Mrs Beatie Morgan averred, their own fault. In their prosperous days Mrs Earnshaw had received occasional presents of money from her parents, but Mr Earnshaw had never been anything grander than a teacher at the scrubby little private school. They had squandered money. Even the Woolworth lunches were an extravagance, evidence of Mrs Earnshaw's pathological laziness (except that she laundered the underclothes once a month). Beatie remembered long summer days, with a hired car and a uniformed chauffeur, mile after mile of hot countryside, a hamper under the trees or a cold luncheon at an inn where cattle stood knee-deep in water: there were photographs. Mrs Earnshaw had worn a tam for such jaunts, Mr Earnshaw a panama, and Beatie a wide-brimmed straw hat over pretty but sulky features, her sense of humour not being in evidence. But things changed. War broke out, Beatie married Idris, and Mr Earnshaw had a long illness. He retired early, without a pension. Mrs Earnshaw's parents, who both died about this time, left virtually nothing. For years they had lived in style on their capital. (Beatie remembered a week spent at the villa in Twickenham, the whirl of dinner-parties and visits to the theatre, which she enjoyed as if she had been the Earnshaws' daughter rather than their maid.) For a while after his retirement the Earnshaws lived much as they had always lived. The furniture at Builth Crescent was sold piecemeal and they lived on the proceeds. When there was no more furniture to sell, they descended to the basement. They intended, of course, to let the upper part of the house.

'You can see the sea from here,' said Mr Earnshaw, gasping lungfuls of dusty air, and they crossed the room to the barred window. 'Mrs Earnshaw means to let this part of the house. The view makes it an attractive proposition.'

Dr Morgan knew full well that Mrs Earnshaw had been meaning to let the house for nearly twenty years. She had heard all about it. That evening in 1948 when the Earnshaws had arrived in Tawe Road with the medallion and the cuff-links, they were intending, so the massive handwriting that leaked tar-like from Mrs Earnshaw's dominating pen had assured the waiting Morgans, to at last 'do something' for their erstwhile maid, Beatie Bevan that was. The something, glowered Idris Morgan, after the Earnshaws had gone away again at midnight, in a taxi, was surely (though it had never actually been mentioned) the offer of an unfurnished flat in that great barn of a place in Builth Crescent. A resident housekeeper more like, he had growled, and a jack-of-all-trades to keep the old place from falling down. But the Earn-shaws had sat in the snug house that Beatie kept 'like a little palace' (as the neighbours whispered, not charitably but truthfully), and eaten grossly of Beatie's hot supper, and presumably realized, despite being thick-skinned, that no-one in their right mind would exchange even a council house for a draughty, run-down flat with a couple of ailing, ageing people (distressed gentlefolk you might call them) crawling for help in the basement. The Earnshaws went home, and never did let the house. If they had let the accommodation unfurnished, they would have had no control over their tenants (filthy loud-mouthed scum who would kick the panelled doors and scrawl graffiti on the walls). They had no money to refurnish the rooms, and in the meanwhile they paid no rates on the three bare floors above their heads.

Dr Morgan was trying hard to see the sea through the dark clammy rain that made no sound on the window-panes. She had no sense of the ludicrous, but she saw that what her parents had rejected she might inherit. Her suspicions were confirmed.

'Shall we go down?' asked Mr Earnshaw. 'The rooms on the first floor are pleasant. Nice ceilings. But of course they don't have the view. The ground-floor rooms are, of course, exquisite. Beautiful plaster-work and those rather nice tiles I'm sure you noticed in the hall. But naturally a suite of rooms like that would be rather expensive for newly weds.'

Mr Earnshaw's ignorance of the residential arrangements at the hospital – and of his visitor's future plans – was total. Dr Morgan saw that the old man's velvet jacket was inadequate protection against the sub-arctic temperature in those rooms. It was unusual for her to be pained by the plight of an individual human being. Her benevolence was naturally diffuse. An acute sense of another person's suffering would have made the practice of her profession intolerable.

'Yes, let's go down. You must be getting cold, Mr Earnshaw.'

Mr Earnshaw ran the tips of his fingers down the scarlet mohair of her coat sleeve, from shoulder to elbow.

'Just like your mother. Beatie always used to look after me.'

She looked conscientiously over the first-floor rooms, and then over the ground-floor rooms, but briskly because of the cold. It was too dark to see the plaster-work in any detail. They crossed the hall, her heels clicking on the slippery tiles. They went down the basement stairs. Mrs Earnshaw was waiting for them among the newspapers in the lobby. She was grinning expectantly into the darkness. She was holding the pension book.

Dr Morgan was engaged to an evangelical young man with abnormally strong feelings about the plight of the Third World. She would have to explain this. Under the forty-watt bulb, she explained to them, her blue eyes smiling on a distant prospect of medical missionary work with the beloved David and the Nepalese, in the mountains, in the sun.

'It's the least we can do,' she said meekly – she who had, with her betrothed, inherited the earth. 'We've been so incredibly fortunate, haven't we?'

Blind Date

JANE EDWARDS

(translated by D. Llwyd Morgan)

I'VE borrowed this frock from Gwen; it's a pink one with a mauve velvet ribbon around the waist. Everybody knows it's a choir frock, but it's prettier than the one I've got, though it's much too big and miles too long. I've been standing for hours in the glass, studying myself, turning and twisting the frock all ways to see if I can make it look better. Gwen has warned me not to pin it in or tack the hem. It's that sort of material that shows everything.

'What if we lapped the waist like this over the ribbon,' said Gwen, 'and pretend that it's a blouse and skirt you've got.' But to no avail. 'Don't worry,' said Gwen, 'I'll lend you my high heels. It won't look so long then.'

'I'm not size fours yet,' I said peevishly.

Then we heard Margaret's voice talking with Mam in the kitchen. 'Comb your hair. I'll go and tell her you won't be two hoots,' said Gwen.

Margaret had on her a brand-new frock not yet out of its creases. A yellow one, with butterflies. 'Pretty. New?' I asked.

'From the club,' she answered, 'a big parcel from Littlewoods arrived on the L.M.S. yesterday.'

'Lucky you,' I said, turning to look at Mam.

She was feeding the baby, and struggling to tuck one breast under her clothes before getting the other out. Her teats were long and red and dripping. I really don't know why she couldn't have gone to the parlour to feed. I'd say *teats* was the ugliest word in the world.

'You've had a bath,' I told Margaret, seeing her nose shining and her blonde hair a cluster of curls on her shoulders. She lives in a council house. About a year ago all the council houses got a bathroom with hot water heated from the fire, and a toilet with a chain outside. We get our bath in the wash-house every other Saturday when Mam puts a fire under the boiler. It's ever so warm there. You can't see farther than the tip of your nose for steam. Dad still holds that there's nothing like a bath in front of a roaring great fire. But Mam says this is more private, and that it's important for us to keep with the times. 'That costs money,' says Dad. He's an old spendthrift. He'd be astounded to know that the bath costs three pounds ten. Mam pays half a crown weekly, by postal order.

'Where did you get that pink lipstick?' I asked Margaret.

'Borrowed some from Helen next door,' she said. 'I'm going to buy some next time I go to Woolworth. Outdoor Girl: only costs tenpence.' I'd be ever so glad if Mam believed in buying a new one instead of that red thing that tastes old like Adam.

'Are you ready now?' Margaret asked. She was looking at her watch as if she was on tenterhooks.

'What's the hurry? Nothing calls,' said Mam.

'Doesn't she know then?' said Margaret when we were out of the entry.

'Gracious me no, or none of my feet would be out. Does your mother know?'

'She never bothers.'

We walk for a while without saying a word. That's the effect talking about mothers has on you.

Margaret said: 'That pink suits your suntan.'

'It's a bit big though.'

Margaret is a tall well-built girl and I'm a small skinny scrag. And when we walk together everyone turns his head to look at us. But because it's Saturday night there aren't so many about. Neli Harriet as usual is in the telephone kiosk. 'Looking for lovers, that's what she's doing,' said Margaret, 'they call it Neli Harriet's bungalow.'

Then Deina Jones Tyddyn toddles out of her house, a

stained shawl over her shoulders. She stands stunned-like in our path, thrusts her nose into our faces. 'And where are you two going on a Saturday night like this, all made up as there never were a pair?'

'Date,' Margaret boasted.

'Points at your age! Home scrubbing floors or learning verses, that's your place. Does your mother know?' she asked me.

'She will now,' said Margaret, stepping out of her way.

'Is that a choir frock you're wearing?' she asked, feeling the stuff with her forefinger and thumb.

'Cheek!' I said to Margaret.

'A real busybody.'

It was beginning to get chilly by now. The sun had gone behind a cloud, and a breeze was blowing a leaf or two across the street.

'Where's that pretty green frock with long sleeves you had?' said Margaret.

'The one that made a paper noise? Gone too small.' It was Bill who liked that frock. 'I like your frock,' he said one afternoon as we stood by Nelson's Tower looking at the others throwing stones into the river. 'It makes a noise like tissue paper.' His voice was different as if he were hoarse, or as if it were nearly breaking. 'Mam made it,' I said shyly, and left him. We didn't speak to each other for weeks afterwards. And we're still a bit bashful.

'I've got a pen-friend,' said Margaret. She pulled a piece of paper from her pocket. 'Through Radio Luxembourg. Perhaps I'll write to him tomorrow. Terry's his name, Terry Wayne O'Brien. Here's his address.'

'I like your handwriting,' I said.

'From London.'

'So I see. Gee, you've got good handwriting. Much better than mine. Everyone's saying you should have passed scholarship.'

'No one to push me.'

A kick for me, that one.

'Would you like Terry to find you a pen-friend?'

She was saying the name *Terry* as if she'd known him all her life. I honestly didn't like the way she said it.

'I wouldn't dare. Mam would half murder me.'

'Needn't worry, he could put his letter in with Terry's. We wouldn't be any the worse for trying. Perhaps he'd get a student for you.'

A student. Like Mr Harrington, who came to teach us Scripture and biology. Mr Harrington from somewhere far away like Surrey, his hair yellow as gold, his eyes blue and soft. Mr Harrington who was always so kind and tender. Mr Harrington who would duck under the desk every time he heard an aeroplane. Mr Harrington.

Margaret said, 'You're very quiet.'

'I was thinking.'

'Thought so. Perhaps you're nervous.'

'A little.'

'You're shivering.'

'Cold.'

'You should eat more. I get two dinners every day. School dinner and another when Dad gets home.'

That's why she's bonny. I can't stand food. That's why I'm scraggy. 'Perhaps I'd better nip home and fetch my cardigan.'

'There's no time. The boys won't wait for us. Hey, do you like my scent? It's Evening in Paris.' She lifts her hair so that I can sniff behind her ear.

'Mmm ... nice. Nain had some of that from Auntie Meri as a Christmas box. A small blue bottle with the Eiffel Tower on it. Nain only uses it for chapel. Two spots on her hand-kerchief.'

'You're not supposed to put scent on clothes.'

'Leusa says the nuns say that only people who don't wash use scent,' I said, to stop her having the last word every time.

'Huh! They need it. Do you know what I hear?'

'What?'

'That they go to bed in their clothes.'

'Never!'

'Do you know what else I heard? They daren't look at

themselves in a glass or in a shop-window, or look at their breasts when they change underwear.'

'I don't either,' I said shyly.

'Well, you should. How will you know one isn't bigger than the other? Or that you haven't got three like that woman in the *News of the World*?'

The *News of the World* is terrible. It's got stories to raise the hair on your head, and keep you awake all night. True stories about women turning into men and men turning into women, and every calamity that could hit you.

I've got goose pimples all over me. My inside is shaking like a jelly. My feet are like ice blocks and my scalp is tight and hard. My nose is red. Red and ugly as usual.

I said, 'What about turning back?'

'Turning back? No fear. Afraid or something?'

It's easy for her to talk: she knows this Frank boy. Been with him before. But not one of us has ever seen Henri, though she seems to think he's a farm-hand.

A farm-hand! My dreams don't include farm-hands. My dreams turn round students. Tall handsome students with long scarves around their necks. Students with piles of books under their arms. Merry, noisy students like those I see from the bus at Bangor. Nice respectable students – ministerials like the ones who come for a walk with us to Llyn Rhos Ddu before evening service. Like Mr Harrington.

'How old is this Henri?' I asked as we neared Fern Hill.

'Same age as Frank, I suppose.'

'How old is Frank?'

'Twenty-one.'

'Twenty-one? Heavens above, that's old.'

'You've moaned enough about schoolboys being too young for you. Don't worry. Everything will be all right as long as you don't let Henri put his tongue in your mouth.'

'Put his tongue in my mouth? Ugh!'

'It's a boy's place to try, a girl's place to refuse him.'

'Does Frank try?'

'Every boy tries.'

'What did *you* do?'

'Tell him not to.'

'And he listened?' If anyone tried it on me he'd never see the colour of me again.

'Of course he did. Do you know Olwen? Do you know what Olwen did to a boy from Llangefni way last Saturday night?' She looks into the quick of my eyes and smiles. 'She bit off a piece of his tongue.'

'Bit it off?' I can't swallow because there's a lump like a potato in my throat.

'He had to go to hospital for four stitches.'

I feel quite ill, am cold all over from thinking what I'd do should this boy Henri try such nonsense. Henri's a silly name. An old-fashioned, ugly name. A name to put anybody to shame. How can anyone with a name like that be handsome?

'Why?' I asked coyly, 'why do boys want to put their tongues in your mouth?'

'To make you sleep, of course.'

'Oh!'

'And while you're asleep they lift up your clothes, pull down your knickers, and give you a baby.'

I feel my legs giving under me. I feel my inside caving in. I was always a one for jibbing it.

'I'm not coming,' I said, looking in the roadside for a comfortable place to sit.

'Don't talk rot. Come on,' said Margaret, taking hold of my cold hand with her warm white hand. It was like a picture of a hand in a catalogue.

'I'm shivering,' I said and showed her my arms. 'Look how cold I am. I'd better go home before I catch pneumonia.'

'You won't, stupid. Henri'll warm you up like a piece of toast. Anyway, it's too late for you to turn back now.'

It's never too late. Never ever ever too late. I can run as if the devil himself was after me.

'I can hear a motor bike coming,' said Margaret. 'It's them, I tell you. Here, straighten your frock.'

It's Frank who owns the motor bike. 'Hello, girls,' he says after slapping the pedal with his heel and raising his goggles to have a look at us. He's trying to smile like a film star.

'Here's my friend,' said Margaret. And she gave me a shove towards the boy on the pillion.

'Has she got a tongue?' Frank asked.

'A tongue! Did you hear that?' said Margaret, laughing and winking at me.

'Henri, give Mags your helmet, and then we'll leave you two in peace,' said Frank.

'You needn't go,' I said sheepishly.

But away they went, and before I knew where to turn I was in Henri's arms, my head out of sight in his armpits. And I'd have stayed there all the time, even though his coat was coarse and smelled, like someone's breath in the morning. But in a while he asked, 'What about a kiss?' 'What about a kiss?' he said a second time, and put his thumb under my chin.

He had a red face and red hair and a voice that made you think of manure and pigs and muck-raking and the like.

'You're much too tall for me. I've got a crick in the neck,' I said, fed-up with his wet kisses.

'What about going to lie down in the fern?' he said.

Only lovers with bad intentions lie in the fern. 'We'll sit on the roadside,' I said.

And there we sat for I don't know how long without speaking or looking at each other.

'A motor bike's lovely,' Margaret said after the boys had turned for home. 'Would you like to have a go some time?'

'You were a long time,' I said, close to tears. 'I'd got tired of waiting for you.'

'You've got grass stains on your frock,' she said. 'Grass stains are difficult to get off. Your mother'll be raving when she sees it.'

Mam was in the wash-house, carrying hot water from the boiler and was in a lather of sweat.

'Where have you been, girl?' she asked, though she couldn't see anything through the steam.

'Only for a walk,' I said, 'only for a walk.'

Morfydd's Celebration

HARRI PRITCHARD JONES

(translated by Harri Webb)

SHE had good reason for celebrating. She raised her glass carefully with her left hand, she tried to avoid burning the fingers of her right hand with a cigarette, and a shy smile hovered around her nose.

There's wonderful it was to be having a celebration all on your own, especially like this, with strong drink and all. She felt fine, sitting in front of a cheerful fire with a bag of peppermints, and her feet up on the little stool. It would have been nice to have had Janet opposite in for a chat and to join the celebration, but there, that one's hearing was none too good, any more than her own. Never mind, she was going to have a spell and get her thoughts together, and then she was going to enjoy *Miss Universe* on the television later on, with that nice young man doing the introducing.

Morfydd was an old maid; she had never had much to do with men, but she thoroughly enjoyed watching the young girls shaping it up in their lovely long frocks and their saucy short ones. Like all the plants on the windowsill in the parlour, they were a sign of life and fun. These days you hardly ever saw a girl going out in shabby and shapeless clothes, thank goodness. The world was meant to be a happy place. Perhaps even she could have looked attractive. Only once had she ever been out properly with a boy, when she went with Leusa as company for her young man's friend, but he got as drunk as a wheel, and she hadn't broken her heart.

But there had been times when Morfydd's spirit had almost broken. Three times in her seventy-two years. The

first time was when her father had died. She was eighteen
then and looking forward to going into service at Newport,
a living-in job with a chance to see something of the world
after four years in the baker's shop. But that was not how it
was to be. Fair play to her mother, she had not expected
her to stay at home, but she could not be left on her own.
And Jack was away in Seven Sisters, married and working
underground.

The second time she had nearly gone under was when
her mother died, ten years ago, just about. But Mr Beynon,
bless him, had been very good to her. For twenty-eight years
she had kept his office in the town clean and tidy, coming
in every night, but he saw now that she needed to have her
evenings to herself, to go out and meet people. So he arranged that she should have day-time work instead, in his
house in Radyr, in place of the two women who shared it
between them. If the weather was bad, his wife would come
the quarter-mile down the hill and pick her up from the
quarter-to-nine bus before taking the youngest girl to school
and then going on herself to the hospital where she was a
doctor.

Morfydd loved the big posh house. You could have lost
her own little back-street place in the huge luxurious living-
room and the outside patio. She had every appliance she
needed for washing, cleaning, dusting, waxing, and polishing, but to start the day she preferred elbow grease, to get
warmed up and supple. She washed the dishes by hand
and then made the four beds. Unless there had been a party.
Then there'd be more glasses and crockery than you'd believe, and sometimes a good number of beds to make. During
the school holidays some of the children would be home,
having late and leisurely breakfasts, playing about in the
bathroom, or running out to dive into the swimming pool.
About mid-morning, Morfydd would begin to see some
shape on things, and she would sit down with a cup of tea
and listen to the wireless, then she would eat her sandwiches
with another cup of tea and a biscuit or two. In the afternoon
she would go to the shops for the mistress and scrape and

clean the vegetables for late dinner. Then she would lay the table. For some reason she would always leave cleaning the sinks and toilets and bathrooms and the washbasins in the bedrooms until last thing, before starting out to catch the five-past-four bus. If the weather was very bad she was supposed to wait, and the mistress would take her down to catch the quarter-to-five bus in that big, silent car. But she didn't often do that.

It had been a good thing to make a fresh start like that after losing her mother. That free time in the evenings had been a new experience, and she did not find that losing all the care of her mother during the day was too much of a change. There was plenty to do in the evenings, going to the pictures, going to bingo, going out with Janet for coffee in the Sun Parlour. And she had another pound on top of her ten pound ten to pay for it all. But she had never gone into a public house, although she had come pretty near to it after her third bad knock. And she'd had a few drops to drink at Christmas and her brother's wedding and her mother's seventieth birthday.

Her mother had had her last big stroke three years before she died. Before that she had still been able to go out in the wheelchair, down to the park and along the Taff, with the view of the cathedral. Sometimes they would go to the florist's in Llandaff and buy the liquid fertilizer for the cacti and the burning bush. From the far end of the park her mother could see the towers of Castell Coch, and that would put her in mind of the view from them over her old home in Tongwynlais. In bad weather she would ask whether the top of the Garth was white, and then Morfydd would be sure to see snow on the roofs of the cars coming down from the valleys soon afterwards.

After that last stroke her mother could hardly manage to cross the doorstep, she could only be carried out to sit on a chair in the sunshine if it was not too hot, but it gave her the chance to exchange a few laboured words with people passing by to the sub-post office or to the allotments across the main road. It was very restricting on Morfydd, of course, but she could have a nice chat now and then with the girls from the Rhondda and Pontypridd going down in the train to work in the Cardiff offices. And she could read about the goings-on in the world in the *Echo*, on her way home in the evenings. Things were going very nicely for her, the neighbours were helpful, one of them was a distant relative, and they kept an eye on her mother when Morfydd was out at work or shopping. Some Sundays Jack would come over and take both of them for a little run in the car. But that was before mother's last stroke. After that he would only come for a chat and a cup of tea and bring a packet of biscuits. But fair play, his wife had come with him to the funeral and had helped with the ham salad and the tea. She would have liked to have children, she told Morfydd one day. But she had only seen her twice since the funeral, on Boxing Day when Morfydd had gone over to help eat up the remains of the goose. And Jack had been over a few times since. He had taken her to see the landlord's agent when that terrible letter had come. She had gone as far as to phone him at his work, as she had done when her mother had died, because she needed to talk to him, she was so upset. It had been something of a shock for him, too, he was at a loss to know what was wrong this time, but, fair play to him, he had come over straight away after work that night.

Tenant at will, indeed! And almost straight away after her mother had gone. She knew that her mother had not been a freeholder, but she was under the impression that she had been a leaseholder on a ninety-nine-year lease or some such terms. But that notice of termination of tenancy had been like a command that she should begin to die. It never entered her head to speak to Mr Beynon about it. She went across the road to see Janet, but she was out somewhere. She felt as if someone had kicked her in the stomach. She went back to the house and helped herself to a drop of the brandy that her mother had always kept in the top drawer of the chest of drawers in the parlour. She made herself a cup of hot tea with plenty of sugar, and then Janet came on the scene. She had been helping the woman in the end house to tend to the back of the old man there who was bed-ridden. After a cup of tea and listening to Janet cursing at the landlord she felt well enough to go to the phone with her and ring up her brother.

It never occurred to him, either, to enlist the help of Mr Beynon. But he spoke of getting a lawyer and promised to ask the advice of a friend of his about which one would be the best to get hold of in a case like this. Mr Beynon, after all, was a barrister with a specialist practice in patent law. But a lawyer is a lawyer. Morfydd was crying into the sink when the mistress came back earlier than usual and found her. She made her wait until Mr Beynon came home, and he arranged for her and her brother to go with him next day to the office of a colleague who specialized in leasehold law.

Neither of them understood much of the discussion that went on between the two lawyers about her fateful document. But they were reassured and within three weeks word came that she was to have a life tenancy, and a new agreement was to be drawn up and signed. This was done one evening in Mr Beynon's house, with his wife as witness. Wasn't she lucky to get someone like Mr Beynon to help her out? What would she have done without him? She was loud in her thanks and praise for him. She bought Dr Beynon a bottle of the expensive scent she had seen on her dressing-table, Climat, and a big box of Havana cigars for him, both presents from the expensive shop by the Park Hotel in the city. She bought silk scarves for the girls and a Shaeffer fountain-pen for the boy. Nothing seemed good enough to express her thanks to the generous family who had given her security of ownership in her home, where she and her mother had lived so long, where all her possessions were kept and treasured.

And tonight, here she was, surrounded by them, and happy. Celebrating her good fortune in the parlour, after receiving her signed copy of the new agreement. And around her were her mother's old chest of drawers and corner cupboard, a photograph of her father in his First-World-War

army uniform, and two solid brass shell cases he had brought
back from France, that her mother had kept polished ever
since, like the fender and the two ornamental pokers. They
were all shining brightly. The three-legged stool came from
Maesteg, she'd had it after her grandfather on her father's
side. There were snapshots on the mantelpiece of Jack and
his wife at their wedding, and another of them on holiday
at Tenby, one of Jack when he was a young boy, and one of
the four of them all together before Jack went away, on the
windowsill. On the mantelpiece too there was one of those
toys that you shook and sent a snowstorm over a woman in
Welsh costume, a brass letter-rack, a pin cushion, and a
lustre jug where she kept her money and important documents like her television licence and her pension book. On
the wall opposite the fireplace, above the hard-backed couch,
there was a plate. A Present from Treorchy. Janet's chair,
that used to be mother's, was empty. She put her swollen
right foot up on it for a spell, but she had difficulty in keeping it there, because she had to keep hold of her cigarette
and her glass, and she was swaying.

She poured herself some more sherry, lit another cigarette,
and put up both her feet on the little stool. After these, she
would call it a day. She was beginning to feel sleepy and
she wondered if she hadn't dropped off a minute or two ago.
She felt pleasantly satisfied, but the smoke kept going down
the wrong way, making her cough. The rocking chair whispered her feelings of complete satisfaction. The fire was full
of pictures and memories, without any smoke to darken the
perfection of her evening. The firelight played on her tired
face, her big bony red nose and the hair under the nose,
and her wiry eyebrows and the locks of her thinning, curly
hair. She had a broad face and quiet grey eyes, but the corners of her mouth turned up and there were a few wrinkles
about her eyes. Her cheeks seemed to be full of high spirits,
but it had always been like that with her. If Janet came
over tomorrow night, that would be an excuse for another
celebration. Perhaps she ought to frame the document that
lay in its important-looking envelope on top of the biscuit

tin alongside the bottle and cigarettes on the little supper table. This would be a nice way to die, knowing that she was sure of her place, and feeling happy and at home there. After all, it would be heaven, like mother, she hoped.

Then Morfydd got up rather shakily, put her glass on the table and the stump of her cigarette in the ashes of the grate. She bent down with one hand on the stool and rolled the mat back for fear of sparks. She put the guard in front of the fire, locked the back door, went back to the table, and put the all-important envelope behind the jug on the mantelpiece. Then she went slowly upstairs to bed and the hot-water bottle.

A Writer Came to Our Place

JOHN MORGAN

THERE was a note on the desk informing me that Mr Sumner, journalist, would be arriving during the night. I was to show him around the factory, allowing him to see anything and anyone.

'You'd think,' I said to Sid, who shared the room with me and who was resting his feet on the desk, 'that I had nothing better to do.'

He turned out to be plump, Mr Sumner, and he wore an expensive grey suit. Over his arm he carried a new pair of overalls. As soon as he was in the room he smiled charmingly at both of us and shook us by the hand. Sid, ironically courteous, offered Sumner his seat and himself sat on a tin can in the corner of the room. Sumner immediately offered cigarettes. We only took one each.

'I hope,' Sumner began, 'that I am not putting you out at all.' He enlarged his smile and looked at us both steadily, in turn. 'My idea, basically, is to look at industry from the other side. One has the management's point of view, of course. But I want to know,' the white, plump hand circling the face, as if he was hypnotizing himself, and falling with the italicized word, 'how the *worker* feels about industry.'

'Shagged,' said Sid.

'Most of the time,' he added.

Sumner laughed. His laugh like his voice was steady and soft, discreet, establishing mutual sympathy and understanding. He behaved, and looked, like an M.P. for a constituency not to be found around here, in which outward elegance was not the mark of a traitor.

'That is the kind of thing I want,' he said.

Above the noise of the cranes as they passed the window

we could hear a wail, beginning like one cat in pain but growing until it might have been ten in a variety of agonies. Sumner jumped in his seat and dropped his cigarette. He was going to stamp on it but I picked it up and gave it to him and he put it back in his mouth. The door was kicked open and Lennie, who had been making the noise, came in swearing. Sumner could not hide his astonishment at Lennie's appearance, at the red hair to the shoulders, the lens-less spectacles, the red, six-inch-long nose, the black, heavy moustache.

'Lennie,' I said, 'meet Mr Sumner, a writer for the papers.'

'Thank God,' said Lennie, taking his spectacles off. Since the false nose and moustache were attached to them they also came off. He removed the wig. Lennie was grey-haired and solemn-faced; his nose was still abnormally long. 'Pardon me,' he said to Sumner; 'I thought you was one of these fancy managers. No offence.'

'Take that other bloody nose off, Lennie,' said Sid.

'Some people can't take a joke,' said Lennie, taking another false nose off. 'Any manganese?' he asked Sid, who was, among other things, responsible for manganese.

'How the hell should I know?' said Sid. He told Lennie to go away. We could hear him make his cat noise as he went.

'You'll have to excuse Lennie,' said Sid to Sumner. 'He owns too many houses. The rents have gone to his head.'

Sumner made a short speech about a property-owning democracy and asked some questions, but I was on the telephone and couldn't follow.

'Let's go down the shanty, my friend,' said Sid, 'for a cup of tea.' He stood up and kicked the tin he'd been sitting on across the room. Sid was very fond of that sort of pointless violence, like throwing the inkstand at the window, hurling chairs against the wall.

We walked onto the stage where a furnace was about to tap. Sumner said he would like to see the operation and so we went behind the furnace, arriving as the leaping, red-hot steel began to flow. Sumner's mouth opened a little. After he had stared for a full minute I told him it was dangerous to stare at the metal without dark glasses. He shut his eyes immediately and looked away.

'Unbelievable,' he said. 'Unbelievable.'

Two hundred tons of metal flowed into the ladle, the sparks flying upwards in the darkness.

'Isn't it dangerous,' asked Sumner, his eyes closed, gesturing, 'for those men there?'

'Very,' said Sid.

'Are there, have there, been accidents?'

'You want the truth?' asked Sid heavily.

'Certainly,' said Sumner, seriously, half-opening one eye.

'Not here,' said Sid, 'but where I once worked five men fell in the ladle.'

'Good God,' said Sumner. 'Did they ever . . .'

'There are motor cars,' said Sid, 'on the roads of Britain, my friend, with bodies in them – in more senses than one.'

'How awful,' said Sumner. He seemed very upset. I liked Sumner.

Our visitor didn't say a word as we walked the length of the shop to the shanty, a lot of people making obscene gestures to Sid as we passed. Sumner, in his brand-new overalls was obviously being accepted as an engineer of no importance. There were ten people in the shanty. Officially it was called a Rest Room and was made of brick. Everyone, except the Welfare people, called it a shanty. When we went in, men put down their copies of *Reveille*, *Weekend Mail* and the most recent and carefully preserved *News of the World*. The man who was reading Sartre's *Baudelaire* kept on doing so. When I explained who Sumner was, the facile expressions reserved for inspecting directors were removed.

'Have you come to see the Illuminations?' asked Davy, one of the crane-drivers, sarcastically. Davy was politically active and so despised all journalists. He hated the newspapers for their strength in a bad cause, the journalists for their weakness in contributing to that strength.

'Now, now, my friend,' said Sid. 'Don't be rude. Offer us a cup of tea.'

We had a cup of tea each, the cups cracked, dirt embedded

in the cracks. Sumner handed cigarettes around. He would be remembered as long as cigarettes or these men existed. Someone said that Sumner would go back to London and tell the world that the worker had no right to more money unless there was higher productivity. Sumner argued this out, sipping from his cracked cup, smiling; and then answered a great many questions about the salaries of Fleet Street journalists and the sexual peccadilloes of the theatrical profession. Since this was what he had come for, Sid and I left him there for an hour. When we returned, Davy was standing, one foot on a brick, one hand clutching a lapel, and making an angry speech about the firm's profits. Sumner was sitting on the floor, a notebook on his knee, seemingly entranced. When we left, he talked about the tenacity with which people clung to outmoded political ideas. He said it came as a surprise to him that these ideas still survived. 'One assumes,' he said, 'wrongly, of course, that, when a scheme is obviously desirable, it becomes immediately acceptable to the people it most seriously concerns.'

Sid said that Sumner was all wrong thinking he'd learn anything by visiting a factory. The only people interested in anything but the things he, Sid, was interested in (he listed them in one word) were the religious maniacs and the 'sly boys' who found themselves good jobs through trade-union work. The political ideas of these people were the same as the ideas of the people in London, except that they were only half-understood. He then started out on his one idea: that the British people were becoming progressively more ignorant. He asked me to name one man cleverer than his father. I suggested himself. 'At least,' I said, 'the police have never caught you.'

Sumner obviously wanted to go, and began a pretty speech of thanks. But Sid told us both to wait outside the office. He went in and came out quickly – carrying relics of Guy Fawkes night, a rocket, a catherine wheel, and a handful of smaller fireworks. 'Watch this,' he said. He laid the rocket against a piece of pipe on the floor, pointing it upstage. He lit the fuse and simultaneously lit the other fireworks. The rocket soared away and he threw the other fireworks after it. Sid was dancing and shouting as the furnace-men ran for shelter. 'Look at that fool,' he screamed, when an elderly first-hand, remembering old explosions, threw himself to the ground; he leaped at Sumner and grabbed his arm. 'Look at them, the s.o.b.s.' He pointed at a man running like the wind, shouting 'Fire,' 'Help.' The fireworks exploded and spun; men peered out from behind trucks and furnaces. Sid was laughing crazily and then stopped suddenly and stared at Sumner, baring his teeth.

'Have a good time with those actresses,' he said, and went back into the office.

A Roman Spring

LESLIE NORRIS

I HAVE this place in Wales, a small house set in four acres of pasture, facing north. It's simple country, slow-moving. I look down my fields and over a narrow valley, green even in winter. I go whenever I can, mainly for the fishing, which is splendid, but also because I like to walk over the grass, slowly, with nobody else about. The place is so silent that you discover small noises you thought had vanished from the world, the taffeta rustle of frail twigs in a breeze, curlews bubbling a long way up.

It's astonishing the old skills I find myself master of when I'm there, satisfying things like clearing out the well until its sand is unspotted by any trace of rotten leaf and its water comes freely through in minute, heavy fountains; or splitting hardwood with a short blow of the cleaver exactly to the point of breaking. I've bought all the traditional tools, the rasp, the band saw, the edged hook, the long-handled, heart-shaped spade for ditching. After a few days there I adopt an entirely different rhythm and routine from my normal way of living. Nothing seems without its purpose, somehow. I pick up sticks for kindling as I walk the lanes; I keep an eye cocked for changes of the weather.

We went down in April, my wife and I, for the opening of the salmon-fishing season. The weather had been so dry that the river was low, and few fish had come up from the estuary, ten miles away. I didn't care. We had a few days of very cold wind, and I spent my time cleaning the hedges of old wood, cutting out some wayward branches, storing the sawn pieces in the shed. After this I borrowed a chain saw from my neighbour, Denzil Davies, and ripped through a couple of useless old apple trees that stood dry and barren in the garden. In no time they were reduced to a pile of neat, odorous logs.

They made marvellous burning. Every night for almost a week I banked my evening fires high with sweet wood, and we'd sit there in the leaping dark, in the low house, until it was time for supper. Then, one morning, the spring came.

I swear I felt it coming. I was out in front of the house when I felt a different air from the south, meek as milk, warm. It filled the fields from hedge to hedge as if they had been the waiting beds of dry ponds. Suddenly everything was newer; gold entered the morning colours. It was a Sunday morning. I walked through the fields noticing for the first time how much growth the grass had made. From some neighbouring farm, perhaps Ty Gwyn on the hillside, perhaps Penwern lower down the valley, the sound of someone working with stone came floating through the air. I stood listening to the flawless sound as it moved without a tremor, visibly almost, towards me. 'Chink,' it came, and again, 'chink', as the hammer chipped the flinty stone. I turned back to the house and told my wife. We had lunch in the garden, and afterwards we found a clump of white violets as round and plump as a cushion, right at the side of the road. They grew beside a tumbledown cottage which is also mine, at the edge of my field where it meets the lane. The cottage is called Hebron. It wasn't so bad when I bought the place – I could have saved it then, had I the money – but the rain has got into it now, and every winter brings it closer to the ground. It had only two rooms, yet whole families were raised there, I've been told. We picked two violets, just as tokens, as emblems of the new spring, and walked on down the hill. Ruined and empty though it is, I like Hebron. I was pleased that the flowers grew outside its door. As we walked along, a blue van passed us, and we stood in the hedge to let it through. Our lane is so narrow that very few people use it – the four families who live there, and a few tradesmen. But we didn't recognize the van. We heard the driver change down to second gear as he swung through the bend and into the steep of the hill, outside the broken cottage. We had a splendid day. In the afternoon we took the car out and climbed over the Preseli Hills to Amroth, in Pembrokeshire. The sands were empty; the pale sea was fastidiously calm. It was late when we got back.

The next day was every bit as perfect. I got up in the warm first light, made some tea, cleaned the ash from the grate, and went into the field. I took a small axe with me, so that I could break up a fallen branch of sycamore that lay beneath its parent in the bottom field. Beads of dew, each holding its brilliant particle of reflected sun, hung on the grass blades. I pottered about, smiling, feeling the comfortable heat between my shoulder-blades. Over the sagging roof of Hebron I could see the purple hills of Cardiganshire rising fold on fold into the heart of Wales. I listened idly to my neighbour, whoever he was, begin his work again, the clink of his hammer on the stone sounding so near to me. It took me a little while to realize that it *was* close at hand. I was unwilling to believe that anyone could be away from his own house on so serene and beautiful an early morning. But someone was. Someone was chipping away inside the walls of Hebron.

I ran through the wet grass, reached the cottage, and looked through a gap where the stones had fallen out of the back wall. I could see right through to the lane. The blue van was parked there, and a thin, blonde girl stood beside it, her long face turned down a little, her hair over her shoulders. The wall was too high for me to see anyone in the house.

'What goes on?' I said. I couldn't believe that my ruin was being taken away piecemeal. The girl didn't move. It was as if she hadn't heard me.

'Who's there?' I called. 'What do you think you're doing?'

A young man stood up inside the house, his head appearing opposite mine through the hole in the wall. He was dark, round-faced, wore one of those fashionable Mexican moustaches. He had evidently been kneeling on the floor.

'Just getting a few bricks,' he said, his face at once alarmed and ingratiating. He waited, smiling at me.

'You can't,' I said. 'It's mine. The whole thing is mine – cottages, fields, the lot.'

The young man looked shocked.

'I'm sorry,' he said. 'I've had permission from the local Council to take stuff away ... They say it doesn't belong to anyone ... I'm sorry.'

'The Council are wrong,' I said. 'This cottage belongs to me.'

I felt stupid, standing there, talking through a ragged gap in a wall three feet thick, but there was no way of getting around to him, except by walking back up the field, through a gate, and down the lane to the front of the house, where the white violets were. The thin, silent girl was standing almost on top of the flowers, which made me obscurely angry. I turned around and hurried off, alongside the hedge. As I went I heard the van start up, and Hebron was deserted when I got back. I opened the door. They'd taken the frames out of the windows, the wooden partition which had divided the little house into two rooms, and an old cupboard I had been storing there. I was incredulous, and then furious. I looked down at the floor. All my marvellous quarry tiles had been prized up and carried away. I could have wept. Nine inches square and an inch thick, the tiles had been locally made over a hundred years ago. They were a rich plum colour, darker when you washed them, and there were little frosted imperfections in them that caught the light. They were very beautiful.

I ran up the road, calling for my wife. She came out and listened to me, her obvious sympathy a little flawed because she was also very amused. She had seen me stamping along, red-faced and muttering, waving aloft the hatchet I had forgotten I was holding.

'No wonder they vanished so quickly,' said my wife. 'You must have looked extraordinary, waving that tomahawk at them through a hole in the wall. Poor young things, they must have wondered what sort of people lived here.'

I could see that it was funny. I began to caper about on the grass in an impromptu war dance, and Denzil Davies came up in his new car. As far as Denzil is concerned, I'm an Englishman, and therefore eccentric. Unmoved, he watched me complete my dance.

But I was angry still. I could feel the unleashing of my temper as I told my story to Denzil. 'They had a blue van,' I said.

'It was a good market in Carmarthen last week,' said Denzil carefully, looking at some distant prospect. 'Milking cows fetched a very good price, very good.'

'Took my window frames, my good tongue-and-groove partition,' I mourned. 'My lovely old cupboard.'

'I believe the Evanses are thinking of moving,' said Denzil. 'Of course, that farm is getting too big for them, now that Fred has got married. It's a problem, yes it is.'

'A young man with a moustache,' I said. 'And a girl with long, fair hair. Do you know them, Denzil?'

'I might buy one or two fields from old Tom Evans,' Denzil replied. 'He's got some nice fields near the top road.'

'They stole my quarry tiles,' I said. 'Every bloody one.'

Denzil looked at me with his guileless blue eyes. 'You've never seen my Roman castle, have you?' he said. 'Come over and see it now. It's not much of an old thing, but professors have come down from London to look at it. And one from Scotland.' Kitty excused herself, saying she had some reading to catch up on. I sat beside Denzil in his new blue Ford, and we bumped along the half mile of track that leads to his farmhouse. I'd been there before, of course. Denzil's farmyard is full of cats. After evening milking he always puts out an earthenware bowl holding gallons of warm milk. Cats arrive elegantly from all directions and drink at their sleek leisure.

We left the car in the yard, and climbed through the steep fields to a couple of poor acres at the top of the hill. Although high, the soil was obviously sour and wet. Clumps of stiff reeds grew everywhere, the unformed flowers of the meadowsweet were already recognizable, and little sinewy threads of vivid green marked the paths of the hidden streams. Right in the middle of the field was a circular rampart about four feet high, covered with grass and thistles, the enclosed centre flat and raised rather higher than the surrounding land. I paced it right across, from wall to wall, and the diameter was nearly seventy feet. There was a gap of eight or nine feet in the west of the rampart, obviously a gateway. It was very impressive. Denzil stood watching me as I scrambled about. Everything I did amused him.

I took an old, rusty fencing stake to knock away the thistles growing on top of the bank and force its pointed end into the thin soil. I didn't have to scratch down very deeply before I hit something hard, and soon I uncovered a smooth stone, almost spherical and perhaps two pounds in weight. I hauled it out and carried it down to Denzil. It was grey and dense, quite unlike the dark, flaky, local stone used for building my own cottage. And Hebron too, of course. I scored my thumb-nail across it, but it didn't leave a scar. It was incredibly hard. Faint, slightly darker parallel lines ran closely through it, and a small, irregular orange stain, like rust, marked its surface on one side. Denzil nodded. 'That's it,' he said. 'That's what they made the walls with. Hundreds and hundreds of those round stones.' My stone had been worn smooth and round in centuries of water, in the sea or in a great river. We were nine hundred feet high and miles from the sea or any river big enough to mould such stones in numbers, yet the Roman walls were made of them.

'They're under the road too,' said Denzil. 'The same stones.'

I looked down from the walls of Denzil's castle. It was easy to see the road, now that he'd said it. A discernible track, fainter green than the land around, marched straight and true, westward from the Roman circle, until it met the hedge. Even there it had defied nearly two thousand years of husbandry. Generations of farmers, finding that little would grow above the stones, had left its surface untilled so that the road, covered with a thin scrub of tenacious blackthorn, went stubbornly on. We saw it reach the road two hundred feet lower down, halt momentarily, and then continue undeterred until it was out of sight. I knew it well, on the other side of the narrow road. It was the boundary of my fields. I had often wondered why I should have had so regular a strip of difficult and worthless shrubs.

'Just wide enough for two chariots to pass,' said Denzil. 'That's what one of those London men told me. But I don't know if he was right.'

We looked with satisfaction at the straight path of the Romans.

'I've got new neighbours,' Denzil said. 'Down in Pengron. Funny people, come from Plymouth.' He looked gently toward Pengron, a smallholding invisible in its little valley. 'They hadn't been here a week,' he went on, 'before they cut down one of my hedges. For firewood.' He let his eyes turn cautiously in my direction. 'Young fellow with a moustache,' he said, 'and a fair-haired girl.'

'How interesting,' I said, with heavy irony. 'And do they have a blue van?'

'Strange you should ask that,' said Denzil mildly. 'I believe they do.' We smiled at each other. 'Can you see,' Denzil said, 'that the Roman road must have passed right alongside Hebron? There must have been a house on that spot for hundreds and hundreds of years, I bet.' He was right. The old cottage sat firmly next to the dark accuracy of the traceable road, its position suddenly relevant. Carrying my stone, I walked back through the fields to have my lunch.

In the afternoon I drove over to Pengron. The house, its windows curtainless, seemed empty, but a caravan stood in the yard. The thin girl came to the door of the caravan, holding a blue plate in her hand. 'Good afternoon,' I said, but she didn't answer.

I've never seen anyone as embarrassed as the young man when he appeared behind her. He jumped out and hurried towards me. 'I know,' he said. 'You want me to take everything back. I will, I'll take it all back this afternoon. I certainly will.'

I felt very stiff and upright, listening to him. I could see all my tiles arranged in neat rows, six to a pile, on the ground. He must have taken over a hundred. He'd been at it for days, chipping away with his hammer while I wandered around in happy ignorance.

'I can understand,' I said in the most stilted and careful manner, 'that someone surprised in a situation as you were this morning is likely to say something, as an excuse, which may not be exactly true. But I have to know if you really have permission from the local Council to remove material from my cottage. If this is true, then I must go to their offices and get such permission withdrawn.'

He was in agony, his face crimson with shame. I felt sorry for him, as I stood unbendingly before him.

'No,' he said. 'No, I don't have any permission. It's just that someone up the village told me that he didn't think the old place belonged to anyone. I'll take everything back this afternoon.'

I looked at my tongue-and-groove partition, my window frames. Unrecognizable almost, they formed a heap of fire-wood in one corner of the yard. Waving a hand at them in hopeless recognition of the situation, I said, 'It's not much use taking that back, but the tiles, yes, and my cupboard, and anything else you haven't broken up.' I walked back to the car, and he followed, nodding vehemently all the way. I was glad to leave him. When I looked in at Hebron later on, the tiles and the cupboard had been returned. I didn't enjoy myself much that day. It's stupid to be so possessive. The old cottage is an unprepossessing mess, not even pic-turesque. I ought to have been pleased that someone was finding it useful, but I wasn't. The lingering remnants of my anger pursued me through the night, and I was pretty tired next day. I took it easy.

I can't think why I went down to Hebron in the cool of the evening. I walked listlessly down the hill, becoming cheer-ful without energy when I found a wren's nest in the hedge. There never was such a place for wrens. They sing all day, shaking their absurd little bodies with urgent song. It was a good evening, cloudless and blue, a little cool air tempering the earlier warmth. I began to whistle. At quiet peace with myself, aimless and relaxed, I approached the cottage. When a man pushed his head and shoulders through the gaping window I was totally startled.

'How much for the house, then?' he said. He withdrew from the window and, stepping carefully, reappeared at the door, closing it slowly behind him. He was a very small man. Despite the mildness of the evening, he wore his reefer jacket wrapped well around him, and its collar high. He couldn't have been a couple of inches over five feet.

'It's not worth much,' I said. He pushed his tweed cap off his forehead and smiled at me, a sweet, wise smile, but incredibly remote.

'No,' he said, 'not now. Oh, but it was lovely sixty years ago.'

'Did you know it,' I asked, 'all that time ago?'

'Longer,' he said. 'More than sixty years ago. Since first I saw it, that is.'

He stood outside the house, his hands deep in his pockets. He stood very carefully, protectively, as if he carried something exceedingly fragile inside him. His breathing was gentle and deliberate, a conscious act. It gave him a curious dignity.

'Know it?' he said. 'For ten years I lived in this house. My brother, my mother, and me. We came here when I was five years old, after my father died, and I was fifteen when we left. I'm sixty-seven now.' We turned together to walk down the hill. He moved slowly, economically. We had gone but a few yards when he stopped, bent down, and picked up a thin ashplant, newly cut from the hedge.

'I've been getting bean sticks,' he explained. 'I've left them along the lane where I cut them, so that I can pick them up as I go back.'

We talked for a long time, and I warmed towards him. He was a great old man. We stood there, the evening darkening around us, and he told me of people who had lived along the lane in the days of his boyhood, of his work as a young man in the farms about us, of the idyllic time when he lived in Hebron with his mother and brother.

'But there's no water there,' I said. 'How did you manage for water?'

'I used to go up to your place,' he said. 'To your well. Times without number I've run up this road, a bucket in each hand, to get water from your well. We thought it was the best water in the world.'

Slowly we moved a few yards on, and the old man lifted the last of his bean sticks from where it lay. Then he turned, faced resolutely forward, and prepared to make his way back to the village, perhaps a mile away over the fields.

'I've got to be careful,' he said. 'Take things very slowly, the doctor said. I'm very lucky to be alive.' He placed his hand delicately on the lapel of his navy coat. 'Big Ben has gone with me,' he said. 'Worn out. He doesn't tick as strongly as he used to.'

'Let me carry those sticks for you,' I said, understanding now his deliberate slowness, his sweet tolerance, his otherworldliness. He was a man who had faced his own death closely, for a long time, and he spoke to me from the other side of knowledge I had yet to learn.

'I'll manage,' he said. He bundled his sticks under one arm, opened the gate, and walked away. It was so dark that he vanished against the black hedge while I could still hear his footsteps.

In the morning I went into the field below Hebron. It's not my field; Denzil rents it from an absentee landlord, and keeps a pony or two in it. There's a steep bank below the hedge, below the old Roman road, that is, and Hebron's garden is immediately above this bank. As I had hoped, the ground there was spongy and wet, green with sopping mosses. I climbed back up and into the garden, hacking and pushing through invading bramble and blackthorn, through overgrown gooseberry bushes. In the corner of the garden which overhangs Denzil's field, everything seemed to grow particularly well; the hedge grass was lush and rampant, the hazel bushes unusually tall. I took my hook and my saw, and cleared a patch of ground about two yards square. It took me most of the morning. Afterwards I began to dig.

It was easier than I had expected, and I hadn't gone two spits down before I was in moist soil, pulling shaped spadesful of earth away with a suck, leaving little fillings of water behind each stroke of the blade. By lunchtime I'd uncovered a good head of water, and in the afternoon I shaped it and boxed it with stones from the old cottage, and while it cleared I built three steps down to it. It was a marvellous spring. It held about a foot of the purest coldest water. I drank from it, ceremonially, and then I held my hand in it up to the wrist, feeling the chill spread into my forearm. Afterwards I cleaned my spade meticulously until it shone, until it rang like a faint cymbal as I scrubbed its metal with a handful of couch grass. I knew that I would find water. For hundreds of years, since Roman times perhaps, a house had stood there: it had to have a spring.

I put my tools in the boot of the car and drove up to the village. If I meet my old friend, I thought, I'll tell him about my Roman spring. I saw him almost at once. He stood, upright and short, in front of the Harp Inn. There was nobody else in the whole village, it seemed. I blew my horn, and he raised both arms in greeting. I waved to him, but I didn't stop. Let him keep his own Hebron, I thought. Let him keep the days when he could run up the hill with two buckets for the best water in the world, his perfect heart strong in his boy's ribs. I had drunk from the spring, and perhaps the Romans had, but only the birds of the air, and the small beasts, fox, polecat, badger, would drink from it now. I imagined it turning green and foul as the earth filled it in, its cottage crumbling each year perceptibly nearer the earth.

I drove slowly back. The next day we packed our bags and travelled home, across Wales, half across England.

Before Forever After

RON BERRY

It was tamping down, September gale rain drowning Wales, sodden donkey coats steaming in our canteen, the huge pot-bellied stove leaking squiggles of sulphur smoke, half a dozen card schools on the go; discussions, arguments all round, a rowdy, becursed, shifting quint of football, women, horses, work and money.

A group of us were playing pontoon, Strapper Cullen banker, my mate Chris down to a few tanners, his dragged-in mouth jutting his knubbly chin – he looked like a pensioner elf. Big Strapper with the bronzy, hard-skinned tan of a buck Huron, he said, 'What's for you, Chris?'

'Turn it over,' Chris said.

Strapper twisted a black nine.

Chris returned his cards. 'Too heavy. Strapper, there's no form, no run of play, there's nothing to go by. With you it's all luck.'

'Lend you half a bar,' offered Strapper.

'When I borrow money to play cards I'll pack in altogether,' Chris said.

The navvy ganger said, 'I'll stick.'

'Me, I'll stick,' I said.

Pete the crane driver bought for a tanner. 'Enough,' he said. 'I'm satisfied.'

Strapper turned over his pair. 'Eight.' He turned over the ace of clubs. 'Nine.' He turned over a deuce. 'Eleven – boys, I can't bust.' Another deuce, Strapper grinning like an advert. 'Thirteen. Pay pontoons only.'

He collected the stakes.

The navvy ganger fisted the table. 'If he fell in our dub

he'd come up with milk choc'late. Deal me out, I'm finished. I couldn't win a game of Oxo.'

'Jammy sod,' explained Chris. 'Typical. Some day he'll marry a whoor who'll drag him down to where he belongs.'

Strapper skidded a few shillings across to the navvy ganger. 'Bus fare to go home,' he said. 'As for you, Chris, win or lose you moan like a granny. Wait till you see this bird I'm knocking around with these days. She'll make you wish you were stone blind, you chopsy old tiger.'

Friendly Strapper Cullen, most favoured character on the building site. A wide-open man, generous, brotherly. Everybody loved him.

The navvy ganger rattled his bus fare, walked across to the stove.

I said, 'Where's she from, this gorgeous bit of yours?'

'Berw Vale. She drives her Triumph Herald over the mountain road at ninety. Perfect timing. She's perfection itself.'

'Blonde girl in a white sports car?' I said.

Strapper dealt the cards. 'Yeh. Seen us, have you, Dai?'

I said, 'Rebecca Pearce. Her old man's rolling in loot. He's chairman of Berw chamber of commerce, he's on the corporation, he's got shares in Marvel-bread bakery, he's a director in the chain-works . . .'

Zealot through to his marrow, Chris choked on private disgust. 'Taliesin Pearce be damned! He's a social criminal of the first water. Born crooked, lives crooked, and he'll die the same.'

Pete the crane driver signalled for hush, Strapper smiling pleasantly, saying, 'Quiet now, ah, if you don't mind?'

'Dirt sticks,' insisted Chris. 'When you're my age you'll appreciate what it means to speak your mind with a clear conscience, knowing full well that you have never taken advantage of your fellow workmen. Consequently, boy, I won't have you telling me to be quiet. In my experience, size and strength don't count. What counts is the state of a man's conscience. Mine's clear.'

I chanted a little mock of praise for my old mate Chris.

'Clear as isinglass. Transparent forever. Stand aside, make way for Christopher Llewellyn, the white knight of the A.S.W.!' – we're both chippies, see, side by side, concrete shuttering, boxing R.S.J.s on this new factory project.

He said, 'Very clever, Dai. When it comes to conscience as regards expenditure of public funds, I can supply certain facts relating to Councillor Tal Pearce.'

'Rebecca's luscious,' I said. 'We were in school together, her little whass-names dancing inside her blouse the day we finished last in the three-legged race.' I sucked a few hostler noises, street corner erotica. 'Bee-eautiful 'Becca,' I said, 'blonde as raffia, cool as . . .'

Strapper twirled his podger on a loop of thong. 'Shut up, Dai.' He was grinning though, eyes pale blue as sunshine on bits of ice, the podger a blur, harmless, disappearing, dropped back into his belt.

'Cool as a menthol cigarette,' I said.

He pressed one finger on my sternum. 'You and Rebecca went to the same school?'

'All the way from infants to itchy adolescence. She's al'right, genuine, but her father, he's pure Welsh Mafia.'

'Hundred per cent,' confirmed Chris, placing his spade ace face-up over a picture.

Pete stuck.

I stuck with nineteen.

Strapper turned over his pair. Ace of diamonds. Black queen. 'Sorry, Chris,' he said.

Chris left the table. The rain slashed down. Mack whistled us off the site at three o'clock. Cockney born, Mack showed all the brave style, but too many G.F. jobs on too many cut-price sites had ulcerated his stomach. We shared a decent bonus system on this new factory, after weeks of ca'-canny, the usual mixture of threats and syrupy sweet reason. The job flowed: steel stanchions, concrete, more steel, more concrete, steel roofing trusses, big Strapper cat-walking the topmost R.S.J.s, black against white clouds, like a visitor from somewhere anti-gravity. Old Pete operated the crane, a droll, neckless, throw-back Celt who seemed to tap into Strapper's mind.

Came one crisp Friday as we straggled towards the pay office, and Rebecca Pearce drove her white Triumph across the site.

Chris spat neatly aside. 'That her, Strapper's piece?'

'None other,' I said.

She's wearing a leather two-piece, oatmeal colour, long blonde hair shawled around her shoulders, wolf calls and parrot whistles answering the hunting music of her twin klaxons. Cockney Mack watched from his office doorway, our happy enough general foreman licking Rennie tablet rime off his lips. Again that musical yelp from the Triumph Herald. I'm looking for Strapper. He's airborne, slowly revolving, floating down like a sun god, old Pete in the crane cabine, lowering his jib out over the roadway, dangling Strapper above the car, joggling him forward until he jinks smartly off the chain hanging from the hook, spanners and podger jingling on his belt. Without taking his eyes off Rebecca, he waved up-and-away to Pete.

A seven-second tableau, Strapper's thick brown mane bent towards blonde Rebecca, then he's loping away to the canteen for his jacket.

'Clown,' decided Chris, 'endangering himself and others.'

I said, 'See you tomorrow morning. I'm going to have a chat with Rebecca.'

'Obvious to me the girl's a parasite,' he said. 'She's using Strapper. The boy's on hire.'

Meagrely built, a really small man, but old Chris is loaded with ethics. I walked over to the Triumph.

'Hullo, 'Becca.'

'David Samuels!' She switched off some utterly shitty pop on the car radio.

'Long time no time for,' I said.

'So this is where you work.'

I asked her, 'Are you still with that dot and carry one insurance company?'

She pushed treble-sized sun-glasses high up on her blonde hair, toned herself into old-fashioned Welshy, and by the Christ she looked beyond the reach of us all. 'I've climbed to private secretary. Aye indeed, Dai Sam. Awful responsible it is.'

I pinked the windscreen. 'Win this banger in a raffle? I can't afford a Hong Kong gambo. As a single man I'm taxed to five nights a week drinking club beer, and pleasant daydreams.'

Rebecca said, 'Twenty-second birthday present off my father.'

'Four years ago he gave you a holiday in Spain.'

'I haven't seen you since, David.'

'Bitter-sweet tears flowing from her angelic eyes,' I said.

She blew a demure raspberry, subsiding to a snaky hiss. '*Tempus fugit,* 'Becca.'

'The flower clock in Swansea! I remember. Whit Monday. It rained. You caught a cold. I went to Spain the following week.'

'Remember our three-legged race?' I said.

'*You* weren't concerned about the race.'

'I cannot hurl the lie back at your milk-white teeth. *Tempus fugit.*'

'Ha, ha, ha. Funny.'

'How do you find Strapper?' I said.

'John found me' – flatly under-stressing her God-given grandeur.

'Everybody calls him Strapper. He's a fine bloke,' I said. 'Handsome, all the makings of a hero. I admire him. You too, girl, I've always admired you.'

She fiddled with the sun-glasses. 'I missed you in Spain. We were only kids, but it was awfully nice.'

'Niceness is nice,' I said.

'It doesn't last, perhaps it isn't supposed to beyond a certain point.'

'Are we talking about the same thing?' I said. 'The one and only experience past all telling?'

'I don't understand.'

Who would, I thought, conceding an influx of worms in the bud. 'Falling in love,' I said.

'But it works both ways. We also fell out of love.'

I said, 'What happened, 'Becca?'

'I wish you wouldn't call me 'Becca. It takes me back to hockey sticks, the smell of liniment when I sprained my knee . . .'

'And that P.E. mistress with a voice like Humphrey Bogart,' I said.

She frowned. 'I felt sorry for her.'

'It's contagious,' I said.

'All right, Dai Sam, what are you hinting at?'

'Dead-end passion.'

'You always were a cruel boy.'

'No, I reckon there's a niche for everybody, even me.'

'Cynic, seek and ye may find,' she said.

I saw Strapper coming down from the canteen, tee-shirt and jeans bulging with the power of him, denim jacket swinging in his hand. 'Here's your spider-man, 'Becca.' To Strapper I said, 'We've been laying flowers on dead memories.'

The untouchable grin, confident as a prince under protocol. 'Forget-me-nots?'

'David's referring to the flower clock in Swansea, O ever such a long time ago.'

I said, 'Aye, *tempus* and *fugit* and so on and so forth.'

Strapper vaulted into the car. 'Watch your language, matey. Away, Rebecca, before I lace his ankles around his neck.'

She smoothly whoofed one-two-three through the gears, and I felt myself bowing like a toy mandarin, as if my groins carried rise-and-fall hinges.

Mack came out from his office. 'Strapper's found himself a real classy skirt. Wouldn't mind myself. She's a goer, stands out a mile.'

I said, 'Her old man's a tycoon.'

He freed his tongue from a juicy puddle of alkaline. 'Don't say. What's his line of business?'

'It's a Welsh disease, ancient as these scab-faced hills and valleys.'

'Come off it, Dai.'

'Our inheritance from times of tribulation,' I said. 'If you can't beat 'em, turn cannibal.'

Mack lowered his head, his shiny all-welded shoes reading ten to two, the empty smile of a doxy failing to comfort his hagged eyes. 'I'm worried. See that last line of trusses. Tricky situation. Jib's too short. Worse, I'm seven weeks behind schedule. Can't expect my scaffolders to hang scaffolding on sky-hooks. What'll we do, track back, swing that last truss in from outside. Use ropes, coupla ropes. Strapper can do it, him and Pete. They work good together.'

I drew my wages. Mack and the navvy ganger were still out on the site, Mack waving his arms, trying to prove his case to the wrong man. Pete the crane driver was homeward, sleeping on a Western Welsh bus. Big Strapper and Rebecca were clocking ninety over the mountain road to Berw Vale.

Next day Saturday, half-day, thank God. We were up on the second deck, toggling beam-side shutters around an R.S.J., old Chris venting his brand of Socialism, with Strapper and Rebecca included in a selective purge when the revolution came. I'm his sounding board, less than half his age, plus double his immunity to consequences, etcetera, etcetera. We've argued politics, morality, economics six days a week for two years. Like Robert Tressall of Hastings, he's truly bent to buggery by his craft. Times change. Backstabbers belong everywhere. We inherit chaos. It's unconditional.

'For example,' Chris said, 'take a muscle-bound moron like Strapper Cullen. Double-time every week-end since his firm came on the site. Before he's fifty, he'll be worn down to a shadow, what with Tal Pearce's young bitch after him and all. Steel erectors, I've seen more intelligent men sweeping the roads. Glorified labourers, that's their status, glorified labourers.'

'You're afraid of heights,' I said.

'Listen, Dai, there's more than one kind of nerve. Put him

up on a platform in front of five hundred trade union members. Could he explain the pros and cons of negotiation? Could he enlighten the rank and file, the backbone of our society?'

'Your father should have named you Jesus,' I said.

He pulled his elvish face. 'Check this shutter with your level. I'll toggle the wire.'

I suggested: 'Take five, man. We've done our whack until tea-break.'

'Where d'you learn that attitude? You youngsters, you're bankrupt as regards scruples. It's all grab, grab, grab. How you'll manage when the hard times come, I do not know.'

We levelled the shutter.

'They can pour this beam first thing Monday morning,' he said. 'Now, as I was saying, there's such a thing as common decency. They were rolling about, her squealing like a stuck pig on the bank outside my allotment. Full harvest moon last night, remember. Midnight, them two bathing in private water. Privilege again, Tal Pearce pulling strings so's his daughter and that big moron can swim in Berw Lake, a body of water which serves for domestic purposes under certain emergencies. The likes of that girl are taking the cream off the backs of the likes of you and me. What I'd do is draft her into skivvying for a few years. Laundry work and dirty dishes. She'd earn the right to flash around like some loose slut because then, Dai, *then*, personal experience teaches the lesson. If society makes profit off a girl's body and nothing else besides, she conducts herself accordingly. Cheap in her own eyes. Follow my meaning?'

'You're a bloody dictator,' I said. ' 'Becca works for an insurance company.'

'Only parasites flog insurance. Vultures they are, profiting on public and private sorrow, not to mention property.'

I hammered a two-and-a-half-inch nail, fixing the lower beam-side to the soffit.

He said, 'I'll remind you about that nail when we come to strip this shutter. She'll tighten up when they pour.'

'Yes, Jesus, but in your company I can afford to be careless once or twice, surely?'

'Better ease her off the soffit, Dai. Do it now.'

'Okay, Jesus,' I said.

'Neither does it pay you to sneer at a man old enough to be your father,' he said.

Strapper leapt off the R.S.J., clean over my head as I prised the shutter away from the soffit with a nailbar. He laid the three-foot spirit level on the palm of his hand, watching the bubble. 'Hullo there, pimper,' he said to Chris. 'Did you get an eyeful last night?'

Chris stiffened up, clenched for self-defence. 'Careful what you're saying. There's a witness standing right behind you.'

Strapper gently wielded the spirit level, royally bestowing grace, tapping Chris on each shoulder. 'I'm entitled to know, old matey.'

'And *I* should like to know who gave you permission to swim in Berw Lake? That Lake belongs to the corporation. Furthermore, for your information, what I witnessed by sheer *accident*, I wouldn't repeat to a living soul.'

I had to say it, 'Old fork-tongue.'

Strapper said, 'I'll come to you, Chris, if there's any gossip.'

Undeterred, Chris raised up on his heels. 'I'll cope with anything you can dish out.'

'I'm not threatening you, old matey. I'll leave that to Mr Pearce.'

'Him! I'd step over Tal Pearce if he was curled up in the gutter.'

'Who owns your house?' asked Strapper.

'Never you mind who owns my house!'

'Mr Pearce,' said Strapper.

I chipped in, 'Well-well-well-well,' sing-song style indicating mood and nous.

'Yeh, he's the owner,' affirmed Strapper, and he jumped up off our scaffold, balanced on the R.S.J., the tight cheeks of his buttocks high above his long legs as he walked across to the last line of roofing trusses.

'Happy thought to suit the occasion,' I said. 'Strapper might become your landlord some day.'

'She's got him for stud, pure and simple. It's bloody wicked. Little bitch like that, she'd match a poof better than a bloke like Strapper Cullen. She's whooring around, Dai, that's what she's doing. Look, I'd be the last man on God's earth to create animosity. As for yourself, it's dead rotten when two workmates can't exchange a few confidential items. I'm off down the ladder. Call of nature. See you in the canteen. Tea-break in a few minutes.'

A marathon arguer, old Chris kept the topic going, the navvy ganger sitting opposite us in the canteen, eating half a cooked chicken.

'Puritan,' I accused, 'you're a dog-in-the-manger puritan, with no authority at all to pass judgement like some spunk-bound old shag-bag. Offer me a Woodbine – I forgot to buy fags before coming to work this morning.'

'You'll learn, boy. Wait until you're married, reared kids, hair dropped out, no teeth left, then you'll shut your mouth. You'll think first instead of throwing insults. Here I've been trying to explain pollution, the possibility if either Strapper or that sloppy girl had a dose of syph or something. Time you realized a country is only as good as the people who live in it. Ever read *The Citadel*?'

'I'd drink 'Becca's sweat,' I said, stalling the ganger on a thick bolus of meat.

'It's in *The Citadel* you'll find an example of pollution such as we've never experienced.'

'I'm more familiar with the "Song of Solomon",' I said, straightaway spouting another little beneficial chant: ' "Thy navel is like a round goblet, which wanteth not liquor; thy belly is like an heap of wheat set about with lilies: Thy two breasts are like two young roes that are twins. Thy neck is a tower of ivory; thine eyes like the fish-pools of Heshbon, by the gate of Bathrabbim; thy nose is as the tower of Lebanon, which looketh towards Damascus." Mind passing that cigarette now, please, Christopher?'

He munched his lettuce-and-tomato sandwich – lettuce cut

around midnight the night before. 'As a life-long agnostic, the outcome of serious thought, I nevertheless respect any man's religion. In a democracy . . .'

'It's poxy,' I said.

Delayed response, nicely balanced between unction and righteous scorn. 'Navel like a goblet, huh, out of all proportion to common sense. Exaggeration beyond reason. Rubbish, boy, romantic rubbish. That's the trouble, today's youth won't face reality. Real issues upon which decisions have to be made for the betterment of mankind. Solomon's got fuck all to do with us building that factory out there. Try Solomon on Mack. Try Solomon on those scientists who leave their bags of urine floating around in space. I'll tell you the plain gospel for the man in the street. It's economics, always has been since we dropped down from the branches. Even a stupid fella like Strapper Cullen appreciates the power of a quid note in his hand. Wouldn't surprise me if he's knocking out thirty-odd a week.'

I said, 'Jealous?'

Give in to Chris, he's dauntless. He lit my cigarette, his pursy mouth set tidy. 'Take a so-called Socialist writer like Mister George Bernard Shaw. He left umpteen thousands. Some of our hypocritical Labour leaders are financiers in their own right. By comparison Tal Pearce is just a potcher, yet we've seen his corruptive influence in Berw Vale politics. I think it's shameful, that young pusher in her bloody sports car, chucking herself at a semi-skilled worker. It's enough to make a good man spit blood.'

I said, 'Bile is what I feel like throwing up.'

The connection skewed, went wrong; Chris wasn't listening, muttering to himself, 'Too true, boy, too true.'

'You're putting my holy ghost through a mincer,' I said.

He looked around the canteen. 'Where is Strapper?'

'Out on the site with Pete and Mack.'

He smirked nastily. 'Some principle, working through teabreak.'

'We did the same last week, stand-by while they poured that column on number two deck.'

'Emergency, Dai. Anything goes all to balls on the site, us tradesmen land in the pickies.'

'Mack's in trouble,' I said. 'They can't swing in the last truss. He wants Strapper to bring it in with a couple of ropes. How does she look in the buff?'

Chris scowled ten years on his worn face, the grunt escaping like an air block in shoddy plumbing: 'Ah?'

' 'Becca Pearce,' I said.

'Oh, al'right so far as I could see. White, exceptionally white, I thought. Goes with her being a blondie, I suppose.'

'Duw-Duw,' I said.

He said, 'Aye.'

We were back up on our section of scaffold when he found another little burst of spleen, vowing, 'I should have stung her backside with the airgun I use for killing rats in my compost heap. Teach her a lesson.'

Far up above our heads, a scaffolder was singing 'Your tiny hand is frozen' – choir tenor, undoubtedly. It was Indian Summer weather, spiritual in a way, Berw mountain in the distance, changed to rust, fawny-grey, dark blobs of hawthorn cringing ready for winter; black leghorns scratching in the yard of a condemned (progress being what it is) smallholding below the new factory, a yellow 'dozer ripping out great arcs of bramble behind the smallholder's two up and two down cottage. Smells everywhere. Green stuff dying.

Right.

'Chris, Mr Jesus,' I said, 'much sadism in your family?'

'None at all. I come from good, honest Welsh stock. There isn't a trace of mongrel blood in me.'

I said, 'You look pure, too, especially in profile. Any love-children in your family?'

'They're no disgrace. Mind, I believe in discipline, decency all round, not love thy neighbour and at the same time brain-wash him till he can't think for himself. Ever see a bishop humping a tool-bag? Ever see a parson emptying ashbins? They're the biggest shower of bastards in our Western society. Fascists to the core, every man jack of 'em.'

'She's very white then,' I said, because, against a man like Chris, tactics are justified. The slow-motion surrealist gambit.

He gave me one of his sincere scrutinies, signifying word of honour. 'Dai Sam, take my advice. Find yourself a lovely open-minded Welsh girl, and marry her. To be quite frank, boy, there's a strange kink in your mentality.'

We moved across the scaffold, began fixing another soffit while I told him the story about our Whit Monday in Swansea. The flower clock, the rain, how I sheltered in the gents, Rebecca in the ladies, and about the ravaged old bloke with one arm who talked to himself in one of the cubicles. Grumble-grumble behind the bolted door: 'Gerroff, this is my seat. I was here first. This is my seat.' That lunatic flower clock, the minute hand jerking around like Armageddon camouflaged by Walt Disney. I gave old one-arm the price of a Woolworth's meal ... but it rained all day.

Chris remembered the bombing of Swansea. Changed forever since, not so friendly.

'*Tempus fugit*,' I said.

'What?' he snapped, as the burping roar of Pete's crane cut out. We turned, a gasping moan ascending from the site, Strapper Cullen deflecting off an R.S.J., falling all-shapes, the visible bounce of his body on the ground-floor concrete. Seconds ticked off, glacial, then frenzy, men racing towards ladders, flying down scaffolding like monkeys.

He looked a goner for sure, blood seeping from his ear, his nostrils, the greyness of death on him.

Chris took charge. He issued the orders. Mack phoned for an ambulance. Men sprinted to the canteen, brought their coats; Chris draped them over Strapper. Pete was crying, down on his knees, crying, 'Strapper-boy, it's me, Pete. Can you hear me?'

Chris cuffed backhanders against his chest, jarring the grief out of him. 'Dai, come here. Take care of this man,' he said.

Old Pete broadcasting how the swinging truss clouted Strapper on the shoulder. Chris said, 'Shut it – Dai, shut him up. This isn't a case of negligence. Act of God.'

I dragged Pete through the crowd, Chris yelling: 'All you men, stand back! You (to Mack), keep everybody away.'

Mack followed the navvy ganger round and round the ring, arms spread out, blabbing, blah-blah-blah. And big Strapper, he looked to be dying. Skull fracture, fractured spine, pelvis crushed. He fell on his spanners and podger.

Still dangling from the crane jib, the truss spun very, very slowly, barely whiffling the hanging ropes.

All this happened before.

A year later we were second fixing in the administration block, the only two chippies left on the job. Clean craftwork, inside, no frozen hands and feet from north-east winds. We weren't Mack's blue-eyed boys either. First on, last off, the seniority rule.

Another October day, blustery, the lifeless smallholding, empty cottage vandalized, naturally, our timber canteen dismantled, taken away, replaced by green sward landscaped down to the roadside. Contemporary planning. For every new factory, a few square yards of turf, token allegiance to the chlorophyll which buries civilizations.

We were hanging beech-wood doors. Flush-panelled hardboard doors down on the factory production floor, of course, again perfectly natural. That's life. Chris was contented, pushing his steel jack-plane, drooling over the beautiful, tight-grained timber. He sniffed shavings like an addict – it's on the wane though, the servant/master hand of man is alien to concrete and plastics. Craftsmanship is doomed.

I lifted the *Morning Star* out of the rear pocket of his overalls. The date clicked: 23 October. I said: 'It's a year to the day since Strapper Cullen had his accident.'

'Bad day,' Chris said. 'Youngster like that, hardly in his prime, ruined for life.'

'Fate,' I said, 'bastard fate.'

'True, Dai. I can't contend otherwise.'

We offered up the door again, Chris inside, me outside. Perfect fit. I didn't hear Rebecca's footsteps, her quiet voice snapping the dream between my ears. 'David?'

Irascible as a starved virus, Chris shouted, 'Hold on to the bloody door!'

I said: 'Wonderful to see you, 'Becca.'

'Introduce me to Mr Llewellyn,' she said.

We lifted the door away from the jambs.

She was transformed, facially harder, her bobbed hair untidy, less outright blonde, her girl-shape lost under a black PVC windcheater, all slanting zips and press studs, a dingy sweater, old jeans, and scuffed jackboots.

'Want me? What for? What's the trouble?' demanded Chris, intolerance deepening the crow's feet around his eyes.

'My husband would like to speak to you, Mr Llewellyn.'

'Husband? I don't know him. Who is he?'

'John Cullen. I think you might possibly see him from that window.'

We looked down. Big Strapper all right, standing hunched over a pair of alloy crutches. Parked at the kerb behind him, one of those three-wheelers for disabled persons. And behind the three-wheeler a ropey looking Bantam two-stroke, with a tatty crash helmet perched on the saddle.

Chris affected bonhomie. 'Congratulations. How is he?'

'John insists on speaking to you personally. Won't you come down to the road?'

'Glad to, Mrs Cullen.' He grabbed my arm. 'Dai, c'mon, we'd better go together.'

'Certainly, you too, David,' she said.

Exactly the same Strapper Cullen, heavier, confident as ever, his short-reached handshake making Chris wince.

'Reason I'm here, I want to thank you for looking after me when I took my big tumble. While I was in hospital, old Pete told me how you organized things.' Strapper patted his jacket pockets, teetering a little. Rebecca darted forward, placed a cigarette between his lips, lit it for him.

'Ta, love,' he said, smiling, her face calm, lowering, their cheekbones touching, a brief nudge of affection. 'Anniversary of the day!' he said. 'Know something, Chris, I'm *born* lucky. Rebecca married me while I was still wearing a plaster cast.'

'The worst is over,' she said quietly.

'Over,' repeated Strapper. 'My lovely, we can't fail.'

'John swims every afternoon in the sea,' she said.

'Well done, boy, well done,' approved Chris.

Strapper chuckled pleasure. 'I'm like a drunken crab until I get into crawl stroke. Hey, love, give them our address. Listen, Chris, we bought this six-roomed bungalow down in Pembroke. Pay us a visit. Stay a couple of weeks. Any time.'

She handed Chris an addressed envelope from Strapper's wallet. 'Bring your wife, Mr Llewellyn. We shall be happy to have you stay with us.'

Chris mumbled. He didn't know what to say.

Rebecca buckled on her crash helmet. 'It's a long drive home, dear. I think we'd better get started.' She opened the car door, Strapper flopped in sideways; she tucked in his useless legs, collapsed his bright alloy crutches, and stowed them in the boot.

We shook hands again. Rebecca said, 'You're a good man, Mr Llewellyn. Good-bye, David.'

Two kicks on the Bantam and she was ready.

'Cheerio, Chris,' bawled Strapper. 'See you, Dai. So long for now!' – Rebecca riding on ahead, slowly, Strapper zig-zagging the tiny three-wheeler, his horn blaring *Bhaap-bhap-bhap-bhaap, bhaap-bhap-bhap-bhaap* up the road.

I said: 'That's what I call guts, him and her.'

Chris squared his shoulders, ground out his feelings like dogma: 'Yes, boy, they do make a man feel small, they definitely do.'

Hon. Sec. (R.F.C.)

ALUN RICHARDS

ELGAR DAVIES lived alone with his ancient widowed mother on the far side of town in one of those rare detached houses built in a brick festooned style known as Rhondda baronial. It was large, squat, grey, multi-chimneyed, and ugly and much too big for the widow and her bachelor son. However, there were times when it seemed that it was not large enough for Elgar who, despite all the appearance of the dutiful son, escaped from his mother when he could. He was helped in this by his long-standing position as secretary of the Pontlast Rugby Football Club, where he displayed a love of the game and his fellows that was deeply felt, so much so that when any disagreement occurred, say, between players and officials, he would return home and seat himself in his study and ponder on the matter with intense seriousness, shutting himself away from both his mother and the world, his small podgy bespectacled little frame, short legs, and tiny feet lost in the large hide armchair bequeathed to him by his father. Elgar was the son and grandson of local heroes, both much-decorated veterans of the wars whose distinction had overawed Elgar all his life.

'Your grandfather was one of the tunnellers of Messines,' his mother was wont to say, and a framed Distinguished Service Order with attendant decorations was proudly displayed in the hallway of the old house. Elgar had not known his grandfather, and had scarcely begun to know his father when he died of wounds sustained when the first batch of territorials went to France in the second war. For years Elgar had felt rather shamefaced at his own lack of distinction, since he had escaped the battlefield and, indeed, he was soon made aware that he was not the man his father was. As a child he had been puny, given to bronchitis, and was much cosseted by his mother and a bevy of aunts who had lived with them, and later, in college, where he went – inevitably, it seemed – to become a primary-school teacher, he was one of the quiet sort who have difficulty asserting themselves. Things did not improve until later life when he began to take an interest in the administrative side of sport where his quiet efficiency and adroit book-keeping skills were much valued, and when he began his secretaryship of the rugby club, he had at last found a position and status in life of which the menfolk in his family would have thoroughly approved. By now he had developed a love of the game of rugby football, and in his late forties he spoke knowledgeably of past games and players, sometimes forgetting his own complete lack of prowess as a player. As Secretary he was also a selector and a man of some influence, and it was in this role that he tangled with a young man known as Bashie Williams who had recently been recruited to the club and who, while distinguishing himself on the field, had been heard in the showers to refer to Elgar as 'a bit of a pouf'. It was a vulgar and completely uncalled for remark, Elgar thought, and it cut him to the quick.

'Not meant, Elgar boy,' said Abe Beynon, the Chairman as they walked from the changing-rooms to the club-house itself. Abe, once praised as a forward – 'slow but dirty' – towered over Elgar's short figure and, when he spoke, he could look down and see the full circular rim of Elgar's sporty pork-pie hat and wide-skirted riding mac swishing beneath it. 'You know what these lads are. No idea of what an effort it takes to run a club. Unappreciative is not the word.'

'I just happened to overhear it,' Elgar said. He stared at the path as he spoke, an intense stare as he scowled through rimless lenses.

'Overheard and overlooked, I trust?'

'He's not a very good forward and a lout into the bargain.'

'Oh, don't say that. He's built like a tank.'

'Robust, I give you.'

'Robust? He's got shoulders on him like a young bull. And what a worker!'

'He gives the appearance of working,' Elgar said pointedly; 'but if you ask me, there's nothing much else, certainly not upstairs.'

'Oh, come on, Elgar, it's not a dancing class we're running.'

'I didn't think it was.'

'Well, whatever he is off the field, he's a lion on it. If ever I've seen international potential, he's got it.'

'Really?' Elgar was surprised.

'Never been surer. You watch. He's one of those who'll rocket to the top. A bit of an animal around the house, I daresay, but he's not here to ice the cake.'

Elgar did not pursue arguments about the game if contradicted by so knowledgeable a person as Abe Beynon, but he did not disguise his dislike for Bashie Williams. The boy was indeed built like a tank, standing six foot and sixteen stone with the short neck and powerfully developed arms and shoulders which make for mastery of the front-row trade. His face was moon-shaped and pock-marked, thick, sensual lips constantly lolling open below a short cropped haircut which added to the ferocity of his appearance. In any other circumstance Elgar would have described Bashie's forehead as Neanderthal for there was about his appearance more than a hint of things primitive. But what annoyed Elgar was the boy's truculent and disrespectful manner when in the presence of club officials. To break wind in the showers or coming off after a game was one thing, but to do it when Elgar was reminding players of the promise to wear black arm bands on their jerseys to mourn the death of an old and trusted servant of the club was another. It showed lack of respect both for the dead and the living, and, more, was no doubt a directly aimed insult, if aimed was the right word.

Then there was his insolent reply which Elgar could only term 'naturalistic'.

'I can't help it, Mr Davies, faggots it is. The old girl keeps a stall on the market.'

There had been a general titter since Bashie was the maker of statements which some found amusing, but, as his coarse wit was generally at the expense of someone else, Elgar found it inexcusable. He had blushed scarlet in front of everyone, a childhood habit which he had thought long conquered, and he could do little more than turn on his heel, thereby increasing the effectiveness of the slight and no doubt causing prolonged comment behind his back. How could he tell the others that he was no prude, and always liked a laugh with the boys? He could not, of course, and had no answer for these farmyard habits which distressed him more than he could say, so much so that he dwelt upon it for weeks. Putting it mildly, Bashie Williams was not the sort of person you liked to meet indoors anyway. He was somehow too big for rooms. When he was in them, things tended to get knocked over. Chairs creaked, sagged, split; door slammed, shuddered, and shook as if in protest at Bashie's potential for physical damage. Everywhere he went, his size created problems and everything about him was too much, Elgar felt. Bashie was a beyond-person, and big-mouthed with it. That he was a splendid forward into the bargain was a pity. They always had wilder spirits in the club. When Morlais Morgans and Dai Price had been arrested after an altercation in a Warwickshire fish and chip shop, Elgar had gone personally to see the local police superintendent and taken a brace of stand tickets for the English international with him.

'You know what these lads are, sir,' he said in a man-to-man fashion, and later everybody had complimented him on the way he'd smoothed things over when the charge sheet was kept clean. Elgar was a fixer, people said, and there were innumerable occasions when a well-chosen word in the right ear had worked wonders. Elgar had a very nice manner. He knew when enough was enough. He did not take advantage and he knew when to stop asking. Then he was very good at remembering the people who helped the club, the grocer who supplied them with free tea, all the local tradesmen who helped out, and it was noticeable that

the club's annual dance had progressed from a scruffy hop
to a gala night with Elgar in charge and the police safely
seen to in the back kitchen of the local hotel. No one dis-
puted his work and no one had ever publicly said a word
against him, but ever since Bashie Williams had been recruited from a soccer team (and didn't that say it all really?),
bringing his sixteen stone over the mountain from a foundry
in neighbouring Aberdarren, Elgar had noticed a subtle
change in his relationship with the boys, as they called the
players. It was a change that began imperceptibly, altering
little things, seeming in Elgar's eyes to spread out like rising
damp from one central spot. And the core of infection was
Bashie, Elgar knew. It was not that anyone said anything
specific, but that, in an extraordinary way, like the girl with
body odour in the television commercial, Elgar now felt
people to be moving away from him. There was one more
very noticeable effect that gave him hours of regret, but
again he was slow to realize the cause.

For some weeks Elgar noticed that his fellow committee-
men tended to head him off when he made his way from
the grandstand to the dressing-room after a match. He had
thought this interruption to be a coincidence at first. He
was used to being spoken to constantly, often being asked
to consider this problem or that at the most inconvenient
of times. He usually acquiesced, so that, on several Saturdays
running, he was buttonholed at exactly the same time, at
the very moment when the players were changing in the
showers, but he had thought this to be a coincidence. Then
the same thing happened before the match when the players
were stripping in preparation for play. This also occurred on
several occasions. Now another committee-man would get
hold of him and Elgar became aware that he was being held
in conversation for the specific purpose of preventing him
from entering the players' changing-rooms. He was not welcome there any more, before or after a match, and at first he
could not believe it, for there was no atmosphere he loved
more : the players sprawling about half-dressed, stamping
their feet into the metal-studded boots, some rubbing them-

selves with embrocation – legend said Bashie Williams drank his the first time he saw it! – and one or two of the younger lads nervous if the opposition was to be feared. Hands were laid on shoulders and there was a great deal of frisky jollity, but best of all Elgar loved Ikey Owens's, the skipper's, pre-match instructions, and Elgar almost felt himself to be a member of the team then, standing in the background, blazered and gloved amongst the lads as Ikey spelled out the plan of the day or enumerated the likely sins of well-observed sinners who had known criminal records.

'If that fella McCool starts anything, you bloody cool it, not him. Give him his head and leave him to me, I'll cobble him quiet.'

And Elgar would grip his gloved little hands fiercely and the downward curve of his thin lips might well be taken to mean that McCool would be well observed from the committee box and had better watch it with him.

It was on these occasions that Elgar, perhaps more than at any time in his life, felt truly at one with the boys who were sprawled attentively on the benches before him. When they got to their feet, Ikey in the lead, he watched them go out into the tunnel, savouring the roar of the crowd as Ikey led the team on. Elgar always locked up after them, then hurried to his seat in the stand. If a player were carried off with a serious injury, Elgar would open up again, and had been witness of some special in-jokes. Once he had been Ikey Owens's companion when Ikey lay there groaning with a broken leg, muttering at the boos which floated in from the terraces as the play continued outside.

'I dunno,' said Ikey as the crowd continued their disapproval; 'this is the only club in the world that plays before a hostile crowd home and away!'

It had made a good story in Elgar's annual report at the dinner, and when, a year later, the offending McCool had a little difficulty seeing out of one eye, Elgar was in the know in a way few others were. Being in the know, being indispensible, being the man to whom people turned for the keys or the cash, mattered to Elgar, and better still, after a hard match when the warriors returned, boots scraping on the concrete floor, their bodies muddied and bloodied, Elgar had his factotum, Moss Thomas, get the shandies ready and he loved it then, the chatter and the final diagnosis.

'How was it, Morlais?'

'What a cow of a ref! Braille give him up when he went for the test!'

Then there were the complaints.

'Look at this lump by here! Good Christ, I'm moulting.'

It was sweaty, masculine, of the earth, earthy, and when they started singing in the showers, the songs were often bawdy and delighted Elgar.

> Here we come full of rum,
> Looking for wimmin who'll peddle their bum,
> In Pontlast R.F.C.!

Certainly no prude, Elgar was in his oils on these occasions, standing near the showers long after the steam had clouded his spectacles, inventing excuses to linger on, sometimes strutting importantly with his little red cash book and gold propelling-pencil, casting a blind eye upon those who were leaning heavily upon him with their expenses and giving as good as he got when there was any backchat about money.

'*Iesu Grist,* Elgar, three shifts, I lost.'

'Three kicks you missed too.'

'Oh, come on, Elgar, I got two maintenance warrants owing.'

'Training night Monday then. You'd better notify Securicor.'

It was such fun there in that hot-house atmosphere with the steam rising and the gorgeous smells of sweating flesh, liniment, and sodden gear, a kind of weekly male orgy which Elgar felt privileged to savour to the full. But ever since Bashie Williams had come, trailing his other soccer uncouthness, there had been a definite shading off in the approval with which Elgar felt himself to be regarded. After three Saturdays of pointed interruptions when on his way to the dressing room, he was more than sure of his exclusion, although Abe Beynon put it very delicately despite his fractured English.

'The boys want to be on their own, I daresay. There's been too many people getting in through the doors. Kids and that. You know what the language is like.'

'I don't mind a bit of language. Good Christ!' Elgar swore impressively.

'Gets a bit overcrowded in there.'

'But there's the expenses?'

'Ikey suggests Mondays. In the club-house.'

'Well, I usually lock up after?'

'Moss is doing it.'

'I wouldn't trust Moss with a packet of crisps.'

'The boys prefer it.'

'The boys?' Elgar caught his breath.

'You know how it is,' Abe Beynon's lantern-jawed undertaker's face was wet lipped and evasive. He had a large polychromatic nose, more a badge of office than an organ, and he rubbed it embarrassedly. 'They'd rather be on their own. Anyhow, be better if you opened up the club bar. They've got very slack there lately.'

Elgar, always glad of an opportunity to exercise his authority, saw the sense of this as there was a big-bosomed, sharp-tongued girl behind the bar who had clearly got out of hand on one occasion and who needed an eye keeping on her in more senses than one, being a bit of a drop-drawers, according to Abe. But since this conversation quite clearly referred to after-match procedures and there could possibly have been some doubt about Ikey's unstated objection, it came as a double shock to learn that another member of the committee thought it would be better if Elgar supervised the ticket collectors immediately before the match.

'Ticket collectors?'

'There's people creeping under hedges – everything.'

Elgar knew that this was patently untrue.

'What d'you want me to do?'

'Well, me and the committee ... like, well, perhaps, 'stead

of going into the changing-rooms while the boys is changing,
we think that you could be very useful at the gate, like?
That's the general idea.'

So there was no doubt. Elgar was being very definitely excluded from the dressing-room, he, the secretary. At first,
although he took care to show as little of his concern as
possible in the presence of his cautioners, his first inclination
was to protest openly. He could have given a polite but very
firm reminder of exactly how much he had done for the
club, and just how very important he was at this precise
moment since he was acting as guarantor for a much-needed
extension to the club-house proper, and without him the
bank manager would very probably have hesitated. But he
checked himself. He had not survived for so long in this
ultra-male world without acquiring certain skills and he
knew that a moaner was never appreciated. Never a squealer
be, they said in the collieries, and it was a code that was
implanted in many others besides the colliers. Also it would
not do to protest openly since there was clearly an under-
current of feeling that he did not fully understand. On its
face value, the objection to him – for he was sure that it must
be personal – could not be that he was officious or disliked
as an authority figure. He contradicted no one, certainly not
the players. He never expressed an opinion before a game,
and generally did not contradict those who held strong
opinions afterwards. His habit was to listen firmly to all, then
come down firmly in the middle. When two of the boys
had been sent off after a nasty business involving a well-
known trouble-maker from a more famous West Wales
club, he had taken the line that the referee was overawed
by the occasion and had seen, not the original offences, but
the retaliations. Elgar had a genuine sympathy for those
punished and had made it his business to have a cheery
but inoffensive word with them in the bar. Then, after a
particularly violent fracas involving more than the odd
punch, he might add a comment like: 'And they're sending
missionaries to China!' which was a good enough crack in
the aftermath of a particularly bloody afternoon, but he took

care never to offend. As far as he could see, he had done nothing wrong. He had said nothing, certainly not to Ikey Owens with whom he was on the best of terms. What then was the reason for the change? And why was Abe Beynon being so tactful?

Elgar searched his mind for reasons, and he could come to only one conclusion. His enemy must be Bàshie Williams.

It was at this time that Elgar began to return home earlier than usual, leaving others to lock up the club-house. His mother, now in her seventies, was a sportswoman herself and on Saturdays would invite her cronies into the house to play contract bridge. This group, a gaggle of women in their sixties and seventies, were sometimes jokingly referred to as The Last of the South Wales Posh, for they were the widows of colliery managers or important officials, those who in the lean years had known such luxuries as maids, foreign travel, or clothes sent on approval up to their houses from the leading Cardiff stores. They were women whose investments had prospered, part of a group whose wills were the subject of great local interest. Money had been made in the old days, even considerable sums, since the wisest had not invested in the coal industry but in the booming multi-purpose stores of England, but the women had lived longer than the men, and Mrs Blodwen Davies's bridge parties were the last occasions for the display of jewelled finery represented by lumpy garnet brooches and occasional Italianate cameos, the souvenirs of Mediterranean cruises of long ago. Besides Mrs Davies, Elgar's mother, there were three other women known to Elgar by the nicknames he remembered as a child. Mrs Owsher-Bowsher, Mrs Eadie Beadie Jones, and Miss Caldi Caldicott-Evans, the sole spinster, who seemed to have been a chain smoker all her life. They dressed inevitably in sombre clothes, drank the occasional port and lemon, leaving behind a mixed aroma of cigarette smoke, eau-de-Cologne and damp talcum powder in any room used.

When Elgar came home early from the club, it was a matter of politeness that he should put his head around the

card-room door, but since this was a Saturday-night world
of his mother's, and one in which he had no real interest,
he usually did no more than utter a few pleasantries and
soon excused himself. Elgar did not play cards and now and
again sensed that his mother's cronies seemed to view him
with a compassionate amusement that made him feel uncomfortable. Mrs Owsher-Bowsher he privately referred to
as That Disgusting Chocolate Person, since her husband had
made a small fortune in the manufacture of sweets and his
widow was a splendid and visible sampler of sweetmeats all
her life, while Mrs Eadie Beadie had been born poor and
retained the occasional crackling malice of one who did not
quite belong amongst the corpulent hoi polloi of long ago.
Miss Caldi Caldicott-Evans, known as The Caldi, a doctor's
daughter who had been to Roedean, was wont to chivvy
Eadie Beadie in matters of grammar or decorum, and was
the thinnest of the quartet still, well known for such eccentricities as entering the local shoe shop, saying; 'Have you
shoes? I mean, have you *good* shoes?' when confronted with
shelf upon shelf of proprietory brands. When Elgar entered
the room, all eyes turned to him except his mother's. Only
The Caldi smiled, as she always did, her spinster's heart remaining the warmest.

Elgar had a stock joke for Eadie Beadie who held the cards
between her thick beringed fingers as if they were enemies
who might get away.

'Everything all right? They're not taking you to the
laundry, Eadie Beadie?'

'Not with tram tickets,' said Eadie Beadie scowling at her
cards.

'You're home early?' said Elgar's mother with a sideways
glance.

'Do with an early night.'

'Anything happened?' said Eadie Beadie maliciously.

'We won six – nil.'

'I thought you'd be drinking when you didn't take the
car,' Eadie Beadie said.

'Always a bad sign,' said The Caldi with a fluttering if crinkled ageing debutante's wink.

'I walked,' said Elgar, returning her smile.

'You'll be walking if you call on a hand like that again,' said Mrs Davies menacingly to Miss Caldicott-Evans. 'If Ely Culbertson ever came down to this valley, he'd go back mental!'

The Caldi flushed while Mrs Owsher-Bowsher, replete in the majesty of her fourteen stone, said nothing and began painstakingly to count up points on the tips of her fingers.

The women, no less than the men, had the gift of repartee and while Elgar nodded pleasantly in the doorway, his mother's determination to get on with the game was quite usual. He was not going to be cross-examined. Elgar nodded at the back of his mother's head, smiled once more at Miss Caldicott-Evans who gave another coy wink, then excused himself. For years now, he and his mother had existed in a state of uneasy truce, each pursuing a separate life, coming together at meals and passing the time of day but little else unless either happened to be out of sorts when they would fuss over each other with habitual clucking solicitousness. Elgar knew that she was disappointed in him, at his failure to marry or to get a headship, but both subjects were now left alone by unspoken consent, and it was accepted that Elgar should live his own life between school and rugby club, with dutiful visits to chapel once on Sunday when he drove his mother to the one remaining chapel several miles away. That it was a bleak life in which the spirit was crushed by the aridity of long-established habits did not occur to him, although now and again he cast his eye on the images of the outside world as presented by the television screen, and sometimes heaved a sigh. He had travelled little because he would not leave his mother, who always gave him the idea that it was best for him to remain where he was well understood and where the family name (Davies, D.S.O.s) still counted for something. He was also delicate and there was his weak chest and the old embarrassing loss of hair

which had been miraculously arrested so that he was
no longer a sufferer from alopecia, thanks to the prescrip-
tions of the local general practitioner who had expectations
under Mrs Davies's will. Best for Elgar to stay put, both
had long ago agreed, while Mrs Davies, it should be said,
remained in remarkably good health, a big-boned,
strong woman, quite unlike Elgar in appearance with a
firm strong line of jaw and sharp, piercing eyes which
looked Eadie Beadie firmly in the face when she answered
Eadie Beadie's piercing questions, stating categorically
that Elgar had made his place with her and that was the
end of the matter. It was a mistake to think that Elgar
was deep. He was not deep, just liked the simple life at
home, being a very good boy to his mother, and if she had
any disappointment, it was that he was not musical as she
had hoped when she first named him. It was against this
background that Elgar had found a way of life for himself which was manageable until that one word floated
across to him from the sneering lips of Bashie Williams.
It might have been the breach in the dam which caused the
dyke to burst.

'Pouf,' he repeated to himself as soon as he had left his
mother and settled himself in his study chair. It was extraordinary that one word seemed to have done so much
damage. What on earth did it mean? Why should it have
such consequences? Why should he be singled out as untouchable when he was so companionable? If it meant
effeminate, it was absurd since he was the most sporty of
men and his entire wardrobe of blazers and ties proclaimed
his attachment to this sporting group or that. In a curious
way, it made him feel childlike to be so set apart and he had
a renewed understanding of those children who were sometimes excluded by their fellows because of the uncleanliness
of their appearance. It was a pariah word, no doubt about
it. But what could he do?

   With his legs tucked under him in his study chair, he
came to a decision. There was only one thing he could do
and that was soldier on, he said to himself, using a phrase of

his mother's which must in turn have been passed on to her by his father.

'Soldier on, John Willy! Best foot forward!' Better still if he could manage not to give the slightest indication of his hurt. He had a number of favourite exhortations to the team when things seemed to be going against them, and now and again applied them to himself when he tended to get down in the mouth. He stood up now and reached for his correspondence file with a typical rallying cry which he applied strictly to himself for once.

'Come on Pontlast – show your class!'

He knew he had to come back from behind as the boys had done on many occasions, and immediately his good nature showed itself. There was something he could do for Bashie Williams as the club were about to make their annual tour of the West Country, and Elgar always made it his business to write personally to employers, seeking permission for the players to absent themselves from their places of employment. It was a formality, since most of the local people accepted the penalty of employing rugby players, but it was one of those routine little tasks which Elgar did extremely well. He saw to it that the letters of application were followed by letters of thanks, and knew that the provision of international tickets was a useful lubricant when favours were required.

He decided that he would write first on Bashie Williams's behalf to the manager of the Aberdarren foundry and he settled the headed notepaper on his lap full of good intentions only to find that he could not remember Bashie Williams's Christian name. Once again an immediate good intention was abruptly followed by an irritation, as it always was when that young man's name came up. He could not put: *re Mr Bashie Williams* at the head of his letter. But the wretch must have a Christian name. *B.* was inserted in the programme and he was inevitably known as Bashie. But that would not do. Elgar decided to telephone the clubhouse, which was still open, in order to ask Abe Beynon.

'Abe?'

'Who is that?' Abe usually had a skinful on a Saturday night and his voice was thick and accusatory, as if a wife might have actually dared to intrude on his Saturday night privilege. 'What is it? Hurry up, if you please. It's nearly stop-tap.'

'It's Elgar. Small point. The Easter tour. What's Bashie Williams's first name?'

There was a moment's hesitation at the other end. Elgar could imagine Abe's babyish pout at being drawn away from his bottle at the bar.

'Leave the bugger alone,' Abe said.

'Listen, I must know his name. I've got to write to his employer.'

'His employer?' Abe sounded alarmed.

'If he's going to miss three days' work his employer will have to be notified. I do it every year.'

'Are you sure, Elgar?'

'What d'you mean, am I sure?' Elgar's annoyance increased.

'I mean,' said Abe carefully at the other end of the telephone – and Elgar could hear him sucking his teeth as he always did when suspicious; 'are you sure it's only leave of absence?'

'I'm not thinking of having him here to tea!'

Abe did not reply directly.

'Look. I've got to head the letter.'

'Basil,' Abe said finally but clearly after deliberation. 'B. for Basil.'

'And he's in the blacksmith's shop, I take it?'

'Yes.'

'Thank you. That's all I wanted to know.'

Once again there was a hesitation in Abe's manner, another note of reservation indicating an area of concern about something that was not directly mentioned and Elgar did not understand it. Did Abe think he was going to socialize with the fellow? If not what did he think? Could it be that Bashie Williams had done him further harm and did Abe think he was going to retaliate in some way? The puzzle remained and Elgar had no answer. He sighed at this latest nuisance but soon dismissed it and give his mind to his particular expertise. As his mother always said, Elgar wrote a very nice letter. He also had a very good hand.

Dear Mr Warbuoys, [he wrote]

re Mr Basil Williams (Blacksmith's)

As you know the Club will be making its annual tour of the West Country prior to Easter Week, and I write to ask if the above-named can be released from the foundry at 12 p.m. on Wednesday, the 15th. I am sure you will appreciate how important it is that the Club should be well represented against the English clubs. I would like to take this opportunity of thanking you for all your cooperation in the past. As usual, I have reserved two stand tickets for you and Mrs Warbuoys for the international encounter at Twickenham, and if there is anything else I can do, please do not hesitate to ask.

Kind regards.

> Yours sincerely,
> Elgar J. Davies.
> Hon. Sec.
> Pontlast R.F.C.

Elgar wrote a number of such letters and received expected replies but in the case of Mr Basil (*né* Bashie) Williams nothing was ordinary it seemed, and when the reply came Elgar was furious.

Dear Elgar,

re Mr Basil Williams

Thank you for your letter concerning the above-named, and also for your offer of tickets which Mrs Warbuoys and myself will be only too pleased to take up. As you know, I have done everything I can to help the Club in the past, and, indeed, will continue to do so in the future, as I quite agree that it is very important for us to be well represented in our annual battle with the English clubs. In the case of Mr Basil Williams, however, I cannot grant him leave of absence as you request, since he has already applied for seven days' leave of absence over the period in question in order that he should attend the funeral of his grandmother in Ireland.

Regards to your mother.

> Yours sincerely,
> E. F. Warbuoys
> Manager.

'Look at this – lying in his teeth!' Elgar said when he showed the offending letter to Abe Beynon. 'He's no conception of what I do to keep up the good relations for the Club.'

But Abe exploded with laughter until the tears showed in his rheumy eyes.

'I pisses myself every time that Bashie opens his mouth,' Abe said hoarsely. 'That'll be another one for the dinner, Elgar boy.'

'The dinner?'

'Your speech, man. Grannie in Ireland. What a character!'

Wisely, Elgar did not comment. Clearly, others saw things which he did not, and, as it happened, Bashie's status as a character had recently been increased by the fact that he had been returned comatose in a drunken condition to the club-house by an irate girlfriend who, exasperated at being kept waiting outside, had pushed him back in through the door, saying, 'You can have him back. I don't want him!' Once again, everybody thought this hilarious except Elgar, but Elgar kept his peace. If everybody thought Bashie Williams a character, then a character he must be. Elgar soon busied himself finalizing the details of the tour and, in the weeks that followed, he nodded cheerfully enough to Bashie whenever he saw him, but Bashie did not speak, merely gave a caustic nod in reply, and there were times when Elgar would look down the corridor outside the committee-room, hesitating to go down it unless accompanied in case some further remark of a loitering Bashie would add to his discomfiture. Although busy, he had a sense of something building up between Bashie and himself. It was uncanny, his apprehension, and he confided in no one, but it remained, and every time he saw Bashie lolling at the bar or playing darts with the boys, Elgar had a sixth sense of danger which sometimes caused his throat to dry and he was often the victim of intense nervousness. He took care not to stand near Bashie at the bar, and once, when he passed him on the way to the Gents, was forced to dig his hands deeply in his trouser pockets to disguise their tremble. Of course it was absurd since no one in the club would have allowed Bashie to offer him even the threat of physical violence, and there was no indication that Bashie was even considering it, yet his glances seemed to Elgar to be full of threat.

Bashie had let his hair grow longer, so that his forehead was crowded by an untidy fringe and he appeared more uncouth and villainous than ever. In an odd way, Elgar felt that Bashie had found him out, and if he had no clear idea of exactly what Bashie had diagnosed, his huge aura of bustling masculinity seemed to contain an explosive charge when it passed Elgar's puny little frame. It was quite absurd, and yet it was quite real. The man's presence was like a taunt which was repeated whenever they met and yet there was not a further word spoken. One night Elgar dreamed about Bashie. The two of them were locked in a cage with people coming to visit them and, in his dreams, Elgar saw Abe Beynon standing complaining to other spectators outside the bars. The complaint was that it was not fair to put the two of them together, and as a spectacle, the fact that they were together was in some way a cheat on the public purse. No violence was offered even in the dream and, while Elgar would not have confided with a living soul about this extraordinary occurrence, his obsession caused him to resume the sleeping tablets which he had long abandoned. Indeed, he packed them when the time came to leave on the tour of the West Country and he was aware that he must have given something of himself away because his mother affected a rare concern for his welfare.

'Are you sure you're all right, Elgar?'

'Of course, I'm all right, mother.'

'You look pale, and you're very restless in the nights.'

'Nonsense.'

'Yes, you are. You're up at the crack of dawn, and there can't be any good in you drinking all that water.'

When under stress, Elgar drank water continuously. It was one of the giveaway signs of his tension.

'You're not doing too much are you, Elgar?'

'Probably.'

'Well, give yourself a bit of a holiday.'

'I will.'

'Eadie Beadie can't come to Llandrindod Wells for the Bridge Convention.'

'Oh?'

'She reckons she'll be rooked. Mean, if you ask me.'

His mother's mind soon passed on to her own concerns and, when the time came, Elgar was relieved to see her off in the hired car which she shared with Owsher-Bowsher and The Caldi. Owsher-Bowsher sat of necessity in the front with the driver while his mother and The Caldi sat firmly apart, proudly demonstrating the room between themselves in the rear, the latter's lined and dotty face wreathed in cigarette smoke as they gave him a final scrutiny before the car pulled off to be driven at a prescribed speed along a prescribed route. They went to one or other of the watering spas every Easter while Elgar joined the boys, taking his seat at the rear of the club coach, where Abe Beynon sat, flagons clanking in the outsize pockets of his poacher's overcoat, his gay check trousers and co-respondent's shoes in strange contrast to the hoarse solemnity of his cracked voice as they sang their way up and out of the valley.

'Tonic Sol-fa on the brain,' Abe would complain every year, but he underscored '*Sanctaidd*' and the more maudlin of the Welsh revivalist hymns with the rest. They began with the hymns, careful to hit the right note under the caressing voices of the tenors, making their getaway like cliché-haunted actors in a television commercial, the repertoire changing to a cheerful obscenity at the first sight of the Severn Bridge and foreign England. Here Abe and Elgar hooted wantonly with the rest, and, with no more than an hour or two's separation in time from his mother's firm admonition to check that the sheets of his bed would be properly aired that night, Elgar, bright-eyed and pink-cheeked, would bawl in his high, piping tenor with the others:

> I done her standing and I done her lying,
> If she'd have had wings, I'd have done her flying!

It was true abandon, one of the joys of Easter, and for Elgar, happy to be on the move once more, it should all have been normal. But why was it that even now, safely tucked up beside the faithful Abe, he imagined hostile glances were being cast in his direction? Bashie, seated far down the coach at the front, was constantly visible, since by some bizarre coincidence his face appeared in the interior driving mirror and, as if that were not enough, Bashie actually turned from time to time and peered down the length of the coach, his eyes appearing to seek out Elgar and resting scornfully upon him, so that Elgar looked away, at the same time crossing and uncrossing his neatly trousered legs and smoothing their creases with a nervous gesture. Throughout the trip Abe Beynon gave him puzzled sideways glances, and even when they trooped into the hotel which was persuaded each year to accept them, Abe continued to watch Elgar with a genuine concern that added to Elgar's embarrassment.

It, said Elgar to himself, whatever *it* was, was beginning to show.

Immediately, they had other problems. There had been flooding in the area, the hotel could not accommodate them all and the party had to be split. The hotelier had made alternative arrangements. Would Elgar care to inspect the rooms in the adjoining boarding-house, and would he also decide which members of the party would use them? At first Elgar suggested that the committee be separated from the players.

'Oh, hell, no,' said Abe reproachfully. 'There's got to be someone responsible in each place.'

Elgar had a sudden terror of being in close proximity to Bashie Williams.

'Perhaps you and I could go with a few of the youngsters?'

Abe was anxious to remove his shoes since his feet swelled on long journeys.

'You go, Elgar.'

'But . . .'

'Just nip down, have a dekko.'

The whole party now stood in the foyer of the hotel and the baggage was being unloaded on the road outside. A decision was needed at once.

'Quick Elgar. 'Fore they gets the gear off the bus.'

But Elgar could not decide. Through the doorway, Abe saw the last bag come out of the boot of the coach.

'Here,' said Abe. 'Mog, Dai, Mush, and you, Bashie, get hold of your gear and nip down the road with Elgar. What's it called, this place?'

'Harbour Rest,' said the manager.

'That'll be changed,' said Abe knowledgeably. 'Go on, Elgar, I'll sign us in by here.'

So Elgar found himself leading the party through the streets of the little Cornish town, Bashie bringing up the rear, the toothbrush which he described as his luggage sticking out offensively from his top pocket. The Harbour Rest was a tall, Victorian boarding-house set in a terrace and the landlady believed in making space go round, since normal-sized bedrooms were partitioned into two, with single beds jammed up against each partition. If Abe had intended that Elgar should inspect each room, he had not reckoned with Elgar's apprehension, for no sooner had the party entered the building than the players began to deposit their luggage, and it was all Elgar could do to ensure that he had a room of his own on the ground floor. The players were anxious to rejoin the main party; there was no inspection and Elgar began to unpack his suitcase with a continued sense of his own inadequacy. Once again the presence of

Bashie Williams had disturbed his sense of equilibrium. He simply must pull himself together.

'Where the hell you bin?' said Abe when he returned eventually to the others.

'Perhaps he's got a bit of stuff there already?' Bashie said loudly.

Elgar was silent. Normally his practice when confronted with suggestive remarks of this kind was to give a sly wink and mysteriously imply that the jester was closer to the truth than he realized, but with Bashie he had no such confidence. What might the fellow say next? Bashie, as it happened, was distracted by the arrival of a pint, and Abe drew Elgar to one side.

'I didn't mean you to stay down there yourself.'

'I could do with an early night.'

'Yes, you're looking a bit peaky.'

That night, Elgar dosed himself with tablets and awoke in a drugged stupor which had the effect of lessening his unease. Surely his fear must be a grotesque product of his imagination? What was needed was a return of his old confidence. If only he could find some remark which would cut Bashie down to size. He remembered his silence on the previous night in the face of Bashie's snide remark and tried to rehearse replies which he might have made.

'Perhaps he's got a bit of stuff there already?'

'Not under the same roof as you!'

That was better than silence. How he envied those like Abe to whom remarks of this kind came as second nature.

'You are,' Abe had once said in a famous reply to an offender; 'about as much bloody use as a chocolate fireplace!'

If only he could sharpen his tongue and learn to defend himself. He would do well to learn from Abe, but then Abe had a street-corner facility for repartee. Perhaps the best he could do was to continue to make himself indispensable to the club and seek what shelter he could beside Abe who knew very well how much he did for them all.

'There are some,' said Abe on one occasion, 'who could

talk the robin off a packet of starch, but our Elgar is a worker, I say no more.'

Such praise as this, proclaimed when the committee was in full session, Elgar with his head modestly bowed beside his chairman, was for the Hon. Sec. the ultimate in acclaim, and the memory of it after a night of assisted sleep marked a return of confidence which was immediately bolstered by an odd occurrence at the breakfast table. Bashie, as might he expected, was late getting to breakfast. When he did arrive, bleary-eyed and unshaven, he sat at the end of the table in his shirtsleeves, blinking at the remainder of the party who were already beginning to eat the bacon and eggs which formed the main course.

The landlady approached Bashie with some diffidence and held a menu card in front of him. Elgar feared that he might come out with some uncouth remark but, as he studied Bashie's scowling face, he saw his lips moving unfamiliarly as if trying to form the shape of a letter. Out of politeness, the landlady, thinking perhaps that her handwriting was causing the difficulty, read the menu aloud.

'Would you like cornflakes, cereal, fruit juice, or grapefruit?'

Bashie glowered once more at the menu, then at her, then cast a resentful glance up the table where several rashers remained on other plates.

'Wassamatter?' said Bashie aggrievedly. 'Can't I have bacon and eggs like the other boys?'

Elgar gave a little gasp. Bashie's thick lips bending themselves about the letters on the menu card was an oddly familiar gesture and Elgar suddenly realized that Bashie could not read. He was also illiterate in all probability, for Elgar now remembered his attempts to evade making his signature on the accounts book on several occasions, and, when he did, he made a hasty scrawl, one foot in the door as if anxious to escape. So that was it... Elgar's own isolation from his fellows had given him a certain understanding of the problems faced by others, and now it occurred to him that Bashie's belligerence was explained by this inferiority.

Illiterate! Would you expect him to be anything but hostile to a schoolmaster? Perhaps the whole thing was an educational matter.

When the opportunity arose, Elgar dropped the news casually to Abe.

'Can't read?'

'No, he couldn't even manage the menu.'

'You didn't say anything, did you?'

'Of course not.'

'All I hope is, it don't put him off his game.'

Abe had other worries and their first game did not go well. Blooded by visits from other Welsh clubs, the local side had made preparations and the first half was fiercely fought, a ball-denying contest with many abrasive confrontations up front, frequent whistling-up by the referee whose nervousness far exceeded that of the players. It was not a game for the connoisseur, maul succeeding maul, scrimmage following scrimmage, and kicking up field predominated, so that the ball-to-hand agility of such stalwarts as Ikey Owens who in the past had displayed a thief-in-the-night quality when outwitting opposing outside halves – he had previously been nicknamed Ali Baba – was not obvious. It was grey football on a grey day, and Abe Beynon complained and complained and complained.

'I wish I never got out of bed.'

'Come on Pontlast – Show your class!' entreated Elgar courageously from the side of an opposing committee-man half his size.

'Boneless,' said Abe, all loyalty vanishing. 'If they was dogs, I wouldn't give 'em house room.'

'Up and under Pontlast!' shrilled Elgar. 'Vary it a bit.'

'Vary it?' said Abe. *'Vary it?* Vary what? With what?'

'There's still time.'

But Abe grunted. He was inclined to take the game with religious seriousness and, when it passed below minimal expectations, would brood in a sullen sog of memory, images of better days flowing through his mind while his face took on the saturnine expression of a man confronting total and expected disaster of Asiatic proportions. In the vintage years, when there had been violent arguments over the respective merits of two world-famous Welsh centres known to him as Bleddyn and Dr Jack, he had quarrelled with his brother-in-law and not spoken one word to him for two whole years, thereby putting his undertaker's business in jeopardy, since his brother-in-law had county-council connections and was instrumental in passing over the bodies of paupers and mental defectives at two pounds ten the single journey. It had cost Abe dear, this passion for Bleddyn, and when a game went wrong, as it did now, Elgar often felt that Abe was grieving, seeing not the present but the past, although Abe still maintained his capacity for cutting everyone down to size.

Elgar tried a new shout.

'Feet and take!' he yelled squeakily. 'Feet and take!'

Abe's eyes swivelled from under his cap.

'They're planting rice,' he said. 'Didn't you know?'

Elgar concentrated on the game. Now the play seemed to be cemented under the Pontlast posts, which rose like two sombre headstones above the steaming packs of forwards. Ikey Owens, hands on hips, stood with his back to his own line, but the bodies in front of him might have been digging their own mass grave and as the forwards slithered about, ball lost and never seeming likely to emerge, Elgar saw Bashie's face break from the rear of the maul, his mouth hanging open as he gazed blankly before him. On this occasion, he packed on the blindside, the side nearest the touchline, but his appearance for once was devoid of threat. All promise of a game had vanished. Even the rough stuff was carried on in slow motion as if by men suffering from influenza and Bashie's gaze resembled that of a foraging cow. Elgar saw him detach himself from the maul and wander forward, passing the centre line in his search for the ball, still moving forward while the ball was dexterously held by the opponents and kept invisible, and now both Elgar and Abe saw the trick coming, one of the oldest in the book.

'Oh, look at him! Look at him! What's he waiting for? – Milking-time.'

They watched helpless as Bashie wandered offside, and kept their silence as the referee blew and the inevitable penalty was awarded and kicked. Now ragged cheers from the few remaining local supporters rent the air. Pontlast had lost, penalty goal to nothing.

Abe shifted his false teeth a notch, readjusted them, then sucked his breath as if rationing saliva for the remark that would inevitably come.

'I always said he didn't have much upstairs,' Elgar said as they walked over to the dressing-rooms.

Abe made no reply.

'Of course, he's big enough, but, well ... is he worth the trouble?'

Abe continued to make no reply.

'I mean, of course, it was a pisscutter of a day,' said Elgar, using a graphic phrase of Abe's. 'But I mean, the oldest trick in the book?'

Abe walked on bitterly, hands ground into his overcoat pockets. Flecks of mud splashed upon the flanks of his sporty check trousers, but again he held his tongue.

'A bad start to the tour,' Elgar said gravely. 'And needless. I mean, a draw would have suited us fine.'

Abe seemed inconsolable, did not return an opposing committee-man's cheery 'Well done!' and Elgar followed him into the visitors' dressing-room where the exhausted players lay in various attitudes of despair about the benches. Bashie, as it happened, was standing examining various marks about his body and displaying certain scratches, the consequences of binding, as if these wounds were in any way an expiation of his cardinal ignorance. Offside under the posts ... Was there any worse crime?

Bashie saw Abe enter, Elgar beside him, shark and pilot fish together.

'Oh, don't you bloody start,' Bashie said defensively to Elgar, but the fact that he had picked on Elgar first was itself an indication of weakness.

'I've nothing to say at all,' said Elgar. But it was untrue. He felt decidedly perky. Now Bashie Williams positively looked as if he couldn't read. 'In fact, you're not even on the menu,' Elgar said sharply.

Bashie made no reply and Abe, overcoat open and thumbs to his braces. leaned forward to look into Bashie's face, his eyes narrowing and lips curling, creating another Pontlast legend as he delivered the *coup de grâce*.

'Basil,' said he, using the name which young Bashie must have dreaded in street-corner confrontations as a child; 'Basil, my son, blind side don't mean shut your bloody eyes, you know!'

Bashie flushed, then turned away sheepishly. They would all change their views, of course, since the rugby world would come to know Bashie Williams, from the high veldt to the packed stadiums of the Pyrenees, as there were honours, both amateur and professional, awaiting him, and Abe's initial judgement was right, but now the lizard-like stare of Abe did not leave its prey, and Elgar, taking courage, capped Abe's remark with a pearler of his own making.

'Yes,' said he, also going for the throat, Abe Beynon's family motto; 'On reflection, it would have been better if you had attended your grandmother's funeral in Ireland.'

If ever there was a Pax Britannica, it did not extend to Pontlast R.F.C. at home or away, and the event marked a temporary decline in the career of Bashie Williams, for that night, a chapter of accidents occurred that was not believed afterwards. Fifteen pints down, Bashie blundered by mistake into the landlady's bedroom, an occurrence that was made worse by his entire sixteen stone being in the nude. The landlady summoned the police. The police would not come. Then she roused Elgar and Elgar summoned Abe. At three o'clock in the morning a committee of investigation was set up.

'What was you doing in the altogether?'

'I thought it was the lav.'

'But she says you got hold of her?'

'Yes.'

'Well, then?'

'I thought she was the light.'

'Thought she was the light!' said Abe disgruntledly. 'You're not in the foundry now, you know? How much had you had?'

'Fifteen.'

'Pints?'

'Yes.'

'And shorts?'

'No shorts.'

'Thank God for small mercies anyhow.'

'Leave it to me,' said Elgar.

'Entirely in the altogether!' said Abe disgustedly. 'I mean, he's got a stalk on him like a cauliflower even in the cold showers. What was the poor woman to think?'

'I'll have a word with her,' said Elgar blushing.

'After that penalty, this is the last straw,' said Abe.

'Please,' said Elgar.

'No, no, no,' Abe said. 'One thing leads to another, and as for that penalty . . .'

'As it happens, I've got a box of mintoes in my case,' said Elgar helpfully, 'and we passed a flower shop on the way here. I've got my Barclaycard and . . .'

Now Bashie Williams looked more humble than Elgar had thought possible, for he eyed the floor between the investigators like an abashed lout outside the headmaster's study.

'Well, what have you got to say to Mr Davies by here? Where have he got to go now and on whose behalf, if I may ask?' fulminated Abe in his vintage county council English. 'Well, *Basil*? Say something, or have your tongue got mixed up with your what-d'you-call?'

'Sorry, Mr Davies.'

'I should bloody think so too. What a start to a tour! Go on, Elgar! Go to it! Tell her he was born in the workhouse, didn't use a knife and fork till he was ten. Tell her he's an animal and we'll chain him to the coach for the rest of the tour. Tell her what you like. I'll leave it to you. I mean, Good

God, it's not as if he'd met her before, is it? Never mind, go to it, Elgar. Bleddyn or no Bleddyn, all I hope is that Cardiff try to book in here next week.'

Elgar went to work and it was one of those occasions and one of those feats for which the Hon. Sec. was justly praised.

'What he done at the material time,' said Abe when the full committee were assembled, 'was to take charge at once. No messin', no adgin'. Without him, we'd have had a rape case on our hands, more'n like, very unsavoury and not at all for the good of the game.'

A vote of thanks was in order and a vote of thanks was given.

'Well, did you enjoy the tour?' said Mrs Blodwen Davies when her son returned.

'Drew one, lost one, won three,' said Elgar. And that was all.

'D'you know, I think he's put on weight?' said The Caldi from behind her inevitable Benson and Hedges. 'Look at his little cheeks!'

'Nonsense!' said Eadie Beadie.

'Yes, he has, he's positively glowing,' said The Caldi, coughing continuously.

'I have found out certain things about that woman,' said Mrs Davies darkly when the visitors had gone. 'Public school indeed! She is the sort of woman who needs a recipe for toast.'

Elgar paid no attention. Remarks, remarks, remarks, he thought. They were surrounded by remarks which cut about their ears like knives, but remembering his own improved performance, he smiled. Not bad, that one about the funeral of Bashie's grandmother in Ireland. He had turned that to his own advantage, and it would keep. Then he might also dig up something about a box of mintoes being as essential on tour as Mush's embrocation. Having learned to bite, there was suddenly no end to the number of points he might make in his speech at the annual dinner.

The reinstatement of the Hon. Sec. was complete.

Black Barren

ISLWYN FFOWC ELIS

(translated by the author)

Aye, lad, I sold the last batch of lambs at the mart yesterday. A fair enough price they fetched too. Mind you, the ewes are yearning: been bleating away all night long. I didn't wean the lambs this year: only sold them off as they came ready. It's all early lambs now. Aye, the poor old ewes are yearning. Like to see them? I'm just going to have a look at them now.

Sheep are my life, you know. Fond of sheep I am. If I was a poet I'd write an ode about sheep. The lambs are so pretty in the spring, bouncing like snowflakes all over the meadow; I can watch them for hours. A pity they have to grow. Still, there's something attractive about them at every age – like people, I suppose. Take yearlings now; smart they are; in the bloom of life, as you might say. A penful of warm wethers, out of breath after gathering; there's nothing like pushing through them, feeling them, enjoying them with the tips of my fingers. Kind old mother ewes like these I'm going to show you now. A proper Samson of a ram, head up, staring into the distance, pleased with himself after a good season's work. And the odd old barren that couldn't take a ram, empty in a field full of in-lambs. Feel sorry for them I do. Nature's hard on some.

Aye, I've got a barren or two every year. But I've got one – if she's really mine – you'll see her in a moment – I've had her for twenty years. Hard to believe, isn't it? Black she is, with two curly horns like a Welsh ram. Curlier if anything. Where she came from I haven't a clue. Perhaps you can explain it when you see her. But I'm telling you: she's been here twenty years, and growing bigger every day. She's bigger than any ram I've ever had. She's huge. But you'll see for yourself in a moment.

I'll tell you when I saw her first. I'd just been to Oswestry mart buying two dozen ewes. I'd turned them into the field and had my tea. After milking and letting the cows out, I popped over to see how the ewes were settling down. And damn, there she was, black and horny among them. An ugly, skinny, long-legged thing, staring at me like any cheeky brat.

Well, the following Wednesday I went to the mart. I'd bought the ewes off a chap from down-country, round Clun that way, a redhead, name of Briggs. I went up to him and told him that I'd bought two dozen ewes off him but that I didn't want the ugly black one that he'd put in with them, and would he take her back? God, no, he hadn't sold me a black ewe. She was never his. He hadn't had a black sheep on his land.

I was in a bit of a fog now, like. I went round the neighbours. No, none of them had lost a black sheep. I went to the policeman. I told the sheep-steward. And I put a small ad in the local paper. Then I waited. Heard nothing. No one claimed her. And of course she had no ear markings as she's obviously never been on a mountain and no red paint or any mark of any kind on her wool.

Well, I said to myself, I've got a black sheep. Nobody owns her. Or, at any rate, nobody claims to. It's as if she's dropped from another world. I'm telling you, I'd hated her at first sight, but I could do nothing now but keep her .

Right. The hard winter came. That winter, if you remember, when it rained ice. Inches of ice on top of feet of snow, every twig and blade of grass cased in a finger of ice. All these Berwyn mountains were like glass. I was having to carry dry hay to the flock; I carried, and kept on carrying, load after load. They'd stuck in a row at the top of the slope behind the house, and I had to strap each burden of hay on my back and crawl up towards them on all fours. And when I'd almost reached the top I'd slither back down the slope to the bottom and had to start all over again. The hay had finished in the loft above the shippon and I was watching the hay in the dutch barn falling lower and lower every day, with no sign of an end to the freeze-up. I was tiring, and I was worrying.

The sheep had gone almost too weak to eat. But this black sheep, she ate like a hungry horse. She'd munch heartily under the others' noses. She'd snatch hay from their mouths. I never saw anything like it. And then, the fever started. The ewes were dying one by one, and not from cold. The ewes that died were those with twin lambs inside them. I carried one after the other into the shippon and laid them in the alley in front of the cattle's steaming nostrils to give them some warmth. The alley was full of them, like a row of woolly skeletons, but die they did, do what I might to save them. But do you think there was any chance of that old black barren dying? No fear, lad. While the others died in heaps in the alley, she stood at the top of the slope in the teeth of every blizzard, *growing*. I'd never seen her look better than she did that winter. She hadn't got twin lambs inside her like those that were dying. She'd got nothing inside her except hunger.

The winter passed, but I'd come to hate this old black sheep so much that I decided to sell her. When mid-spring came I picked five other barrens and put her with them, and off I went to the mart. I got precious little for them, but I was quite glad to be rid of them; pasture was scant enough. Fine, I said: that one's gone, and good riddance to her.

But hell, when I got home and went to look at the ewes that were still dropping lambs, what should I see right among them, as bold as ever, but her. Great heaven, I said, how did *she* come all the way back here, when I've just sold her ten miles away? She was like a big black blot among my little white sheep, staring at me like a curse.

That, for a while, was that. The time came to wash the sheep ready for shearing. And I washed her, though I'd meant not to. I hated the thought of putting her murky black

fleece with the white wool of the others. Anyway, I was standing at the edge of the washing-pool with a wooden douser
in my hand, ducking each sheep with it on the neck as she
passed, holding her under water for a minute or so. Then
Dick, Gelli, threw in the black barren, though he swore
afterwards that he didn't. Well, first of all, she made such
a splash that I was wet from head to foot. Then the douser
got caught in her fleece, as if that cursed wool of hers had
curled itself round it. The next thing I knew was that I was
with her up to my neck in the mucky water. To finish the
job properly she landed me a crunching kick in the ribs
before leaping over the floodgate after the others. Taking
revenge on me she was. You can laugh, lad, but I know that's
what it was.

That year passed, and the year after. The black barren
wasn't behaving too badly now, but I hated the sight of her.
If she'd produce a lamb to pay for her keep that would be
something, but she was good for nothing as she was. All
she did was grow. She stood head and shoulders above every
other sheep on the place, her horns like two coiled snakes
on either side of her head.

I'd just bought a new ram. A big Leicester. A noble creature with a nose like an eagle's beak and white socks and a
fine carpet of wool on him. He'd served all the ewes in his
field as far as I could judge, except the black barren. Oh, I
said to myself, she won't take this one either. The murky
madam was keeping a field's breadth away from him.

But one evening, what should I see but her and the big
Leicester together in the corner of the field. So, I said, she's
found her lord and master after all. I might get a lamb from
her this time, though I hope it'll be a better thing than she
is. And I went home feeling oddly satisfied. Next morning
I returned to the field. The big Leicester was lying dead as a
doornail, his belly torn open by a pair of horns.

I went home at once, crying like a child. That ram had
cost money. I snatched the gun from its corner, loaded it
and ran back to the field. She was grazing on her own on the
hillock, grazing fast and furious as if she were starving. You

shall starve, my beauty, I said – for ever. I'd never had a better target. It was as if she'd been set there for me.

I raised the gun. I aimed. I fired. But just as I fired, she moved. And what should I see behind her but another ewe that had been grazing in her shadow. That one dropped dead, her head full of shot. But the black barren? None the worse. She carried on grazing fast and furious; the shot hadn't even disturbed her.

I nearly shot myself. That was the next thought that came to me. I couldn't fire again on the black barren lest I killed another of my precious ewes. It was the first time she really put fear into me. I was sick with fear.

But the following day would be Wednesday. You wait till tomorrow morning, my lovely, I said, and you'll go. This time for sure. But when the next day came she didn't go. Whether it was the fear or not I can't say, but I felt too weak to go to the mart. So she stayed.

She kept on growing. Year after year she grew. She's grown twice as big as the rams. I sheared her, but her fleece was useless. It just frittered away in my hands. And she never bore a lamb. A barren she was, by nature.

Anyway, one evening I was rounding up the sheep. It was hot, sultry weather with thunder about, and a lot of the sheep were crawling with maggots. It fairly hurt me to see them, twisting and turning and raking themselves against the posts in the hedges, their backs raw naked flesh. But her? Oh, she was fine, grazing away in mid-field, her useless fleece whole and her skin as healthy as could be, without a fly or a maggot near her. God, I got mad. I was that tired after being at it for hours on end with the shears and the ointment, and here was this evil creature as fit as a fiddle amid all the suffering. I just couldn't stand it. I crept quietly up behind her, caught her round the throat with my crook and held her. She was strong and kicked like a horse, but I held on. I managed to pull some cord from my rucksack, fettered her feet and threw her on the grass. Then I took out my clasp-knife.

Now, Lady Soot, I said, we'll see which of us is the stronger.

It's not a gun I've got this time: there's no danger of my killing one of the others. I'm going to finish you. My life's not worth living.

I grasped her throat, spreading the wool to make a clear space for the blade, then raised my hand high enough for one clean blow. But just as the knife was on its way down she looked at me, her eyes afire, and gave a sharp shudder. And the blade plunged into my left wrist. The last thing I saw was my own blood. After that, all went black.

When I came round, I was lying in the house with the doctor bending over me. Dick, Gelli, had happened to come by and had seen me flat on the field, bleeding. I asked him what about the black sheep. He'd seen no black sheep, only a piece of tangled cord on the grass at my elbow.

I must have lost pints of blood. I lay for three days, and it was some time before I got strong enough to take a walk round the fields. But when I did, the first thing I looked for was her. If I hadn't seen her I would have felt strangely disappointed. But she was there, right enough. She was all there.

Till then, I'd been fighting her, and I didn't know for sure which of us was master. But the fighting came to an end. And this is how it happened.

There's an outcrop of rock about a quarter of a mile from here. Evans's Rock we call it, because there was a quarry of some sort there many years ago. On this side the land is level, but on the other there's a sheer drop of several hundred feet. I'd had to put up a strong fence round it to prevent the sheep and heifers and young steers from getting near it, because I'd lost more than one lamb that had fallen over, and I'd found a heifer on it once with a broken leg. Not one of the sheep had got through that fence. But milady got through it, as you might expect. She'd get through anything.

If she'd gone on her own I could have forgiven her. But she drew three yearling ewes with her. And when I saw them they were standing in a huddle on the highest boulder. My heart took a turn when I saw them. How the devil am I going to get those from there without frightening them over the edge? I said to myself. Somehow, I'll have to catch them and fetter them and carry them one by one on my back.

Well, I tied the dog to the corner post in the fence and started to crawl towards them on all fours, moving as stealthily as I could from boulder to boulder, keeping my head well down. I was close by them now, and they hadn't seen me. But I had to come into sight because there was a strip of open ground between us. My heart pounded like a mallet as I thought of that precipice beneath them: one slip would be enough.

Very slowly I raised my head. And she saw me. It was she, the black barren, that saw me first, you can be sure. She bleated and stamped her foot. One of the yearlings took fright, and jumped, and fell into the gulley below. Well, that's the end of that one, I said. A pretty young ewe that would have bred for years.

On I went, gnashing my teeth. When I was within five yards the black barren spun like a top and pushed one of the remaining yearlings with her rump, sending her spinning into the abyss with a long-drawn-out cry like a child's.

I was crying myself now. I couldn't help it. There was only one thing I could do: rescue the last little yearling, come what might. So I reached out my crook as gently as I could, trying to get the handle round her throat before she could jump. But just before the crook reached her what should the old black barren do but plant her horns under the yearling and lift her. And the last one vanished out of my sight in that awful depth.

I stood up then and cursed the barren, I don't need to tell you. I cursed her to hell and beyond. You go after them! I shouted, my tears spurting. Go, damn you! Go! She just stood there, her black lips curled off her teeth in a maddening leer. And if I was ever maddened I was maddened then. I gripped my crook and gave her a ferocious prod with the ferrule, and another, and another. But I couldn't move her. It was like as if her hooves had been soldered to the rock. And d'you know what she did next? Her leer died on her lips, and she gave me a most pitiful look as if she were saying, 'Are you going to leave me on this old rock to starve?'

I suddenly felt strange all over. I just couldn't stare her in the eye. And the next thing I knew was that I'd lifted her, huge as she was, on my shoulders and was lurching with her over the rocks and slippery grass back towards the fence. I set her down in the field. She turned once and looked at me like the devil himself, as much as to say, 'You silly fool.' And off she went.

I knew that the fighting was over. There was little doubt now who was master.

Well, there we are. I'll just open this gate and we'll go into the field. There they are, see, the old ewes. Still bleating after their lambs, poor creatures. There aren't as many of them as there ought to be. I've lost a lot of sheep in twenty years.

Now, then, let's see . . . Where is she? She must be here. You can't possibly miss her, she's that big. There she is. See her? Under that rowan tree in the corner . . .

What did you say? You don't see her? Of course you do. There she is now, moving towards those two ewes by the hedge. You can't fail to see her unless you're blind.

Are you . . . quite sure? I can't understand it. I can't understand it at all. Dick, Gelli, says he's never seen her. My wife says that she's never seen her, that she doesn't know what I'm talking about. Dear God, how am I going to bear it?

Sure, I'm well enough, as far as I know. No, I haven't got a guilty conscience. Why d'you ask? I never harmed a sheep; I've told you, I'm fond of sheep, always have been. I never harmed a *sheep* for certain . . . No, I've never been very happy. I don't really know what happiness is. Does anyone? For me, life has always been something to get through as best I could, hoping each day that the next day would be a little better. A sort of crawling up the slope and slithering back down to the bottom and starting all over again. Isn't that what life is?

Are you sure you don't see her? Yes, of course I can see her. She's watching me now like a stoat, her horns coiled on either side of her head like two snakes. She's black as midnight, she'll bleat in a moment and I'll be sick when I hear her.

I can't understand why none of you see her. But there it is: I understand hardly anything now. One thing I know: I'll never be rid of her. And never is a long time. Isn't it?

Mel's Secret Love

EMYR HUMPHREYS

I

SUMMER was firmly established in the city. The leaves spread everywhere, from the park in the centre, down those tree-lined streets which had been considered in late Victorian times as more than wide enough for any conceivable expansion of traffic. In Margam Road, terraces of three- and four-storey houses, with gothic touches in their heavy stone façades, were partially hidden by high hedges and trees. It did not seem possible that such an area, so solid, so permanent, could be scheduled for demolition. When the plan for the new link with the motorway was first divulged there had been a great outcry. A defence committee of residents had been formed and the secretary had appeared on television; but now, after two years, indignation had worn thin. Residents had begun to move. It was rumoured that weeks rather than months stood between the long row of dignified houses and total demolition.

In the second-floor bay window of one of these, a girl called Mel sat smoking a cigarette and admiring the play of sunlight in the movement of the tender leaves. She had eaten cold beef and salad for her Sunday lunch. Beef was cheaper because of the hot weather. Sunday papers were on the chair opposite but she wasn't inclined to read them. With her bare elbow nestling in the palm of her left hand, she held her cigarette an inch from her lips and from time to time pouted and sucked contentedly at the filter-tip. She was comfortable in her cool summer frock and there was no demand for any movement on her part, beyond toes wriggling in sandals brought out for the first time this summer: peace and quiet should last at least as long as her cigarette.

It was the day before her thirty-sixth birthday, but she was unmarried and she still thought of herself as a girl. She was Miss Madock in the office, but Mel at home and Mel to her friends and Mel above all to her boss when they were alone together, when he became Arty instead of Mr Gender of Smoke, Simons, and Gender and Co. She bent her head so that she could touch her hair with the finger-tips of the hand that held the cigarette. This was her crowning glory, a colour that could shift from bronze to gold, colour that caught the light and drew attention. All her life it had been commented on and, when it was washed, it was inde-structibly youthful; 'morning sunlight on the waving corn' as Arty called it on Monday mornings, quite boldly, even when there were other people in the front office. In one of his moods of reckless gaiety, he would go on about it until she blushed with embarrassment and he laughed delightedly and jumped about the room. Arty was forty-nine but he still loved to sing and dance. 'I wanted to go on the stage, so I became an auctioneer' was one of his regular jokes. When he laughed it was like the bubbles rising in a bottle of soda water. He was only five foot five, but wherever he went his personality filled the room and he made everybody feel more alive. Mel would find no difficulty in spending an afternoon alone, thinking about him so that the muscles of her tight pale face would relax, her soft drooping nose tilt upwards and furrows clear from her high forehead.

Voices downstairs and footsteps and breathless laughter put an end to her session of thinking about Arty. The heavy front door slamming into place echoed through the house which had so many empty rooms. The house belonged to Mr Ferrata who owned a café-bar near the station. He and his wife occupied the basement flat. Sunday was their busiest day. Little Mrs Ferrata laboured at the coffee machine, worrying about the empty rooms in the house. The future was so uncertain. She had not enough English to follow

what was happening, so her husband had to tell her bluntly
in Italian: '*Another two months, another three months . . . I
don't know . . . who knows?*'

   – Mel! Are you there, love?

It was Winnie, the only other tenant left in the house. Her
two rooms were across the landing. She seemed to enjoy the
emptiness of the house. She certainly shouted on the stairs
far more than she used to. She was talking now to a companion at the top of her voice, excited and cheerful. Mel
went to the door and stood on the landing, prepared to greet
them for Winnie's sake, rather than any eagerness on her
own part for company.

   – Mel!

Winnie was out of breath with talking and climbing the
stairs. She was a large fat girl with a smooth sallow skin and
she wore a mauve trouser-suit which was too tight for her
and carried a gossamer scarf of the same colour which she
waved about as she talked.

   – Mel, love . . . This is Judy. You've heard me talk about
Judy. Used to work in our office. Many a long year ago.
Judy's getting married!

Judy looked at Mel expectantly to see if she was someone
willing to participate in the spirit of the occasion. She was a
bony peroxide blonde with a protruding lower lip and, as she
shook her limp hand and congratulated her, Mel searched
rapidly for an attractive feature which she could keep in
mind so as to enter more sincerely into their mood of joy.
She had been brought up in the country and was inclined
to be shy. Judy's ears were in view and they seemed to Mel
to be small and very comely. As warmly as she could she
invited them into her room for coffee.

   – Bless you, Winnie said, my room is in a heck of a mess.
Mel's got a lovely room – haven't you, Mel?

Winnie directed Judy's attention to the old prints on the
wall, the Chinese carpet which Mel had picked up two years
ago in a sale, the black, red, and white motif on the heavy
Welsh *carthen* over the divan and the view from the window
of the trees in the street.

– All I can see is weeds in the deserted gardens, Winnie said. Nobody's planted anything this year. Honestly, it's that depressing. It's like the end of the world.

Winnie continued to draw her old friend's attention to objects in the room while Mel went into the kitchenette to make coffee.

– Where did you get this bit of Staffordshire, love?

Mel hurried to the doorway, holding a tin of coffee and blushing nervously. Winnie was clumsy and now with dangerous freedom she was waving the Prince Albert statuette that Arty had given Mel.

– Ah! Say no more!

Winnie put it down with exaggerated care. She spoke with the broad West Wales accent she used when she wanted to make people laugh. Pouring hot water from her electric kettle on the coffee powder, Mel jumped at the noise of a piece of furniture being knocked over.

– It's all right, love. It's only me. I'm a terror, aren't I? It's my feet, love. I can't help it. They're killing me.

All three laughed and the two visitors accepted their coffee very gratefully. Mel touched two chairs and a glass-topped table, restoring them to their normal spatial relationship, before she sat down to hear more details of the forthcoming wedding.

– How many tiers?

Winnie pushed her head forward as far as it would go, to show insatiable interest.

– Three, Judy said firmly. I think three's quite enough. You remember my cousin Meg? She had four. Daddy said I could have four. But I think four's too much. Don't you?

– Tears?

Mel looked puzzled.

– On the cake.

Winnie built a wedding cake up in the air.

– Oh.

Mel looked ashamed of her ignorance and began to blush.

– I thought they were some kind of pearls, to wear, you know . . .

– What a lovely idea, Winnie said. I would wear them all over.

She lit her second cigarette and Mel pushed an ash-tray in her direction.

– Thanks, love, Winnie said.

– You work at Smoke, Simons, and Gender, Judy said. Winnie was telling me. Gareth . . .

– Her husband to be, Winnie said cosily.

– Gareth . . .

– Gareth Pollock-Jones, Winnie said. She'll be Mrs Gareth Pollock-Jones in three weeks. Sorry, love. I can't help interrupting.

– Gareth has a friend in your office. Colyn. Colyn with a y. He's coming to the wedding.

Mel smiled politely. 'Colyn with a y' was Arty's phrase as well. It was possible that everybody used it. It did not follow that Judy meant it sarcastically as Arty did. There was no means of knowing either what 'Colyn with a y' might have been telling his friends about life in the offices of Smoke, Simons, and Gender. The wisest course was to keep a neutral face and show only mild surprise.

– Small world, isn't it? Winnie said.

She turned her head towards Judy and Mel in turn, quite happy to be a spectator if their encounter should develop into a contest, but anxious too that the match should remain friendly.

– The reception will be at the Anchorage. Right by the water. Should be lovely if the weather's all right.

– I was just going to say that, Winnie said.

– The lawns, you know, they run right down to the river. It belongs to Gareth's uncle so we'll have special terms of course.

– That's marvellous, isn't it?

Winnie's head moved again to look at Mel and conjure some response.

– How many guests? Winnie demonstrated an eager interest although she already knew the number.

– Just over two hundred. I wouldn't like too many.

Judy's lip hung down a little hesitantly. She was prepared to let flow a flood of information; but Mel sat so upright and silent in her chair, she was discouraged. All had promised well with an audience of two until she mentioned Colyn. If there was something wrong with him, surely it was Mel's place to tell her; it was certainly too awkward for her to ask. Mel sensed her hesitation and struggled to show a keener interest. She asked about the wedding-dress and offered more coffee.

– It's full-length wild silk, Judy said. Decorated around the neck and cuffs with guipure lace. A matching headband of wild silk, with a short veil.

– A white wedding. Isn't that marvellous? Nothing like it, is there, in the end?

Winnie was nodding with enthusiasm.

– The bouquet will be lilies of the valley and miniature gladioli. The bridesmaids will wear duck-egg blue.

Judy caught Mel glancing through the window. Within a minute or two, in the middle of a description of some of the more impressive wedding presents, she remembered it was getting late and she had another friend to visit. When she consulted her watch, her engagement ring flashed in the afternoon sunlight. Winnie escorted her downstairs. Mel could hear her expressing her admiration for every detail of Judy's triumph.

– It's once in a lifetime, love, she was saying, and her words echoed through the empty house, so you make the best of it. Now there's a bit of advice from an old maid if you like. You load yourself up, love, with the treasures of a lifetime. Your ship's in port as they say. I think mine must be stuck on the rocks somewhere . . .

Whatever Judy said was lost in the reverberation of Winnie's laughter. Winnie was committed to being cheerful. Fastidiously Mel emptied the ash-tray Winnie had filled and opened a second window. The front door was closed after loud and affectionate farewells. There was a long silence before Mel heard Winnie dragging her feet up the stairs. Hurriedly she made for the bathroom which they shared and prepared to wash her hair.

– Mel! Can I come in?

Winnie raised her voice above the running water. Wearing her nylon dressing-gown, Mel opened the bathroom door. There was a chair painted white alongside the bath and Winnie sat on it gloomily.

– She was let down ever so badly, she said. Some years ago now, of course. This Gareth chap is all right. A bit dull for my taste. Works in the bank. Mad on tennis and squash. Too energetic for me . . .

Mel lifted her head out of the water.

– I can't hear, she said.

– Doesn't matter, love. It's not worth hearing. I'm just a jealous old bitch. For God's sake, what's she getting? A mother-in-law, a semi, and a couple of snivelling kids. I'm cheering up minute by minute.

Winnie laughed noisily. When Mel had wrapped her hair in a towel, they went back to the sitting-room and Winnie said she'd warm up some more coffee. She was eager that they should sit in the bay window and smoke and talk. Mel asked the time. It was a quarter to four.

– I must go to chapel tonight, she said. I haven't been for weeks.

– Who's counting?

– I saw the minister's wife in the Kardomah Friday morning. She comes from my part of the world.

– 'Green green grass of home!' Winnie said. When I think of all those long Welsh verses I used to have to learn. I can't think why you go, love, to be quite honest. Nobody bothers any more. It's a thing of the past, isn't it?

– I quite like going.

Winnie stared at Mel, quite mystified.

– I never know about you Mel, quite honestly. You live in a world of your own. You're not like me at all, slopping it all over the place. You keep it all in here.

Winnie crushed her fist into her chest. Mel said nothing. Winnie offered her a cigarette. Mel shook her head, but

Winnie jumped to her feet and pushed a cigarette between
Mel's lips.

– How's Arty?

Winnie put the question with immense discretion, exhal-
ing cigarette-smoke from the corner of her mouth while
staring straight at Mel.

– He's eating too many chips, Mel said.

It gave her real concern and Winnie knew better than to
smile. It was her role on Sunday afternoons, such as this, to
give Mel sympathetic intense attention. Even though they
were alone in the house, their voices dropped. The sepulchral
quiet of the house advanced right into the room. They
crouched together smoking in the bay window. Within hail-
ing distance of the visible world of the street, Mel's voice
had become a confessional murmur.

– He loves them, you see. Crisps, chips, potatoes. They give
him awful wind. He hasn't been to the office since Thursday.

– Fancy Judy knowing 'Colyn with a y', Winnie said. I
nearly burst out laughing. I thought of you saying that Arty
had started calling him *Colyn Ploryn*. Marvellous the way
Arty invents names for people, isn't it?

Mel looked at her suspiciously.

– I never would, of course. Something told in confidence . . .
I'll never forget how true you were to me, Mel . . . You know
I'd never breathe a word, Mel, I'd rather die first and that's
the truth.

Winnie became so earnest, she might have been renewing
an oath over sacred relics.

– He certainly has a bad effect on Arty. He's got eyes like
ferrets. Peeping into everything. I have to keep all our files
under lock and key. Every one of them. It's very embarrassing for Arty, I think. Just because Mr Simons is his uncle,
this Colyn thinks he can wander through the whole place
pushing his nose into this or that. Nobody in the office likes
him. He's a snooper, Arty says, and nobody ever likes a
snooper.

– You're telling me, Winnie said. We've got one too. Only
ours is female. That's worse if anything.

– We went to the Red Rock Beach estate last Tuesday.

Mel spoke very calmly and Winnie held her breath. She leaned forward, her eyes shining.

– There's a new block of flats there, you know, just finished. Arty's handling them. Three-bedroom flats at £7,500, ninety-nine-year lease. The top one is furnished and we had to check it was all in order before the public are asked to view. We had a bit of an argument really. I said to Arty I thought it was over-furnished.

– Well, Mel, Winnie said. You're an expert there all right.

– He let me rearrange it a little. We had a wonderful time.

– How long did you stay there?

– There's a wonderful view of the Estuary. Arty was so funny. He said let's pretend it's ours, he said.

– What time was that?

– About three in the afternoon. He made me go to bed with him. I never want to do it really, as you know. But he's so persuasive. We were there all afternoon. I had to make him come away. I said your car is outside, Arty. Some-one is sure to notice. He never thinks of things like that.

– How did it start, Mel? You know, when did you first . . .

Winnie looked intense and truthful. Mel seemed to hesitate.

– People would say there's no future in it, Mel said. I know that's what people would say. But I don't look at it like that. That's not the way I look at it. I've been with him now for over seven years.

– I quite agree, Winnie said. It's love that matters after all. This is real love. This is what I'd call love if you asked me.

– When we were in the flat on Tuesday. You know what he said?

Winnie shook her head. She was about to light another cigarette but she waited to hear what Arty had said.

– 'Mel,' he said, 'you know how much I love you,' he said, 'but you've got your life in front of you, kid.' I was a bit tense. The door was locked but I thought I heard somebody on the stairs. It wasn't impossible. We could have been fol-lowed.

Mel paused to consider the implications of what she had just said. She looked closely at Winnie, only prepared to say more if she made a sign that she fully appreciated the critical nature of the situation. Winnie half closed her eyes to show how well she understood the need at all times for the utmost secrecy.

– 'You want to get rid of me,' I said. I didn't mean it. 'Now listen,' he said, 'I'm trying to be unselfish and it's an effort. You might want to settle down. I won't mention it again. But if the chance comes, kid, take it.' 'I'm very happy, Arty,' I said. 'I've got everything I want.' I meant it and yet I was crying. Isn't that funny? I didn't mean to cry. As you know I hate crying.

– He is a thoughtful man, Winnie said.

– I know.

Mel spoke with reverent appreciation.

– There's nothing he'd like better than to come here, you know, just for a meal or something. He knows I like cooking. But he's so careful never to embarrass me. I said to him last week, 'Arty,' I said, 'The house is virtually empty. You ought to come before it gets knocked down.' 'Well I will,' he said. 'I'll not refuse an invitation. A week tomorrow.' That was last Tuesday. So he'll be coming here on Wednesday evening.

– Gosh.

Winnie looked excited.

– You can join us if you like.

Winnie shook her head.

– Only for coffee, she said. And keep me some lemon mousse if you're making any.

– There won't be any potatoes. Just a few crisps. You know when I went with him to Shrewsbury on business last February, Janet rang up the office and asked me specifically to watch that he didn't eat potatoes up there. She made me promise. She's a bit fussy, but she's a good mother as Arty says to the children.

– Does she know, do you think?

This was a question they had considered together before but it never lost its puzzling freshness.

– I don't think so. And yet sometimes . . .

– What does Arty say?

– Arty says she suspects everybody except his mother and me. That's his joke of course.

– What's she like, Mel?

– Small. A bit fussy. Rather nice-looking in a way. Dark.

– Ah . . .

– What?

– She hasn't got the morning glory!

Winnie stretched out her arms towards the towel on Mel's head.

– Morning rats'-tails you mean.

Mel tightened the towel around her wet tresses, pulled out her neat little vacuum cleaner and led the way across the landing to clean up Winnie's room. This was the way their sessions in the window often ended.

– Come on, she said.

Winnie was a little reluctant to start work.

– Come on, let's get this done before I go to chapel.

II

Mel was preparing a frugal breakfast with her normal, quiet efficiency when she heard Winnie shouting. Her electric kettle was in her hand. She was making a pot of china tea to drink with a slice of lemon. Winnie rushed in. Her cylindrical curlers wobbled on top of her head. Her pale blue pyjamas were hemmed with a broad black and white check. With the excited gestures she was making and her baggy pyjama-trousers she resembled a clown making an entrance in the circus.

– The bulldozers are coming, Winnie said. They're in the back garden! They'll knock the place down while we're still in our beds.

– You've been dreaming, Mel said.

Winnie suffered from bad dreams. She blamed them on

her fondness for toasted cheese and cheap sherry. Mel said it was because she smoked too much.

– Come and look then, Winnie said. They're there! Oh my God . . .

– Keep calm, Mel said.

From Winnie's window there was a desolate view. Two long rows of neglected gardens with broken fences and over-grown hedges divided in the middle by a narrow lane. Many of the houses opposite were already empty and covered with a fine dust that made the windows look like sightless eyes. Only Margam Road on the margin of the motorway scheme still carried on the fight for existence.

– It's not a bulldozer, Mel said.

– What is it then? Look at the size of it. They could be starting across the way. Think of the noise, Mel, and the dust.

– Arty said they wouldn't start until the Margam Road argument is settled. And that won't be for ages. I told you before. It's a breakdown van. That's what it is. A big break-down thing. Look at the crane. Come to fetch somebody's car I expect.

– Are you sure?

Winnie's relief was as large as her alarm. She clutched Mel's bare forearm with her hot sticky hands. Mel turned her head away quickly to hide her distaste. But Winnie had already exploded with a new excitement.

– Mel, she said. Mel, love. It's your birthday! Many Happy Returns!

Winnie kissed her vigorously on the cheek.

– I haven't got it now. I'm bringing it home this evening. Anyway here's your card. Has the post been? Shall I go down and see?

Mel tried to prevent her, but Winnie enjoyed rushing up and down stairs in her pyjamas. She said it gave her a sense of freedom and she liked the exercise and it helped her to look her calorie-card in the face.

– It all helps, she said, as she puffed her way up. Only two, love, and a bill for me. That's all.

Mel looked at the handwriting on the envelopes.

– My father, she said. And Miss Lewis. Poor old Miss
Lewis. Never forgets my birthday. She's in an old people's
home now, but she never forgets.

– That's nice, isn't it? Winnie said.

– I had my card from Gwladys last week. Always sends it
too early.

Gwladys was Mel's sister married to a policeman in Rhodesia. Winnie stood on the landing waiting for more information. There was nothing from Arty. Not a word.

– Miss Lewis is seventy-nine, Mel said. You wouldn't believe it. She's so sweet and smiling. My mother goes to see
her every week.

– That's nice, Winnie said.

– I'm late, Mel said.

She became determinedly animated to show that she had
to get to work quickly and nothing could be allowed to stop
her. Winnie tried to remind her again about looking out for
a flat they could share since she worked in one of the biggest
estate agents' offices after all, but Mel was too intent on
leaving quickly to do more than nod. It was in any case a
ticklish problem. She did not fancy sharing a flat with Winnie. As a neighbour across the landing she was fine, or at
least bearable; but in the same flat, filling the ash-trays at
week-ends and never changing the sheets on her bed ... It
was something to discuss with Arty when the mystery of the
birthday-card had been solved. She had in fact mentioned
it to him about three weeks ago. But he was troubled about
his son, and she did not want to add to his worries. Her job
was to relieve him of his burdens as far as she could. The
boy was fourteen and devoted to his mother. On the first day
of term he had run away from school. Arty had taken him
back. He said the headmaster had been very 'sniffy'; Arty
was very sensitive about that. He was a working-class lad
who had worked his way up, unlike Mr Simons, who was
brother-in-law to a bishop and conducted his business with
ecclesiastical solemnity. If a new flat were to be found, it
would be for Arty's convenience, not Winnie's.

Mel found a seat on top of the number four bus. It was twenty-five minutes to nine on the first Monday morning of her thirty-seventh year. The route was tree-lined in the way she liked and she was prepared to celebrate her birthday in her own mind and in the transparent lightness of the leaves. Her fine head of golden hair glittered bravely in the fitful morning sunlight. She caught glimpses of it on polished surfaces and window-panes and it made her feel youthful and defiant in her own quiet and well-behaved way. The man next to her was old and fat and took up more space than he was entitled to, and she held on tightly to the chromium-plated bar on the seat in front ... Whatever the reason for Arty not sending a birthday-card, the mystery would be solved shortly, in the office. Perhaps there was already hidden in the top drawer of her desk, under the carbon paper, a bottle of the perfume he knew she preferred. He hid a box of chocolates there once; three Christmasses ago. Or a silk scarf under the cover of her typewriter. He had done that too. Arty was a personality, unpredictable, full of surprises. One birthday, four years ago, he had ordered her out of the office and into his car. Before she knew it, they were on the steamer to Weston, and he was looking down at the foaming wake and chuckling at her undiminishing surprise. Perhaps today, if he remembered what day it was, they would do the same again. Although Arty hardly ever did the same thing twice ... From the moment in June 1961 in the second empty bungalow – on the Foreshore Estate when he kissed her for the first time ... *What about your wife, Mr Gender? she said. I like you all the more for asking, Mel, he said. Call me Arty.* From that day their understanding had grown. Of course he was temperamental. Success made him laugh and shout. There was a bowler hat on the hat-rack. It was two sizes too small for him, but when he felt like it he would wear it and he would sing and dance. He taught her to clap and laugh. He didn't do it so often now, because he was forty-nine and short of breath. And all last year 'Colyn with a y' had been getting more and more on his nerves. When he was troubled Arty bit fiercely at his knuckles and drank lots

of coffee. They had worked together now for over seven
years, and during working hours they were fully entitled to
be close together. During their working hours they lived
and breathed together in a rare partnership of understanding and love ... Perhaps he had bought her a new window-
plant. Perhaps there was a card or even a letter in the office
post ... ? After all, he had to be careful. The boy was fourteen now and devoted to his mother and very difficult. As
Arty said, there could be tricky seas ahead. They had to be
extra careful and she was more than willing to make
any sacrifice so long as they could keep their deep secret
love.

Messrs Smoke, Simons, and Gender and Co. (R. G. L.
Simons, F.A.I.; Arthur L. Gender, A.A.I.; Colyn M. de S. Melas)
occupied the ground floor of an office-block opened in 1963.
Little Olive was already in the front office sorting out the
mail. Olive belonged to a religious sect that didn't allow its
members to go to the cinema or the theatre. She was always
very chatty and cheerful. She was learning to type and went
to night-school and she was very loyal to Mel. She had a
way of calling out her name that Mel found very appealing.
But this morning when she saw Mel coming in she rushed
off down the corridor to *the ladies* without saying a word.
Mel thought this was odd.

  Nancy, a large gloomy woman of fifty who was Mr
Simons's clerk, hadn't arrived yet. She had a demanding
old father and sometimes she just couldn't leave the house
in the mornings. Arty said she was a victim of persistent
mental cruelty ... He was always so kind to Nancy and
Olive. It was a very happy office before Mr 'Colyn with a y'
Melas joined the firm. There was nothing wrong with old
Simons himself, as Arty said. He was lazy, but Arty never
minded that. And he was a social climber. And that was
why Colyn got in. Mr Simons's wife was his aunt by marriage
and Colyn's mother was very big in cathedral cities because
her late husband had been a suffragan bishop in Africa. And
Mr Simons's life ambition was to get on the Governing
Body. According to Arty it was as simple as that. 'Colyn

with a y' fancied himself. He had a bad complexion but rather nice curly hair and he wore a variety of green waist-coats and he watched every little thing. 'The spy with a y,' Arty said. He had complained to Mr Simons about Arty telling smutty jokes at a Public Auction and doing harm to the firm's good name and high-class reputation. Arty was hurt. And very angry. She could tell by the way he was biting his knuckles all day. And his wind. He was belching all day. It was worse for his stomach than potatoes.

She looked through the mail very quickly. There was nothing addressed to her and marked personal. She picked up all the letters addressed to Arthur L. Gender, A.A.I. and carried them off to his room. There was no point in wasting time. She would start answering some right away and have it all neatly ready for him by the time he came in. He always liked that. He always expressed his appreciation no matter how short the phrase, such as 'there's my girl' or 'good kid' when he was preoccupied or in a hurry.

She was very surprised to see the door of his room already open. Could he have come in early . . . her birthday perhaps? From the open doorway she saw Colyn Melas sitting in Arty's new chair, the with-tilt, constant-height, Tycoon-Director's chair about which he was still making jokes. Colyn Melas's uncle as he called him, Mr. R. G. L. Simons, stood with his back to the door, dressed immaculately as usual, but today in a black suit. Colyn saw Mel first. He seemed to be looking at her freshly washed hair. He rose to his feet with grave respect.

– Miss Madock?

Mr Simons then turned and stared at her.

– Oh . . . ah . . .

They looked at each other, Mr Simons and Colyn Melas, quite unable to decide what to say next. Colyn moved away from the tycoon director's extra-deep cushioned seat and she found that a relief.

– Miss Madock . . . Mel . . . you haven't heard?

He made his distinguished features take on a sorrowful expression by frowning so that his eyebrows almost touched.

– Heard what?

– Your ... Mr Gender ... Arty ... passed away. Yesterday, in the Infirmary. You hadn't heard?

Her grip tightened on the bunch of letters in her hand. All the colour left her face, her head sagged forward, and before Mr Simons or Colyn Melas could catch her she fainted.

III

– I see that Mel's home then?

Big Miss Humphries leaned across the counter, smiling with her customary benevolent curiosity. Her smile was fixed in the direction of Mel's father, who was operating the bacon-machine, but her eyes were computing an inventory of objects normally hidden from a customer's view. Bryn Marian Stores was out of date and the owner knew it; but as he said himself it had never been his main interest. In the thirties there had been a moment of excitement when the drapery counter was introduced. Certainly at that time Mel and her sister Gwladys were the best-dressed children in the village and their father took great pride in them. But the counter now was just a melancholy monument to a bygone age. The one concession to technology was a frozen-food container strangely isolated in the centre of the shop and overhung with a desolate collection of mops and brooms hanging from the ceiling.

– Just a few days, Mel's father said.

There was a minimum custom he needed to keep the shop going and he had established a minimum courtesy to sustain it. Every customer who came through the door had made the effort to journey well away from the centre of the village to where the shop stood in isolation on the edge of a wilderness of gorse and outcropping rock.

– I thought I saw that beautiful head of hair, Miss Humphries said. Being so tall, she could look over hedges and she had seen Mel sitting on the garden seat under the apple tree. She also noticed that no one had cut the grass and the sad neglect of the garden. Big Miss Humphries always walked slowly through the village swaying slightly from side to side, and taking note of details that would escape the attention of the casual passer-by.

– She doesn't get it from me.

It was the usual mechanical joke he made when anyone referred to Mel's hair, always passing the palm of his hand above his own bald head as he spoke. At the same time he held forward the sliced bacon on the sheet of grease-proofed paper for the customer's inspection.

– I hope she's not ill . . .

Miss Humphries was picking coins out of her purse.

No doubt Miss Humphries had noticed how motionless Mel sat on the garden seat: as unresponsive as a stone statue. He had given the customer the change she was entitled to and he was not prepared to give her anything more. Her eyes moved in her head, surveying the shelves behind him, but he knew very well her meagre shopping was over. There was no further need for him to speak. At last she retreated, swaying purposefully as she passed through the narrow half of the door that opened.

When she was well on her way back to the centre of the village, Mrs Madock, Mel's mother, appeared out of the shadows, sighing as she always did, but today punctuating her sighs with a clucking noise as a sign of additional distress. Together in their gloomy shop they gave each other wordless melancholy support: each was always comforted to know that the other was somewhere about in the shadows. However bad the news, murmuring across the empty shop from one counter to another, there were always crumbs of comfort to be picked up. There was a time when Mrs Madock kept a few hens. They all died of some mysterious disease. They discovered by going over the details in the shop while waiting for custom that it cost far less to buy the eggs from John Corn Hir, an old admirer of Mel who was glad of the excuse to call twice a week and find out the latest news about her.

– She won't eat a thing, Mrs Madock said. I made her scrambled egg. She wouldn't touch it.

His mouth opened but he said nothing. His wife then spoke as if she were answering a question.

– I suggested it, she said. I said, why don't you go for a long walk, Mel. A nice long walk. John Corn Hir would love to see you.

– She wouldn't come down when he called, Mr Madock said.

– Well if you won't go to Corn Hir, I said, take that walk your father used to take before his leg began to trouble him. Through the wooded gorge and up the side of the mountain until you can see the sea. That's the walk, I said.

– She doesn't like the name, Mr Madock said.

– What name?

– Corn Hir. It's an old name. I can't see anything wrong with it.

She doesn't like John either, Mrs Madock said. Such a nice fellow. Always agreeable. A very good farmer too.

These were all words they had used many times before. Mrs Madock sniffed nervously and pitched the new question on a higher note.

– Have you any idea what's happened?

Mr Madock only shook his head.

– She says she's going back tomorrow. I said, you know you can stay as long as you like, Mel, and she said, I know that, Mam.

Mrs Madock took some comfort from that.

– She wouldn't come to chapel, Mr Madock said.

Mrs Madock made noises to show her extreme distress. In chapel Mr Madock played the organ. This was his greatest pleasure. He played fluently and his taste was all for sweet melodious hymns in the minor key. A new organ had been installed for nearly a thousand pounds, three years ago, and Mr Madock had mastered it by long hours of dedicated practice which was greatly appreciated by all the senior members of the congregation. It had become the very centre of his life and it grieved him deeply that his daughter, home on unexpected leave, did not want to come and hear him play. She did not want to be seen in the square chapel where she had been baptized and confirmed and where, one day, her parents had always hoped she would be married.

– Young people, Mrs Madock said. None of the young people want to come.

– Mel was never like that, her father said. Mel always liked coming. And Gwladys too. Gwladys always liked coming.

– It's the spirit of the age, Mrs Madock said.

– Not in her case, Mr Madock said. Or in Gwladys's either. They've always appreciated being brought up in a good home. There's something the matter . . .

– Nothing she will tell us about, Mrs Madock said.

– I'll have a word with her, shall I?

Mrs Madock nodded, but she did not look hopeful. Her husband made his way down the dark passage that led to the house and he limped through the parlour and the kitchen and blinked in the sunlight in the garden. He wiped his hands on his white apron. Mel smiled at him politely as she used to when someone came in when she was minding the store.

– It's quiet, he said.

She agreed it was quiet.

– I like sitting there, he said. I like listening to the birds. There's a lot to be said for living outside the village. You won't believe it, but I heard a woodlark here the week before last. On a Sunday afternoon. There's a lot to be said for living in the country.

She did not speak and he did not sit down. He stretched out his arm and leaned against the trunk of the apple tree.

– I think John Corn Hir was very disappointed, not seeing you. I told him you weren't well. He's a very nice lad John. He bought a new Land-Rover last week. I teased him, you know. Buying a new car one week and buying a new Land-Rover the next. Some people, I said, must be living on a goldmine.

He stopped speaking when he realized that Mel had
stopped listening. It was clear to see that she was locked up
in her own thoughts.

– I'll sit a minute, Mr Madock said.

Perhaps if he were closer she would hear what he was
saying.

– We're not as young as we used to be, he said. Your
mother and I. I've been thinking you know, it would be very
nice if you stayed home. You could help me with the business. You could modernize if you like. New methods and
all that. When we've gone it will all be yours. It isn't much
of course, but it's a house and it's a business and it's a bit
of land. It will always have some value. I know I'm not a
businessman and never was. I would have gone to a college
of music if my mother could have afforded it, but that's all
in the past, of course. Anyway, Mel, if you want to stay home
you know you'd be very welcome.

– I must go back tomorrow, Mel said.

She spoke very quietly, but her father knew it was final.
He went back to the shop.

IV

Mel spent a week alone in her flat in Margam Road before
she returned to work. Most of the time she spent in bed.
Winnie looked in every evening to see if there was anything
she wanted. Mrs Ferrata came up on Tuesday and offered to
clean the room. Mel nodded. She lay in bed watching Mrs
Ferrata at work. She was energetic enough, but badly organized. She backed into the table on which the Staffordshire piece stood, and knocked it over. It chipped badly
against the edge of the table and half the head came off.
She began apologizing and then she saw that Mel was crying, her tears soaking into the pink nylon pillow-case. Mrs
Ferrata began crying herself. She cried aloud that her house
was doomed; she stood in the bay window and waved her
arms towards the sky. Afterwards Mel felt a little better. She
got up and by the time Winnie came home from work she

had made a sponge-cake which they were able to enjoy together. Winnie looked at the statuette of Prince Albert and said it should not be all that difficult to repair it so that at least it would keep its sentimental value.

– To think, Mel said, I was with him for over seven years and I don't even know where he's buried.

Winnie reached over dangerously to take Mel's hand, knocking over her tea-cup, and they were both overcome by a bout of weeping.

When she returned to the office everything appeared astonishingly the same. She put out a hand to feel the thickness of the counter in the front office. The free-standing display cabinet with photographs of properties on the market stood in its usual place and all the photographs seemed familiar. She was tempted to inspect a glamorous picture of the block of flats at Red Rock Beach. Instead she closed her eyes and turned to look at little Olive who told her that Mr Colyn Melas had moved into Mr Gender's office.

The idea took a little getting used to. Nancy was very thoughtful and arranged for Mel to go into Mr Simons's office that first morning to take dictation. She noticed that Mr Simons had a habit of examining his appearance in the mirror and not finishing his sentences. He would also interrupt himself by making social calls on the telephone in the middle of a business letter or examining the state of the clothes he kept in the closet behind his desk. She had to go over every letter and memo with Nancy who knew his style so well that she was able to make some sense out of the strange jumble. But it all took time and meant working late.

Mr Colyn Melas was very sympathetic. He spoke very softly to Mel and asked her directly whether she would mind working with him, so that she could hardly refuse. His voice seemed to have changed. And his complexion had definitely improved. The pores on his spreading nose were wide as ever and there were blackheads still in his neck and red patches from a recent attack of boils, but he kept himself conspicuously tidy. His shirts and his ties were different every day. He wore attractive waistcoats and he stared at her unblinkingly, for long periods at a time. When she was in his room and the door was closed he spoke so softly sometimes it gave her the impression she was sharing his most intimate thoughts and she had to look up at his face and see if in fact his lips were moving.

– I'm so glad we are going to work together, he said in a quiet, sincere tone. I'm so glad you don't mind working with me. I'm so glad, Miss Madock, you don't mind ... if there's ever anything you need ... If you need anything ...

It took her some time to get accustomed to his manner. His stare, particularly, and his eyes, which seemed to change colour so easily, like the sea, sometimes green and sometimes blue and a constant source of movement and mystery. Even more difficult was seeing him sitting in the chair that Arty had chosen for himself from a glossy brochure on office furniture. His method of work, however, was easy to grasp, rhythmic, efficient, quiet. There were the occasional shocks. Finding Arty's comic bowler hat in a cupboard for example. And one day, in his quiet voice, Colyn Melas said:

– I'd like you to know something. The night that Mr Gender died I said to my uncle, 'I think Miss Madock ought to be informed.' He agreed with me, but he didn't know your address so I said to Janet – Mrs Gender – I said, do you happen to know where Miss Madock lives? I think she ought to be informed. She just shook her head. Of course at that time I couldn't press her.

Mel looked as if she might cry, trying to smile a signal of gratitude. She wanted to say that the woman knew very well where she lived, but her lips stretched and she said nothing.

– You can always talk to me, Miss Madock, he said. Always think of me as your friend. I think it will help a lot if we confide in each other.

He stared at her. She was accustomed now to the stare and in a curious way she found it comforting.

– Time is the great healer.

He spoke so softly and unexpectedly that she put up both hands to cover her burning cheeks.

Every day he had something new to tell her about himself. It didn't appear to come easily. He would sit hunched in Arty's chair as if bringing his shoulders so far forward helped him to squeeze out what he had to say. Sometimes he would hold his breath, so that she was compelled to look up in alarm, wondering why the room was not alive with the murmur of his voice.

– I know I'm not very likeable.

Mel felt obliged to make some sign of disagreement.

– Oh, I know it. I'm not like Arty Gender. You were so loyal to him. Can I say that? Your loyalty was beautiful. Do you mind if I say that? I used to watch it, you know, from the outside. Through the glass so to speak and I used to envy him. I used to say to myself I'd like to have that kind of loyalty. How old do you think I am, Mel? Can I call you Mel? Are you sure you don't mind?

He talked regularly about himself.

– I know I'm evasive, he said. I can't help it. I was bullied terribly at school. I suffered from boils, you know, and the boys used to laugh at me. I don't blame them, of course. I was a bit of a squirt, I'm sure. It does me so much good, Mel, to be talking to you. I hope you don't mind.

Mel said she didn't mind. Even when it meant working late it was soothing somehow to sit listening to him talking about himself.

– I married too young. I was so glad anybody would have me, I suppose. But it means I've not had the freedom, you know, to do the things I would have liked to do. After all my father was a bishop in Africa. There's adventure in my blood. You know I feel sometimes I shouldn't be sitting here in an office. I should be somewhere out there in the bush. Discovering something. Finding things out. Completing my education. I never completed my education. That's half my trouble.

One evening it was raining heavily and he kept her working late. He began to talk about himself. The office was empty. Mel felt a little uneasy.

– I wish you'd talk to me, he said. I'd like to think that you thought of me as a real friend. Do you think of me as a friend, Mel?

He stood behind her chair and she thought she felt him touching her hair.

– We've got to help each other. I feel this very strongly. I wish you'd talk to me sometimes. Tell me what you're feeling. Will you do that, Mel?

He leaned against his desk and stared at her anxiously.

– I admit I'd like to kiss you. We're alone in the office. But I'd never do that. I'd never frighten you like that. You believe me, don't you?

Mel cleared her throat.

– I'd like you to tell me, Mel, about you and Arty. Not now. When you feel like it. It would do you good. That's why I'd like you to tell me. So that it will do you real good. Okay?

He smiled as frankly as he could, until she was compelled to smile back.

– That's good. Now I'll take you home. I want to see where you live. So I can wave up at your window.

In the car Mel tried to make conversation.

– They're scheduled for demolition, she said. It's a shame really. They're such nice houses.

He parked his car under a dripping tree. She pointed out her room on the second floor.

– Did Arty ever come up?

Mel remained silent.

– Of course you don't have to answer. I want to show real understanding. It's not just curiosity, Mel. It's a practical question. Do you share the room?

Mel explained the position. As she spoke he nodded encouragingly as if she were a child who had to be coaxed a little to repeat her lesson.

– You ought to think of Christchurch Close, he said. Think very seriously.

Christchurch Close was a small precinct of luxury flats and maisonettes being built on church land near the cathedral.

Smoke, Simons, and Gender were the main agents, and Mel knew how expensive they were.

– I'm quite serious, he said. There will be the odd small flat at a moderate rent. The housing committee have insisted on this in case of criticism. If you say so, Mel, I'll make it my business to see one of them comes to you.

– That's very kind of you, Mel said. Can I just think about it?

Colyn smiled admiringly.

– You know what you've got, Mel, he said. You've got inner dignity. I admire that very much. I haven't got it myself so I admire it very much. I hope you don't find me too repulsive.

Mel said no, and then they laughed together as if he had made a joke.

v

Winnie met Mel on the stairs one evening when she came home from work. She whispered excitedly and made many gestures. Mrs Ferrata stood in the hallway and looked up expectantly as if she expected to be included in the secret.

– There's a man in your room, Winnie said. He's been there for more than two hours. Mrs F let him in. He's got a funny little Hitler moustache and his face is all sunburnt except for his bald head which is shiny and white. Who is he, Mel? I'm dying to know.

Mel sighed.

– It's John Corn Hir, she said. From home.

Winnie leaned against the banister and sagged to show that she understood the news was an anti-climax. She made a gesture of disappointment to Mrs Ferrata, who went back into her kitchen.

John Corn Hir sat on the edge of the divan, clearly ill at ease in such a feminine room. He looked down at his large brown boots as if he would have liked to wrap them up in a parcel and post them back to the farm.

– Hello Mel, he said. Nice place you've got here.

– What are you doing in Caer? Mel said.

Winnie stood in the doorway fascinated by the change in Mel's tone of voice. It had become quite bossy. John Corn Hir was humble and apologetic.

– I'm on the Regional Pig Board now, he said. I'm up for the quarterly meeting.

Mel pulled a face at the word 'pig'. Again Winnie marvelled to herself at Mel's rudeness. She made no attempt to make her visitor welcome.

– I promised your dad I'd drop in and see how you were, he said.

– You'd better have a cup of tea then, Mel said.

John seemed more than grateful not to have been turned out on the spot. He looked at Winnie who still stood in the doorway and nodded at her agreeably.

– The house is coming down then. The landlady was telling me. I didn't know that. Must be a bit funny, living in a house that's coming down.

– Would you like a cup of tea, Winnie?

Mel called from her kitchenette.

– I'm on my way out really, Winnie said. I'm going to take a peep at Judy's new home. They're expecting me, you see.

She looked carefully at John Corn Hir to study his reactions. Again he smiled at her encouragingly and nodded. She felt obliged to explain who Judy was.

– Judy is a friend of mine who got married just over six weeks ago. Her husband works in the bank.

– Can't work in a better place, can you? John said cheerfully.

Mel found Winnie a little annoying. She had said she was going and yet she hovered about even when Mel pushed in a trolley with tea and cakes.

– She's a marvellous cook, Winnie said.

– Oh I know.

He agreed enthusiastically.

– Know? How could you know?

Mel sounded quite cross and she looked very disapproving as he loaded the third heaped teaspoonful of sugar into his tea. Winnie left at last, but when she had gone Mel wished she were still there to make some kind of conversation and relieve the uncomfortable silence. John drank four cups of tea and ate four pieces of cake. This kept him smiling and busy.

– Your dad's not well, he said. Not well at all. His leg.

– Is it worse then?

– It's not better.

He looked at Mel and passed his tongue over his dentures to remove the last traces of cake before speaking on a solemn subject.

– I've brought you a letter, he said.

– From Dad?

– No. From me. Shall I give it you now?

– If you like.

He fished inside his heavy sports jacket and took out an envelope.

– I meant to give it you just before leaving. Don't open it until I've gone. I showed it to your father. He said it was all right. Well, I won't keep you now.

He stood up, ready to leave, and Mel shifted the envelope about, uncertain now whether or not to accept it. When John Corn Hir put on his long stiff trench-coat he looked to Mel a figure from a distant past, old-fashioned, and like a tree or a wall incapable of real change.

– I enjoyed the cake. Give my kind regards to your friend.

He pointed with his cap to the door and Mel realized that he meant Winnie.

– Yes, well ... I'll say good-bye now. I didn't know it was coming down.

He pointed his cap at the walls of the room. He seemed cheered by the news. Mel made him promise not to mention the fact to her parents. He told her not to bother to come down and she listened to his heavy tread echo down the stairs.

His handwriting was laboriously upright. The sight of the pale blue lined notepaper seemed to distress her. It smelled of fish-meal.

Dear Mel,

I am writing this note to ask you to marry me. I know that the house at Corn Hir is not in good condition as at present, but I am quite prepared to make any alterations you would want should you agree to my proposal. As you know Corn Hir is a very productive unit. You may not know that I have a substantial bank balance in the region of ten thousand five hundred pounds, also five thousand in the war loan after my uncle and three thousand unit trust investments. As you know I have always felt very warmly towards you and I know it would please your parents to have you near,

> Your sincere friend,
> John.

When Winnie came back from the last bus she was full of enthusiasm for Judy's new home.

– You should have seen the kitchen, Mel. You would have loved it. Fridge, washing-machine, super cooker, food-mixer, the lot. She's got it made, girl. All she does is wander around the house polishing her wedding presents. I can tell you, love, I was mad with envy. And he's quite nice too. Quiet you know and can't do too much for her. It's the only thing you know, Mel, in the end. At the end of the day, as old Harold says, you put the cat out and lock the door, up to slumberland and hear him snore. Nothing like it.

Winnie hooted with laughter. Mel, who was in her dressing-gown and ready for bed, handed Winnie John's letter to read. Winnie opened her mouth wide and flattened her hand against her breast.

– Mel! This is a proposal!

– Look at the way he's written it, Mel said. He's so ignorant. He annoys me. Now I'll have to write him an answer. It's very embarrassing.

– What's it like, Mel?

– It's a dump. Stuck up in the hills, overlooking a river. Pigs everywhere and poultry. Ponies and sheep in the garden. Old bedsteads in the hedges. It's such a mess. You've never seen anything like it. Hasn't even got indoor sanitation. He's got some cheek, I must say.

Winnie had become serious as Mel was talking. She lit a cigarette and waved away the smoke.

– You know what I think, Mel? Do you mind if I speak quite frankly? If I were you I'd accept him.

– Accept him!

Mel was as indignant as if Winnie had insulted her.

– You've had a bad time, Winnie said. I'm your friend and I wouldn't be a good friend if I didn't tell you. What's gone is gone, but what about the future? We'll have to get out of here very soon now and where will we go? Point number one. We're not getting any younger. Point number two. We're not well paid. Point number three. He may be a bit of a hillbilly, but he's got the cash and that's what counts. We can't live on romance for ever. We've had our fling and now's the time to settle down . . .

– You marry him then!

Mel snatched a cigarette and furrowed her forehead.

– I would like a shot if he asked me. You're the romantic type, Mel. And you want to watch out. There's nothing wrong these days living in the country. You'll have a car of your own. And the telly. Put central heating in . . .

Winnie picked up John's letter and read,

– 'Any alterations you would want'! Take out the war loan and you could build another house in the next field, Mel. You accept him. Don't be daft. This is a wonderful chance. You take it.

– He's got a nerve, Mel said. Writing to me like that.

– Any woman can train a man if she puts her mind to it, Winnie said. Look at Judy. She's got her bank-clerk sitting up and begging. You could do just the same if you wanted to.

– Well I don't want to . . .

– Sleep on it, Winnie said. Sleep on my words and take my advice. Say 'yes' first thing in the morning. Don't give him a chance to change his mind.

VI

– I'm proud of you, Mel. I really am.

They could still hear the noise of the angry client shouting at little Olive in the front office. He was some kind of college lecturer, as far as Mel knew, who claimed that he had been misled by Colyn about the state of the woodwork of a house he had bought for £4,850.

– Ridiculous fuss, Colyn said. He'd had the place for next to nothing anyway.

They listened to his last shouts of protest and condemnation.

– I think he's gone, Colyn said.

– I'll just see if little Olive is all right, Mel said. She's very sensitive about these things.

Mel had faced the intruder calmly. He had a large fierce beard and he demanded to see Mr Melas. Colyn was hiding in the cleaner's closet. Mel managed to make the man believe that he was out of the office for the whole day.

– When clients come in here and they see you, you give the place tone. I was saying this to uncle this morning. You can ask him if you like. I was saying your salary should be increased. No matter by how small a margin. As a symbol. Just to show how much the firm appreciates you.

Mel blushed and he took her hand in his in the most tender way, and lifted it to his lips.

When she got back to Margam Road that evening she told Winnie that the firm was going to give her a fifteen-shillings-a-week rise.

– 'Colyn with a y', Winnie said.

She used such an insinuating voice that Mel went straight to the bathroom and locked the door. She sat there for so long on the white chair that Winnie realized that things had changed a great deal at Smoke, Simons, and Gender, and that Mel was very offended. It was quite unacceptable now to remind her of anything Arty had ever said about 'Colyn with a y'. She made a special effort to please and gave her

own room a cleaning as an open token of repentance. Later
she said:

– You'll kill me for saying this, Mel. But if you've got any
sense left in your head, you'll take that John Corn Hir's
offer. Have you answered his letter?

Mel shook her head.

– Well for God's sake answer it, love.

Mel had also intended to tell Winnie about Christchurch
Close. But she resented her tone and her advice so much that
she said she wanted to go to bed early. She had a headache.

She woke up with a headache the following day. In the
office Colyn Melas was very sympathetic and talked at length
about some of his own disabilities.

– I'm so glad you told me about your headache, Mel, he
said. I want to help you in every way I can. I expect something's worrying you. Bad news at home perhaps? That
brings on a headache. Did I tell you I dreamt about you
last night? Very interesting dream. I dream a lot, you know.
I need my dreams.

After a long lunch with a client Colyn came back to the
office in a merry mood. He had a new pack of playing-cards
in his pocket. He shuffled them with great dexterity and
Mel was fascinated.

– Pick one, he said, go on. Pick a card.

– I didn't know you were a conjurer, she said.

– It's all practice. Constant practice. Go on Mel. Pick a
card.

He was smiling, at his most frank and friendly. His teeth
were in excellent condition and the inflamed open-pored
skin did not seem to matter. His hands fluttered delicately
in magical control of the pack of cards. Each time she picked
a card he closed his eyes and this made her feel strangely
sympathetic towards him. He reminded her of a minister
standing in the pulpit with his eyes closed praying. And
then when his eyes opened and the trick succeeded, he
chuckled delightedly and showed a new confidence in himself with such appealing simplicity that she could not but
share it.

– I'd like to ask your advice.

Mel spoke softly, but he heard at once.

– Yes.

He was breathless and eager as if this would be something he had been waiting a long time to hear.

– It's not urgent . . . It's a personal problem.

– Yes.

His hands were perfectly still now, the cards scattered on the desk.

Mel took out John Corn Hir's letter from the pocket of her overall. Colyn placed the letter on his desk and flattened it carefully with the palm of his hand, pushing a few cards off the blotter pad. He took so long to read it that she became acutely aware of the room in which they worked together. She spent far more time in the room now than she had when Arty was alive. Because of the grief she had suffered and because Colyn was always saying how much he understood and how much he needed her, the room had acquired something of the atmosphere of a place of worship. It was here that they worked late for so many evenings a week and she listened to him talking about himself and the difficulties of his life; it was here that she carried out daily ritual tasks and assisted him to display the different sides of his character; and it was here that he showed so much respect and admiration for her, sometimes touching her hair, but never even asking for a carnal kiss. Often he spoke of their relationship with a touch of awe in his voice. Whatever it was, she realized that he had created it and that she was participating in some mysterious way in a cult in honour of something on a higher plane than anything she had experienced before.

– I don't know what I would do if I lost you.

After a long silence, he had spoken. He sounded so subdued that she became alarmed.

– I realize how unlikeable I am, but you have made me feel . . . I must say this . . . an altogether bigger man, a finer person. You gave me so much, perhaps you don't realize how much . . .

– I've no intention of accepting!

Mel sounded determined and vigorous.

– I just wanted your help in framing an answer.

– It's such a wonderful offer, he said. Let's be realistic about this. He's obviously quite well-to-do. I don't know how big the farm is but by present-day prices it could be worth a great deal. Suppose he owns a flock of five hundred ewes, well there's several . . .

– I'm not going to marry him.

Mel sounded quite angry.

– I don't know how I'll be able to face this office without you here, Mel . . .

– I'm not going . . .

– It's so clearly in your interests to accept.

– But I won't.

He had slumped in the tycoon-director's chair. He stared unhappily at the letter and at the playing-cards scattered on the table. Gently, but deliberately, to relieve him of his misery, Mel unbuttoned his waistcoat and placed her hand over his heart.

VII

Winnie had been given a Siamese cat. At first she was deeply disturbed by the cat's persistent wailing. 'This bloody cat' she called it for the first two or three days, but in no time at all she became extremely fond of it. She called it Twinkle and it strode about the house in a masterful way, demanding tributes of milk from Mr or Mrs Ferrata and admiration from anyone who crossed her path. She would wander about any room with an open door but her favourite spot was on Mel's divan. She looked her best in Mel's room as Winnie freely admitted. The presence of Twinkle helped to conceal the growing estrangement between the two women.

There had been a Sunday evening in late summer when Mel tried to convey to Winnie something of the spirit of the relationship between Colyn and herself. She wanted to explain in her own words, slowly and accurately, that nothing improper had ever taken place between them, that he had

not even kissed her on the lips. But Winnie was too un-
sympathetic.

– I'll tell you what you should have done, my girl. You
should have married John Corn Hir, she said. That's what
you should have done.

The cat jumped into Mel's lap and that was the last occasion when she tried to take Winnie into her confidence. They
were always pleasant enough with each other and they
always found the behaviour of the cat a source of conversation. Nevertheless Mel left it very late before telling Winnie
that she was moving into a small new flat in Christchurch
Close.

– When?

Winnie was nursing Twinkle. She looked as if she was
unable to swallow.

– A week tomorrow.

Suddenly it became clear to her that Mel had made no
effort to find a flat that they could share; that she had
known for weeks that she was leaving, that she might even
have told Mrs Ferrata not to tell her. She stared at Mel's
freshly washed golden hair and realized with a sudden panic
how little she knew about Mel Madock whom she had always
taken to be her best friend or at least the friend nearest to
her. She held Twinkle more tightly and made a determined
effort to hold back her tears.

– Aren't they very expensive?

– The firm has paid my rent for the first quarter, Mel said.
As a token of appreciation.

– Not for services rendered?

Winnie tried to smile to take the hostility and spite out of
her words.

– That wasn't a very nice thing to say.

– Well it wasn't very nice to go fixing yourself up on the
quiet without saying a word . . .

– I am not obliged to account for every single step I take, I
hope.

Winnie could control herself no longer.

– Don't ever come to me for sympathy again, that's all I say . . .

The tears flowed faster down Winnie's cheeks. What maddened her was Mel's calm. She stood there like a receptionist in a grand hotel turning someone away on the grounds that she was too common and untidy and vulgar to be admitted.

The day the van came to collect Mel's furniture, it seemed that they were reconciled. They embraced each other and vowed to keep in touch. Winnie promised to bring Twinkle to see the new flat. But as soon as the taxi moved off with four cases taking up most of the room on the back seat, Mel knew that she was parting from Winnie for ever.

VIII

Mel was delighted with her new flat. As Colyn said, it was a perfectly designed living unit, labour-saving and aesthetically satisfying in every way. At night the subtle lighting suggested warmth and comfort and wherever she sat it seemed to flatter her head of golden hair. In the day-time she took great pleasure in the view of the north-eastern corner of the cathedral and the impressive charnel-house. She began to read books about the cathedral and became knowledgeable about its architecture and its history. She knew the dates when the north-eastern tower had been pulled down and when it had been rebuilt and who had been responsible for the restoration. She took out books from the city library as though she were determined to make herself an expert on the subject. Colyn seemed very impressed by this unexpected interest. As often as possible she cooked him a little meal and he never left without their drinking a generous helping of green chartreuse. They came to regard the sweet liqueur as a symbol of their relationship and to attach a ritual significance to the pouring and the drinking. They often discussed whether or not they should become lovers. And he managed to persuade her to tell him everything about her relationship with Arty. One night she was telling him in detail about a trip she and Arty had made in secret to the Cheddar Gorge. Suddenly, as she repeated a phrase Arty had used – 'Mel, you make me feel young again' – she realized she had told him the whole story before. Possibly more than once. Without understanding why, she stood up suddenly and asked him to leave. At first he was puzzled, and then, deeply understanding, he took her in his arms so that she could weep on his shoulder.

When the spring came, his visits became less frequent. Mel understood perfectly. He was a married man. His mother was the widow of a bishop and something of a figure in cathedral circles. She lived near by. He had to be careful. In the office he began to make plans for week-ends that they would spend away together. There were business trips to London that had to be made and to the Midlands. There was every good excuse for her accompanying him as indeed she had accompanied Arty. Daily he impressed upon her it was what he wanted. Mel smiled patiently and said it didn't matter. What mattered most to her, she said, was their friendship, their spiritual relationship in fact. Colyn said he thought this was marvellous and kissed her hands, but she would have to forgive him for longing to possess more and more. They did in fact make one trip to Tenby together. But it was not a success. All the way there in the car, Colyn was morose and uneasy. In the town, he found the streets either too crowded where they would be sure to meet someone they knew or too empty where they were too conspicuous. The hotel was pleasant enough, but in the course of the evening it became clear he was unwell. He had a carbuncle on his left buttock. It was painful and embarrassing. Mel came to his room to bathe it with hot poultices of lint and boracic. He was not well enough even to enjoy the ceremony of drinking green chartreuse.

Near Easter she came to the office and found Colyn playing with a fishing-rod. All morning his manner had been puzzling. He produced two packs of cards and wanted to perform tricks and was most unwilling to pay any attention to work. In the afternoon he said he was going home early.

– Family holidays, Mel, in fact, he said. I don't want to go of course, but what else can I do? My mother says I'm neglecting Lawrence. Do you know how old he is now, Mel? Did I tell you? He's eight next month, my son is. Think of that. That's how time flies.

– How long will you be away?

Mel smiled bravely.

– Fortnight. Maybe a little longer. Scotland. My mother is coming with us. Speyside. I'm supposed to teach young Lawrence to fish. I said I'd be home by 4.30.

Mel looked at her wrist-watch.

– It's gone four now, she said. You'd better hurry.

– Yes, I suppose I had.

He hesitated. He held out his hand and she gave him hers, but instead of kissing it, he squeezed it tightly.

– You're so loyal, Mel, he said. I am such a poor sort really. I don't deserve a secretary so loyal, so true.

He hurried out with dramatic speed. It was only the next day that she noticed he had gone without the fishing-rod. In the afternoon Mr Simons asked her to step into his room. In his office there was a full-length mirror. He was wearing a new suit and from time to time he moved about to see how well it fitted.

– How is your father, Miss Madock? he said.

Mel was puzzled. It was a question he had never asked her before.

– Not getting any younger, I suppose? Any more than any of us?

He sat down reasonably content at last with the details of his appearance. Now, however, his throat seemed to be troubling him. He gave a series of dry coughs and fingered his stiff collar.

– I'm sure you must wish sometimes that you lived nearer home so that you could see him often. Your mother is still alive, is she not? As they get older, you know, parents like to see more of their children. It's a law of nature. Now with an only child like yourself . . .

– I have a sister, Mel said, in Rhodesia.

– Is that so?

He looked as if he had many interesting things to tell her about Rhodesia but he had made an uncharacteristic effort to concentrate.

– Well, there you are. It proves all I've been saying, doesn't it? You ought to look for a position nearer home. I'll do all I can to help you. D'you know Bodkin Richards of Bodkin Richards and Ross, Penhesgin? Very old friend of mine. I know they are looking for an experienced clerk. Just the place for you. A very nice old-established business. Do a lot of church business. Not more than seven miles from your home, is it? You could buy a little car. It could be very pleasant. The kind of place I'd enjoy myself to tell the truth. I'm a countryman at heart you know. Yeoman stock. You can't beat it really. Backbone of the country. Take a month's holiday with pay. We'd like you to have that, starting next week. Take a trip abroad; I would if I were you. Have you ever been to Venice, Miss Madock? Wonderful place. My wife and I were there last year . . .

Mel sat as still as a graven image, only the breeze from the open window lifting the light edges of her hair to give her a vague halo.

– I don't think you've ever met Mr Melas's mother. Or his wife. They do a lot of good work you know. Especially my sister-in-law. A born committee-woman. Ruthlessly efficient. And Marjorie's much the same. Some people would call them hard women. They would have done well in business, I'm pretty sure of that. They're both English you see. It makes a difference. Very determined women and very resentful. They were particularly annoyed about the flat in Christchurch Close. It's not that they're without feelings, but they have a very highly developed sense of justice. I did suggest they should come and see you. I told them how valuable you were to the firm and so on. But nothing else would do . . .

Her silence was beginning to unnerve him and he was running out of explanations.

– Poor Colyn of course is just clay in their hands. Very soft clay too.

He suffered her silence for as long as he could, and then he said:

– I'm very sorry, Miss Madock. But there's nothing else I can do. Would you ask Nancy to come in a minute? Come and see me again, of course, before you leave.

Mel was unwell most of the following week. When she came to the office, she complained of a headache. She closed the venetian blinds in Mr Melas's room and sat there alone in the semi-twilight. When Nancy asked her what was the matter, she said nothing about her dismissal. She complained of sleeplessness. Nancy was sympathetic. She gave Mel a tiny bottle of sleeping-pills and said that she really ought to go off sick and see a doctor. But Mel came in each day and stayed later each evening saying there was a great deal of desk clearing to be done in Mr Melas's office. On her last day no one except Mr Simons knew she was leaving. He assumed that she was following his advice in every detail, since she had never contradicted anything he had said.

– Good, he said. Well I'm sure everything will work out very well. Bodkin is a first-rate auctioneer. One of the old school. I'm sure you'll take to the place. Have you decided where you'll be going on holiday?

Mel nodded obediently.

– Good. Good. Well I'm sure you'll have a marvellous time.

On Sunday, just before lunch, Mel left Christchurch Close carrying a small suitcase. It was a warm day and the leaves were already out on the trees. She took a bus to Margam Road. Walking from the bus-stop carrying her small case she looked up at the houses. They were empty. At long last demolition had started. Bethesda blue slates were stacked neatly in the front gardens. The front doors were open and the dust of the early stages of demolition had gathered thick on the stairs.

She was able to go up unhindered to her old room. The door was shut and when she opened it something of the former neatness was still left: the pattern of the pale yellow wallpaper, the window-seat and, oddly, the little white chair that used to be in the bathroom. The Ferratas hadn't taken it and neither had Winnie. She had forgotten that she had brought it home once, from a sale Arty had conducted, and painted it white herself.

She placed the chair in the bay window and sat down as she used to in the old days to look out at the trees and at the traffic in the street. She opened the suitcase. Inside there was a bottle of green chartreuse and the two liqueur glasses she and Colyn always used. She filled them both and looked at the sunlight in the young leaves. It was still a pleasant view and still a place to sit and dream away a Sunday afternoon. She sipped the green chartreuse, filling one glass after the other, and when she felt cold she took the sleeping pills.

The demolition-workers found her body the following afternoon. A hole had already been opened through the ceiling and she was covered with a layer of grey dust, except for her head which was propped up against the bathroom chair. A beam of sunlight picked out the bronze and gold colours in her hair.

MORE ABOUT PENGUINS
AND PELICANS

Penguinews, which appears every month, contains details of all the new books issued by Penguins as they are published. From time to time it is supplemented by *Penguins in Print*, which is our complete list of almost 5,000 titles.

A specimen copy of *Penguinews* will be sent to you free on request. Please write to Dept EP, Penguin Books Ltd, Harmondsworth, Middlesex, for your copy.

In the U.S.A.: For a complete list of books available from Penguins in the United States write to Dept CS, Penguin Books, 625 Madison Avenue, New York, New York 10022.

In Canada: For a complete list of books available from Penguins in Canada write to Penguin Books Canada Ltd, 2801 John Street, Markham, Ontario L3R 1B4.

04